Ethel Carnie H.

This Slavery

Trent Editions

*Trent Editions aims to recover and republish landmark texts
in handsome and affordable modern editions.*

Radical Fictions series
Radical novels and innovative fiction, with an emphasis on writers of the British Isles.

*Series editor: John Lucas (Emeritus Professor of English, Loughborough and Nottingham Trent
Universities)*

H. G. Wells, *The Croquet Player*, ed. John Hammond (1998)
Patrick Hamilton, *Impromptu in Moribundia*, ed. Peter Widdowson (1999)
Ellen Wilkinson, *Clash*, ed. Ian Haywood and Maroula Joannou (2004)
Storm Jameson, *In the Second Year*, ed. Stan Smith (2004)
Stanley Middleton, *Harris's Requiem*, ed. David Belbin (2006)

Our other series are
Poetry Recoveries
Reconnecting poets to their own time and ours
American Recoveries
Key texts from the cultural memory of North America
Early Modern Writing (silver covers)
Recovering radical manuscript & printed texts from the cultural margins

Postcolonial Writings (maroon covers)
Radical voices of the colonial past, speaking to the postcolonial present

Radical Recoveries
The history & development of working-class, radical & popular print culture

Trent Essays (white covers)
Writers on the craft of writing

For further information please contact Trent Editions, School of Arts & Humanities
Nottingham Trent University, Clifton Lane, Nottingham NG11 8NS, or use your internet
search engine to find our web page.

'The excellent Trent Editions...' (Boyd Tonkin, *The Independent*)

Ethel Carnie Holdsworth

This Slavery

Edited with an Introduction and Notes by

NICOLA WILSON

Trent Editions

2011

First published by the Labour Publishing Company 1925

This edition published by Trent Editions, 2011

Trent Editions
School of Arts and Sciences
Nottingham Trent University
Clifton Lane
Nottingham NG11 8NS

http://english.ntu.ac.uk/trenteditionsnew/default.htm

Typeset and designed by Callum Lewis & Rebecca Kirby, Department of Typography and Graphic Design, The University of Reading
Printed in the UK by ImprintDigital.com

ISBN: 978 1 84233 141 5

Front cover image: strikers at Woodside mill in Darwen, Lancashire, April 1907. Reproduced with kind permission from Darwen Library local history collection and Blackburn Central Library.

CONTENTS

BLACKBURN Rᵈ
Gᵗ HARWOOD

J.R.Brunton

IGHTENHILL
PARK LANE,
BURNLEY.

Ethel Carnie c. 1908

INTRODUCTION

'What I feel is that literature up till now has been lop-sided, dealing with life only from the standpoint of one class'

> Ethel Carnie, 'Rebel Pen Club of Working Women',
> *Christian Science Monitor*, 10 January 1914, p.31

'He wails that I see nothing in poverty but poverty. Certainly, as one who was half-starving in the richest city in the world only three years ago, with husband and two kids, I can see nothing in dry crusts but – dry crusts'

> Ethel Carnie Holdsworth, 'The Books They Write',
> *Sunday Worker*, 26 July 1925, p.6

An Ex-Mill Girl

ETHEL CARNIE (later Ethel Carnie Holdsworth, or Ethel Holdsworth) was born into a Lancashire weaving family in Oswaldtwistle, four miles south-east of Blackburn, on New Year's Day, 1886.[1] Her parents both worked in the local cotton mills and, when Ethel was six, moved the family to the growing textile town of Great Harwood. Located in the midst of Lancashire's north-east cotton towns and close to Blackburn, Great Harwood was described by the socialist leader Robert Blatchford as 'a monstrous agglomeration of ugly factories, of ugly gasometers, of ugly houses – "brick boxes with slate lids".'[2] Here, like many of the local children of the time, Carnie Holdsworth entered the mill half-time at the age of eleven while still attending school, and two years later she went into the mills full-time as a winder. In her later fiction and journalism Carnie Holdsworth was a voracious critic of the factory system and the life it offered to its 'slaves', and in 1909 she published a series of damning articles on life in the mill towns, championing the rights of the men and women of the factories to youth, health, beauty and culture:

Factory life has crushed the childhood, youth, maturity of millions of men and women. It has ruined the health of those who would have been comparatively strong but for the long hours of unremitted toil and the evil atmosphere. The children leave the ugly school-house [...] for the mill. [...] One grows up quickly by the side of the roaring loom. [...] The lips are not for discourse and laughter, but to draw cotton through the shuttle's eye; the fingers were moulded to grasp the skewer, and to fling the shuttle, and the wonderful mechanism of the eye, that arch of light and beauty, to pore into the reeds looking for broken threads.[3]

In spite, if not because of, the ten hour days at the mill – those 'long hours of unremitted toil and the evil atmosphere' – Carnie Holdsworth was a passionate autodidact throughout her teenage years. Her reading was extensive. As a young woman she devoured the works of many of the great canonical writers, Romantic poets and nineteenth-century novelists – Shakespeare, Dickens, Wordsworth, Walter Scott – as well as the translated works of 'Oriental' writers such as the hugely popular poetry of the Persian philosopher, Omar Khayyám, and the *Arabian Nights*. She was able to get her hands on this print culture through the borrowing facilities of the local Great Harwood Co-operative Society (in *This Slavery*, Rachel Martin also borrows books from the Co-operative Lending Library). In later interviews, Carnie Holdsworth extolled the educational work of the Co-operative Movement and recalled how 'as a half-timer, I have waited my turn in queues at the top of the newsroom stairs, and have often had to be content with four hours sleep'.[4] Her incessant reading, both during the evenings and during the daytime at work, caused her to confuse what she described as 'the day me' with 'the night me'.[5] In one of her later articles for the *Woman Worker* she recalled the experience of trying to read during the working hours of the mill: 'You understand ever after the feelings of Pip's convict in Dickens's book *Great Expectations*, when he glanced around at the dismal, salt marshes with the irons on his leg that he had brought from the hulks, and knew that sooner or later he would be caught'.[6] Forgetting about her immediate work, she would come to herself 'to find the bobbins too full, one rubbing against the other, so that it would take hours to right them again'.[7]

Carnie Holdsworth began to write poetry at an early age and, by the time she turned eighteen, was getting some of it published in Black-burn's weekly papers. This brought her to the attention of her 'first literary friend and advisor', W. H. Burnett, newspaper man and president of the Blackburn Authors' Society, who championed her locally and helped her to publish five hundred copies of a small six pence volume of poetry, *Rhymes from the Factory*, in 1907.[8] This sold out within a month (in the preface to the second edition she attests to receiving up to forty enquiries a day for it), and Carnie Holdsworth was encouraged to publish an enlarged one shilling edition. It was through this that she achieved national rec-ognition.[9] In July 1908 the popular socialist author and Clarion leader Robert Blatchford visited Carnie Holdsworth at her home for a fea-ture-length interview with his newspaper, the *Woman Worker*. Previous women in the paper's 'Portrait Gallery' included such influential and well-known figures as Margaret McMillan and Mrs Pankhurst. Ethel Carnie Holdsworth appeared under the title 'A Lancashire Fairy' and was described by Blatchford as 'a small, quiet young woman, with quiet grey eyes, a quiet smile, and a dimple in her chin. [...] Just a typical Lancashire factory girl, in a typical Lancashire house'.[10] What Carnie Holdsworth thought of Blatchford, who admits to feeling 'more like a big, rough dog than usual' at this first encounter, we do not know – she would later have a bitter split from him – but the meeting, for which Carnie Holdsworth was fined for taking unauthorised leave from her loom, initiated a rela-tionship of patronage that would transform her life expectations. She later commented, 'what I should have been had Robert Blatchford not taken me out of the cage goodness knows – I do not'.[11]

With Blatchford's influential encouragement, Carnie Holdsworth left the mill at the age of twenty-two to take up a writing career full-time. She moved to London and wrote verses, fairy stories, and factory sketches for a number of newspapers, including the *Clarion* and the *Woman Worker*, which she also edited between July and December of 1909. Through such work she became acquainted with prominent left-wing figures like the independent labour MP Victor Grayson, the shop workers' trade unionist Margaret Bondfield, and Blatchford's daughter, Winifred, all of whom shared a platform with her at the *Woman Worker's* first annual reunion in November 1908.[12] This appears to be the only time in her career that

Carnie Holdsworth deliberately sought to mix with the leading socialists and left-wing 'celebrities' of her time. (Perhaps surprisingly, there is no evidence that she ever met Annie Kenney (1879–1953), Hannah Mitchell (1872–1956), or Ellen Wilkinson (1891–1947), women of similar politics to herself and of similar backgrounds). We cannot now know what she made of the London socialist crowd during her first stay in the capital during 1908–9. It seems that she enjoyed London itself, for she praised it in both her poetry and journalism. An article for *Women Folk* in 1910 announces that 'London is the key to all the mysteries of life, [...] if ever you have enough money have a peep at London'.[13] Ruth and Eddie Frow suggest that Carnie Holdsworth's increasingly political and feminist editorials on the *Woman Worker* may have caused Blatchford to reassess his protégé. Yet whatever the reasons, and they may also have been family-related, when the paper collapsed at the end of 1909 Carnie Holdsworth returned to Lancashire and 'took the line of least resistance and went back into the factory again'.[14] She listed her occupation for the 1911 census as 'cotton winder and journalist'.[15]

The return to the mill was only to be a temporary measure however. Over the next few years, before she married the local poet Alfred Holdsworth in April 1915, Carnie Holdsworth published her first novel, *Miss Nobody* (1913), a second volume of poetry, and several children's stories. She travelled in Germany (writing about her experiences in *The Wheatsheaf*, the journal of the Co-operative Society), engaged in shop work with her mother, and attended Owens College in Manchester as a non-degree student where, she later said, she felt like 'a duck in pattens' (wooden clogs).[16] During 1913–14 she worked at Bebel House Women's College and Socialist Education Centre in London, where she founded the 'Rebel Pen Club', a literary group for working women of an aspiring literary and socialist bent.[17] Bebel House, named after the influential socialist-feminist, August Bebel, was part of the Central Labour College's programme of adult education. Unlike the Workers Educational Association (w.e.a.), which believed in a liberal education and Matthew Arnold's notion of culture as a great civilising force, the Central Labour Colleges championed what was known as the 'Independent Working-Class Education Movement': a partisan education centred upon the Marxist tenets of class struggle.[18] Unlike the Yorkshire novelist Margaret

Storm Jameson, who also worked at Bebel House and would later portray what she deemed to be the damaging effects of its educational practices in her novel, *The Green Man* (1952), Carnie Holdsworth remained a vigorous champion of 'class education'. The tone of her letter to the *Cotton Factory Times* in 1914, lambasting the policies of the w.e.a. and calling instead for 'Armour not Culture', is immediately recognisable as belonging to the narrator of *This Slavery*:

> From cradle to the grave the worker is being chloroformed. The worst chloroform of all is that administered by 'non-political, neutral-impartial' education. [...] What brain power we have left after being exploited we had better spend in concentration on the narrow, rigid, and distinctly not impartial facts deduced from the experiences of our own exploited class.[19]

Despite her more dogmatic rhetoric and the constant allusions in her writing to the spectre of the Red Army, Carnie Holdsworth was throughout her life opposed to violence. She avoided contact with the suffragette movement because she disapproved of its more militant tactics, but dedicated to Emmeline and Christabel Pankhurst two of her poems, which were subsequently set to music by the composer Ethel Smyth and performed as part of Smyth's 'Three Songs' by the London Symphony Orchestra in 1913. As a firm believer in the solidarity of the working classes and the international labour movement, Carnie Holdsworth was ardently opposed to the First World War. She chaired meetings of the local British Citizen Party, which opposed conscription, and saw off her husband Alfred, when he was called up in 1917, by waving a red flag.[20] At the end of the war, after first being reported killed, Alfred returned home from a prisoner of war camp. Carnie Holdsworth later fictionalised his experiences in her novel *General Belinda* (1924), in which a character describes the prisoner of war camps as 'a picture of a hell where famished and verminous men had degenerated into beasts, tearing at each other for scraps of food'.[21]

Carnie Holdsworth had two children, Margaret (b.1916) and Maud (b.1920). After an unsuccessful stint in a deprived post-war London and a period living with Carnie Holdsworth's parents for financial reasons, the family moved to Hebden Bridge in West Yorkshire. For the local people Ethel and her husband cut a distinctive pair. Alfred set up a political debating society called 'The Forum' in the local Trade Club, whilst the Ex-Mill Girl author's smoking habits earned her the dubious nickname from local children of the 'Chain Smoking Lady'.[22] Between 1923 and 1925 Carnie Holdsworth and her husband edited and produced the *Clear Light* from their home in Hebden Bridge with their own funds. Anti-fascist and anti-militarist, the journal urged a united front of labour, communism and anarchism and became the organ of the National Union for Combating Fascism in 1924. It is not clear how involved Carnie Holdsworth was with the newly formed Communist Party of Great Britain in the 1920s, though she was in close contact with William Holt, the Communist councillor for Todmorden, throughout the years that she lived in Hebden Bridge, and Alfred later became a party member. By 1927, she had joined the Labour Party and described herself in its Who's Who of that year as an 'author and home worker'.[23] Four years later, when her last novel, *Eagle's Crag*, was published, Carnie Holdsworth had published ten novels in addition to three volumes of verse, three collections of children's stories, and numerous other serial stories. She continued to write journalism for much of her life, though her troubled marriage, another 'fascist' war, and the decline of her physical health depressed her. She died in Manchester, largely forgotten as a former 'literary celebrity', in December 1962.[24]

This Slavery: The Land of Moors and Mills

With its scathing narrator and Marxist-feminist class politics, *This Slavery* is a radical, polemical novel and a key intervention in the history of British working-class writing. There are no obvious comparisons to be made with the literary works of Ethel Carnie Holdsworth. The competing demands of work, family and home (what the politician Hannah Mitchell described as having 'to work with one hand tied behind us')[25] have meant that, historically, female novelists from a working-class background have been few and far between. A number of Carnie Holdsworth's contemporaries – working-class women of similar backgrounds – have written autobiographies (Annie Kenney, Hannah Mitchell, Alice Foley), but the narrative and material challenges of writing novel-length fiction have largely worked against the appearance of female working-class novelists.[26] The closest literary comparison we can make with Ethel Carnie Holdsworth is probably Ellen Wilkinson (1891–1947), who was born not more than twenty miles away from Carnie Holdsworth into an upper working-class family. But Wilkinson was a Member of Parliament when she came to write her novels (her first, *Clash* (1929), was written on the train as she travelled between London and her constituency), making her material conditions at the time of writing very different to those of Carnie Holdsworth's. In this respect, Carnie Holdsworth's fictional achievements are all the more remarkable.

This Slavery is set in the archetypal working-class landscape of urban Lancashire, the honorary home of what Friedrich Engels in the 1840s called the first real industrial proletariat 'from which all labour movements emanate'.[27] The novel centres on the lives of a matriarchal family of cotton workers: sisters Hester and Rachel Martin, their mother Mary, and their maternal grandmother. Through them, the material conditions of life in the mill towns are acutely drawn after a fire at the mill shatters the family's 'respectable poverty' (5), leaving them unemployed, uninsured, and close to starvation. The narrative draws on the long-standing traditions and history in working-class Lancashire of political engagement, close-knit community (which sometimes cripples its members by forcing them to adhere to a straightening respectability), and women's work outside the home. This is the more radical heritage of the British working-classes which continues to attract the interest of historians, sociologists, novelists and film-makers.[28] Yet from the opening pages of the novel, which are located in the Martin family's kitchen, overlooked by pictures of the 'gentle' socialist forefathers William Morris and William Liebknecht, it is clear that Carnie Holdsworth's take on this radical heritage offers a rather different version from that which is often told. Firmly locating the kitchen as a core space within her story of class politics, Carnie Holdsworth's 'slavery' is an important reminder of the roles played by women in the labour movement and the significance of the daily world of the home, as well as that of work, as a formative site of class experience and consciousness. As Leonora Eyles's contemporary account of the lives of 'thousands of inarticulate women' as good as caged in their uncomfortable domestic interiors would pronounce: 'I believe that the political revolutions that end in bombs and massacres begin with the tired, neurotic women in the Little Houses'.[29]

Through the diverging stories of sisters Hester and Rachel Martin, Carnie Holdsworth offers a story which is both radical and romantic, heroic and pathetic, simultaneously drawing upon the mythos of the 'pluck' of the urban Lancashire mill workers while consistently undercutting that 'spirit' by condemning the economic and social conditions which so graphically produce it and determine its subjects' lives. From the author's opening dedication – 'To My Mother and Father, slaves and rebels, I dedicate this little book; with a Daughter's affection and a Comrade's greetings' – the politics of the novel are everywhere apparent. The plot, style and language of the text are infused with the rhetoric, ideologies, and songs of the international labour movement. The hero, Jack Baines, is an activist of the Social Democratic Federation – a vanguard organisation intent on educating the workers in economic theory and the fundamental importance of the class struggle – and during her enforced unemployment Rachel reads Karl Marx's *Das Capital*, declaring that she will become a 'scientific Revolutionist' (90). It is surely the Red Army that Stephen – the crippled, Christ-like child of Hester and Sanderson – can hear as he listens to 'The Feet' outside approaching the mill-owner's home. Other key influences in the novel are the ideas of the utopian socialist William Morris, whose picture peers out into the Martins' kitchen and whose *News from Nowhere, or, an Epoch of Rest: Being Some Chapters from a Utopian Romance* (1890) inspires the dreams of both Martin sisters, and the Persian poet Omar Khayyám, whose work colours the thoughts of Stiner, the Martins' hapless neighbour, another Christ-like martyr to the cause of Labour. Yet one of the most important intertexts in the novel, and the one that would have been most familiar to its contemporary audience – socialist or not alike – is the Bible, allusions to which pepper the narrative. Those whom the narrator portrays as its more hypocritical and misguided earthly disciples are subjected to some of the novel's most withering critique.

At the centre of *This Slavery* is a passionate feminist-Marxist critique of both economic and sexual slavery, coupled with a plea for women's freedom under socialism. In forgiving her mother's past adultery, Rachel delivers one of the key feminist speeches in the text, criticising the available roles for women in the labour movement as she does so:

> 'I believe our morals are determined by our necessity an' the economic conditions we live under. [...] I don't see that sex is any more sacred than genius, and to sell one has no more ill effects than to sell th' other. [...] I wonder when women'll be free, mother? An' chaps, too, of course. But we, we somehow have a tradition behind us besides an economic slavery. We've got the race on our shoulders, an' all th' other besides. An' all they think we're fit for down at the SDF yonder, is to cook a thumping big potato pie, when there's a social, or go round canvassing the names when a councillor puts up.' (54).

The idea that sex, or the female body, is no more sacred than the mind – both of which Carnie Holdsworth suggests are sold to the profits of capitalism – is still a radical one, and strikes at the heart of conservative ideologies of women's feminine sanctity. Indeed, Carnie Holdsworth was doing something very radical in linking the economic exigencies and cross-class liaisons of working-class women in the mills with the late nineteenth and early twentieth-century panic about the trade in female prostitution – the so-called 'white slavery'. In suggesting that Mary Martin and her daughter Hester should be forgiven their 'transgressive' adultery and marriage respectively (or their sexual prostitution to capitalism, as Jack Baines would have it), Carnie Holdsworth offers a serious interjection into contemporary debates about working-class women's sexuality and the economic, physical and material realities underlying women's resort to prostitution. The sympathy with which Mary Martin and her daughter, Hester, are treated is well-nigh unique in the history of the novel up to this point (George Bernard Shaw's late nineteenth-century play, *Mrs Warren's Profession,* which offers a moral and realistic take on the social evils behind prostitution was not licensed for performance in Britain until the late 1920s). It was more common to portray the grasping or myopic working-class woman's trade-up through her sexuality. In Elizabeth Gaskell's depiction of the sexually transgressive working-class woman in *Mary Barton: A Tale of Manchester Life* (1848), for instance,

Introduction

Esther Barton, the eponymous heroine's aunt, haunts the margins of the text like a shadow. She is unable to cross over the threshold of the respectable working-class home and her 'fall' is inadvertently blamed for the death of her sister, Mary's mother. Carnie Holdsworth's use of an echoing name in *This Slavery* (Hester Martin/Esther Barton) is surely deliberate and meant to call the reader's attention to the earlier industrial tale. The retention of both Mary Martin and her daughter Hester as key characters in *This Slavery*, both 'fallen' women who remain central figures of love and authority within the family home, is a radical intervention on Carnie Holdsworth's part in the depiction of working-class women's sexuality.

The industrial novels of the nineteenth-century novelist Elizabeth Gaskell are clearly an important influence on *This Slavery*, and the reader may recognise the novel's ironic inversion of Margaret Hale's defence of John Thornton in *North and South* (1855). Yet the most significant influence on the novel in terms of both genre and plot are the sensational serial stories produced in the contemporary penny weeklies for working women and young girls. As dark-haired, opinionated and independent mill-girls, Hester and Rachel Martin would have been immediately rec-ognisable characters to a contemporary reading public well-versed in the trials and tribulations of the fictional mill-girl. The inter-war period's plethora of new fiction weeklies aimed at the female breadwinning public included popular weeklies such as *Peg's Paper* and *Ivy Stories* (to which Carnie Holdsworth later contributed), all of which offered cheap and vicarious entertainment through long complete novels, romantic serial fiction, and 'matey' advice. What is so fascinating about *This Slavery* is the way in which Carnie Holdsworth adapts this popular, widely-read genre – a clear pull for the contemporary mass reading public – and adds a socialist and woman-centred framework to the classic mill-girl melodrama of virtuous heroines, headstrong factory girls, and lecherous overseers.

As well as recalling the moral panic about women's 'white slavery', the 'slavery' of the title is also a direct reference to the factory system. This draws upon a rhetorical tradition of comparing the lives and working conditions of British mill-hands with the slavery endured by enslaved peoples in the colonies that goes back to the Factory Reform debates of the early nineteenth century.[30] If it is one of Carnie Holdsworth's aims in this novel to focus her readers' attention on the 'slavery' suffered by the people not so far away in Lancashire, the wider struggles and deprivations of the international labour movement are never far from the narrator's mind. The novel offers a blistering critique of the inequities of global trade and the economics of Empire, the system upon which the wealth of the few in the Lancashire mill towns had been built, where British traders were able to flood colonial markets with manufactured goods that cost less than it was possible to produce locally. Thinking scornfully of the British Empire 'built by the labour of generations of […] uncounted lives', Rachel immediately equates the suffering and starvation going on in her own town to that endured by 'hundreds of thousands' across the world: 'Millions in Eastern countries lived like beasts' (71). In Stiner's vision of the town, 'the town with the great Indian trade, the high wages, the high speed, where bits o' lasses drowned themselves for dark fear that they could not reach the average wage' (25), the divisions between the working classes – between shop girls and mill-hands, bank clerks and weavers – are explicitly compared with the divisions of the Indian caste system. Throughout her life, Carnie Holdsworth would campaign for an international front of the 'exploited' labouring classes in the face of the global systems of capitalism, empire and fascism; for all the workers of the world to unite.

The date at which Carnie Holdsworth wrote *This Slavery* is open to question, but the novel certainly seems to conjure up a pre-war world. The reference to a woman's loss of her son in the Boer War, the failure to mention figures such as Rosa Luxemburg (one of the joint leaders of the Spartacist Uprising in Germany in 1919) or the Communist Revolutions in Russia, and the lack of knowledge about the work of the Salford-based painter L. S. Lowry (1887–1976) ('no painter had ever painted it' (101), suggest that the novel was written either during or before the First World War. This is also when the debates over 'white slavery' were at their height. Rachel's reference to the death of the Spanish-Catalan leader Francisco Ferrer (1859–1909) as a recent event certainly suggests that the novel is set in the pre-war period. Chris Lynch points out that Carnie Holdsworth's depiction of the strike in the novel may have been based on her experience of the Great Lancashire Lockout of 1911–12, when the

Weavers' trade union brought their members out on strike after failing to get three non-union workers dismissed. One of the non-unionists, Miss Margaret Bury, lived in Great Harwood, and Carnie Holdsworth would no doubt have been witness to the angry demonstrations and violence which met her decision, as well as the misery and hunger that the strike caused.[31]

The lack of historical specificity in the text has concerned some critics reading *This Slavery*. Ian Haywood comments that 'for all its strident politics, the novel lacks a defined historical sense. [...] Given the rarity of the novel, the modern reader feels some frustration that an opportunity was lost to engage more fully with contemporary events'.[32] Perhaps, as Phyllis Mary Ashraf has suggested, the novel was an earlier work which it only became possible to publish in the post-war phase of rising militancy and political unrest (the General Strike, of course, was to occur just one year after its publication), or perhaps it was the reduced state of the publishing industry in the First World War, or personal circumstances, that encouraged Carnie Holdsworth to seek publication of the novel only after she had settled in Hebden Bridge in the mid 1920s. Whatever the reasons for the eventual appearance of the text in novel form in 1925, there is little to be gained by criticising the lack of contemporary references. The novel as published marks a key intervention in socialist-feminist debate of the interwar period, a period when 'class' still heavily predominated over 'sex' as a political and analytical category in the various strands of the British labour movement, and it is in these terms in which *This Slavery* should be read.[33]

Aside from the Marxist-infused rhetoric of the novel, the didacticism and some of the stylistic bombast, what may most jar on the ears and sensibilities of the modern-day reader may be its disturbing depiction of disability as punishment and its sometimes cruel portrayals of 'class traitors': particularly the police and domestic servants (Carnie Holdsworth was not consistent on this later point, her novel *General Belinda* follows the fortunes of a sympathetic domestic servant who is heavily exploited). If Carnie Holdsworth's political radicalism and the narrator's enthusiasm for the footfalls of the Red Army also disturb the contemporary reader, one should remember the widespread intellectual investment in the far-left as a viable and respectable alternative to capitalism in the early years of the twentieth century, before the horrors of Stalinism in the 1930s and other regimes were made known. In a time when it is again possible to think that we might 'Make Poverty History', *This Slavery* seems to have a continuing relevance.

Reception and Recovery

This Slavery was the most radical of the 'Ex-mill girl' author's novels. After first appearing in serial form in the *Daily Herald* (October 1923 – February 1924), it was published in book form in 1925 by a left-wing press called the Labour Publishing Company. A short-lived publishing venture of the 1920s, created by the Labour Research Department with the aim of making books of interest to the labour movement more readily available, the Labour Publishing Company published original works and reprints of, amongst others, Lenin, Marx, Tom Mann, Winifred Horrabin and Leonard Woolf. *This Slavery* joined its list as one of only a handful of novels, and was sold at two shillings and sixpence, the common rate for cheap reprints of recently published novels (first editions were generally sold at seven shillings and sixpence during the interwar period). The fact that the first edition of *This Slavery* was sold at 2s 6d was remarkable enough of a venture to warrant a note of optimistic praise from the reviewer of the *Plebs*, 'first, congratulations to the publishers for producing a novel for working-class readers at something like a working-class price'.[34] Yet even at this price, the likelihood of such a reader being able to purchase the novel new, rather than borrowing it from a library which was much more common a practice, was slim.

Carnie Holdsworth's decision to publish *This Slavery* with the Labour Publishing Company seems to have been due to its rejection by her usual publishers, Herbert Jenkins, specialist purveyors of light romantic fiction who boasted amongst their authors of the 1920s the massively popular P. G. Wodehouse with the first of his acclaimed *Jeeves and Wooster* series. After publishing *Helen of Four Gates* in 1917, Jenkins's had bound Carnie Holdsworth into a further six-book contract which was broken by their failure to publish *This Slavery* (she returned to them with her next book, *The Quest of the Golden Garter* (1927), making

Jenkins's total of Carnie Holdsworth novels six, not the envisaged seven). By offering *This Slavery* to Jenkins as her contracted publishers in the first instance, Carnie Holdsworth was presumably deemed to have met the terms of her contract with them, and their decision to pass it seems to have come as something of a surprise. In the autumn of 1924, at least, when Carnie Holdsworth admitted to one of her fans that '*This Slavery* is not yet out in book form, truth to tell I have not had time to paste out all the serial cuttings completely yet', she believed that it would be 'out in Spring, published by Jenkins & Co. At about 2/6'.[35] Sadly the archive of the Labour Publishing Company has been lost to history and there are no surviving letters relating to the fate of *This Slavery* in the Herbert Jenkins archive. This means that we cannot know precisely how or why *This Slavery* came into the hands of the Labour Publishing Company – it was the only one of Carnie Holdsworth's ten novels to be published by them – nor how much Carnie Holdsworth received for it, or what the production and sales figures might have been. It was published in Russia in 1926 and Carnie Holdsworth also talked of it being translated into German, though whether a German edition ever appeared remains unclear.[36]

By the time of the publication of *This Slavery* – the novel for which Carnie Holdsworth is now most often remembered – she was well established as a novelist. *Helen of Four Gates* (1917), her second novel, had been compared in the press to Thomas Hardy's *Tess of the D'Urbervilles* and the novels of the Brontë sisters (particularly Emily Brontë's *Wuthering Heights*, which the novel heavily draws upon), and was a popular bestseller. It was made into a silent film, directed by Cecil M. Hepworth and starring the popular actress Alma Taylor, in 1921. Carnie Holdsworth's other novels published after the First World War – *The Taming of Nan* (1920), *The Marriage of Elizabeth* (1920), *The House that Jill Built* (1920) and *General Belinda* (1924) – dealt variously with northern domestic life, working-class motherhood, the ethics of philanthropy, and the hardships of life in domestic service.

Though many of the themes in *This Slavery* were present in Carnie Holdsworth's earlier work (and particularly the serial story 'The Iron Horses', serialised in the *Co-operative News* from July to December 1915), the scathing tone of the narrative voice in *This Slavery* and the book's undisguised, trenchant class politics represented a serious challenge to previous readers of her work. Its bitterness was too much for her erstwhile local champion, the *Blackburn Times*, whose reviewer took much offence at what he deemed to be an unfair representation of Lancashire factory life. Carnie Holdsworth was deeply hurt by this criticism and defended her 'first attempt to portray a horrible social struggle' on the grounds that *This Slavery* was a symbolic representation of an ongoing global class struggle, stating that it was the economic conditions themselves, and not the author, that should be blamed for 'the brutality, the hatred, the waste, the degradation of all that is finest and largest and best in humanity'.[37] The novel caused a stir in the labour press, reviewed in the *Plebs* (the journal of the National Council of Labour Colleges) as 'A Propaganda Novel' suitable for the unconverted which 'strikes the real, proletarian note'.[38] Yet Carnie Holdsworth was roundly criticised by the male establishment on the left for mixing politics and romance. The reviewer of the communist paper the *Sunday Worker* was particularly trenchant in his criticisms, declaring that Carnie Holdsworth's use of 'the usual love situation as the pivot of the machinery of the whole tale' was part of the author's 'inheritance from the bourgeois fiction writers', an education that had also apparently caused her to lose sight of the 'revolutionary significance' of poverty.[39] There was no recognition of the wider audience that the inclusion of a love story within a socialist tale might bring. Carnie Holdsworth's rejoinder was spirited, declaring that 'he talks like a middle-class mamma who cannot tell love from sentiment', and further arguing that there was nothing for the labour movement to gain in glorifying the material poverty of everyday life: 'a dry crust with a scrape of margarine is a dry crust with a scrape of margarine'.[40]

After her disappearance from the publishing scene in the late 1930s, Carnie Holdsworth's work slipped into oblivion. The research of the German scholar H. Gustav Klaus, which from the 1970s has sought to recover the writing of 'lost' working-class writers, has therefore been indispensable to the rediscovery of Ethel Carnie Holdsworth and her work in the later part of the twentieth century.[41] Important early work on Carnie Holdsworth's novels was undertaken by Phyllis Mary Ashraf and Edmund and Ruth Frow, who recovered a lot of biographical material in the late 1980s and were able to speak to Margaret Quinn, Carnie

Holdsworth's eldest daughter, shortly before her death.[42] Interestingly, the contemporary critique of *This Slavery* on generic – and distinctly gendered – lines, has continued to set the tone for the way in which the novel has been read by some parts of the left. In an insightful study of the place of *This Slavery* in the context of the literature of 'The Radical Twenties', for example, John Lucas argues that the novel fails because of its romantic focus on the individual:

> The attention Carnie Holdsworth pays to the outbreak of a strike in the cotton industry is to a large extent wasted. […] By paying so much attention to Hester, Carnie Holdsworth loses sight of the representative nature of the issues her novel ought to be addressing.[43]

At the same time, Carnie Holdsworth's work has come to be of interest to feminist scholars who have sought to locate the author's novels within the longer tradition of the socialist romance, going back to the popular socialist fiction of late nineteenth-century women writers such as Isabella Ford (1855–1924) and Katherine Bruce Glasier (1867–1950).[44] Carnie Holdsworth's novels also make interesting comparison with the late Victorian fiction of the socialist author and journalist, Margaret Harkness (1854–1923). The most important feminist intervention in the reading of Carnie Holdsworth's work in recent years is that made by Pamela Fox, who has sought to recover the 'radical potential' of the romance as a complex literary genre, arguing that it can function as a 'complex resistance strategy', as well as the more obvious reinscription of a dominant convention governing gender, class, and literary relations'.[45] After being lost from the literary horizon for over fifty years and unavailable in print for even longer than that, the fact that *This Slavery* continues to inspire such debate is sure proof of its narrative power and wide-ranging interest as a novel.

Original British dust jacket, *This Slavery* (London: The Labour Publishing
Company, 1925)

NOTES

1. For clarity I refer to her as 'Carnie Holdsworth' throughout this introduction, except where referencing the publications which she produced in her maiden name, Ethel Carnie, or later as Ethel Holdsworth.

2. Robert Blatchford, 'A Lancashire Fairy. An Interview with Miss Ethel Carnie', *Woman Worker*, 10 July 1908, p.155.

3. Ethel Carnie, 'The Factory Slave', *Woman Worker*, 3 March 1909, p.214.

4. Anon., 'Ethel Carnie Holdsworth: A Notable Lancashire Woman Novelist', *Woman's Outlook*, September 1920, 294–5 (p.295).

5. Anon., 'With Authors and Publishers', *New York Times Book Review*, 16 September 1917, p.6.

6. Ethel Carnie, 'Factory Intelligence', *Woman Worker*, 10 March 1909, p.219.

7. Anon., 'With Authors and Publishers'.

8. Ethel Carnie, 'The "Benevolent-Minded"', *Cotton Factory Times*, 5 June 1914, p. 8. See also the dedication to Burnett in Ethel Carnie, *Voices of Womanhood* (London: Headley Bros., 1914).

9. Ethel Carnie, *Rhymes from the Factory*, second edn (Blackburn: Denham, 1908).

10. Blatchford, 'A Lancashire Fairy'.

11. Ethel Carnie, 'How Colour is Introduced', *Woman Worker*, 7 April 1909, p.323.

12. Tickets at one shilling were available through the Independent Labour Party, the Social Democratic Federation, and 'all womens' and labour organisations'. 'The Pioneers' Opening Night: To London Readers', *Woman Worker*, 28 October 1908, p.505.

13. Ethel Carnie, 'One Girl to Another', *Women Folk*, 30 March 1910, p. 835. See also the poem 'London' in *Songs of a Factory Girl* (London: Headley Brothers, 1911), p.35.

14. Anon., 'Ex-Mill Girl Who Became Literary Celebrity', *Yorkshire Observer*, 5 April 1932, p.11.

15. *Census of England and Wales 1911*, The National Archives, RG 14/25009/283.

16. Anon, 'The Authoress of Our New Serial Story', *Co-operative News*, 21 July 1915, 998–9 (p.999).

17. Anon., 'Rebel Pen Club of Working Women', *Christian Science Monitor*, 10 January 1914, p.31.

18. The Central Labour Colleges became the National Council of Labour Colleges in 1921. For a history of the tensions between the Central Labour Colleges and the Workers Educational Association see Jonathan Rose, *The Intellectual Life of the British Working Classes* (New Haven: Yale Nota Bene, 2002); and Jonathan Rée, *Proletarian Philosophers: Problems in Socialist Culture in Britain, 1900–1940* (Oxford: Clarendon Press, 1984).

19. Ethel Carnie, 'The Class Struggle and "Learning"', *Cotton Factory Times*, 6 March 1914, p.4.

20. For more on the little-known British Citizen Party see Roger Smalley, 'The Life and Work of Ethel Carnie Holdsworth, with particular reference to the period 1907 to 1931' (unpublished doctoral thesis, University of Central Lancashire, 2006).

21. Ethel Holdsworth, *General Belinda* (London: Herbert Jenkins, 1924), p.302.

22. Hebden Bridge Local History Society Archive. MISC 6/20. *Helen of Four Gates:* filming in West Yorkshire generations ago. Dilys Dean. Undated.

23. *Labour Who's Who* (London: Labour Publishing Company, 1927), p.105.

24. Anon., 'Ex-Mill Girl Who Became Literary Celebrity'.

25. Hannah Mitchell, *The Hard Way Up: The Autobiography of Hannah Mitchell, Suffragette and Rebel* (London: Faber & Faber, 1968), p.130.

26. Annie Kenney, *Memories of a Militant* (London: Arnold, 1924); Mitchell, *The Hard Way Up*; Alice Foley, *A Bolton Childhood* (Manchester: Manchester University Extra-Mural Department, 1973).

27. Friedrich Engels, *The Condition of the Working Class in England*, trans. by Florence Kelley Wischnewetzky (London: Allen & Unwin,

1892; repr. Penguin, 1987), p.82.

28. For this archetypal community see the autobiographies of Robert Roberts, *The Classic Slum: Salford Life in the First Quarter of the Century* (Manchester: Manchester University Press, 1971) and *A Ragged Schooling: Growing up in the Classic Slum* (Manchester: Manchester University Press, 1976). In the 1930s Walter Greenwood captured this landscape in *Love on the Dole: A Tale of the Two Cities* (London: Cape, 1933). For important historical work on the Lancashire area and its history see Jill Liddington and Jill Norris, *One Hand Tied Behind Us: The Rise of the Women's Suffrage Movement* (London: Virago, 1978); and Elizabeth Roberts, *A Woman's Place: An Oral History of Working-Class Women, 1890–1940* (Oxford: Blackwell, 1984).

29. Margaret Leonora Eyles, *The Woman in the Little House* (London: Richards, 1922), p.25; 16.

30. The industrial reformer Richard Oastler wrote to the *Leeds Mercury* in October 1830 with a letter entitled 'Yorkshire Slavery', since credited with initiating the Ten Hours Movement. Oastler sought to bring the attention of the contemporary Anti-Slavery Society to the slavery going on in the city's own streets. For more on the rhetoric of freedom in the early nineteenth century industrial debates see Catherine Gallagher, *The Industrial Reformation of English Fiction: Social Discourse and Narrative Form, 1832–1867* (Chicago: University of Chicago Press, 1985).

31. Anon., 'Miss Bury Driven from Home', *Daily Mirror*, 11 January 1912, p. 3.

32. Ian Haywood, *Working-Class Fiction: From Chartism to Trainspotting* (Plymouth: Northcote House, 1997), p.46–7.

33. For the 'woman question' in this period see Karen Hunt, *Equivocal Feminists: The Social Democratic Federation and the Woman Question, 1884–1911* (Cambridge: Cambridge University Press, 1996); June Hannan and Karen Hunt, *Socialist Women: Britain, 1880s to 1920s* (London: Routledge, 2002); Pamela M. Graves, *Labour Women: Women in British Working-Class Politics 1918–1939* (Cambridge: Cambridge University Press, 1994); and Christine Collette, 'Socialism and Scandal: The Sexual Politics of the Early Labour Movement',

History Workshop Journal, 23 (1987), 102–11.

34. H.O.B., 'A Propaganda Novel', *Plebs*, October 1925, p.408–9.

35. Hebden Bridge Local History Society Archive. MISC 8/4. Postcard from Ethel Holdsworth to W. Hardisty. 10 September 1924.

36. In correspondence with W. Hardisty in 1924 (see above), Carnie wrote that 'a translator wishes to turn it into German, and I wish it too'. Chris Lynch has conducted an extensive search for this translation but it remains unfound.

37. Ethel Carnie Holdsworth, 'Mrs. E. Carnie Holdsworth's New Novel', *Blackburn Times*, 27 June 1925, p.16.

38. H.O. B., 'A Propaganda Novel'.

39. 'Peachem', 'The Books They Write', *Sunday Worker*, 5 July 1925, p.9.

40. Ethel Carnie Holdsworth, letter in 'The Books They Write', *Sunday Worker*, 26 July 1925, p.6.

41. H. Gustav Klaus, 'Silhouettes of Revolution: Some Neglected Novels of the Early 1920s', in *The Socialist Novel in Britain: Towards the Recovery of a Tradition*, ed. by H. Gustav Klaus (Brighton: Harvester, 1982), pp.89–109.

42. Phyllis Mary Ashraf, *Introduction to Working-Class Literature in Great Britain*, Part II (Berlin: Ministerium fur Volksbildung, 1979); Edmund and Ruth Frow, 'Ethel Carnie Holdsworth: Writer, Feminist and Socialist', in *The Rise of Socialist Fiction 1880–1914*, ed. by H. Gustav Klaus (Brighton: Harvester, 1987), pp.251–56.

43. John Lucas, *The Radical Twenties: Aspects of Writing, Politics and Culture* (Nottingham: Five Leaves Publications, 1997), p.159.

44. On this earlier tradition see Chris Waters, 'New Women and Socialist-Feminist Fiction: The Novels of Isabella Ford and Katherine Bruce Glasier', in *Rediscovering Forgotten Radicals: British Women Writers, 1889–1939*, ed. by Angela Ingram and Daphne Patel (Chapel Hill: University of North Carolina Press, 1993), pp.25–42.

45. Pamela Fox, *Class Fictions: Shame and Resistance in the British Working-Class Novel, 1890–1945* (Durham: Duke University Press, 1994), p.145.

SUGGESTIONS FOR FURTHER READING

Archives

THERE are no known archives containing the personal records or correspondence of Ethel Carnie Holdsworth. The Working-Class Movement Library in Salford holds Edmund and Ruth Frows' biographical research, notes and correspondence from the late 1980s. See http://www.wcml.org. uk/holdings/carnie.htm

Contemporary and Primary Sources

Blatchford, Robert, *Merrie England* (London: Scott, 1894)

—*Britain for the British* (London: Clarion Press, 1902)

Bridges, Winnie, *Educating Grandma* (Bristol: Falling Wall, 1988)

Eyles, Margaret Leonora, *The Woman in the Little House* (London: Richards, 1922)

Gaskell, Elizabeth, *Mary Barton: A Tale of Manchester Life*, 2 vols (London: Chapman and Hall, 1848; repr. Penguin, 1994)

—*North and South*, 2 vols (London: Chapman and Hall, 1855; repr. Penguin, 1994)

Foley, Alice, *A Bolton Childhood* (Manchester: Manchester University Extra-Mural Department, 1973)

Ford, Isabella, *On the Threshold* (London: Arnold, 1895)

Harkness, Margaret, *A City Girl: A Realistic Story* (London: Vizetelly, 1887)

Kenney, Annie, *Memories of a Militant* (London: Arnold, 1924)

Khayyám, Omar, *The Rubáiyát of Omar Khayyám*, trans. by Edward Fitzgerald (London: Quaritch, 1859; repr. New York: Dover, 1991)

Klaus, H. Gustav, ed., *Tramps, Workmates and Revolutionaries: Working-Class Stories of the 1920s* (London: Journeyman, 1993)

Mitchell, Hannah, *The Hard Way Up: The Autobiography of Hannah Mitchell, Suffragette and Rebel* (London: Faber & Faber, 1968)

Morris, William, *News from Nowhere, or, an Epoch of Rest: Being Some*

Chapters from a Utopian Romance (Boston: Roberts Brothers, 1890; repr. Oxford: Oxford University Press, 2003)

Wilkinson, Ellen, *Clash* (London: Harrap, 1929; repr. Nottingham: Trent, 2004)

Woodruff, William, *The Road to Nab End: An Extraordinary Northern Childhood* (London: Abacus, 2002)

Secondary Sources

Alves, Susan, '"Whilst Working at My Frame": The Poetic Production of Ethel Carnie Holdsworth', *Victorian Poetry,* 38.1 (2000), 77–93

Ashraf, Phyllis Mary, *Introduction to Working-Class Literature in Great Britain: Part II, Prose* (Berlin: Ministerium fur Volksbildung, 1979)

Boos, Florence S., *Working-Class Women Poets in Victorian Britain: An Anthology* (Peterborough, Ontario: Broadview, 2008)

Bourke, Joanna, *Working-Class Cultures in Britain 1880–1960: Gender, Class, Ethnicity* (London: Routledge, 1994)

Bridges, Winnie, *Threads of Lancashire Life* (Blackpool: Landy, 1997)

Collette, Christine, 'Socialism and Scandal: The Sexual Politics of the Early Labour Movement', *History Workshop Journal,* 23 (1987), 102–11

Fox, Pamela, *Class Fictions. Shame and Resistance in the British Working-Class Novel, 1890–1945* (Durham: Duke University Press, 1994)

Francis, Pat, 'The Labour Publishing Company 1920–9', *History Workshop Journal,* 18 (1984), 114–23

Frow, Edmund, and Ruth Frow, 'Ethel Carnie Holdsworth: Writer, Feminist and Socialist', in *The Rise of Socialist Fiction 1880–1914,* ed. by H. Gustav Klaus (Brighton: Harvester, 1987), pp. 251–56

Graves, Pamela M., *Labour Women: Women in British Working-Class Politics, 1918–1939* (Cambridge: Cambridge University Press, 1994)

Hannan, June, and Karen Hunt, *Socialist Women: Britain, 1880s to 1920s* (London: Routledge, 2002)

Haywood, Ian, *Working-Class Fiction: from Chartism to Trainspotting* (Plymouth: Northcote House, 1997)

Hunt, Karen, *Equivocal Feminists: The Social Democratic Federation and the Woman Question, 1884–1911* (Cambridge: Cambridge University Press, 1996)

Johnson, Patricia E., 'Finding Her Voice(s): The Development of a

Working–Class Feminist Vision in Ethel Carnie Holdsworth's Poetry', *Victorian Poetry*, 43.3 (2005), 297–315

Kirk, John, *Twentieth Century Writing and the British Working Class* (Cardiff: University of Wales Press, 2003)

Klaus, H. Gustav, 'Silhouettes of Revolution: Some Neglected Novels of the Early 1920s', in *The Socialist Novel in Britain: Towards the Recovery of a Tradition*, ed. by H. Gustav Klaus (Brighton: Harvester, 1982), pp. 89–109

Liddington, Jill, and Jill Norris, *One Hand Tied Behind Us: The Rise of the Women's Suffrage Movement* (Virago, 1978)

Lucas, John, *The Radical Twenties: Aspects of Writing, Politics and Culture* (Nottingham: Five Leaves Publications, 1997)

Melman, Billie, *Women and the Popular Imagination in the Twenties: Flappers and Nymphs* (Macmillan, 1988)

O' Rourke, Rebecca, 'Were There No Women? British Working Class Writing in the Inter-War Period?', *Literature and History*, 1.4 (1988), 48–63

Rée, Jonathan, *Proletarian Philosophers: Problems in Socialist Culture in Britain, 1900–1940* (Oxford: Clarendon Press, 1984)

Roberts, Elizabeth, *A Woman's Place: An Oral History of Working-Class Women 1890–1940* (Oxford: Blackwell, 1984)

Rose, Jonathan, *The Intellectual Life of the British Working Classes* (New Haven: Yale Nota Bene, 2002)

Smalley, Roger, 'The Life and Work of Ethel Carnie Holdsworth, with particular reference to the period 1907 to 1931' (unpublished doctoral thesis, University of Central Lancashire, 2006)

—'Ethel Carnie Holdsworth: Her Place in the Lancashire Protest Tradition and her Distinctive Propaganda Style', *North West Labour History Journal*, 32 (2007), 51–3

Swindells, Julia, and Lisa Jardine, *What's Left? Women in Culture and the Labour Movement* (London: Routledge, 1990)

Todd, Selina, *Young Women, Work, and Family in England, 1918–1950* (Oxford: Oxford University Press, 2005)

Wilson, Nicola, 'Politicising the Home in Ethel Carnie Holdsworth's *This Slavery* (1925) and Ellen Wilkinson's *Clash* (1929)', *Key Words: A Journal of Cultural Materialism*, 5 (2007–8), 26–42

NOTE ON THE TEXT

The various errors and inconsistencies of spelling, capitalisation, punctuation and usage in the original edition have been standardised and corrected.

In all other respects the text follows that of the original edition.

ACKNOWLEDGEMENTS

For their interest in this book and their efforts to make Ethel Carnie Holdsworth's work available to a wider audience I would like to thank Alan Duckworth of the Community History Department at Blackburn Central Library, Kathleen Bell, Gill Frith, Ian Haywood, Maroula Joannou, Cora Kaplan, H. Gustav Klaus, Alison Light, Carolyn Steedman, and the staff at the Working-Class Movement Library in Salford.

For permission to quote from works in their collections I would like to thank Esther Dean and Nigel Smith of the Hebden Bridge Local History Society. Elizabeth Ludlow advised on the biblical references and Helen Brown has generously provided several family photos, including the photo of Ethel reproduced here. The front cover image, 'Strikers', was found by Alan Duckworth and the reproduction of the dust cover of the original British edition is thanks to Roger Smalley.

Chris Lynch and Roger Smalley have supported this edition with much enthusiasm and offered many helpful references as well as advice on the biographical material in the Introduction. I would like to thank Christian Fox and John Goodridge of Trent Editions for their careful copyediting, John Lucas for his editorial suggestions, and Callum Lewis and Rebecca Kirby of the Department of Typography and Graphic Design at the University of Reading for designing and typesetting the book and helping to see this project through to completion.

Ethel Carnie Holdsworth

This Slavery

To
My Mother and Father, slaves
and rebels, I dedicate this little
book, with a Daughter's affection
and a Comrade's greetings.

BOOK ONE

CHAPTER I

Mrs. Martin was out. Without her restless, bustling energy, the kitchen had an air of peaceful dreaming. Firelight hid the worn look of the oilcloth. The battered bust of Beethoven on the mantel-shelf between prosaic tea-caddy and coffee-canister frowned splendid courage in the shadow. Glints of flame from the fire were reflected in the glass that screened the face of gentle William Morris.[1] Liebknecht,[2] the companion picture, looked out in the shadows, as though contemplating with twilight grief the respectable poverty of this Lancashire household.

The old woman in the rocking-chair in the corner grew restive under the silence. She was quite sure that either the fire wanted poking, or the cat wanted letting out, or the yard door wanted bolting lest those O'Briens stole the coals. She coughed twice – a manufactured cough, to attract the attention of her grand-daughters. All in vain. When she heard the pages of a book turn, she had her cue.

'Put that book down, Hester,' she requested.

'Hester isn't reading,' answered Rachel's strong voice.

'Oh! What is she doing on, then?'

'Darning her stocking.'

'Wi' her foot tucked under her skirt, I'll bet,' guessed the old woman. Soft treble laughter answered her. By that sound the blind woman located Hester.

'Isn't the fire deein' down,' she asked. 'I feel perished.'

She heard a book laid down. Rachel's strong hands took hold of the chair, and the old woman felt the warmth of the fire.

'That's better,' she said. She spread out her hands to the flames.

Hester, looking over the stocking she was mending, noticed the old hands silhouetted against the glow. How she wished she could paint them, just so – toil-twisted, humble, the hands of a woman who had slaved almost from cradle to grave. Often thoughts like this came to Hester.

But then – how could any working girl find time to do that on which men and women spent a lifetime? Ten hours a day, body weariness, odd jobs to do in the house, Sundays that were recuperating hours to gather strength for the next week's grind. Hester sighed. It was indeed a tremendous hole she had found peeping over her clog-top.

'Haven't you lit up yet?' asked the old woman.

'Oh, we can still see,' Rachel told her. 'Mother hasn't got over that last gas bill yet.'

'You'll know about it when your day-leets is ruined,' sighed the old woman. She huddled nearer to the fire.

Silence fell again.

The garden gate clicked.

'Oh, Lord! Somebody's coming,' ejaculated Hester.

'It'll be thy mother.'

'It's the wind. I left the gate unfastened,' broke in Rachel. 'Hester – Clodd's ³ fine. Read this when I've done. Knocks Genesis to blazes.'

'Eh, lass, I don't wonder we've such ill-luck when you talk like that,' said the old woman. She huddled nearer to the fire.

'There's no such thing as luck,' argued Rachel. Then she stopped in answer to a look from Hester – Hester of the child-like soft heart, who never argued with grandmother on Socialism because it upset the old woman.

'But – there is somebody at the gate,' said Hester nervously.

Rachel flashed her a look.

'Expecting somebody?' she asked.

'Nay,' denied Hester.

'Anyhow, nobody could see tha'd thy stocking off in this leet,' Rachel told her, dropping into the vernacular as she did whenever deeply interested. Rachel was interested.

'I'm not bothered,' Hester denied. But her delicate face flushed. She grumbled mildly about the big hole. There was a shy secretiveness about Hester Martin which sometimes made even those who knew her best suspect her of motives for certain lines of action of which she never dreamed. Then the spark of indignant fire would burst forth – the true reason of the line of action would be given, and the astonished friend would find that Hester's motives were almost non-understandable in a

6

world where 'the devil take the hindmost' is the accepted rule of existence.

'Has Barstocks got any more orders?' asked the old woman.

Rachel was deep in Clodd.

'They'd the chance o' one. But there wasn't much profit to it,' explained Hester, 'so they didn't take it.'

The old woman huddled nearer to the fire and sighed.

'The Lord'll provide,' she quavered, clinging to the tenets of her old faith. *'The Lord is my shepherd. I shall not want. He leadeth me by the still waters. He maketh me to lie down in the green pastures.'*[4]

'The Lord might have had a try at making Barstocks take an order with a lower percentage of profit than they expected,' broke in Rachel. 'Happen He did – and had to give it up. Anyhow, if me an' Hester didn't turn out at a quarter to six every morning, we should all have clean teeth.'

In spite of this almost brutal statement of the honest truth Rachel had used the plural in order not to remind the old woman that she was dependent on their toil. Rachel held by the sword of truth. She used it fearlessly, but not without some fine reserves of chivalry.

'With the manna did He feed them,' quavered the old voice. *'He will remember His own.'*[5]

Hester laid a finger across Rachel's lips. Her grey eyes looked black as they gleamed on her sister. What is the good of it? That was the question those eyes asked.

'I know,' murmured Rachel, in a whisper. 'But when you think of the *clemmed*[6] folk there were in this town last year – and to hear her talk like that.'

'What she thinks won't alter it,' said Hester in a low voice. 'Leave her alone.' And so afraid was she that her grandmother was disturbed that she went barefooted across the hearth, ostensibly to poke up the fire, but really to stroke her grandmother's hand with a little, quick, bird-like movement.

'Tha'rt a good lass, Hessie,' murmured the old woman. 'Bless thee. Thy father'll never be dead whilst tha lives.'

She began to sob as she always did when she mentioned her son-in-law, the cobbler who died at his bench.

'In heaven we all shall meet,' she said.

Only the fervent faith and the old pathetic voice saved the platitude from banality. Rachel compressed her lips. Tolerance of the heaven-dope for all earth's indignities was sickening to her. She had not Hester's sharp, intuitive imagination, which saw beyond the slavishness of the slave the forces which had conspired to produce such a mentality.

'There!' was all Rachel could make herself say. 'Don't upset yourself. Pop the kettle on, Hessie; I've filled it. She might well be low-spirited after a washing day like this has been. Cheer up, gran. Me an' Hessie'll take you out by the Banks on Sunday, if it's fit.'

A knock on the door was a welcome relief.

'It'll be our Mary loaded,' said the old woman.

'It's Jack Baines. Nobody knocks like him,' asserted Rachel.

A quick note of eagerness sounded in her deep voice.

'Oh – I didn't hear a knock,' said the old woman. 'Come in, Jack, lad.'

'Jupiter! I've my stocking off,' said Hester. She ran under the stairs, pulling the door to after her.

'Where was Moses when the light went out?' asked a man's voice.

'We're economising,' Rachel told him. 'Pull a chair up.'

Jack did as he was bid. He pulled the chair up so near that Rachel could smell the tobacco odour of his coat, an odour so strong that it drowned the smell of the factory – that moist, sickly smell of steamed shoddy unlike anything else on earth. She noticed that his pocket bulged with books. They were fine excuses, those books. For the last two months they had accounted for one weekly visit from the finest debater in the smoke-veiled old s.d.f.[7] club-room.

'Hester out?' inquired Jack casually.

Rachel did not get a chance to reply.

'She ran under th' stairs to hide her foot,' laughed the old woman.

'Come out, Hester! Tha'rt whipped,' said Jack.

The stairs door opened. Everybody laughed as Hester emerged. Hester laughed, too. But her air of discomfiture could not very well be hidden.

'I think we might as well have a light on the subject,' said Rachel. Two seconds later the room was flooded with the white light of incandescence. The Martins were the only dwellers in the row who had adopted it.

Jack Baines stole a glance at Hester. There were bits of grey fluff in her dark hair. She had not yet taken off the winder's belt, with its pitted indentations made by the sharp pressure of the cop-skewering.[8] There was a smudge of blacklead on one soft, delicate curve of the pale cheek. She was to him something surpassingly beautiful. Her utter unconsciousness of the fact that all his hopes, apart from the Revolution, of course, were wrapped in that straight-fronted, high-bibbed, hideous apron, became Tantalus.[9] The talk drifted on to the town-topic of Barstocks' refusal to book the order. Jack tried to be interested in it. He knew that the stubbornness of Barstocks would spell bad times for at least four hundred people. But to-night he was strongly individualistic. Somehow this thing had got to be settled. He had been beaten twice in an argument in one week. If only Rachel would ask Hester to run for some chips, he would get the chance to offer to go with her to carry an umbrella. So he sat on and on, discussed books with Rachel, saw the old woman sent off to bed, after being spoon-fed by Hester, saw Hester disappear into the scullery, cautiously closing the door behind her, heard her splashing water, saw Rachel take her the comb. When Hester emerged, he made up his mind.

'You might ask me to my supper,' he chaffed. 'What price some chips?'

'Who'll fetch chips in this stuff?' asked Rachel.

'I will,' volunteered Hester.

'But it's raining cats and dogs,' Rachel told her.

'I'm not sugar; I'll none melt,' was Hester's independent answer.

'I'll go wi' thee,' Jack told her.

Hester put on her shawl.

'Don't be long. I'll have all ready,' Rachel called after them.

She stood staring into the fire when they had gone. A cob of coal fell. She still stood staring. Her face had a white, shaken look as she wheeled round, crossed over to the old dresser and opening a drawer took out the white Sunday cloth. So it was Hester. She heard the rain slashing the windows. Her grandmother coughed and disturbed by the cough, moaned in her sleep. Rachel sat down again. A little sobbing sound fell on the air of the kitchen. The dog came from under the shabby couch, stole towards her and thrust his nose in her hand.

'Go under, Jip,' she told him, in her usual tone. He stared at her, as one convicted of having made a mistake. Then he went 'under.'

Out in the poorly-lit street, Baines and Hester were fighting their way against the wind. Primitive, savage, its great wet wings beat out music like the surge of an old sea on an untamed shore. The box-like houses, dimly lighted for the most part, revealed on their blinds human shadows crossing and re-crossing. Here and there was the shadow of a hanging plant or bird-cage. They passed the opaque blackness of two high-walled factories, silent, gloomy as prisons, their wheels waiting within for the cold dawn that would bring back their hurrying slaves, slaves who could hope for no reprieve till death.

'It was sad about that chap had a stroke on his way home from work,' said Jack.

'Is he dead, then?'

'Ay. There'll be half a week's wages for his wife to draw. Sixty-six, he was, that day. He's kept his end up, very weel.'

A gust of wind blew Hester's shawl out of her grip. The wet fringe flicked Jack's face. It tantalised him. He placed the shawl within her hand, reaching out for it. Their fingers touched and fell quickly asunder, thrilled. Nature made her inexorable appeal, in the sordid trap of monotonous streets where slaves lived, eager to let none escape her; Nature, democratic, universal, was there, mocking, seductive, singing her old siren songs – though the specific purpose of her being there was merely the continuation of the species, whether they were slaves or freemen. She was there, speaking to Jack Baines to snatch this opportunity to assert his masculine positiveness. She was there, whispering to Hester to retreat. Hester hurried her steps filled with the old feminine desire to escape, which is caused by some antagonistic sense of what it will all mean.

'Shall I carry the bowls, Hessie?' inquired Jack.

'No; I can manage.'

She was struggling against the wind.

'Well – catch hold o' my arm.'

'Eh – I can manage.'

The dark, rhythmic music of wind and rain surged around them, sighing, shouting, dying away into long sobs. Suppose – she did not like him.

'I-I-I – say –' began Jack.

'There'll be a lot of damage done,' said Hester.

'Ay.'

'Fool, fool; coward,' sang the old democratic, brooding spirit. Jack groaned inwardly. They turned a street corner. How easy this sort of thing appeared in books. He appreciated for the first time the advantages of the ages when all one needed was a club. At least one could be spared all this.

The smell of warm chips a few feet ahead was wafted to them. The carrier of the chips walked unevenly. He was singing. The burden of his song was that the full ones don't care what the empty ones feel. Hester tried to dodge him. He was a heavy man. The impact was terrible. A bowl slid to the flags. Hester gave a stifled cry of pain. Jack's fist shot out, but Hester hung on to his arm and the blow missed.

'Nothing b-broken, is there?' asked the staggerer. 'Hope I didn't h-hurt you – young woman.'

'Get home, Stiner,' Jack told him, recognising him. 'And be thankful it's thee. I don't know what we have such like in the movement for. Some hopes of a Revolution out o' your sort, isn't there?'

Stiner pulled himself together.

'I've been c-chalking th' th' flags at th' front o' th' chapel w-where Barstocks g-goes,' he explained. 'The psalm-singing, slave-driving devil. Who th' hell can b-be sober, allus, in a w-world like this. "O, Love, could'st thou and – ich – I – with Fate conspire, to b-break this"[10] ich – never mind. I've been chalking the flags.'

'The rain will wash it off,' Jack told him.

'I'll write it again, then,' said Stiner, doggedly.

'Go home,' said Jack.

'Have a chip or two –'

He held out a rain-soaked scrap of newspaper.

'Must have lost 'em,' he muttered. 'Good-neet.'

His voice, singing of the sorrows of the empty ones and the callousness of the full ones, came back to them, on the wind.

'I could kill anyone hurt thee – a hair o' thy head,' said Jack. 'There; it's out now. Wilta have me, Hessie?'

They did not see the rain-wet streets, with the lamp-lights dully reflected in the shining flagstones. They did not notice the factory stacks, the black chimneys like evil pillars of the Temple of Toil. They forgot their rain-soaked, shoddy clothes – the livery of those who do the work of the world. The great winnowing wings of wind and rain beat around them, storm-music chorus of old love, old dream, old hope, which keeps the earth alive and young. Under the sodden shawl Jack found Hester's hand. It made a little, futile bird-like attempt to be free – then lay still in his.

'I'll work my fingers to the bone for thee,' he said huskily. 'Wilta, Hessie?'

'I-I – like thee,' came the northern acceptance.

They passed a street lamp.

The face of Hester, touched with lamplight, was tremulous, pale, bewildered.

'I'm only a weaver.'

'What am I?'

'But – tha'rt Hessie,' murmured Jack.

The rain was abating as they reached Ryan Street. Ryan Street was busy with swilling brushes, sweeping out water from the front to the back door of its houses, men cursing and women lamenting, tasting the discomfort of a small flood. Women in shawls were standing in the roaring gutters, water up to the clog-tops, screaming out to sleepy children huddled in doorways to keep in out of the wet. To-morrow at dawn those still damp shawls would be swarming out towards the factories. Ryan Street was always like this in heavy rain. People lived in Ryan Street because it was cheaper. Ryan Street had bugs. Ryan Street had drunken people and people who fought together. Ryan Street was a little circle in the Hades [11] of poverty, varying in degrees of degradation, but for ever the same old Hades, the inevitable parallel of the heaven of ease, leisure, culture, refinement which would shudder back from Ryan Street – and yet which is purchased by the sordid miseries of thousands who cannot escape from Ryan Street because they are trapped there.

Something of all this throbbed in Jack's mind. The horrible realities of life rushed at him suddenly.

A passionate desire for the beauty of the earth, the wild, sweet, mad scent of it – for trees – for the sense of infinity in the night skies – for something to harmonise without, with the fire of dreams and love within – seized him suddenly.

'Let's just walk till we can feel we're away from it all,' he asked. They walked, following the old cry of a world once young and unsmirched by inequalities, artificialities and mocking resemblances to a freedom not yet arisen. From the beginning of the Long Meadows they dimly felt the presence of the hills. The rain was over and gone. Filmy veils of moonshine hung around the tree-boles. Then the moon would dodge under a bank of clouds and all would become the infinity of dark, unfenced fields again. A planet came into sight, mysterious world about which Science guessed and theorised and argued. Beauty shot out at them in her hundred disguises, mystic with the light of an old moon to which multitudes once prostrated themselves. The air was full of romance, beauty-born. Problems of existence dissolved into nothingness before the grand elementals of life. The practical discussion of what street they would live in, how many children they would allow themselves to have, and whether Hester would go to the factory or pinch and scrape with one wage, was forgotten here, as it was meant to be forgotten.

They kissed with shy modesty, and the earth assumed new, undreamed of meanings. They said in the vernacular, in tremulous voices, things that had been said in old Babylon, classic Greece, by the shores of Mitylene[12] and through the mouth of Avon's bard. They stepped over the borders of a county into the universal land of poetry, where lovers walk, and little children with their hands full of flowers, and dreamers of new worlds, and fighters against wrongs intolerable. Nature laughed her subtle, triumphant laughter. Toil stood frowning at the slaves who had forgotten her bonds, waiting, threatening and revengeful. A church clock struck, they turned round, and walked back to the ugliness, the smoke, the fried fish shops, factory chimneys, and dirty songs sung in dirty streets; back to the slime of a civilisation in which the few, a dark, brigand band, gather the roses of culture, idleness and power. They passed through the familiar streets, wrapped in their cloak of dreams. It was Hester who remembered that they had passed the chip-shop. They went back, and finally emerging with the chips, they came to an excited crowd gathered about a dark doorway.

'What's up?' asked Jack.

'It's Ben Gillimore. He's cut her throat. She brought an affiliation order against him last week. The police are bringing him out.'

They brought him out – struggling, handcuffed, cursing, a weedy sample of sordid fatherhood.

'Come on, Hessie,' said Jack. He felt sick.

It was not until they turned the top of Oak Street that Jack remembered Mrs. Martin. He would have to ask her consent to Hessie's walking out with him. He did not anticipate any opposition. But it was an embarrassing job with which it would feel good to be done. They knocked at the door in a spirit of childish gaiety and Rachel opened it to them.

'I thought you were growing the spuds, an' all,' she told them. 'Mother's come.'

Jack braced himself.

Mrs. Martin was at the kitchen table putting up the breakfast for the mill in the morning. She nodded to his nod.

She was a middle-aged woman with a care-worn countenance, not without nobility.

Rachel sat down to Clodd again.

The table was set – a cup for himself, he noted.

After supper Jack faced Mrs. Martin. For the first time he remembered that he would be taking a breadwinner and leaving her with a harder struggle. It was galling, but it was reality. His own poverty was borne in on him as it had never been before. He was a little pale and his words sounded stilted when they came.

'I suppose you won't mind me an' Hessie walking out together?' he asked.

Mrs. Martin looked straight at him.

Her own face lost some of its colour. She struggled to find words and failed. He thought she was going to break down. Then her face grew more determined.

'She's too young,' she said with decision.

Rachel turned over a page of Clodd.

'She's too young,' Mrs. Martin repeated.

'She'll grow older.'

'Ay. She'll grow older fast, too – if she gets wed and has to scrat along on twenty-five bob a week or else go out carrying kids to be nursed. I've fought and fended to bring 'em up. All I could give 'em I've given 'em. I didn't think they'd want to be off – so soon.'

The reproach levelled at Hester had a crushing effect on her. It was almost as though she were being told that she had not yet paid off the debt she owed for having been brought into the world and worked for – till she was eleven years old. She sat on the kitchen chair, silent, and with a sense of the guilt of an ingrate having been thrust upon her. She had an almost fanatical spirit of filial respect. It bound her in iron thongs. She sat dumb, through all the torturing scene that followed. They were fighting over her like two dogs after a bone. The same terrible realisation of the sordidness of life which had been hers when, as a child of eleven, she had crept from under a machine with fluff-filled nostrils and had realised that this must go on for ever, till she grew old, seized her again. A dim sense that she belonged to neither of them flitted through her chaos of thoughts, thoughts all jumbled with the agony of hearing the two she loved best speaking fierce words.

'I'm going on for fifty. I've worked nigh on forty years in the factory. I'll have to go till I drop I'm thinking. I can't keep three on us on our Rachel's bit o' brass. We'll be half clemmed when our Hessie's gone.'

It was too brutal.

But – it was true.

Hester Martin grabbed at her soaked shawl, tossed it over her head and ran out.

'Come back,' shouted her lover.

But she was running up the street like a wild thing, choking with sobs. It was sordid. It oppressed her like a death sentence. To be argued about, to hear it argued about, the great primitive, sacred impulse, the only romance that touches with angel-hands the grovelling ignomy of a slave's life. It was too appalling. She laughed once, throatily. A policeman stared after her, then walked on his unholy beat, a member of the great class which exists to keep slaves in their places. When she saw him through a mist of tears she crossed over to the other side of the road, obeying an instinct. Hers were not sentimental tears, but the scalding tears of rebellion against the sordidness of her lot.

Jack Baines meanwhile sat back in his chair. The rain had started again. The knowledge that Hessie was out, getting wet through, worried him. But he held on, fighting for his own. Knock down one argument of Mrs. Martin's and up came another. She refused to be helped after he and Hessie were married. He had either to surrender or to accept the accusation that he left the household to suffer short rations. Being unable to do either, the thing went round and round in a vicious circle. And through it all he had the conviction that Mrs. Martin was not fighting against him for her own sake, or for the household's sake, but for some hidden motive more noble than the one to which her own words gave colour.

'Go and fetch that lass in. She'll be coughing for a week or two,' Mrs. Martin commanded Rachel. Rachel went out after Hester. Her satirical sense of humour had helped her to endure the scene. She was as amazed as Jack at her mother's attitude, and she wondered, as he did, what lay under it. She called her sister a silly bitch, mentally, for not putting up a fight. But the odd tenderness she always felt for Hester, relic of the morning when she had taken Hester to tent for her, sheltering her from the snow under her shawl, conflicted with this criticism. Suddenly through the wind and rain, a child's cry of terror fell on her ears.

Pulling her shawl away from her eyes, Rachel saw a child's small form crouching over the gutter. The cursing of a man came to her. A match spluttered into flame, then went out.

'Oh, don't do it again,' came in terrified, shrill tones.

'What's up?' she asked, reaching them.

'She's lost a sovereign.[13] A sovereign,' came in furious tones. 'By God – if she doesn't find it – .' The child began to sob again.

'Serves thee reight for sending a child out on a neet like this with a sovereign,' Rachel told him.

'If it's aught to do wi' thee, take thy share out of it,' he retorted. 'It's more'n half o' my week's wages, not thine, which maybe makes a difference.' Rachel recognised his voice. It was Jabez Speak, lately left a widower. He was buying shares in the new factory that was being erected. He was a type of working-class thrift, trying to become a capitalist.

'If tha marks that child, I'll report thee,' Rachel told him.

She went past, wondering if the whole of the working-classes had not better take laudanum and have done with the whole beastly struggle, whilst the comical wonder as to whether there would be enough of it to go round, kept her poised above the emotionalism she hated.

She took her way up the wet pavements of an almost perpendicular street and realised that she had not quite got rid of her anaemia. You may beat down the palpitation of the heart caused by a forlorn and broken love-dream, but not that which comes from a monotonous, mechanical life. She stopped at the top of the street. A shawled figure flitted into view.

'Hester,' she shouted.

The figure stopped. It was Hester.

Rachel drew a deep breath when she caught up with her sister.

'Why did you go out and leave it all to him?' she asked with unwonted fierceness.

'Oh, shut up.'

Hester's voice was monotonous, low-pitched.

'But why?' persisted Rachel.

There was silence. The wind sobbed in the trees of the vicarage garden as they passed.

'It's all so sickening,' said Hester suddenly. 'To have to fight for everything – bread, love, everything – like beasts. Shut up. I don't want to talk about it.'

'Why didn't ta tell her it were naught to do with her?'

'Oh – I – there were so many things I couldn't forget – when we were childer and she told us tales in bed and fell asleep talking and got mixing weaving in with it – and – all we owe to her – anyhow, I've sort of made my mind up. If she doesn't say we can walk out, we'll not.'

The utter filial slavishness of it took away Rachel's breath.

'Why, man,' she said excitedly, 'tha can't play wi' a chap like him, like that.'

Hester tossed her shawl over her shoulder.

'I sha'n't,' said Hester quietly. 'I shall give him up.'

'But tha's promised.'

'Oh, shut up.'

'An' – ,' Rachel faltered. Then she spoke it out though it did sound sentimental. 'It isn't likely tha'll ever find another chap will think the same o' thee as he does. And tha'rt such a fool, tha'll wed somebody. Tha can't chuck things o' this sort away.'

'It doesn't come so hard,' said Hester with a proud sort of dignity. 'When you've had your childhood stolen off you, you're prepared to go on surrendering. After all, when you can't get butter you take margarine. Come on. Let's go back.'

'I don't seem to care,' said Hester still trying to explain as they went down the old street. 'Anyhow, it all feels smirched now.'

'Tha'rt born a thousand years too soon,' Rachel told her sarcastically. 'I believe tha's gotten what they call an artistic temperament. And that's no good in the working-class.'

But for all her sarcasm a new appreciation of her sister touched her with surprise and wonder. Touched her also with pity. How the brutalities of working-class life would play havoc with a soul that would sooner surrender a great, sweet freedom than fight for it, fiercely, tenaciously, as the beasts fight for existence. Or – would the resignation of fine sensitive disdain break at last, and Hester Martin become a flambeau in the night of poverty, warning the oppressors that surrender is not infinite, and that the revolt of the gentle is more to be feared than that which spends itself, letting off steam as it goes?

'Mother, is the battle over?' shouted Rachel as they went up the passage.

Jack and Mrs. Martin were both sitting silent. Their faces told that they had said bitter things to each other.

'Well,' said Jack, 'I'll be going.'

Nobody moved or spoke.

Jack hesitated a moment on the mat as if hoping Hester might call him back. He did not realise the steel bonds of modesty, nor the equally steel-like bonds of that working-class virtue, 'Obey your parents.' The door closed. It had a tone of anger in its slamming. Hester did not know that the wind had torn it out of his nervous grip.

There was a long silence. Hester sat like marble.

Mrs. Martin shot a disturbed look at the girl who had never answered her a word.

'Happen tha doesn't think it, but I've saved thee from something,' she said. 'What would a thing like thee do, struggling in poverty? If he's aught about him he'll wait. If he hasn't, well, there's plenty o' fellows in the world. An' in a year or two we'll not be in this hole. We shall be better off – a lot better off – happen we shall be rich. So – dry up.'

'I'm not crying,' said Hester.

She rose from the chair. Her gaze met her mother's. The two glances met and held each other's. For the first time the eyes of Hester met those of the elder woman's without a daughterly look. It was the glance of one woman saying to another, 'You have taken advantage of my affection, of my youth, my modesty, and the fact, which I could not help, that once you kept me when I could not keep myself.'

Mrs. Martin flinched under it.

She began to cry.

'What's that?' asked Rachel, suddenly.

Above the beating of the rain came the clattering din of a battalion of clogs.

Rachel, still pondering the conundrum of how her mother ever expected to be rich, flung open the door. People were rushing past.

'What's up?' she asked.

She asked twice before she could make out the answer. Closing the door, she went in. Mrs. Martin and Hester were holding each other's hands. Hester was trying to smile. Her eyes had that same estranged look of reproach.

'Either Barstocks or Ben Bridge is on fire,' said Rachel.

'Oh, Lord!' gasped Mrs. Martin.

Rachel tossed out the shawls. Locking the house up they rushed after the other toilers. At the end of the street the sky was lit up by the glare. Was it Barstocks or Ben Bridge? That was the great question. With anxious hearts and faces they rushed on through the night. It meant semi-starvation if it was Barstocks. From every direction came the sound of those anxious thousands, shawled figures, men, and even children running to the scene of the fire.

CHAPTER 2

THERE was one slave in Brayton who did not run to the scene of the 'great mill fire.' The sky was a flare of red light visible for miles, but Bob Stiner slept on on the old settle. The alarm clock going off at twelve, through a mistake of Matty's, aroused him. He jumped up, stared dazedly at the clock, and gave a titanic sigh of relief that five hours yet remained before he was forced to march down the eternal slave-rut. He decided to go to bed, pulled off his boots and climbed the stairs, to discover that the beds were empty. Dumbfounded, he thrust his feet into his bluchers, [14] went out with dangling tags, and succeeded in knocking up the collier who lived next door. A window was shot up. A bandaged, ghostly head looked out, and a few oaths were exchanged in all good fellowship.

'Tha'll neither sleep nor let other folk,' protested Bob's neighbour.

'We'll be deyd long enough,' gibed Bob. 'I believe in wakening the working classes up.'

Out of the gloom his voice held a significant tone which told that he was thinking of more than his literal awakening of the injured collier.

'Go to hell,' the collier told him.

'Say. It's thee goes there,' chaffed Stiner. 'How's thy head?'

'Damned sore.'

'Everybody's out at my castle,' Stiner told him. 'What's happened?'

'There's a shade (shed) afire somewhere. My old girl's gone to look at it. They'll be there,' said the collier. 'Good-neet.'

The window was dropped.

'A bit more surplus value gone pop,' mused Stiner. 'Whilst the cat's away the mice'll play.'

He went back into the house, took a stubby piece of chalk out of the caddy, roughly tied his boot-tags, and, without locking the door, sauntered down the silent, echoing street.

Half-way down the street a woman passed him, running, he presumed, towards the drama of the mill fire.

'What slave-hole is it that's on fire?' asked Stiner as she passed.

'Eh?'

Her shadow on the lamplit flagstones made a weird, elongated cartoon of poverty, beshawled and hurried.

'What slave-hole is it that's on fire?'

She caught his meaning, but scarcely its implication.

'It's either Barstocks or Ben Bridge. I hope to God it's not Ben Bridge,' called her voice as she ran, her clogs clattering heavily.

'I wish to God every hell-hole like Barstocks was burnt down,' came the challenge from behind her.

She ran more quickly. A cat crossed Stiner's path. Matty would say that was an ill-sign. He quoted bits of Omar [15] as he went down the street that was like a double row of rabbit hutches. The moon, with its shining glass, reminded him of the beauty of the old tent-maker's stanzas. Khayyam was a fatalist though. An old fatalist with a finer ideal than the religious fatalists. But was fatalism, religious or materialistic, any good as a revolutionary force? Had not all forces for bettering the lives of the masses been challenges to fatalism, which said in effect, 'All is written; nothing can be wiped out; nothing added?' Thus musing, Stiner passed along until he saw another cartoon, on another lamp-lit set of flagstones, another shadow of fatalism, but this time fatalism armed with force. From gardens blowing by Persian waterways, Stiner's fancy leaped to an industrial battle which had been raging overseas.[16] Men, women, and even children had gone down under machine-guns manned by police. Stiner, the man who gazed much on the ground, lifted his head and gazed at the slop. Our own class, too. The concrete symbols of bloody force to be used on any determined attempt to unclasp the hands of legalised robbers from their pilfered possessions. Bought. Our own class. Bought as the old mercenaries of other civilizations had been bought. Stiner could not help it. He spat on the ground as he passed the slop.

O'Neill swung the leaded stick, without which he never went out. He was whistling. Bob went on, responding with 'The Red Flag.'[17] At the corner of the street he looked round. O'Neill was standing, a motionless figure by the lamp.

Two minutes later Bob was kneeling on the flagstones before the chapel where to-night Barstocks, Senior, that psalm-singing devil, was to hold forth on Empire.[18]

They would open the ceremony by singing 'O God, our help in ages past,' or 'Jerusalem, the golden,' and then Barstocks would inject commercial glory poison into their slavish blood. The tunes would be played on the magnificent organ Barstocks had given, an instrument purchased out of the very life-blood of his driven workers. But Barstocks should not have it all his own way.

'My name's Bob Stiner,' muttered the man with the chalk.

It was his way of stating that all the devils in hell, including policemen, parsons, manufacturers, and – slaves should not hinder him from doing his particular bit of unpaid propaganda. The 'moving finger' wrote:

Ye cannot serve God and Mammon.[19]

The rich we have with us always, everywhere – otherwise we would not have any poor.

Christianity has been made a happy hunting ground with the Devil of Greed driving the sheep to slaughter, Christ, the agitator, turned into a dog, barking them on. God has been used to pick the pockets of the poor. If we worshipped the sun we might not be content to live where the sun never shines. We would be better with Odin and Thor [20] *– for they might teach us to use a hammer – like old Wat Tyler.* [21]

Socialism is the hope of the W –

Stiner stopped. Someone was coming. Anyhow, he struck a match, and surveyed his handiwork with that peculiar sense of satisfaction which only comes from unpaid labour, freely chosen.[22] Thousands of people would read that challenge in the dawn. Going down the old cinder path to the mill gates, women who were mothers in their spare time, would read it. Little half-timers would stop and spell it out. Men in greasy caps carrying their bagging-tins[23] would read it. Somehow, somewhere, it would weave itself in with the grind and roar of the ten-hour day.

Socialism is the hope of the W –

'What are you doing there?' asked O'Neill.

'Putting my house in order,' Stiner told him.

He completed the sentence on the flagstones.

'Well, get along, or I'll run you in for loitering.'

The grey-headed weaver got on his feet as the sergeant flashed his bull's eye on the chalked flags.

'These are private flags,' he told Stiner.

'Are they?'

Stiner's good humour was unmistakable.

'They are.'

'Well, it's a public message,' said Stiner. 'Unfortunately, I'm only a poverty-knocker and can't afford to run a daily.'

'Now, get along, and no jaw; get along.'

The dehumanised voice held no tone of anger or feeling, it might have issued from a machine.

The arm moved with it also like a machine.

'None o' thy pushing,' expostulated Stiner.

'Get along.'

Stiner moved, following the line of most resistance, though. He did not move fast enough. The leaded stick swished through the air, and Stiner realised that the cur had taken advantage of the deserted street and the fumes of Lethe[24] in his breath, *to make a case*. He staggered – a keen, stinging pain in his head, a wet, warm, sticky rush of blood blurring his right eye. Demons awoke in him. Far off he heard, as in a mad dream, the ting-ting of machine-guns, manned by mechanisms without feelings. He heard the shriek of women and children – unmechanical creatures with feelings. He felt their presences in the shadowy, reeling street. They were like a procession of blood-soaked comrades, bidding him – remember.

'Here; tha shan't have it all thy own way,' grunted Stiner.

He landed O'Neill a blow that that 'arm of the law' would not have thought it possible this stooping, grey-head of a weaver could have struck. The next moment they were wrestling together. O'Neill brought his stick down again. Stiner grunted. It had skinned the knuckles of his hand. He realised that there was a shop window just behind them. His bleeding hand did not relax its hold of O'Neill. Inch by inch he was being thrust nearer the window, towards the rendezvous of dummies in ready-made suits. His stick struck out, whilst his other hand groped for the whistle. The stick caught the old weaver in the groin. His eyes, wide, dreadful, glared in his pain-writhed face. He bent almost two-double under the agony of that blow which resurrected that old rupture of his. Even so, earth-dragged by pain, his hand retained its clutch on O'Neill. Inch by inch, he had almost got him within hurling distance now. O'Neill blew his whistle. Stiner, taken off his guard, loosened his grip. O'Neill seized the moment. The stick came down with all its force on Stiner's head.

'The moving finger writes,' he grunted incoherently, and crumpled up on the flagstones across the message he had written.

'Drunk – loitering – assaulted me when I tried to move him on,' he heard as they dragged him to his feet.

Had he really assaulted the police? He stared at them dazedly. The lamp-posts were decidedly drunk. Must be drunk. The dim lights flickered before him in weird cotillion. Yes, he must be drunk. What was the matter with his knowledge-box anyhow? He put up his hand and felt his head stiffly. His cap was stuck. The hair pulled. Then – it came back – that shadowy picture. He remembered that O'Neill had struck him first. He laughed throatily, and half stumbled. They construed it into an attempt to give them the slip. A moment later he realised that he was being led through the streets of his home town like an assassin. He had defended himself against a guardian of 'lor and order.' It was too funny. The handcuffs tightened on his wrists. Stiner laughed again, swayed – and collapsed.

They brought him to at the police station with a drop of raw brandy. They sat him before the fire, joked with and at him, examining his injuries with casual glance and deciding that he was ready for the cell – not the hospital. The door closed. Stiner was inside a prison cell for the first time in his life. He had a frenzied desire to punch the damned door to bits. Then reaction overcame him. He sank on the floor – and wept like a child. There were these odds against the people all the time. They were creatures of feeling, feeling not yet deadened fully, and between them and all discontent – stood force all the more potent in that it was a purely mechanical force. It was the triumph of a machine over humanity, the superiority of matter over mind.

The human being on the cell-floor wept, a link with all humanity in its sufferings – even as Christ wept – whilst Caesar held the dungeon, the whip, and the slaves chosen from slaves to keep them in their places.

Physical torture was added to his sense of outrage and ignominy. He fumbled at the worn truss and hurled it across the cell. Broken in body – but by the gods – not broken in purpose, not broken in mind. A prison cell had closed its door on him. The kids were disgraced. Matty would not understand. Moreover – if Barstocks was burned down, no other mill-door in the town would let him through after this. They would choose unconsciously, a more respectable slave. They would book his name and say they'd send for him, but all the odds were against his being sent for.

It meant – trampdom. It meant – lodgings. It meant – respectable poverty no more. It meant – flotsam and jetsam. Added to his reputation for getting now and then over the mark and failing to turn up for a day or two on the old slave route – he had been in prison. It was a cheaper martyrdom than he had ever dreamed of. He wished he had killed the bloody policeman. No, he was glad he had not done so.

Their day would come someday and after all – after all there was still the writing on the flags for the slaves to read in the dim dawn. Flung thus from reaction to reaction, he sat in the dark cell realising force fully for the first time. He saw the town spiritually, morally, materially – the town with the great Indian trade, the high wages, the high speed, where bits o' lasses drowned themselves for dark fear that they could not reach the average wage. He saw its spiritual sky-pilots, gagged, even if they chose like Paul to speak, yoked to an old tradition. He saw workers whose earthly dream of heaven was a thirty pound piano and a plush suite. He saw the small tradesmen, bitter antagonists of Socialism, even while they bewailed the big shops swamping them. He saw the rigid caste dividing shop girls from mill-hands, bank clerks from weavers and spinners. All exploited, yet with an illusion of being 'different.' Hell-fire. He laughed, the tears still damp on his cheeks.

Talk about breaking down caste in India or sending missionaries to the Pacific. Good God, if a man took a world like this seriously, he would go mad. He found a chew of tobacco in his pocket, and as he pulled it up and rolled it, forgetting he wanted a chew and not a smoke, he was humming,

'Whither come they and whence go they?
What is this of which they tell?
In what valley are they dwelling

'Twixt the gates of heaven and hell?
Are they thine or mine for money?
Will they serve a master well?
And the host comes marching on.'[25]

And away and away, clear as a vision in the dark cell, he saw the white endless road where his broken boots would tramp. He saw the fences where he would inscribe sentences on Capitalism. He saw the half-open doors of poor cottages where children would stand and stare at him with the wonder in the eyes that would soon pass when they went out to labour. He saw doss-houses and casual wards where he would still carry the message; a passing ship with the old flag flying, a man without name, unreported – throwing out Marxian truths in pubs, quoting Shelley[26] – to pals who would sleep with him under the cold stars, the fool, the outcast, the drifter – still with one dream unsullied, one purpose never broken, one glory never sold for a mess of pottage.[27] And dreaming the dream he had awakened and slept on for almost forty years, he fell asleep.

He awoke at dawn. The grey light gleamed ghostly through the high-barred window. The sound of clogs going past the wall had roused him. Clogs. It sounded like an army. It was an army, an army of deluded slaves. They were moving on. One pair had dropped out, that was all. Then he recalled the fire. A wild hope seized him. If it was Ben Bridge and not Barstocks that was burned down his looms would still be there. He would still have, whilst they could pay the rent, a sure and certain shelter, his children – his children, thrice dear, thrice beloved, even though they were ashamed of their old dad, because he sometimes got drunk. The queer fibre of almost poetic tenderness dimmed his eyes as he thought of having to leave them. The long road seemed suddenly, in the morning light, the way unto Gethsemane.[28]

The cell door opened.

It was a young policeman in his shirt sleeves. His face was fresh and boyish. He had not yet been dehumanised.

'Dry, mate?' he asked.

Stiner nodded.

He brought him a pint pot of tea.

A curious wonder touched Stiner's soul.

He looked up at the boyish faced man.

'What the hell made you take this job on?' asked the man who would have asked such questions of his executioner.

'Out of work. Good wages. No bad times. It's all right.'

The cell door closed.

Stiner drank his tea.

He knocked on the cell door when he had finished.

The young policeman came.

'What is it?' he asked.

His voice already had a semblance of the official tone. It would deepen, even as the human skin upon him thickened.

'Was it Barstocks or Ben Bridge got burned down last night?'

'Barstocks.'

'Have they saved aught?'

'Some of the cloth out of the warehouse. Fireman got burned badly.'

'To save the cloth and lessen insurance?' asked Stiner.

The policeman was silent.

'Does my wife know I'm here?'

The policeman nodded.

Matty came an hour later. The dark human comedy was staged in the cell. What was he going to do now he'd got himself in this mess? And did he think anybody else would shop him now Barstocks was burned? She would get him bail if he'd quit the town. The children would not be able to lift their heads up.

'All right, old girl. All right, I'll quit,' Stiner told her.

He had not been an angel, that was true. In the dim cell the two pairs of eyes regarded each other with understanding. He had little more than kept himself – 'bacca and beer reckoned off. They could hold up their heads higher without him. They aspired to – caste.

'All right, Matt,' he repeated. 'I'm going after this. But I somehow thought – anyhow – never mind. I'll go. I'm not much damned good except as a slave. Happen I'll be a freer slave.'

She went out with a strange sense of inferiority, and had to look at the commonsense of the matter before she could shake it off. Seven days later Barstocks, from the magisterial dais sentenced Bob Stiner to seven days hard labour in default of a fine of five pounds. Drunk and assaulting the police was the charge. He was a most dangerous man, if they could believe their officer, and they must believe their officer.

'I'll have the seven days,' almost shouted Stiner. 'You psalm-singing, slave-driving devil. What about that weaver drowned herself because she couldn't reach your damned average. How long did they give thee for that? You old hypocrite.'

'Take that man away. One month for contempt of court.'

So Bob Stiner went down. He came out on a rainy morning, and bowed with his unattended rupture, dragged himself past the workhouse. Two half crazy men stood near the gates. They laughed meaninglessly as he went past.

'The whole blasted working-class would do with putting inside a mad-house,' grunted Bob. 'Happen it would bring 'em to their senses.' Then a softer mood followed. After all, the odds, the great odds against free thought on the part of the masses. Generation after generation sacrifice had been taught to them in ethics, religion, and literature. Fear of lack of bread. Fear of policemen, soldiers, law, Church, State. Moneyed Interests forever against them. Taught what to think, when philanthropic forces gave them any education, without question.[29] Taught what to think when they clamoured for learning. Taught what to think before an election. Happen it was a wonder that they had any brains left at all.

The bitter wind seared him through. He walked with bowed head, reading, like Chaucer, his thoughts upon the ground. The sense of being an outcast touched him with burning shame. He was drifting, drifting towards another hell of Capitalism, further down socially than the old respectable poverty, where somehow, you kept your heads just above water till a mill fire came, or your health broke, or the kids got wed. All through the swing of a bit of stick, well leaded. The long, wet roads straggled aimlessly before him. He stood still. Over the borders. He was going over the borders. The wind whistled through the naked trees. A tramp went by. Stiner studied his outlines. They told their own story. Going nowhere – somewhere – anywhere –

'Which is the way to the workhouse?'

Stiner started. It was a young woman, respectably dressed. She was in pain.

'Just along there – pal –' Stiner told her.

With a groan she went on.

Stiner turned round and called.

She halted.

He fumbled in his pockets.

He shoved a shilling into her hand awkwardly.

'For the baby – from its grandfather – just for luck,' he said, mumbling.

She broke into tears.

Social pride showed itself, the damnation or the salvation of the masses, accordingly as it is perverted or converted.

'With an old chap's love – to a poor little pal,' Stiner insisted.

She smiled, groaned, and trailed on.

'Jesus Christ!' grunted Stiner. Over a thousand altars Motherhood wore an halo. The workhouse maternity ward!

He took out his chalk.

'Workers of the world, unite,' he wrote upon the fence. Dimly his mission loomed up before him. To write on fence, on snow or sand – everywhere, the good true, unadulterated message. None would know that he who wrote was an outcast. The broken body, the broken boots would not be known. One Dream shone down the twisted track of his life with a white effulgence of undarkened glory – the dream of the dawn where fellowship would link all roads, all seas together, and Brotherhood make of all men one family. All but the Capitalists, of course, damn 'em. He lit his pipe and walked on, taking his dream with him, knowing that somehow he could never be wholly lost or outcast whilst he kept that, not to sell at a price, but to give. He did not know that in his pocket lining, rain soaked and blotted, was a letter which Hester Martin had given him to give Jack Baines, on the night after he came out of the local police cell. The turmoil of the week that followed had driven it out of his mind. Down the long road he went, towards whatever hell fate held in store for him, with the smudged few words which might have altered several destinies in every way but material poverty. The sight of a withered white rose yet clinging to a black bough set him off singing 'The Last Rose of Summer.'[30] He went down the unknown road singing, and penniless.

CHAPTER 3

THE burning down of Barstocks' mill flung four hundred slaves to join the army already besieging mill gates in the sleet-misted wintry mornings. After getting one's name and address set down there was nothing to do but trudge home and sit by a meagre fire, with a sense of enforced rot. Burial agents ceased to call at some of the houses. Some pianos changed hands, passing from slaves out of work to slaves in work. Driving inside the mills reached an intensity which left the lucky ones like washed out rags at the end of the day. Lips were locked against every indignity. To oversleep and awaken to the yell of the quarter whistle was to rush out into the dank air half-dressed, without bite or sup, life and death dread stamped on the pale faces that flitted like the phantom wraiths through the lamplit sleet. A sick winder who returned to work after being thrice sent for, had to go home again, and was found dead behind the door, key in hand, when her daughters returned from the day's work.

Those 'out,' trudged precious footgear and heart's courage away filing over the dreary switchback to and from the next town. Everywhere it was the same. Not enough work to go round, but those inside speeded up by the threat of those outside. Sleet, heavy rain, followed by bitter snow-feathered winds added to the misery. Turneresque[31] – Demonesque, the land of moors and mills lay under its smoke grey sky, its racks of terrified Toil, and terrified Hunger grinding out profits duly registered in the Financial Times. Leisure came at last to a section of the slaves. She came with the wolf, not the Renascent lamb.[32]

Meanwhile, what of the Martins? Caught in the web of want along with their fellows, the household tried to disguise its shadows. Granny stretched her thin hands to a lower fire. Her faith in the Lord had a faint suggestion of a whimper. Rachel with almost terrible tenacity of purpose sat in her father's greatcoat, itself a banner of poverty, struggling through book after book she got from the Co-operative Library. Hester sat listlessly, housework done, staring out on the desert of back-yard. Mrs. Martin chased up and down the town after cheap scraps of food, undeterred by any weather if she heard that anything was going cheap. The woman next door, with a realisation of the circumstances of the house, would pop a tousled head over the wall and call 'Mrs. Martin, Mrs. Martin' in her tired, shrill voice and say in a low, half-ashamed tone, – and with a look of tired apology, 'I thought you might be able to use this up.' And Mrs. Martin would say that she never refused anything but blows, with a lump in her throat, and love and bitterness in her heart – love for the thought behind the gift – bitterness that she had to take it.

There was something harmonic in the irony that Rachel Martin began to read *Das Capital* [33] under the same terrible conditions as shadowed the titan who analysed society even as it killed him, inch by inch. Of the household perhaps the old woman and Hester suffered most. One eternally tried to warm herself at a fire too low. The other, perceiving the hideous struggle, and unable to see any grand purpose in fighting for brute-survival, wilted like a frail flower dashed about in a storm.

It was not despair. It was not apathy. It was a sensitive perception that to be poor amongst the poor was to have the soul slain, bit by bit, until nothing was left to creep on the earth but a bent body from which the light had faded. Sometimes Rachel looked over her book, to see Hester brooding by the window. Perhaps even the greatcoat failed to keep out the cold. A little shudder ran through her at times, as she lifted her head from the book to see a Hester cameo-pale, staring out through the window. Grandmother from her chair spake platitudes about the longest lane having a turning. She fidgeted with her thumbs a lot these days, and prayed twice as long before getting into bed, with Rachel standing, impatiently waiting to tuck her in and get back to *Das Capital*. In point of time they had not been out of work many weeks. Like the average slave a couple of weeks had made them feel the pinch.

Three generations – an old woman who had toiled more than fifty years, a middle-aged woman still vigorous and active, two young women, one practical and dominant, the other gentle, unpractical, and sensitive as a fiddle-string, they were already half-starving. The world wagged on. They wasted and were wasted. Against this waste of human life in the world no economists cry out. Within these four human beings in this one house was the capacity for social management, for deductive thinking, for artistic creation, for calm, generous rest after a life of service. 'This Slavery' ordained that they should spend their energies frustrated as common rats in traps.

'Where's mother?'

It was another wet afternoon. Rachel had jumped up in her galvanic way to stretch her limbs, stiff and numbed with cold.

'Gone out after ham bones – five for sixpence.'

Hester's gentle voice had no tinge of irony. She merely stated a fact. But there was something in the way the gentle Hester sometimes stated a fact that would have made a diplomat wince. The parson who had stopped in the street to sympathise with her about her father's death had once felt that strange power in the pale, awkward, ill-developed young woman, rushing to her work in the grey factory shawl. She told him that it was not her father's death they sorrowed for, looked him in the eyes and sped past, racing after the whistle.

If anything moved Granny these days it was the mention of food. She caught the words about ham-bones though she had been dropping asleep.

'Aye, an I'll bet she gets some,' she chirped in, 'I'll bet she gets some.'

Rachel stared at Hester.

'I sometimes feel I could fast – from choice,' said Hester. 'We seem to do nothing but talk, and think – about grub.'

'We're like to fire up, aren't we?' asked Rachel, with humour. 'We're not disembodied souls.'

'I sometimes feel like a dis-souled body,' retorted Hester. 'Our bodies seem to get in the way. We're like a set of pigs kept grovelling on the ground.'

Rachel stared, laughed, and Granny cackled. A spark flamed in Hester's eye. Her cheek flushed. She went quickly to the wall, took down her fiddle, and went off into the damp, fireless parlour – to play. Whenever Hester had got to breaking point she invariably made a bee-line towards the fiddle. Then from behind closed door they would hear the splendid, sombre, brown music of Beethoven – of Beethoven, the son of a cook, and the god-child of the gods of Sound. They heard her now at the beloved Sonata. Granny heard it so often that she could follow it.

Rachel held *Das Capital* open with thumb and finger. The mediocre player is often regarded as a genius by his family. The embryo genius is sometimes regarded as a decent player by his family. Hester could certainly play. A very flood of sound, exquisite, unerring, filled the little parlour. To Hester it was merely an open door, an escape from a work where ham-bones at five for sixpence were worth a two miles tramp in the pouring rain. Sad, beautiful, that Sonata – a low tide ebbing, foiled in its passionate attempt to reach the dream-shore, the soft, murmuring sob of the muffled waves beating the moon-flooded sands, the menacing roar of the greater waves still beating on the shingles, crying, mad to rush the shore in spite of all but falling back, back, roaring, undefeated courage even as they went. Perhaps he meant that. Perhaps he did not. That was how Hester made it sound. Rachel, book in hand, crept to the door.

When it was finished she said, with a laugh, 'If we get to "Heigh, lads, heigh," Hester, tha can play an' I'll sing.' Which brought Hester out of the parlour, brooding-browed, and silent as a mule.

With another few mumbled sentences about the ham-bones, and our Mary getting wet, the old woman fell asleep. Hester gently covered her with a woollen antimacassar off the chair-back. They heard her breathing. She mumbled in her sleep, some futile hope of her pension. The two young women looked at each other across her.

'Well?'

'Well?'

'Pretty chronic, I call it,' said Rachel. 'We'll accept the working-class platitude that we shall get through.'

'H'm.'

That was all Hester's answer.

'I think if a millionaire hopped along and looked twice at me,' said Rachel, 'I should feel inclined to marry even that social octopus. There are times when I get sick of the working-class. Sick of 'em. They'll work till they drop, they'll rot without even smashing a window, they'll clem, and shake tablecloths without crumbs to deceive their next-door neighbour. They'll spank their kids because they're tired. They'll give their chaps up because they're too young, or court ten years till they can get – "a nice home." They're no good, and I only stop with 'em because I can't get away from 'em.'

She surveyed her sister.

She had not missed that wild blush of shocked colour which had mantled Hester's face at the left-handed reference to giving up Jack Baines.

She felt rather than saw the quivering demoralisation of her sister at this ruthless attack.

'Has ta written to him?' she asked.

'Not sin' he went.'

The words were almost inaudible. Hester's eyes reproached her sister for this impudent interference. Rachel felt the strange, silent challenge in her eyes. She stared into them unflinching, then her gaze quivered away. After all she had got to know what she wanted. Man was a creature whom some woman hunted down. Hester was a poor hunter. She could not even scramble her way upon a tramcar in the rain, but stood there disgusted at the scrimmage. It was the survival of the fittest. If Hester didn't grab Jack Baines, there was no reason why he should go begging.

'I think I'll have a walk,' said Hester.

'Fiddle-lesson?' asked Rachel, in surprise.

The rain was still slashing the windows.

Hester nodded.

She did not think it necessary to tell Rachel that she was not going up to the old man's house for her lesson, but into a wood on a hill-top where there was only wind and rain and not the shadow of a sordid struggle. Rachel would have been concerned. So Hester went out to the wood on the hill, and Rachel stayed behind and took out writing materials. She fished under the chair-cushions for an old newspaper to spread over the faded cloth on the table. A letter fell on the floor. Rachel picked it up and gazed at it in bewilderment. Why was her mother writing to old Barstocks? She turned it over and over. That offered no solution. What was inside it? She placed it back in its old position. Curiosity burned strong but morality was stronger. But it worried her even as she wrote to Baines. She filled two sheets with local affairs, gave him news of Hester in a postscript, licked a stamp, and had just hidden her letter when she heard her mother's voice calling for someone to open the door.

'I've got 'em,' said Mary triumphantly, and the house seemed to wake up with grandmother, who had to hear all the details of the struggle.

Draggled with rain, panting, and flushed, Mrs. Martin wore a look of triumph. Her conquest was soon on the fire, in a pan. She went upstairs to change her sopped skirt.

'I found a letter under the cushion,' said Rachel, as her mother re-entered the kitchen.

Mrs. Martin stood stock-still. She looked in an agitated way at her daughter.

'Oh, what letter?' she asked.

Then she said, 'Oh, that.'

She gave no explanation.

'Whatever are you writing old Barstocks about?'

'Oh, nowt much,' answered Mary.

She went into the scullery. Rachel pondered. There was something here she did not understand. Could her mother be going crazy? It was the first time she had seen her look nerve-shaken. When later Mrs. Martin asked that Rachel would not go out to change her book that night, as she wished to go out, Rachel felt that there was something here that needed unravelling. When she saw the letter poked into the fire – without appearing to notice – her intelligence became even more engaged in wonder as to what that letter could contain. Evidently it was not safe to post.

Hester meanwhile had left the streets behind. Something seemed to unroll, wild and fresh and almost jubilant in her heart, as the last house was left behind. The shrouded hills and the grey sky had their own melancholy beauty. The coarse grass was beaded with moisture, cold colourless specks like rosaries of tears. Brown birds flew up with primitive ones of fear. It was a sombre beauty. It had almost something of the look of a battlefield. Its untamed wildness made its essential fascination. It was the outward harmony of an inward mood, which cried, 'I also, Hester Martin, am still – Hester Martin, wild though crushed, solitary though jostled and herded.' It was the cry of individualism. There has never been any artist who was not an individualist. She stole into the dark wood, with its wind-bent trees, and played and played and played. She stayed until the sun began to sink. The wood was like a cathedral. It had all the colour, all the dimness, all the music – but it had no heathenish symbols, no priest chanting the repentance humanity so seldom feels. Rather it was the voice of fettered humanity which wailed through the wood, rather it was the soul of the slaves of all generations crying in a wild surge of passionate emotion, 'When shall we be free? Take our bodies, break them. Take all we have – but give us freedom.' Sudden faintness caused her to remember time at last. She thought of the ham-bones, and despite herself wondered if her mother had been a successful hunter. She slipped the baize cover on the silent fiddle, and turned to leave the wood. Only then did she realise that she had an audience. A blatant voice broke the silence.

'I didn't know – you played –' it said.

She saw in the dimness of the wood a man of sleek appearance, and thought his face familiar.

'Oh, yes, I play,' she stammered, resentful, quivering and ashamed.

'You are Miss Martin, aren't you?'

She nodded, eager to escape.

But he walked back into the town with her. Sanderson, he said his name was. She heard him, civilly polite, talking of the weather, trade, the pity it was about Barstocks. He was a yarn agent, he said. Hester listened, irritated, feeling trapped. He held out his hand as he turned on his own way. She placed a chill, unresponsive hand into the fat one.

'I'm mad on music,' he said in explanation.

And the funny thing was – it was true.

Hester went home and forgot him, save as an unpleasant incident. Just an unpleasant incident. But he carried in his mind the picture of her, shawl tossed on to the old pine, swaying to the fiddle, a soul expressing itself. He fell in love with Hester's soul. Which was again – the funny thing about it.

CHAPTER 4

Hester came slowly homewards through the dark streets where lamps were just beginning to twinkle. The lamp-lighter greeted her with a gruff 'good-neet' as he passed, and something of wondering pity in his look. As the light had shone on her face there had been something of almost unearthly beauty and dream on it, something which made him afterwards tell his wife that he thought that lass o' the cobbler's was going the way of her father.

As Hester passed the open doors of chip-shops the smell of food came to her with a dim recollection that it was long since she had broken her fast. She peeped in and saw long lines of shining bowls waiting their turn on the white-topped counters, children on tip-toe, trying to see over, the glint of bright tiles over the fish-pan, and a few shawled old women sitting waiting on the forms against the walls, where heat and moisture made snail-like tracks. She set her will against the thought of food, for she had yet many streets to travel before she reached home. Strains of music yet lingered in her mind. The wind-tossed trees were reflected there, and impressions of the wild, brassy-edged clouds, of birds rising from the coarse bents, and of the grass in the wood dark with shadows and blobbed with dew and rain. The clank of passing clogs on the flagstones grated on the ear that had listened in a wood to the harmony of sweet, wedded sounds. The real world seemed dull, flat and unprofitable. A quick pulse beat in her temples as she dodged past the door that once at this hour had waited for the hand of Jack Baines. She half-feared that someone would open it, and coming out see her shrinking as she went past, yet she stared at it – the door that was unlike any door in the doors of the world, humble as it was. But for her someone within that humble kitchen would have been waiting for a quick step, a cap tossed off, a chair drawn up to the table. She experienced a helpless sense of guilt. Trapped by pride, modesty, and the fact that her wages were needed at home, she, the gentlest of beings, had been made to deal a blow cruel and ruthless. She heaved a quick sigh, and with the help of the steel will with which she could conquer her own emotions, passed on.

'Is that thee, Hester?' came her mother's voice, as she opened the door. 'Ay.'

'It's time tha came. Up an' down in this weet an' cowd, an' had naught to eat sin' breakfast. There's nobody can afford to be ill at this show. We've enough on our plates.'

Hester stepped into the kitchen, dimly lit with fire-glow.

'I've taken no hurt,' she said.

How they bothered about the bit of body that was to fade as grass. How they ignored that thing within it which hungered and thirsted for love and beauty and freedom.

'An' mind that rent in the oilcloth,' her mother reminded her. 'We're going to ha' naught on th' floor, an' if there's aught looks poverty-stricken it's a bare floor. Oh, tha's bin to thy lesson. I thought tha'd bin out in th' cowd.'

Hester hung her fiddle on the wall.

Her mother's glance followed her about, with the half-veiled apology which had stolen into its tenderness at times of late. Taking off her shawl, Hester sat down to the table. Rachel poured out her portion of soup. She drank it slowly, noticing that her grandmother seemed quiet. Mrs. Martin saw the look.

'She's bothering because I've had to let her club run bad,' explained Mrs. Martin.

'You'll get buried all right,' Rachel said, not without softness.

'I wouldn't like to think you'd to borrow brass to lig me away,' said the old, quavering voice. '*It looks so.*'

'You'll live to be a hundred,' Rachel chaffed her. 'God ne'er has gi'en stuff, Gran.'

The old woman laughed uncertainly. She fidgeted with her cap, the cap which gave her the look of a tufted, quick-moving bird.

'No; they say He'll ne'er ha' gi'en stuff,' she said, in a half-laughing voice. Then to their pained surprise she fell a-sobbing. Hester jumped up, flashed Rachel a burning look, and the next moment had the old head cuddled against her shoulder.

'You're an old silly, gran,' Hester told her in a whisper. 'You know how we all love you. You know how we couldn't do without you. This is only a bit o' rough ground we're going o'er. An' if we were really starving, you know we'd cheerfully share out to the last spoonful. Besides, what does it matter how we're buried, when we've folk that love us when we're alive. You pretend to be a Christian, an' you're just an old heathen, bothering about how you'll be put in the ground. 'Tisn't as if you were a spring onion, wouldn't come up if you weren't set right.'

'I allus liked to think – sohowbeit, I'd be buried respectable,' said the old woman.

'Well, you will be,' Rachel assured her.

'You're a fathead,' Hester's eyes told Rachel across her.

'How did I know she'd take it in earnest,' Rachel's glance sent back its message. Ten minutes later peace was restored. Perhaps a rather more sorrowful veil hung invisibly across the kitchen. That was all. Perhaps the old woman sat a little more still in her chair, and Rachel looked a few times over *Das Capital* at her, wishing she had not tried to lay a fear in that way.

'Are you going out?'

There was surprise in Hester's tone as she saw her mother bring down her best coat.

'Ay; you can stop in till you get mould on you,' her mother said.

Rachel was acutely aware that her mother looked paler than this slight cloud would account for. Paler than she had looked since the day when they put her father into the ground.

'It'll do thee good, Mary,' chirped the old woman.

'Ay. I daresay it will,' agreed her daughter.

Rachel just managed to stop herself from saying that they probably had as much appetite as they could provide for. Matter-of-fact as she was, she was keenly sorry that her grandmother had taken her joke so ill. In amends she laid down *Das Capital*, and said, 'How would you like me to read to you out of that pack o' lies?' Grandmother bristled.

'It's noan a pack o' lies,' she defended. 'Ay; I would like thee to read, lass. Read me a bit o' Ruth an' Naomi, wilta?'

'I will,' Rachel told her solemnly, and a laugh went round in which the old woman joined. So Rachel began to read the old beautiful story, noticing as she read, the unbeautiful economic underlying it. Hester sat listening, too, her expression changing with the story, her mind far away in an old world.

'Good Lord! There's somebody at the door,' said Mary, who was fastening her fine figure into a straight robe.

'I'll go,' Hester told her.

As her mother dodged under the stairs she had a keen, quivering memory of the last time she herself did that.

'This is Miss Martin's, is it not?' asked the voice which had so rudely disturbed her that afternoon.

'Yes.'

He peered at her.

'I've brought you some music, a few operas and Chopin and Bach. You'll like his fugues. I was passing and thought you'd perhaps like them. I hope you don't mind.'

'It's very kind of you,' Hester said simply.

'Well, I hope you'll enjoy them,' he answered. 'Good night; I've a train to catch.'

'Thanks,' Hester told him.

She came in with the music.

'Wasn't that Sanderson?' asked Rachel.

'H'm,' said Hester in a conclusive way.

'He's deein' to get wed, but can't get off,' added Rachel. 'Nobody'll take him seriously.'

Hester sat down and studied the music, frowning a little. Then she took down the fiddle and went into the parlour, lit up, and began to play the new music. The devil himself bringing her new music would have been welcome. Whether Sanderson wanted to get wed was nothing to do with Bach, Gounod, and – , her fingers trembled, here was a piece she had wanted to buy for two years.

She could hear Rachel's voice reading the story of Ruth and Naomi.

When she came back into the kitchen, her mother was ready. Granny had gone to sleep, just before what Rachel called that shameless proposal which provided at once both bread and a husband. Rachel went back to *Das Capital*, but did not miss the fact that her mother looked agitated and nervous, and had actually forgotten to remind them to put the saucer on top of the milk-jug before they set it on the window-sill. Rachel reminded her of it.

'Eh, ay; I'd forgotten it,' said Mary flushing.

As she stood up in her best clothes and with that flush in her cheeks, Rachel thought that her mother must have been very wonderful to look at in the days of her youth.

Where could she be going in such state and in such excitement?

'You're not going to catch another, mother, are you?' she asked jestingly.

'Another what?' asked Mary.

But Rachel saw that she knew well enough.

'Husband,' she explained.

Mary smiled.

'No,' she denied simply. She stared into the fire as she pulled on her gloves.

'I'm just going to see how Matty Stiner is goin' on amongst it,' she said.

It was a better attempt at lying than Rachel could have believed to lie in her mother's power.

'All right. If it rains, I'll bring you your umbrella,' she said casually.

'Tha can't,' she replied quickly. 'I sold it – yesterday.'

'Oh –' said Rachel.

Apparently reading, she was conscious of her mother's unusually hesitating movements. She had to stop to poke up the fire. She sat down once, lost in some thought that clouded her fine face. She glanced at Hester in that new way, trying to probe into a Hester who could lock up her soul as she could lock a door.

'Well, I'll be going,' she avowed at length.

She so far forgot herself as to let an audible sigh steal on the air of the kitchen.

'Try to get her to bed by eight,' she said, looking tenderly at the old woman. 'She forgets her troubles when she's asleep.'

The words had more than ordinary significance. They told of some inward thought of despair. She fidgeted with her seldom-worn gloves once more and went down the passage. Rachel went to the door, stood on the step and looked after her.

'Get in, with that thin blouse,' called Mary.

Her tone held its usual solicitude, practical and motherly. Rachel watched her out of sight. When she went back to her book, she still saw her mother walking over the pages. Hester was combing and plaiting her hair, just as though she had work to go to in the morning.

'I'm going for a walk round the houses,' Rachel said.

She tossed a shawl on and went out. But she could not see anything of her mother when she reached the end of the street. There was a couple, 'dressed up,' standing by the curb, trying their best to hypnotise each other. Rachel noted them in her observant way. Polly Jones, a winder with heart-disease. Ben Phillips, a taper's labourer at twenty-three shillings a week. They were trying to talk finely to each other. They looked awkward and shy, and Polly said, 'Yis, I think so, too.' Fools – glorious, valiant, pathetic, ridiculous fools.

'Good-night,' greeted Rachel, just to see them start.

After all, it was a divine tragic-comedy – Love in these mean streets, defying everything. With such insouciance, such courage against all odds, what could the masses not do? But no, the poor fools 'got' each other – and that was the end of it.

'Oh, good-nite, Rachel,' said Polly, with an imitation lisp.

She was showing-off on being seen talking to an admirer. Rachel felt it in her blood. She turned her head, and called, 'It's a fine moonlit neet to-night,' and with that quip against Polly's sudden fineness of speech, passed on.

She was not long in reaching the Stiners'. She heard a gramophone next door to the Stiners' rasping out 'Stop your tickling, Jock,'[34] and a loud laugh within. The damned world was sex-mad, mused Rachel. Sex and food, food and sex, the two great impulses that have brought us from the slime, and left the bulk of the world still in the slime. Then she plunged into the gloom of an unlighted passage, with the same familiar worn doormat, the same oilcloth of anaemic cleanliness.

'It's only me,' said Rachel.

'Eh – is it thee?'

They were sitting round a fire very low in the grate. Matty was clasping her knees. Children of various sizes sat around. It looked a doleful party.

'What are you doing in the dark?' asked Rachel.

'Studying our sins,' said Matty, with an attempt at being cheerful. Her voice sounded as if she had been crying.

'We'd no penny for the gas,' she added. 'So we sat round, and I tried to tell 'em some tales. Only I've sort of forgotten 'em. I used to know one or two bits out o' the school reading book, but you sort of forget 'em. They sort o' go out o' your head.'

'Eh, you'll feel miserable in the dark,' said Rachel.

She sat down.

'You'd have a job to gas yoursel' without a penny to put in the slot,' said Matty.

Rachel laughed.

'We shall live till we dee if the dogs don't worry us,' she gibed.

Then, 'Have you heard from Bob?'

'No.'

Matty's voice was hard, the note of grim humour gone out of it. There was a short silence in which the clock ticked, ticking life away.

'Anyhow,' she avowed, 'he's ta'en his belly an' his back with him.' Rachel said no more, and wished she had not said so much.

'He could ha' done weel for us, if he'd shaped,' went on Matty. 'He were just content to be a poverty-knocker. And the rest of his time were spent chalking flags an' giving out papers at meetings, callin' parsons, an' getting us ill-will, an' going up on committees when there were any gruntin' to be done, an' gettin' sacked for it. If he'd ha' used his headpiece for hissel', we wouldn't ha' bin sittin' here without a penny to put in th' slot.'

Rachel realised suddenly that she had a deep liking for the absentee. Ambitionless, poverty-stricken, fighting the gods that be for the whole of his class, of them, with them, for them. She wondered how many Bob Stiners it would take to be a leaven to the whole. Drinking a bit, now and then – but, drunk or sober, carrying the good torch. Matty, however, had loosened her tongue and was grumbling about his folly in not trying to save himself and his family. It was the old symbol of Noah's ark.

'Twelve shillings a week to keep this lot on,' said Matty, in a muffled voice. 'Rachel, we'd to boil praty peelin's to-day. As God's in heaven, we had.' She broke down, sobbing suddenly. The youngest child crept to her knees and set up a howl, frightened.

'Shut up wi' thee,' said Matty, and squeezed him close to her. 'It's not often I bawl,' she sniffed. 'Shut up, Teddy. Mammy's better. You generally are, after a bit o' eye-water.'

'There's folk as badly off as this all the time,' Rachel told her.

'They're what is called the submerged tenth.'

'Ay,' said Matty. 'I've heard him talk on 'em, but I didn't think it were aught like this – .'

'Well, we're 'em, now – or shall be,' said Rachel, 'if we stop here a bit longer.'

A yell of laughter came from the next house.

'They're having a picnic next door,' said Matty, 'I've never heard music sound as miserable as this has sounded this last hour. I fair felt like knocking on the wall. But it's like he used to sing – them as is full don't care what them as is empty feels.'

'There's somebody at the door,' said Rachel.

'I'll go,' said Matty.

She went down the passage.

Whispered voices came to Rachel's ears.

Then Matty came back, her eyes dim – a huge steaming potato pie in her hands, held by a snow-white towel.

'Come on, kids,' she said, in a strangled voice. 'Pu' your chairs up, an' sam in.' Like savages they rushed round the table. 'Here, thee, tha's got thy share,' Matty told one. She gave him a crack with the spoon, but it did not stop him eating, and from the house next door came a yell of merry laughter, and the rasp of the gramophone.

'I were wrong,' said Matty, throatily.

'Aren't you having any?' Rachel asked her.

'Nay,' said Matty, 'I don't feel hungry.'

'My mother hasn't bin here, has she?' asked Rachel.

'Yigh.'

'When?'

'Oh, just for a minute,' said Matty. 'Oh – twenty minutes sin'. Had ta come after thy titty?' One of the children laughed.

Rachel laughed, too. Then she went out. She turned in the direction of the road that ran up towards the walled house where Barstocks lived, insured against all hunger, whilst they starved like beasts. Two men were talking by the curb. She heard what they were saying.

'It's time some o' the other factories gave us a hand,' said one voice. 'It ought to be brought up as we take up collections at the shed-gates.

We can't go on clemming – an' I'm damned if I'll go to their blasted soup-kitchen wi' Mrs. Barstocks serving it out like she was the wife of God Almighty.'

'Beggars can't be choosers, Sam,' said the second voice.

Rachel passed on.

Beggars! Beggars!!

Out of their labour and the labour of those like them came all the wealth of the world, and all the weapons to defend that wealth. O'Neill passed her. He was swinging his leaded cane.

'Good-night,' he said amiably.

Rachel did not answer. She was thinking of poor Bob Stiner – outcast, starving probably, and starving amongst strangers. She hated O'Neill quite suddenly, hated him with a cold, impersonal hatred, hated all he stood for, the lying symbol of a law and order that was anarchy in its worst sense. Then she realised that she was passing the door of the house where Jack Baines had lived. Someone was standing, a shawled figure, in the doorway. She hurried past, eager to dodge any questions. She stepped out towards Barstocks, even whilst her reason told her that she might be going on a wild goose chase. After all, her mother might easily have been writing to Barstocks to ask him to try get them work elsewhere. She caught the refrain of the Salvation Army,[35] out of the windy, star-hung night.

'My – ba-ad compan-yuns, fare-ye-well,
I w-w-will not go, with you to hell;
I mean with Jesus Christ to dwell;
Wi-ill you go-o – wi-il you g-go?'

And she realised that the idea of the Christian's heaven was only the reflex of earth's selfishness, which could conceive the notion of living happily in an upper and beautiful storey, with the basements of hell frizzling the outcast, the unchosen, underneath. How the old material laws ran through everything – even through our spiritual beliefs.

CHAPTER 5

RACHEL soon felt the pure breath of the country blowing about her. The little cottages with their lighted windows had, many of them, their blinds undropped. Covered by the friendly darkness, she got glimpses, however brief, into other lives. She saw forms of women, moving about 'from hearthstone to sink,' an old man, without jacket, bald head ashine, reading, in his chair, the shadow of a mother and a baby on a white blind, a group around a clothless table eating dully without looking at each other. Life was simple here. It was a simplicity thrust upon these rural people. Rachel knew that out of all these dwellers in this score of struggling houses there was probably not one who was any richer for Shakespeare having been born. She caught sight of crude pictures on the walls.

Probably the cows in the sheds felt more of beauty and harmony in their surroundings than the bulk of these rural poor. A fine day would mean to the women 'a good drying day.' Their lives were rounded with heavy slumber and heavy toil. A poet to them would be a useless article. For Rachel's 'social octopus,' a millionaire, they would have put themselves to the trouble of turning their houses inside out, merely to have him stand on the mat and smile down at them. They would have cheerfully run two miles to stare at a king, that padded effigy of a man, wire-pulled and echoing-mouthed. Had Christ returned to challenge tradition as he challenged it before, they would have seen him dragged off by a skunk like O'Neill, and thought him a mad fool for trying to enlighten their darkness.

She thought of it all as she walked on towards Barstocks', without losing sight of the fact that she was going to Barstocks'; essentially a thinker, the weaver lass would not miss seeing the comedy life was. She enjoyed it in a peculiar way, even whilst she deplored it. Hester would probably have winced, feeling only the tragedy of that group eating heavily and dully, round that higgledy-piggledy table, tired glances fixed on the plates. Rachel thought it funny.

She whistled softly, as she went along, fragments of 'England, Arise,'[36] and 'Men of Harlech,'[37] and the hymn she had found in the Psalm Book, with the name of Robert Nicholls[38] attached. Jack Baines had told them that Robert Nicholls had sold him some literature once – told them how that incident had been the turning-point in his mortal life.

He had given her a little word-picture of the man with the rain on his wild hair, having come through thunder and lightning over the hills, peddling his literature for bare bread, and as Rachel walked the ghostly limestone road between the dark frescoes of the hedges, Robert Nicholls seemed quite near to her, as she whistled his hymn.

She reached Barstocks' house almost before she knew, and halted by the gates, surveying it. Could her mother be inside there? If she was, what was she after? That was what she had come to find out.

She tried the gate. It was fastened.

The brilliant light streamed over close-shaven lawns, and a monkey-tree threw its weird shadow on the brightness of the sward. There was a classic figure of Mercury, a-tiptoe, in a square of light from a French window. How conventional these jumped-up rich were! Rachel would have liked to wave a wand which could change the bronze Mercury into a figure of starved childhood, with heavy feet, and the mud on its thin shoulders. Even as she mused about it the door of the lodge-house opened. The parasite came out, staring at her with that air of 'What are you after?' consistent with the well-trained watch-dog, considering his master's interests because somehow his brute instincts tell him they are his own, that his pottage depends on his faithfulness.

'Hello,' said Rachel.

The man slowly approached the gate. Rachel made up her mind swiftly.

'Is Mr. Barstocks at home?' she inquired.

'Yes; he's engaged.'

He was studying her, this shawled, working-class figure. She had not the hesitant speech usual to such people.

'I know – he's got a visitor,' she said, without a tremor.

'Yes. There's a person called to see him,' he said.

'A *person*,' Rachel told him, 'eats peas with a knife, according to old Kitchener.[39] Well, I'm a delegate on behalf of the burnt-out weavers. Unlock these gates.'

He peered at her and hesitated.

'I've left my card at home,' Rachel told him. Despite himself he smiled.

'He's in a devil of a temper,' he confided.

'High living,' suggested Rachel. 'My gout is poor man's gout.'

'You're quite sure – ?' he asked.

'That I've come on behalf of the burnt-out weavers?' asked Rachel. 'H'm! We're getting a fund up, and want to see what he'll do.'

She stared him straight in the eyes. She had once got a handbook on hypnotism, and it said you should stare people straight in the eyes. She had no faith in the handbook now, having loaned it once to Matty to try hypnotism for keeping Bob out of the drink, but she felt a pulse of surprised pleasure when the man fetched keys out and unlocked the gate. She had told him that she had come on behalf of the burnt-out weavers. Having said so, she would see that once inside, she had come on behalf of the burnt-out weavers.

'Ring the bell,' the parasite told her, 'if you're going in at the front door.'

She stood in a stream of lights, her shawl loose on her head. Her features were well-illumined. He ought to have staggered back and cried, 'My God! The Master's daughter!' But as it was life, he thought her a cheeky piece of goods, and wondered how many there were like her in Brayton.

'Oh! I'm going in at the front door, all right,' she told him, calmly. 'No back ways for me.'

So saying, she marched up the walk, without the slightest self-consciousness, an upright, common-sense soul, undeluded and unawed by the evidences of wealth gained by legalised robbery. She wished once that her father could have seen her triumph. He would have laughed a week over it – sitting crouched over his bench, mending the broken boots of the poor, who would not take the trouble to find out why they were poor. She heard another watch-dog yelling and rattling its chains at the back of the house. She was glad she was a slave of the rich rather than a parasite eating the stolen food, for what *did* old Barstocks do in return for *all this?* He walked through the shed twice a year in a white hat. He bought working-class brains to run his concern for him. He bought hands – with brains also behind them (could an imbecile weave?) – and he bought machinery, made by other hands, with brains behind them. He fastened all these hands and brains down, because they must either be bound or starve, and *this* was his share – and *theirs* – she thought of Matty, and the kids and the dish of potato pie.

The bell rang imperiously.

Soft steps sounded on soft carpet.

The door opened – and beyond the white-capped, silk-stockinged maid Rachel saw a glow of colour and beauty.

'Is Mr. Barstocks in?'

'He's engaged.'

The capped slave was studying the shawled slave, with superiority. Rachel ignored the silent challenge.

'I've an appointment with him.'

'Oh I – Step this way, please.'

Rachel stepped. It was like getting past Cerberus[40] to get a word with this common thief.

There was another of them, some yards beyond, a footman in white stockings, with an expressionless face. She thought he would get about thirty pounds and his food to wear a face like that twelve hours out of every twenty-four, for three hundred and fifty-six days a year. Of course, he could think, behind his face. But what a strain! He also weighed and measured her. She had a demonic desire to wink, vulgar as winking was, just to see if his face would not crack.

'This person has an appointment with Mr. Barstocks,' the maid told him.

The footman opened a door.

Rachel stepped into a room. There was a reading-lamp, a glorious fire, books on the table. Rachel took one up and sat down. 'The Triumphant March of Democracy,' by *Andrew Carnegie*.[41] She whistled under her breath.

Wasn't it funny, wasn't it a scream? *Democracy* and – Carnegie! They were cooking chicken. She could smell it! She looked up and saw Venus rising from the Sea, and a life-size portrait of a woman with a somewhat scornful expression. That would be Mrs. Barstocks. Rachel studied her. Then she stole across the room, her vision still filled with that ugly proud face, ugly because it was so proud, somehow foolishly proud, ignorantly proud. Rachel peeped out. The coast was clear. The maid had gone.

The footman had gone. Carelessly studying the Japanese prints on the walls, as she passed, she listened intently. An echo of a voice reached her. Her mother's. It sounded almost as if – . She passed on, guided by these voices. Old Barstocks sounded as though he was preaching.

This must be the door.

'Anyhow, you owe me summut, surely,' came Mrs. Martin's voice. 'I'm not asking much.'

'Please keep your voice down. The servants – .'

'I shall stop here till you pay me summut.'

Rachel hesitated, then the door creaked under her hand. Not unlike Fanny in 'Hindle Wakes,'[42] she blundered in. Mrs. Martin turned deathly pale as she saw her. Old Barstocks gaped at her.

'What's brought thee?' asked Mary, struggling for authority.

'My legs,' Rachel told her. 'And – business. Strict business. Do I intrude?'

The grey-haired man stared at her.

He lost the self-control his educated wife had tried to give him.

'What's the devil's brought you?' he cried, purpling.

Rachel eyed him. He crumpled a little under her look.

'Haven't I as much right here as you?' asked the Proletarian, frowning at him. She was amazed at the effect of her challenging words, the words of the conscious slave surveying the splendour wrenched out of their very bowels.

'You've told her – you've told her,' gasped out Barstocks.

Rachel stared from one to the other.

'An' what if she has. Haven't I a right to know?' she asked, groping after the solution of this mystery.

'You're a liar and a blackmailer, Mary,' said old Barstocks.

'Say that again!' Rachel told him, with blazing eyes. She walked up to him.

He collapsed into a chair.

'Mr. Barstocks, the Vicar has called about the donation towards the new panelling in the Sanctuary,' said the maid, respectfully.

'Tell him I'm engaged. Ask him to call again,' her master told her.

'Look here,' said Rachel, when the door had closed behind the maid, 'what's it all about?'

Old Barstocks motioned feebly to Mrs. Martin. She did not see him. She was almost shaking. Fierce tears were in her eyes, at this insult. Rachel's movement towards Barstocks when he had called her a blackmailer had stirred something in Mary Martin's heart. She had not lied. She had told no one. Neither was she a blackmailer.

'It's thy faither tha'st looking at,' she told Rachel.

She spoke the words to Rachel.

She hurled them really at old Barstocks.

Rachel changed colour. She stood staring at the man in the chair.

This in place of the man at the bench, mending the broken boots of the poor! But after all – birth was a mere accident – incident. She tried to reason herself together.

'Well?' asked the man in the chair.

He pulled out his watch, his face anxious.

'How much do you want?' he asked Mrs. Martin.

Rachel walked over to her mother. She slipped her hand through her arm.

'Nowt,' said Rachel's young quivering voice. 'Nowt! But if we had bargained – it wouldn't have been blackmail. It would have been compensation.'

'Compensation.'

He glared at her.

'Ay. We ought to be compensated for being born in a world like this. More 'un all, I ought to be compensated for being a sprig off your tree. But just to prove how little of your thievish nature, I've gotten, we'll settle it at nowt. But if you don't do summut for folk is starving in this town – the burnt-out weavers – I'll tell everybody who I am – though it would be cutting my nose off to spite my chops. You're an hypocritical, miserable, thieving devil – an' if ever there's a revolution I'd put a bullet through you with pleasure as *my* share in cleaning the world.'

She dragged at her mother's arm.

'Come on,' she said.

'Here,' called old Barstocks. He had heard, or thought he heard his wife's footstep. Panic had seized him. He drew out a cheque-book.

'Fill that amount in,' he told Rachel.

She took it – stared at it, and threw it back in his face. The door opened softly.

Mrs. Barstocks stood in the doorway.

'What's the matter?' she asked.

Old Barstocks went livid. He stared entreatingly at Rachel. She had a fine weapon of revenge in her hands – if not the gun she had mentioned.

'Nowt,' said Rachel. 'Come on, mother. Let 'em go on eating their chickens, and giving the scraps to the poor. Come on, this place stinks. A ton o' washing soda wouldn't swill the lies out of it. We're poor – but, by God, we're honest! An' that's why they dish us all the time. We think they're like us. But they can't be. This whole house is a stinking lie, materially, morally and spiritually. I'd sooner be born in the gutter than live on the poor, like a cannibal, ay, live on 'em – live by their deaths, and their crushed lives, and their crushed souls. Come on.'

She almost knocked Mrs. Barstocks down.

'Whatever – whoever is – she?' asked that lady.

Rachel's clogs sounded even on the thick hall carpet.

'Some sort of a – Socialist – I should think,' said Mr. Barstocks.

'I should say an Anarchist,' said Mrs. Barstocks. 'I suppose there's a lot of suffering in the town. We ought to open a soup-kitchen. I spoke to the Charity Organiser about it, but they say the young girls are dancing – so if they've money to dance – .'

'Yes, my love,' agreed Barstocks. 'You're right.'

He crossed over to a decanter and poured out a glass of wine.

'Hateful girl!' said Mrs. Barstocks. 'But you can tell them. Reformers can talk and talk. We'll never make silk purses out of a sow's ear.'

'No, my love – never,' agreed Barstocks.

CHAPTER 6

To say that Rachel was surprised at the way she had lost her temper, is to put it mildly. She suddenly realised that she, a reasonable animal, possessed emotions which could carry her off her feet. She realised also the mental shock she had sustained on learning that the man who used to crouch over the bench – tap... tap... tap...tap... – at those pathetic boots, singing in a husky voice, songs of a world where there would be no poor, was not her father.

'What arta thinkin', Rachel?' asked Mrs. Martin, almost timidly.

'Only feeling like I'd buried him twice,' said Rachel.

There was a silence, long and painful to Mrs. Martin. Then Rachel broke down for ever the woman's rising fear that this would make her daughter her judge.

'After all, he *is* my father,' stated Rachel. 'He helped to mould my mind, and that counts more in evolution than merely creating your limbs by an act which a beetle is capable of. I wish I'd not got their big teeth. But a few years – and I'll have false 'uns. But whatever (I'm curious, I'll admit, humanly curious) whatever – made you – fancy old Barstocks?'

'I worked under him,' her mother told her, in a low voice. 'An' – all that winter – thy father were ill. An' he – he saw that I got all the good payers in. An' I could get *him* nourishments. I knew he'd have killed me – but I couldn't see him die under my eyes. I-I were fond o' him. An' – he never knew! The doctor said I'd pulled him out o' th' grave. But oh, Rachel – to see him dandling thee an' singin' to thee under his coat o' neets, an' sayin' that were him o'er again. I went down mysel' like water down a dyke-side, an' he said it were havin' thee. An' – our Hester weren't born for four years after. But I never sort o' had any rest till she came along an' I see him nursing his own. I mended up, then. But when he were deein' – an' said I'd bin one o' th' best – it nearly turned my brain. I wanted to tell him, but I knew it were harder for me, an' kinder to him not to do. So – I didn't.'

I hope there's no future life. I'd like to think we're done wi' when we're deyd, for then – I'd ha' to tell him, wouldn't I?'

Rachel gripped her arm.

For a few shillings a week extra from good payers her mother had gone through *this*.

'An' it sort o' came over me,' continued Mrs. Martin, brokenly, 'a two or three weeks sin', how me an' him had brought thee up – an' that he ought to give us summut back, would ease things a bit. So I wrote and daren't send the letter, for I didn't want to make bothers between his wife an' him. So I went. But he said I'd no proof, an' that nobody would take the word of a woman like me, against his. Meaning, I suppose, that I was poor an' he'd got up in the world. Tha doesn't think too ill o' me, doesta, Rachel?'

'I believe our morals are determined by our necessity an' the economic conditions we live under. Viewed from a human standpoint, apart from economics, you saved a life an' created one – that was two. You made the world richer. After all, I don't see that sex is any more sacred than genius, and to sell one has no more ill effects than to sell th' other.'

Rachel's voice was quite calm again.

She had the feeling of having been lifted up by a whirlwind.

Mrs. Martin could not understand the argument, but understood that Rachel was not going to judge her.

'An' tha doesn't think a bit worse o' me?' asked Mrs. Martin.

She stood still in the road.

Rachel gripped her arm, and pulled her on.

'I reckon you did more'n lay your life down for my Dad,' she said. 'He'll allus be my Dad – to me. I dropped down his chimney, anyhow. He taught me to think. He's part o' my make-up. I wonder when women'll be free, mother? An' chaps, too, of course. But we, we somehow have a tradition behind us besides an economic slavery. We've got the race on our shoulders, an' all th' other besides. An' all they think we're fit for down at the S. D. F. yonder, is to cook a thumping big potato pie, when there's a social, or go round canvassing the names when a councillor puts up. Hello, what's this?'

Someone was running and crying aloud in the darkness. They overtook her, sobbing and praying and panting by the hedge.

'What's up?' asked Rachel.

54

She was a woman of fifty.

'My lad – my Tom – he's 'listed, my only one, all I had. He's been out o' work months. But I'm going to stop him. He's a big lad, six foot in his stockings. They say he's at the station, and I'm going to stop him.'

She was quite unconscious that she had no shawl on. Wisps of grey hair blew about her white face.

'If he's 'listed, he'll have to go, unless you buy him off,' Rachel told her.

'Nobody'll lend us any more,' she murmured. 'We're in debt sin' he's been out. We couldn't starve. O, Lord, help me. His father was killed at th' quarry twelve months sin'. What'll become o' me?'

She ran along, whimpering and praying.

They left her reluctantly, for she seemed half-mad. Still, with blind faith she was pursuing her way to the station to beg the recruiting sergeant to let her Tom go home with her – as he was all she had.

'If ever a revolution comes, in England,' said Rachel, calmly, 'you'll see me with a rifle over my shoulder. I can ring the bell nine times out o' ten at the shooting-gallery. It depends on how much you will have behind your trigger-finger.'

'Eh, Rachel, tha wouldn't kill anybody, would ta?'

'They're killin' us inch by inch all the time,' Rachel told her. *'An' I daresay if they were laid out there wouldn't be half o' the number were killed in the Boer War. You can't alter things without shifting things. Why should it be our blood all the time?'*

Then she was silent, wincing for a moment as she realised afresh that in her blood was the blood of the Barstocks' – cultured, unimaginative, top-dogs, 'human sinks,' who took all and gave nothing.

'I wish I was home,' sighed Mrs. Martin. 'I feel done, Rachel, right through.'

'Lean on me,' urged Rachel, 'we'll soon be home now, mother.'

As they went through the dim streets she was thankful, devoutly thankful, that so far as the proletariat went, the accident of birth did not matter, for was not property the underlying cause of the change from the matriarchal to the patriarchal form of society?

Since they were the propertyless, what did it matter. She was *here*.

'Tha'rt goin' too fast, Rachel,' Mrs. Martin gasped, once.

'Eh – I'd forgotten. I were thinking.'

Rachel slackened her pace, feeling compunction.

Her mother had to stop, gasping for breath. 'I believe – there's summut wrong wi' my heart,' she said.

'Get out,' Rachel told her.

'Ay, I do.'

They toiled on through the streets.

'Good-night,' came a voice out of the darkness.

'Good-night,' answered Rachel.

'Who were that?' asked Mrs. Martin.

'Sanderson – the yarn agent,' Rachel told her. 'They say he's going to be a partner in that new factory.'

'I didn't know tha knew him.'

'I don't,' Rachel told her. 'It's Hester he knows. She met him at lectures, last winter.'

'Oh!'

Mrs. Martin seemed to be thinking.

They reached their own door.

Rachel went in first. Her gaze fell on the woman next door. She could hear Hester speaking to someone upstairs.

'What's up?' she asked.

'Eh, Rachel,' said the neighbour, 'there's more trouble for you. You grandmother's had another stroke. Your Hester's nearly frightened to death. But we've done all we can.'

Rachel, white-faced, flung her shawl over a chair-back and went up the stairs.

'It never rains but it pours, Mrs. Martin,' she heard the woman on the hearth saying.

Hester heard Rachel coming up and crept past the doctor. They met on the square-yard at the top of the stairs.

'I thought you'd never come,' almost sobbed Hester. 'Oh, Rachel.'

'I think it would be a good thing if we were never born,' declared Rachel to the astonishment of the doctor. Then she stopped and walked softly up to the bed where the old woman lay.

Granny was trying to say something. Her left hand went to and fro, to and fro, mechanically, swiftly, like a thing not human.

Rachel bent her head.

'P – Pension!' she thought she heard.

Hester also crept up to the bedside.

'Her Pension papers came – she's a year older than she thought – an' she got excited – an' fell off her chair!'

'Glory!' muttered Rachel.

A second stroke, brought on by the thrilling excitement of a few shillings a week as the crown of a life's labour. She had gleaned,[43] scared crows, been in gentlemen's service, and given six slaves to the world.

'S – Sing!' Rachel heard.

Hester was trembling violently. But the doctor nodded his head.

'All she wants you to,' he told them. 'She – ,' he looked at his watch.

'Enuff said,' Rachel answered, looking towards the bed. Her Granny might hear – if she could not see.

Mrs. Martin was stumbling up the stairs. She opened the bedroom door to see Hester and Rachel, their faces white in the gas glare, standing side by side. They were singing – their grandmother's favourite hymn. Rachel had tears in her eyes. Hester was dry-eyed and like a piece of chalk. The treble and contralto rose together – a little feat.

'Weary gleaner, whence cometh thou,
With empty hands and clouded brow,
Toiling along on thy weary way,
Where hast thou been gleaning to-day?'[44]

The doctor held Mary Martin back as she would have rushed to the bed. He held up his fingers. His lips moved.

'Twenty-four hours,' he told her, in a whisper. 'Let her go – quietly.'

Mrs. Martin sat down on a chair and bowed her head. Even in the rush of grief which came to her like a flood she was wondering how they would bury her, since that policy was lapsed.

CHAPTER 7

THEY sat up, all three of them, in the room where Granny lay dying. The coal-nook in the yard was scraped out to keep the fire going. Their neighbour brought in a bucketful of coal after her husband had gone to work. In the phraseology of the working-classes, he was a 'nipper.'[45] There was a 'monkey'[46] on the house they lived in, and he said folk had enough to do to look after No. 1.

'I'll never be out o' your debt,' Mrs. Martin told her, standing in the fireless kitchen. Clogs were beating the old iron music in the dark streets outside. The whistle shrieked through and over her low, tearful words.

'An' there's a jug o' tea in th' oven. I'll bring it in,' said the nipper's wife.

'You're right kind,' Mrs. Martin told her.

'Eh, it's little we poor folk can do to help one another,' answered the other, and hurried out.

Upstairs Hester crouched over the fire. She could not bear any longer to watch the galvanic motions of that hand. They had tied it gently to the helpless one, once – with an old silk handkerchief of the dead cobbler's. But it had fought itself loose. To and fro, to and fro. It was horrible.

'What do you think she thinks she's doing?' asked Hester in a low tone.

'Probably there's no thought at all at the back of it,' Rachel answered. The long, black night was nearly over. Another whistle yelled, like the voice of a demon who would not be disobeyed. Hester stole to the window and peeped out, staring with tired, dull gaze. Sleet was falling. The street lamp gave it a curious ghostly appearance. Through it, as through a sad film, figures were moving with bent heads. Little figures flitted past, hanging on to their parents. An infant's wail rose, feebly protesting at being carried out of a warm bed. Then the whistle ran into something like a jerky, rising note of exultant, hysterical glee. The clogs answered its note with a quicker music of the iron upon the pavement. The people were very nearly running, pressing on with the sleet blown into their smarting eyes. Then the iron music slackened, changed, the beat of the feet grew irregular and faltered into silence. Then came the sound of someone running – someone who had overslept.

Across the bare, dark ground beyond the flags in front of the house, came the throb of an engine's iron heart – thump, thump – a tireless thing. The whistle dropped down into a gurgling groan like the dying sob of a million, million slaves – finished – at last. Hester turned from the window. Out of this life there was no escape, saving death. To get out of the factory was as difficult as to fight one's way up out of the pits of hell. So hopeless it was, that few thought of it. They were looked on as *contented*. But open the heavy door for them – point a way – and how they would rush.

Their mother brought them up the tea. They drank it round the fire. Hester went and stood looking down on her grandmother.

'Do you know me, Granny?' she asked, in a clear, emotionless voice.

She leaned down. The hand never stopped.

'H – Hessie!' came the old voice. It was twisted and broken, that word. But Hessie knew that her grandmother knew her. She leaned down again.

'What does she say?' asked Rachel.

'I think – "Sweet Beulah,"'[47] Hester told her sister.

All through the night, at intervals, they had been singing to her. The hymns with their promise of a land of peace and joy beyond the grave, were a mockery and insult to the two girls who sang with their hearts breaking, breaking not at the mere passing of their Granny from the corner, but for her life, her hard life, crowned with a death no less hard.

Again they stood by the bedside singing 'Beulah Land,' and 'Galilee,' and 'Shall We Gather at the River?'[48]

'Won't you try to drink?' Hester asked her.

Her clear treble reached the old woman's better than Rachel's deep voice.

'F – Fish?' she asked.

Then Hester crossed the room.

'Where arta goin'?' asked Rachel.

'To get some fish.'

'The shops won't open till eight – an' if they did we couldn't – .'

'I'm going next door.'

'Oh!'

So she went.

'Eh, I am thankful I've a bit in the frying-pan,' their neighbour told Hester. 'It's only a scrap – but happen it'll satisfy her.'

'She might get better,' suggested Hester. 'It looks like it, doesn't it, wanting some fish?'

'Eh, they take fancies when they're dyin',' the neighbour told her.

Hester went back with the fish. She put a crumb of it into the old woman's mouth. She chewed it ravenously, then made a queer noise.

'She wants you to take it out,' Hester told her sister. It was Hester, the unpractical, who understood all her wants.

So they took it out. Then Hester sat holding the hand which did not work. She stroked it gently. The old woman got restless at nine o'clock. They took their breakfasts in turns, a crust each of bread, with margarine, thrust down with difficulty.

'Try to eat, Hessie,' Mary told her daughter. 'After all, we've to go on – livin'.'

Milk carts rattled over the pavements. At noon the doctor came.

'Yes; there's a change,' he said to Rachel. 'I think it is going to be as I thought.'

He looked at Hester, who was putting fresh bed-hangings on the bed. She was coughing.

'If you'll come down, I'll mix you a bottle up for that,' he said to her casually.

'I'll see she comes,' Mary told him. 'But we've bin that upset.'

She followed him downstairs.

'That girl shouldn't come down into this chill kitchen,' he said, drawing on his gloves.

Mary flushed.

'We can only get one bag a week,' she answered. 'We worked at Barstocks, you know. It's – it's kitchen physic she wants.'

He nodded.

'Well, see that she comes for a bottle,' he said without comment, and went out. It was his business to order things, not to mend the rotten social road. Mary stood staring at the fireless grate. Rachel's voice from the top of the stairs, roused her.

'Mother, come up.'

It was the voice of Youth – Youth confronting Death. Mrs. Martin rushed up.

Rachel went down to call the doctor back.

Already the vehicle was out of sight.

'Don't scream, Hester, tha'll steer her,' said Mrs. Martin in a choked whisper. 'An' that'll bring her back, to go through it again. God knows – once is enuff.'

'Mamma!'

The old voice quavered the word wearily. Perhaps once again she was gleaning in the Derbyshire fields, her legs pricked by the stubble. Her sightless eyes had been dark long. There was no light to fade. Somewhere, she was wandering, not sightless, but seeing some scene of childish toil.

Hester's hand caressed the motionless hand.

The other was still working – working.

'Mamma' came the cry. All seemed blotted out between struggling childhood and the grave. Hester's ice-cold hand went on stroking the poor, helpless one. They heard Rachel close the front door.

Then she remembered something of the present.

'Mary,' she breathed. But it would be impossible to write the word as Granny said it, twisted, broken.

'I'm here, mother,' Mary told her.

'G – Good lass! Go – Good lass,' she managed to make somehow intelligible.

Hester came hungrily nearer.

'All good lasses,' she gasped. Then – 'Gi'en stuff.' Hester was sure her grandmother said 'Gi'en stuff.' She was glad Rachel, half-way down the stairs, was not in the room. She murmured something about her pension. Then – it came again.

'Mamma!'

Her breathing came slower, slower – stopped, went on again. One – two – three – horribly, horribly hard. Hester closed her eyes.

'Don't steer her!' beseeched Mary Martin.

She bent over her, listening.

All was silent.

'She's gone,' Mary told Hester. Rachel was creeping in. She heard the words, and ran to the bed, seizing the hand that had stopped working now. She broke down sobbing by the bedside.

'An' to think I upset her, about God not having gi'en stuff.'

'Tha couldn't help it. Tha didn't mean it.'

Rachel looked up, from where she was kneeling.

'If we hadn't been so damned poor,' she said, rising like a white-faced, indignant goddess, 'she couldn't have ta'en it like that.'

Mary stared at Rachel.

Swearing, in a room of death. Rachel's answering glance stated that she would cry truth abroad, with or without swearing, from a gravestone. She passed out of the room. Hester obeyed her mother's order to go to the woman at the top of the street and ask her to come and lay Granny out. Hester was glad to get away. Already, to her shuddering imagination, Death, strange, mysterious, with its shadows of corruption, hung over the house. Mary was staring down at her mother.

'I wouldn't have you back,' she was thinking. 'You're at rest now.'

Then she stole to the window.

How would they bury her?

How in the world would they bury her?

CHAPTER 8

MRS. MARTIN went down to see the Insurance Agent, leaving Hester and Rachel in the darkened kitchen. Upstairs in the bedroom, Granny lay with pennies on her eyes, to close them decently. The dark discs on the white face had given Hester so horrible a suggestion of staring black holes that she had almost tumbled downstairs – away from this *Thing* which seemed like yet so unlike Granny.

All the clothes Granny had saved for long years *in case anything happened and she could go to her grave decently*, she had on. Yet it seemed as though the problem of her burying was going to be a problem.

'They sent us a lapse notice, an' we took no notice,' stated Rachel, out of the shadows. 'So there isn't much hope.'

'No,' Hester agreed, with trembling lips.

She could not shake off the uneasy feeling that the *Thing* upstairs was listening, listening intently as Granny had always listened, when the struggles of ordinary life were discussed.

'I don't see why they don't just dig a hole and chuck us in,' continued Rachel. 'Same as they do on a field of battle. It is a field of battle; an' if they'd stick a cross over us, it would tell everything there was to tell.'

'Oh, shut up,' urged Hester, softly.

She gave a half-glance towards the dim landing upstairs. Rachel saw it.

'She isn't worrying any more,' she said. 'She's finished. It's us has to go on. It's not just burying her. It's how are we going to live. Tha looks like two laths nailed together. An', Hester, I feel I could eat grass sometimes. How are the others doing?'

'Like us,' said Hester, tonelessly.

'If only there were somebody we could borrow off,' said Rachel.

'We should have it to pay back, and when we're in work, we have all on to get what we need,' her sister answered.

'Well, every day'll be Sunday by and bye,' answered Rachel, 'when we're dead, like Granny.'

She rose and wound the blind up another few inches.

'We're half-clemmed,' summed up Rachel. 'Our nerves are shaken with losing her out o' the corner. An' we've to sit in the semi-darkness, just to suit the woman across. To Harry with it.'

She wound the blind up half-way.

'Eh, Rachel!' protested Hester.

'Tha'll be saying that when the revolution comes,' gibed Rachel, without animosity.

Hester flushed.

'Happen not,' she said, briefly, 'but if you'll look at the faces of the folk in Brayton you'll see how far off *that* day is. We're their prisoners, Rachel. We're ready, but they're not. Look at 'em an' ask yourself how much any one of 'em would dare, to win a new world.'

'I didn't know tha looked at 'em,' said Rachel, curiously.

'Sometimes,' her sister told her, 'an' then Rachel, I see more nor flesh.'

Rachel stared at her.

She sat by the window, pale as alabaster, a creature so frail looking, it seemed as though a strong wind would blow her away. Sometimes Rachel almost shuddered when she realised the human endurance Hester possessed. It was so quiet, so unaggressive, so passive, and yet, in some remarkable way, a challenge, with reserves, untold reserves, behind it.

'What's that?' asked Hester, starting nervously.

'The wind in the key-hole,' Rachel told her.

'Oh!'

'I keep thinking I hear her moaning,' said Hester in a low voice. 'And – that hand, Rachel.'

She rose, a shuddering, imaginative pagan, and stood by her sister, warm flesh and blood, for succour.

A little later she sat down again.

'Hasn't the coal man been yet?' asked Rachel.

'No.'

'I'm starved to the marrow.'

Rachel shivered, despite her father's old coat, which made her a grotesque figure, as she sat in the semi-darkness. She felt the *material* hardship; Hester, that which arose out of it.

'Mother'll be coming back. I daresay this last cob o' coal will boil the kettle,' said Rachel, out of a long silence. She planted it on and tried to make the fire brim up with two pieces of wet wood. It was Hester who stood over it for half-an-hour, fanning the tiny flare to induce it to coil round the cob of coal, and make of it a living thing.

Ten minutes later their mother returned, red-eyed, angry and exhausted. They read the verdict at once.

'No go,' said Rachel.

'No go,' admitted their mother.

She flopped down upon the first chair she came to.

'Well, what are we going to do? We can't let her stop on the top o' th' earth,' asked Rachel. 'The decencies have got to be preserved – whatever there is underneath 'em.'

'All the folk I know are as ill-off as us,' said Mary, weakly. 'Give me a cup o' tea, for the Lord's sake.'

Hester took down the caddy.

'There's only a few grains,' she said in a low tone.

'Never mind.'

'It's no good minding,' said Rachel.

Mary suddenly burst into dry sobs. Hester made half a step towards her, then moved towards the window. The clock ticked on evenly. Every tick meant a life coming into a world of such brutal struggle, such sordid miseries as these. Her imagination shuddered back from it. Tick-tick! Tick-tick! Coming into the sordid scramble, the wretched hypocrisies, the jungle-like traditions.

'Couldn't you sell one of your other policies?' asked Rachel, with hope. 'I suppose none of us will be kicking the bucket just yet.'

'I sold 'em – to bury your father,' said Mrs. Martin dully. 'They wouldn't have him in a club. So I sold the others to lay him by.'

Rachel stared at her mother and laughed.

'It's like opera – when it gets past a certain point,' said Rachel. 'I always want to laugh.'

'Well, it's beyond me,' said Mrs. Martin, in a hope-less tone. 'Unless one o' you go up and ask John Rodes if he'll let us pay by instalments – when we've got working.'

'I'll go,' said Hester, quickly.

They stared.

Hester – Hester with her shrinking from the sordid details of working-class life, was going to see John Rodes. She went half an hour later after their neighbour had lent them six spoonfuls of tea, and the cups of tea had brought the colour into their cheeks and warmth to their limbs.

'Don't be long, Hessie,' called her mother from the door. 'An' tell him a plain coffin'll do.'

So Hessie went.

She approached John Rodes in his workshop. Several coffins in process of making were about the room. He was a fat man, whistling as he used his hammer.

'Well?' he said, turning to Hester.

His practical grossness seemed to be hurled at her with all its fourteen stone.

'My grandmother's dead,' said Hester, with stiff, white lips.

'Ay. A lot of folk popping off,' he said. 'Busy! We've hardly time to eat.'

He stared at her, the bit of a white-faced lass, with the band of soft brown hair peeping from under the shawl, which seemed too heavy for her head. Looked like egg-shell china, he thought. He noticed her clog, broken.

'Tha wants that mendin',' he said.

Hester took heart of grace.

'We worked at Barstocks,' she explained. 'That's nothing.' She glanced at the clog. 'But my grandmother's dead. We wondered if you'd be kind enough to make her a coffin. We'll pay you – as soon as we can. We have hands. We'll be sure to pay you. We are honest folk.'

Her heart was beating like a sledge-hammer. Her hands were ice under her shawl. Her pride, a titanic, sensitive pride, was breaking into pieces, stamped underfoot by the thought of Granny waiting for her coffin.

John Rodes stood with the hammer in his hand.

He had bills of his own to meet. Just now he needed ready money.

'We're that busy we've hardly time to eat,' he said. 'I'm afraid we're that busy – hardly time to eat. Look there!' He pointed with his hammer at the coffin lids reared round the walls. She saw the brass plates blaze. The light hurt Hester's eyes. They smarted with tears welling up – thrust back.

She was a quivering human soul talking to – Commercialism.

'Yes,' she told him.

To herself she seemed to cringe – but she was cringing away from the atmosphere cast off by this fat man, this business man.

'I'd hardly like to take it on with all these in. Try Guelders,' he said.

He did not look at her.

Perhaps there was something even in his grossness which shrank from meeting those eyes, eyes clear, penetrating as truth, eyes wonderful as a poet's dream.

She did not speak.

She turned.

'If – if you could pay a small deposit,' came his voice. 'You see, Miss, I don't know your name – I've bills to meet. *I'm a business man.* I've a lot o' money out in this town. I have that. An' I've my stuff to pay for, or else there's black looks. You see – .'

'How much does a coffin cost?' asked Hester.

'That's five pounds – .'

He pointed the hammer head at it.

'This, with silver handles – ,' he began.

'A plain one,' said Hester.

'I could get you one for two pounds, pitchpine. Keeps the water out. The graves up yonder in the church is full o' water, but the clay holds it well. Two pounds – .'

'How much deposit?'

'An' – you could ha' one, not pitchpine, but them keeps the water out best – .'

'Pitchpine,' said Hester. Imaginative Pagan that she was she shuddered back, then forwards, her mental hands clutching at the pitchpine that should preserve that dear shell at home from water, and clay, and worms.

Then – .

'How much deposit?' she said.

'Half – that wouldn't hurt you?' he asked. 'Would it, now?'

'No,' she told him, thinking of the empty bread-bin, the caddy without tea. 'I'll bring it before you. ... When do you want it?'

'Could you come up in the morning?'

She nodded.

'I'll not do bad for you. I'm not hard on folk,' he told her.

She gave him a ghostly smile. Whether it was gratitude, or – .

John Rodes scratched his head as he went back to the coffin. Something damned queer about that lass! Made you feel ashamed; but damn it, what could a man do?

'Your sosiges is ready,' yelled a voice from below stairs.

Whistling, he went downstairs to tell the tale.

'Well – ,' said Rachel as Hester went in.

Their mother was upstairs taking the pennies from the old eyes.

'I've to get a pound,' Hester told Rachel, in a whisper.

'Where from?'

They stared at each other.

Hester's gaze wandered to the fiddle. Rachel's followed it.

'Nay, by God!' protested Rachel. 'Tha'rt not going to – play in the streets!'

'Eh, hush!' said Hester.

She was back again in the house of death, a house sacred to the great, beautiful, terrible Presence.

'If I was mother, I'd sell the chairs, or something,' said Rachel.

'We'd have nothing to sit on,' Hester told her dully. 'There's nothing we can do without. Perhaps, later on, we'll have to sell 'em to eat 'em.'

She began to laugh, hysterically.

Then she became calm.

'Don't tell her,' she said in a whisper, as they heard their mother's step on the stairs.

'No,' whispered Rachel.

'Well?' asked Mrs. Martin.

'John Rodes'll do it.'

'Thank God!'

She tottered to a chair.

Hester and Rachel exchanged glances.

Their mother was thanking God – .

Much He had had to do with it.

'I don't care now, so long as that's done with,' said Mary. 'An' I'm that tired; I'll go up an' sleep, lasses'.

She went.

'You're not going now?' whispered Rachel.

'Might as well.'

'H'm. What'll I tell her?'

'Tell her, I've gone to a lesson.'

'She'll think you're callous.'

'Let her.'

'Where to? '

'Redburn. It's market day. There'll happen be Brayton folk there. I'll have to dodge 'em. I'll play in the back streets, away from where they go.'

'Dressed up?' asked Rachel.

'No. The shawl'll cover my face – .'

'Ay.'

Rachel moved slowly over to her sister. She felt that she ought to kiss her. But kisses were not so cheap in their world as in the bourgeois world. To kiss was to give a bit of the soul – then to stand back again – ashamed, Spartanlike of the softnesses of life.

Then overmastering impulse conquered her reason.

She leaned forward, grasped her sister awkwardly, held her, looked her in the eyes – and her lips brushed Hester's cheek.

'If the *Lord* would only send a millionaire!' she said, comically, 'I'm hanged if I wouldn't be a bird in a gilded cage. It would be a change from rusty iron.'

They smiled, eyes wet.

Then Hester dodged out on her five miles' walk, the fiddle under her shawl. She wavered once. She could *sell* the fiddle. Then the prospect of long months without the instrument tugged at her heart. Besides, it would not bring a pound.

She went on.

Rachel sat down, drew out the last sheet of notepaper, and wrote in her large sprawling hand:

'Please get the next boat back. We're starving like rats in a trap. Granny's dead, and Hester'll be the next. She's breaking her heart for thee, on the quiet, of course.

RACHEL.'

(She who must be obeyed.)

She ran out and posted it herself, without stamp, in a dirty envelope. Then, very quiet herself, she sat by the window. Their next-door neighbour was washing. The miserable cotton underclothes blew about on the line. Thrift! Rachel stared at it. Anyhow, she had done her duty. She had given up the ghost, as far as Jack Baines was concerned. Old maidhood loomed up before her. She pictured herself at fifty, somewhat stout, still weaving, still reading, still gathering knowledge, for no purpose at all, that she could see, except to lessen the general sum total of mass ignorance. Perhaps, to spread the knowledge gleaned under these conditions. She did not know. A hopeful sparrow hopped on the window-sill.

'Nothing doing,' Rachel told it. 'A good time coming to-morrow!'

The dog heard her, crept out, and laid his nose on her knee. His eyes appealed, wistful, hungry.

'Damn it. Take the last,' Rachel told him.

She gave him the crust out of the mug. Then she sat down again, amusing her sense of subtle irony by thinking what profits she, Hester, and her mother had made to Commercial Enterprise nearly all their lives, from half-time days till now. She then passed on, thinking of the accumulated wealth of the world, of England in particular, the great Empire on which the sun never set! Like a world built on a coral reef, built by the labour of generations of shell-life, that came up from the underworld of the sea, uncounted lives, coming, dying – dying *in* their shells, so the wealth of the legalized bandits was built on the lives of the multitudes dead, living, and – to be! A few weeks of unemployment – and *this,* this was the reward of years, long years, of building up the wealth of the world. It was funny. Terribly funny. But for one moment, Rachel's intellect was subdued by her passions, the noble, outraged passions of the caged who would be free. She stared at the dog gnawing the crust. He grew afraid and crept under the chair to eat, away from that strange gaze. She was wondering if Socialism did come, as their poor dead grandmother used to whisper it would, knee-deep in blood, whether it could be any worse than this. Hundreds of thousands were enduring the starvation which they were enduring. Millions in Eastern countries lived like beasts. The whole panorama spread before her mental gaze. She rose up and paced about, like a caged thing. And as she paced, a white flame of indignation in her heart, it was almost as though a voice spoke, close to her ears:

'What have you done – *You* – to pass on what you have learned?'

Rachel started.

'This is the result of all we've passed through,' she thought. But she thought also of Jack Baines – Jack Baines, always doing the work, giving the message. And Stiner, and – a few others. Wide was the field. Few were the labourers. At least if she could not marry Baines, she could stand shoulder to shoulder with him, fighting for the same things. They would be comrades. Perhaps, perhaps of all words, that was the sweetest, purest, the most valiant.

'Eh, Rachel!' cried Mrs. Martin, entering the kitchen an hour later.

Rachel was lying on the floor.

She opened her eyes weakly, saw her mother.

'What's up?' she asked.

'I think it's a faint,' she told Rachel.

Rachel sat up.

'I – managed to faint in a soft shop,' she said laughing weakly, in reference to the fact that she was on the rug.

'Eh, Rachel – .'

'You're as bad as Hester with your "Eh, Rachel,"' said Rachel, testily.

'How doesta feel now?' asked her mother.

'Not so bad.'

She struggled up to the chair, and sat down on it doggedly.

'If you don't get mental inertia, you're all right. That's the thing to fear,' she said. 'Mother, let's go out and cadge our tea. Let's go down to Matty's. Happen – you never know – they might have summut.'

So they went, ashamed, hungry, to see if Matty by some miracle had anything to offer them.

CHAPTER 9

RACHEL and Mrs. Martin did not go down to Matty's in their clogs and shawls. Death was in the house. To lock the door on a dead person and go out, faint and hungry, to cadge a meal, was to do a thing too brutal to be openly displayed to the whole world. Dressed up, they might convey the impression that they were out on the business of seeing about the coffin, shroud, or grave papers. What hypocrisy 'This Slavery' engenders when it must be 'dressed up' to look respectable! What lies it plants on childish lips that will babble of 'home' doings. It is no wonder that there are thousands of human beings who cannot look in another creature's eyes when they speak, mind to mind. What a slimy, evil trail is left all through the social world, so that when a soul is found strong enough to rise beyond all pretence, his natural frankness is so unique that it seems almost an art! Of all the tragedies Freedom *might* bring, could it bring any more degrading than the spectacle of one person saying a thing he did not mean, because another person possessed more things than he did? At least the tragedies Freedom would bring, *if any*, would be an iconoclasm, trampling down the mean, the false, the illusion – not the grand, the true, and the realities of life. Rachel felt something of this, but not coherently, as she and her mother, two sombre, 'dressed-up,' white-faced beings, set out in the mizzling rain, on the chance of Matty having a cup of tea to offer them.

'Why, there's Johnny Grimes,' cried Rachel.

A little, bandy-legged man was walking towards them, his factory cans[49] in hand.

'Hello, John!' called Rachel.

He looked up and stopped whistling.

'Hello.'

'Tha's never got workin'?' asked Rachel, eyeing the cans.

'I have that.'

He grinned all over his face.

'Lucky beggar,' said Rachel.

'Ay. I went down, just on spec, to see if my turn was comin',' he told her, 'an' happen just to smell a bit o' warmth, for it is warm in th' shed. Th' wife were yellin' – an' th' kid were cryin' – for her milk had gone back, through us being a bit short like.'

Rachel nodded, noticing the definition of starvation as 'being a bit short.'

'An' I felt like makin' a hole in th' water mysel' – so I just walked down to the factory to walk it off – an' found th' shed up. Does ta know, Jimmy Taylor?'

'Him as had a little lass scalped sweepin' under, last year?' asked Rachel.

'Ay. Him. Excuse me, I've a bit o' weft or summat in my throat.'

Johnny spat into the gutter.

'Keep out o' that puddle,' urged Mrs. Martin to her daughter. 'Thy shoes are thin.'

Rachel moved away from the puddle of rain a little impatiently.

'He's gone potty,' said Johnny, in a whisper. 'He's bin goin' a day or two. Kept lettin' his looms stop, an' kneelin' down in the alley, prayin' an' singin' like a good 'un. When I landed he were there, at it again, and the weavers couldn't do their work for watchin' his antics. He'd bin preachin', stannin' on a turned-up weft-can, before I landed, and some of 'em had let their looms stop to harken to him. He'd had a text, too – *Love they Neighbour as Thyself.* Eh, aye – you could tell he were barmy. Clean gone. That afternoon he'd ta'en it into his knowledge-box 'at he were Jesus Christ. So, the manager had got fed up with him – they'd an order to get out an' when he saw me he said:

"Get on them looms. We'll have this damned fool out of it."

'By the Mass! It were funny. Jimmy didn't even notice when I set his looms goin'. He said:

"I am Jesus Christ."

'The manager yelled in his ear-hole:

"Well go home, Jimmy, an' see if thy cross is ready. We've an order to get out, here."

'He stared at th' manager, an' walked out – an' such a look in his e'en.

So – I'm workin'.'

'Poor fellow,' said Mrs. Martin.

'Ay. There were one or two women in the factory cryin' over him,' said Johnny. 'But you know, he'll weave no more. What could they do but send him hoam. They say they can't cure religious madness. What could they do?'

'Nowt!' said Rachel, shortly. 'Even Religion hasn't got to interfere wi' gettin' an order out! If it can be manipulated to make you work harder – it's all right.'

'Ay,' agreed Johnny. 'An' now they're workin' our guts out. But that's better nor havin' nowt between your ribs.'

A little silence fell, broken by the sound of a pair of childish feet clattering towards the chip-shop.

'I'll get hoam,' said Johnny. 'She doesn't know I've started. She'll jump sky-high. Good-neet.'

He walked in whistling.

Then – he turned, slowly, very slowly.

'Mrs. Martin,' he called, through the rain.

She stopped. Johnny came back to them. His voice dropped to a whisper.

'I subbed my afternoon's wages – to get some tommy.[50] I know you'd have done as much for me.'

He hurried away.

Mrs. Martin stared at the shilling in her hand.

'No,' she protested feebly.

Johnny went on whistling through the rain.

'His heart's in the right place,' she told Rachel. 'Most of our hearts are,' Rachel told her, and left the rest to be guessed at.

'Are we turning back?' asked her mother.

'No. Let's go on – an' share wi' Matty.'

So they went, walking into what Matty called 'a right glory-hole.' Matty had taken in some washing. The children had been washing the rags off their battered dolls. The fire was almost out. It was dusk, and as they entered the door they heard Matty singing in a flat voice 'On earth I'm a stranger, but heaven is my 'ome.'[51] They stayed whilst Matty cleaned up, and lit the gas. It wasn't much to look at – this shelter – but it was the place which haunted Bob Stiner, an exile in a doss-house.

Half-an-hour later they sat around a table with butter-less bread, sugarless tea, and a dish of potatoes boiled in their jackets, all procured with Johnny's shilling.

'Fingers were made before forks,' apologised Matty.

Rachel knew then that Matty's forks had gone to the pawn shop.

'Where's the kid who reads Shakespeare?' asked Rachel, looking round the table.

'He sells papers, after school. It's only half-a-crown a week, an' he gets wet through. But what can you do?'

'Shoot somebody,' said Rachel quietly.

'If you knew *where* to start,' said Matty, taking it as a jest. Mrs. Martin looked warningly at her daughter.

'After all, if we liked we could alter it without shootin',' she said wearily. 'But you can't get folk all of one mind.'

'An' some wouldn't work if they could,' said Matty, virtuously.

'Them's 'em I'd shoot,' Rachel told her.

She was too subtle for Matty.

'Ay. I could shoot 'em mysel',' she agreed.

Someone knocked at the door.

Matty turned pale.

'If it's the rent-chap, I can't face him,' she said.

'I'll face him,' Rachel told her, shortly.

She marched down the lobby, and opened the door. Sleet blew into her face. Vaguely, through it she saw something that looked like a respectable scarecrow.

'Is this my castle ?' asked Stiner's voice. 'An Englishman's castle is his home, isn't it?'

'They say so,' Rachel told him.

'Good God. He's come back,' whispered Matty to Mary. 'He can't stop. He can't stop. I could take a lodger in and profit more by him. He can't stop.'

'I think we'll be going,' Mary told her, embarrassed.

'No; don't. He'll go sooner,' she begged.

Mrs. Martin sat down very unwillingly.

Stiner came into the kitchen. Its gas-glare showed his unshaven pallor, his rent sleeve, dirty scarf and broken boots. His eyes held the miseries of the past months. He was sober, but his shaking hands told that he had only just 'pulled up.'

'May I sit down on your chair, madam?' he asked.

'It depends where tha's bin,' Matty told him.

'Well, I don't think I'm fit to sit in a *respectable* house,' he admitted.

'Tha allus liked low company.'

'So did Jesus of Nazareth,' he told Matty. 'And anyhow, I've found comrades. *Comrades.* Low comrades maybe. Still *comrades.* Better, or shall we say different, from the washed slaves who ape their betters. May I sit down, madam?'

'Ay. Sit down, tha fool.'

Stiner sat, cap across the threadbare knees of his corduroy trousers.

'Arta takin' me back?' he asked at length, after he had watched Matty clear off the empty plates.

'No; I'm not.'

'That's straight,' Stiner told Mrs. Martin.

There was something of curious, generous gallantry in the way in which he set her and Rachel at their ease, during this discussion of his 'To be or not to be.'

'That's straight,' Matty told him.

'Where's the dog?' he asked.

'We had it blood-poisoned, daddy,' piped a curly-headed child.

'Poisoned, tha means,' corrected Mrs. Stiner.

'H'm!' commented Stiner.

'Can we afford to keep a dog?' asked Matty.

He bent his gaze upon his greasy cap.

'Drunk or sober, rich or poor, a dog never turns,' said Stiner. ' A dog never turns on you.'

'Women aren't dogs,' said Rachel, breaking in for the first time.

'No, they're *not*,' admitted Stiner.

He sat studying the same worn pattern on the same old floor. Poverty-stricken, but still – home. There were no lice here. There were times, pay-nights, when it looked *nice*.

'Is that thy final judgment?' asked Stiner.

He lifted his head, and looked at his wife.

Rachel turned away and stared at the picture of Daniel hypnotising some wooden lions.

'That's final,' said Matty. 'We want to live respectable, like other folk, not ha' thee comin' home at half-past two Sunday afternoons, when the schools are loosing.'

'Oh, Respectability, but for thee!' breathed Stiner.

'Tha wants to come back to it – sohowbeit,' Matty told him sharply.

He looked her in the eyes.

Then he turned to Mrs. Martin.

'You see, I'm a poverty-knocker, madam,' he informed her. 'If I'd earned five pounds a week it would have been *different* – quite different. That's women. Have it as you like. I'd sooner have a decent dog. What did old William say, "Through tattered clothes small vices do appear; gold and furred gowns hide all"?[52] Something like that anyhow. Well, good-neet, folk.'

He went, putting his cap on as he spoke.

Rachel followed him down the lobby.

'Tha hasn't the price of a pint, lass, hasta?' he asked, humbly, and ashamed. 'I'd like to forget – just for an hour or two! An' if I get inside, I can entertain the company. An' when I come out, the hideous misery of it all will look all right, all rosy. An' to-morrow – to-morrow I'll go back to hell. It is a hell, Rachel. Underpaid – flotsam – jetsam – a tramp-weaving shop. Lice! An' to forget the lice in the doss-house, you booze – an' get blue 'uns. Still – one learns – one learns – and forgets folks' faults – in their miseries. And whatever we are – we are part of the great army that makes Commerce possible, and manufactures comfort for those who don't give a damn how we live.'

They were standing on the doorstep.

The rain smoked on the flagstones, and people were running for shelter.

Rachel slipped something into his hand.

'It's a brooch. Hall-marked. Sell it in a pub,' she told him. 'Go an' be happy – *if you can*. But won't you wait till the rain has stopped?'

'I'm not sugar. I shan't melt. Thanks,' Stiner told her.

He seized her hand in the dim light, and kissed it with an incongruous grace – the incongruity caused mainly by his attire.

He went off in his broken bluchers, into the wind and rain. Respectability had no room for him. He was going back to a lower circle, still carrying the red flag, even in hell. And above the sound of the rain Rachel heard him singing the 'Miserere.'[53]

CHAPTER 10

HESTER MARTIN had been playing for three hours in the rain. She had received one shilling. A dream had been shattered as to the royal receipts taken by street players. She kept her shawl over her brow, and her brow was bent over the fiddle. She could see when she lifted her gaze, the stone figure of Queen Victoria looming through the rain. She had left the back-streets of the poor, where a woman had asked her to come in and shelter, and have a cup of tea. Red-hot needles of pride had ceased to prick her. She scarcely felt real to herself, after three hours of it. Moisture from her shawl dripped into her smarting eyes. She saw shining umbrellas bob past and well-dressed people.

She might have done better had she played the simple melodies of the poor. But she had played Beethoven and Bach, and Grieg's 'Cradle Song.' In the ordinary way of romance she ought to have caught the ear of some prosperous musician. But Redburn[54] was more famous for cotton – though it loved music – and it was very wet. She had seen the crowds rushing towards the theatres. They were playing 'The Merchant of Venice' at one theatre, and 'A Royal Divorce' at the other.

A half-empty house was revelling in the beauty and splendour of Portia, the magic witchery of Jessica, and a full house was snivelling over the woes of Josephine, the courtesan wife of Europe's greatest butcher.[55]

Hester, meanwhile, in the grey rain, played on, too numb with cold, too faint with hunger really to suffer. She was only half-conscious. It did not matter now whether anyone heard her or not. She was playing on until eleven o'clock to catch the theatre-goers. Then she would walk home, by the lonely road past the reservoir, and the old toll-house where a man had once been murdered. Imagination did not flinch at the prospect. It lay submerged, dulled. She was just a weary body, with something within that still drove her on to play.

'Miss Martin!'

She started and looked up into the face of – Sanderson. Sanderson, holding an umbrella over his mackintoshed figure.

He stared at her as though still not believing his eyes.

'Whatever are you doing here?'

'Playing,' Hester told him.

'Sort of – er – experience?' he asked.

Hester smiled.

The smile told all.

'Good God!' ejaculated Sanderson. He was one of those who said such things when surprised.

'But I was just going to set off back,' Hester said hurriedly.

'There's a train due now,' Sanderson told her.

'I'm going – the other way.'

'Not – not walking?'

'I suppose all the people who stand in gutters and play tin whistles walk *home*,' Hester said to him. 'I've never heard of them riding in motorcars!' She spoke wearily, calmly stating facts without Rachel's satire.

'But *you* can't walk,' Sanderson answered her.

'I am going to walk.'

She dragged on the green shroud of the fiddle with numb fingers. Then she stopped.

'Good God!' she heard Sanderson say again.

'I'm not – going to faint,' Hester told him. 'Please go away. You are drawing attention to me. *Please.*'

She gathered all her energy together. She went a few of all those paces that lay between her – and home.

'I'm ravenously hungry,' Sanderson said, at her side. 'There's a steak-pudding shop two streets away. There'll be no one in till the theatres empty. Come on.'

He gripped her arm, masterfully.

'Please let go of my arm,' asked Hester.

'You're going to have some food. You'll never walk home, else. It was madness of you to come and play in the streets. Anyhow, I'm going to see you have food and put you on the train. Whatever made you do it?'

'The out of work folk are starving,' Hester told him. 'We can starve quietly. But you've got to have coffins to put your dead in. An' all our friends are in the same boat. So I thought – but I see it was quite mad, now. You hear so much about how street-singers and players earn a pound in a night.'

Her low tired voice was a murmuring music in his ears.

'You could have come to me,' he said.

'Oh – we couldn't have come to you.'

'Why not?'

'Oh, I don't know.'

'We are all human,' Sanderson told her.

'I daresay,' said Hester. 'You forget it, when you've stood hours in the rain and seen them walk by.' She shivered.

'Yes. But the others don't feel it like you do,' Sanderson told her quickly. 'You're a sensitive plant, you see. These others – they are impostors, in the main. They drink, and swear, bad lots generally. You can't class yourself with them, you know. They tell all sorts of yarns.'

'Perhaps the true story they don't tell would be less popular but more terrible,' Hester said gently.

'Your father was a Socialist, wasn't he?'

She did not notice that he was steering her where the streets were shadowy, where there would be no danger of their being seen and recognised by Brayton's 'mob.' Hester Martin, yes, the Hester Martin, who would walk to the altar in white satin and orange blossom, and live forever after in boots, silk petticoats, and tailor-mades, gradually blurring over Brayton's memory that she was the same Hester who had raced after quarter whistles, and trailed out through factory gates at the end of summer days, a white-faced slave, whose shawl, slipping from her weary head, was no more grey than the fluff that clung in hideous bobs to her hair. Above all, Sanderson did not want anyone ever to taunt him with the fact that his wife had played a fiddle in the streets to try and get a coffin for her grandmother. It was damned romantic, of course. Quite so. But Sanderson liked his romance orthodox.

'Shakespeare doesn't appeal to me at all,' confided Sanderson gravely. 'Of course, the dresses are splendid. Must have cost an awful lot. And it's a sort of classy audience. Nice, you know, Miss Martin. Quite nice. Shows up the rotten Jews, and all that. But I've no taste for Shakespeare. Of course, it's myself that's wrong. Must be.'

But his tone conveyed quite the other thing.

Hester was silent.

'I ought to have gone home,' she said, uneasily.

'You'll go home – when you've had food.'

'You are very kind.'

He flinched a little under the simple, gentle gratitude of her look and saw quite plainly that she smarted at having to accept anything savouring of charity. Queer how she had not shrunk from playing. Perhaps she had felt that she was working, in another way, for what she would get, he mused. Romantic and all that, like the old wandering minstrels. But awful thing to do. Why had her mother not stopped her. She looked like a girl who would be easily influenced by anyone whom she cared for. That was how women should be. Gentle and sweet and dependent and dependable. Poor Sanderson! Riding on the tide of the rise and fall of prices, the middle-man recognised evolution in business – but not in women.

Ten minutes later they sat in an eating-house.

The woman, who looked like a pudding herself, stared at them curiously as she wiped up in slap-dash fashion the crumbs left by the last diner at the little table.

Hester, faint and hysterical, with her shawl falling on to her shoulders, the rain on her dark hair, her pallor and her languor, held some resemblance to the beggar maid who sold the dawns and sunsets that her haggard freedom had known, for cloth of gold. Sanderson had, perhaps, some of the pompousness of the old king but scarcely his dignity.

'What are you having?' asked the dealer in steak and kidneys.

'The best you've got,' Sanderson told her, importantly.

'Pies and peas, bacon and liver, steak and kidney pudding with two vegetables,' she told him.

She glanced down at the fiddle.

Hester moved it nervously, a few inches, her cheeks flushing.

And whilst she waited for the order, the cheerful-faced, dumpling-figured pudding-woman wondered *where* on God's earth she had seen Sanderson before.

'Steak and kidney with two vegetables,' ordered Sanderson. 'And tea for the lady.'

The pudding woman walked away.

Where the Hanover had she seen that 'mug' before?

She banged up the little door of the lift and yelled down to the basement.

'Fanny! Steak and kidney and vegs. Two vegs; and one tea pot. Sharp!'

The pudding woman did not like to forget *where* she had seen anyone. It worried her. She glanced at Sanderson, seeing his profile this time, as he sat talking earnestly to the girl in the shawl, and the muck-wet skirts.

'Stir up, there!' she yelled, banging the door of the lift again. From below stairs a voice answered. A tramp came in, and ate a penny bun at the counter. He reeled a little.

'Pint o' tea,' he ordered, and went to sit down, unconscious of any curiosity his attitude might arouse. He sat with his head resting on his hands.

He was muttering strange words – words that frightened the cheerful pudding woman when she brought his tea.

'Set it down,' he said, without looking up and continued muttering his thoughts half-aloud.

'Into this wilderness – and why not knowing,
I came like water – willy-nilly, flowing;
And out again like wind along the waste.'[56]

Hester stared across at Sanderson.

'Queer chap,' he said.

'It's Bob Stiner. *I know him,*' she said gently. 'I-I want to speak to him.'

She did not notice that Sanderson seemed shocked at her desire to speak to a man like this, or that he deliberately turned his back to avoid recognition. Hester was an individualist, and her individualism took stock of souls, not clothes.

'Mr. Stiner,' she said, crossing over to him.

The half-drunken man looked up.

He was crying – crying at the mere idea of it – that we should come like water, willy-nilly flowing, and out again – !

It was beautiful. It was philosophy. It was poetry. It was Omar Khayyam! But would that fatalism do the working-classes any good?

He was staring at Hester.

'Mr. Stiner,' she repeated.

He started to his feet and bowed.

Stiner was always very polite when drunk.

Then the tears and the mists cleared from his eyes.

'Jack Baines' girl, by God!' he exclaimed in a loud voice.

Hester turned crimson, then sheet-white.

'Don't shout so, Mr. Stiner,' she begged gently.

'Jack Baines' girl,' repeated Stiner. 'Come an' sit down aside o' me, lass.'

Hester sat down.

Between the frail, pretty, willowy Hester and Stiner, semi-drunk, with his coat buttoned awry, his scarf hanging out, his blucher laces untied as usual, there was something incongruous, as between a piece of porcelain in clogs and shawl, and a tramp whose face told of doss-houses, lice, and delirium tremens. But there was something curiously alike in their forgetfulness of themselves, their attire, and their dreamy survey of each other. A psychologist would have said that take away all surface differences, the two souls looking out from those two pairs of eyes, were better fitted, *in spite of all,* to travel life together, than were Hester and the man in the mackintosh. Yea, even though Stiner was twice her age.

'Mr. Stiner.'

Stiner bowed his head.

'I-I want to ask you – .'

'Anything,' Stiner told her.

'Did you –'.

'Your tea is ready, miss,' said the pudding-woman.

Hester nodded gently, without turning from Stiner.

'I gave you a – letter to give to someone – a few months ago. Did you give it?'

Stiner stared at her.

'I live a day at a time, lass,' he told her. 'It's enough for my class.'

'Yes. But you can remember, can't you? I gave you a letter –'

Just then the door opened.

Stiner gazed at the policeman, slowly got up, gazed at him thoughtfully, menacingly, and then stooped to Hester.

'I know I shall kill a policeman before I go out like the wind along the waste,' he told her. 'That's my sort of fatalism – I know I shall kill a policeman, lass, as sure as my name's Bob Stiner.'

The words were clearly, slowly uttered.

Hester sat gazing at him thoughtfully, afraid the policeman would interfere with him. Even whilst she sat, afraid and wondering, Stiner walked out, leaving his tea, undrunk and unpaid for.

Hester sat down to the steak pudding. She ate slowly, daintily.

Sanderson gazed at her covertly across the table.

Then he spoke.

'What was that he said about you being Jack Baines' girl?' he asked.

Hester flushed and paled at his presumption. Presumption of this kind always unnerved her. She felt her incapacity to deal with it as it should be dealt with. She cringed away, as she had done when dealing with the coffin-maker.

It was the inability of the gentle and fine soul to struggle with the roughness of the world's practical people.

She sat marble-faced, her heart palpitating. Then her lips parted, and her low words reached Sanderson.

'Mr. Baines asked me to walk out with him,' she said.

'And did you – with a weaver?' asked Sanderson.

The spark in Hester's eyes should have warned him.

'I'm a factory worker, too,' she told him.

'Yes, but – .'

Hester was silent.

Sanderson felt that her gaze searched him through. On the other side of the counter another gaze was searching him. And – another. Fanny and the pudding-woman stood close together, studying him.

'It's the same old dog,' Fanny said.

'Arta sure?'

'Ay; I'd know him in th' dark,' whispered Fanny.

'Tha'rt sure? It's him as goes to that woman in Mary Jane Street? Be sure.'

'It's the same old dog,' said Fanny.

'Try an' warn that lass. She's only a bit of a kipper. I'll keep him at the counter whilst tha clears th' plates off. Tell her he's a wrong 'un. He's tryin' to get round her, you can see. She looks poor, but that's nowt compared wi' other things.'

'And you didn't walk out with him, Miss Martin?' asked Sanderson.

'That was why he went away?'

Rachel would have told him to mind his own business. Hester stared at him helplessly, like a victim of the Inquisition.

'Only once,' she told Sanderson, looking at him helplessly.

She felt again the memory, the fresh wind blowing over the dark fields, the cold drops of rain, the kiss that brushed her cheek – afraid of her youth.

'Oh!' said Sanderson.

He stared into the wonder of her eyes.

They almost made him fail in his purpose.

But after all – .

No damaged goods for Sanderson! He had great ideals.

'There – there was nothing wrong, was there, Miss Martin?' he asked.

'Wrong?' asked Hester, echoing the word in surprise.

Then she almost started up from the table. It was Hester, transformed.

'How much are my pudding and things?' she asked the pudding-woman.

'No – no,' almost groaned Sanderson.

She examined him with the look a child might cast on a snake.

'Ninepence,' said the pudding woman, quickly coming to the table.

Hester put down the shilling she had earned. Then the pudding-woman went for change.

'No – no – ,' came from Sanderson. 'I – you see – I'm so deeply interested in you, Miss Martin. In fact – I wondered if you would – walk out with *me.*'

Hester grew calm at the table.

She looked across at Sanderson.

She had taken him for a human being, disinterestedly kind to another human being. Whereas – .

And she grew tired, tired and sick of this real world, where nobody did anything – for nothing.

She did not even reply to his hopes. She took her change and walked out of the shop. Sanderson sat on – feeling like a worm. A worm! And Sanderson was not used to feeling like that. It made him more determined than ever – to claim the goods.

NEVER would Hester Martin forget that walk by the canal. Imagination returned, triumphant, as the numbness of body faded, after food. There were times when she halted, faced by the wall of impenetrable blackness. She groped her way with her fingers, along the stone wall, away from the black water's edge. But when she halted, the wall of darkness behind pressed upon her, equally terrifying. Old tales, relics of ages gone, told by other children of the poor, in that childhood not yet far removed from her in years, tortured her. Fragments from fantasies of 'Christabel and Lamia,'[57] poems of beauty built out of superstition, would dance in and out of her mind. Once she saw, afar, the flares of a furnace – saw marionettes, which were men, bowing and rising against the crimson glow, an impression in red and black. She stopped, her fingers sore with feeling the rough wall as her guide, soothed, comforted by the Hades-like picture of Labour, earning its bread in the 'dead waste and middle of the night.'[58] The inhumanity of that toil oppressed her. The humanity of Labour, visualised in those bowing and rising figures came close to her, with a great sense of companionship and oneness with her own struggle. For a few moments, at least, she was one of them, not a terrified girl, shrinking fearfully in the heart of night. Sometimes she essayed to run, with spurts of fear-born strength. But she paid for these efforts in greater slowness, when they were passed. A barge passed once, dimly lighted and stacked with coal, with a man looming up, ghost-like and kerosene-illumined. The canal-water was splashed on her from the dripping rope, and a horse went past as she crouched close by the wall. The lights of a flour-mill, its machinery grinding away, enlivened the darkness half a mile from Rushworth. Then all was blacker than ever. When she stumbled upon the road that ran to the church she was almost exhausted. But even fear has its reactions. She leaned against the ivy-covered wall of the dead symbols of a dead church, and understood the courage which shall destroy all hells, material and theological. She had realised that fear was a tradition from heathen times, from primitive man, played on by Church and State. Sodden with rain, leaning against the wall of the church whose crucifix was the sign of the eternal sacrifice asked of the Poor, she stared into the darkness with eyes that were challenging. She ran no more, when she continued her journey, not even when she crossed the bridge from which some weeks before a discharged weaver had hurled herself to slimy death, as the only escape from 'This Slavery'. She walked with unhurried, regular steps from Rushworth to Brayton.

She was conscious of a hushed calm within herself, as she turned down her own street – a quiet sense of conquest. Never again would she fear to walk alone in the black midnight.

O'Neill shone his bull's-eye on her face.

'Late to be out, Miss Martin,' he observed.

She eyed him calmly.

'I've been breaking into a bank,' she informed him.

O'Neill laughed.

'I suppose you missed your train,' he told her. 'I saw Mr. Sanderson. He asked me to look out for you, as there were all sorts on the road, with all this unemployment.'

Hester stared at him.

'There are always all sorts on the road,' she told him, cryptically. 'The folks who are most dangerous are not those tramping after work.'

Rachel heard the click-clack-click-clack of Hester's clogs. She ran to open the door.

'How much?' asked Rachel, anxiously.

'Threepence – when I'd got some food,' Hester told her.

'Jupiter!'

Rachel laughed – then grabbed Hester's shawl.

'Tha'rt nearly drowned,' she said.

Hester walked into the kitchen. It had changed. A fire roared up the chimney. The table was spread. The kettle sung.

'Take her shawl off, Rachel. Letting us down like this,' said Mrs. Martin.

'I'll take it off myself,' stated Hester.

She did so.

'We've had Sanderson, the yarn agent, here, blowing me up for letting thee go playing on the streets. He's lent us ten pounds. We can have more, any day. There's no need to go playing like a beggar.'

Hester stared at her mother.

Her eyes were large and bright in her pale face.

'And you – you took it?' she asked.

'I shall pay it back,' Mrs. Martin said, sharply.

'You'll remember it's your debt – not mine,' said Hester in a low voice.

Mrs. Martin stared.

'That's a nice way to speak to thy mother,' she protested, in surprise.

Hester went to bed.

'What did she say that for?' asked Mrs. Martin of Rachel.

'Because Sanderson's a business man, and business men don't fling ten pounds about – without *interest*, unless it's a further fetch,' her daughter told her.

'Folk are kinder than we think,' said Mrs. Martin.

'Ay. *Our* folk – when they've aught to be kind wi' – which isn't often. Folk like Johnny Grimes. But not *Sandersons*. Do you know what Sanderson is?'

'A yarn agent,' answered Mrs. Martin.

Rachel laughed.

'He's a floater on the tides that change every day. He lives on the differences between to-day's markets and to-morrow's. He's a gambler. He buys as cheap as he can and sells as dear as he can. And the way he gets his living has moulded his mind. Would Sanderson give anything for nothing? Can a pig fly?'

'But what can he hope to gain?'

Rachel whistled – and stared straight at her mother.

Mrs. Martin looked away.

'I shall pay him back,' she said lamely.

'Some fine day – when it snows green,' Rachel told her cheerfully. 'Meanwhile – we're out o' work. Quite frankly – I don't want any.'

'Rachel!'

'I don't – not till I get through Marx. I've worked eleven years without a break, till a fire stopped me, and gave me a chance of studying. I can feel myself *expanding*, evolving. I defy even Starvation to stop me from finding out all I desire to know. And when I've got to know all I can, I shall pass it on to others. I shall become a scientific Revolutionist. But I never thought it would be a *thing* like Sanderson which would make my narrow path easier for me to tread.'

Mrs. Martin stared in amazement at Rachel, at the widely-set, shining eyes, the tossed hair flung back from the great brow – stared at the impudent nose, the mouth with its tender, satirical smile.

'Oh, Lord!' she breathed. 'I wonder who the pair o' you take after.'

Rachel laughed.

'We are breeding *forwards*,' she said, gaily. 'Already we are quite prepared to follow the example of our betters, when they are bust. We are going to live on nothing a year, and carry on our studies.'

'Hush!'

Mrs. Martin whispered anxiously.

'Ay; she's coughing,' Rachel told her.

'Hard, too.'

'She's had a cough a bit.'

'An' quack medicines, bolstered up by big advertisements, to cure it.'

'I'm sure the cough mixture I gave her is good.'

'According to the advertisements it will make new lungs,' said Rachel. 'Ten days ago I was passing by a powder-mine, and got blown up. One box of your ointment put me together again, and I gave the rest away. Large boxes two and sixpence, small boxes – .'

'Shut up,' begged her mother.

She was listening to Hester's cough.

'I think she ought to go to the doctor,' she said, appealingly, wistfully.

'She should have gone months sin' – but we hadn't the price.'

'Well – she must go now.'

Mrs. Martin was determined, now when they had the price.

'Don't scare her with the leet. She'll be asleep,' warned Rachel.

Her sudden tenderness took her mother by storm.

Mrs. Martin's eyes filled with tears, which made the candle-glow dance about. You never knew when you had Rachel, but somehow, she never failed you, when the time came. She would argue and attack, but in the hour of need, she remembered and helped.

She went first into the room where Granny was laid out, made now more ghastly by the paraphernalia of covers, white flowers, and the smell of camphor set in saucers near the bed of the sheeted figure. She could hear Hester 'barking away' in the other room. She lifted the sheet and touched Granny's hand. The flesh was soft. According to Northern superstition that meant another death. So she stood brooding – the woman who had lived forty years a machine-life, but had kept so little pace with industrial development that she yet believed in 'luck,' in 'sighs of death' – not having yet been fully freed from the superstitious of the period of James I. Then with a soft step she went into Hester's room, shading the candle with her hand so that she should not be startled. Even the cough could not make Hester wake up. As her mother stood there, she began to murmur in her sleep. Mrs. Martin bent down, listening, marking the whiteness about nose and mouth, and the colour which had sprung into the cheeks, a flush like that of a wild-rose.

'And the painter's eye of wonder, the marvellous fiddle-bow,
These shall be ours, and all men's, and none shall lack a share,
In the wonderful days that are coming, the days when the world grows fair.'[59]

It was the Dream – the Dream of Morris and Marx, Carpenter and Liebknecht, Wat Tyler and John Ball,[60] Ernest Jones[61] and Robert Owen,[62] Shelley and Heine,[63] and William Blake.[64] It was the old imperishable, immortal Dream, singing itself on the lips of a feverish girl-woman, caught in the trap of Capitalism. It was also the dream of a thousand obscure men, unreported and without lime-light, working for the Cause, not bleeding the movement for themselves, but bleeding themselves for the movement.

Mrs. Martin was frightened.

She did not like folk talking in their sleep.

'Hester!' she called.

Hester answered without opening her eyes.

'Has the whistle blown?' she asked, languidly.

From the Dream she had leaped at once to the brutal realities of whistles blowing – blowing – calling the generations of slaves who had not yet the initiative to determine their own destinies.

'Tha'rt not workin' – it's only one o'clock,' Mrs. Martin called.

Hester did not answer.

She turned her face to the wall, sleeping exhaustedly, murmuring at intervals a broken word of poetry.

'She'll be all right in the morning,' Rachel told her mother, when she went down, saying Hester was rambling.

'Wilta sleep wi' her?'

'Ay.'

Rachel went to bed at two o'clock. She burnt the candle out reading 'The Rights of Man.'[65] Then she arose, wound up the blind stealthily, so that the moon could shine into the room, and laid herself down. She slid her arm under Hester's neck, pulled the thin blankets around Hester's back, and dropped to sleep – awakening to the familiar click-clack-click-clack, and the rattle of the knocker-up's wire on the next door window.

'Is it getting-up time?' asked Hester.

'Sleep on, MacDuff,'[66] Rachel told her. 'Tha'rt tired.'

Hester turned over and slept.

She came downstairs at eleven with the conscience-stricken look at the clock which belongs by tradition of slavery to those whose routine lot is so much bread, so much work, and the minimum of sleep.

Rachel tossed her a glance over Marx.

Hester looked a wan ghost after the experience of the previous night.

'Tha wants to go down to the doctor, Hessie,' was her mother's greeting.

'Oh – I'll go – sometime,' was Hester's answer.

She sat, listening.

'The postman's gone,' Rachel informed her.

Hester flushed, took up her cup of tea with slightly-trembling hand, and kept silence.

'Tha'll go down to the doctor to-day,' her mother told her.

'All right,' she answered, indifferently.

'An' tha can go see about the coffin,' commanded Mrs. Martin.

But Rachel went, with Sanderson's money in her hand. She entered the same room where Hester had stood, twenty-four hours before, hot and cold with shame at asking for a coffin without money.

'Well, I shouldn't like your job,' was Rachel's comment, as she stood by the hammerer.

The fat man looked at her, a twinkle in his eye.

'How's that?'

'It mun have a conservative effect on you, makin' your livin' out o' the dead,' Rachel told him. 'Summut on a par with openin' church pew doors, or reading ancient history. I'd liefer be a midwife.'

'It's not a bad trade,' the fat man told her.

'Particularly in a white winter – an' clemmed folk in the town,' agreed Rachel.

'Ay, ay. Things is rare bad. I don't know what the world is comin' to. We've been that busy we've hardly time to eat, fairly. There's a lot o' old folk poppin' off. This east wind touches 'em up. Brings 'em down like the leaves off the tree.'

He surveyed her, hammer in hand.

'Mostly poor folk,' Rachel told him.

He blew his nose.

'Ah well, lass, there's a lot more poor folk nor rich folk, so there's like to be more deaths.'

He looked at her triumphantly.

'But you've allus a better chance when you've plenty to take to, an' big fires, and not such a struggle,' Rachel persisted.

He scratched his head.

'Ay. I daresay that's true.'

'No daresay about it,' Rachel challenged. 'It's true because it's reason.'

'What arta tryin' to get at?'

'I were tryin' to lead up to the fact that whenever anybody dies because they can't get grub, and warmth – whether they die slowly or fast – THEY'VE BEEN MURDERED,' asserted Rachel.

He stared at her dumbfounded.

Then he stared away, his gaze resting on a coffin-lid with a woman's name on the shining plate.

'She's left five,' he said in a whisper. 'Five. There weren't a thing in the house, to eat nor sup. Worked at Barstocks', she did. An' there were another comin' along – so she did as she shouldn't ha' done, lass. The Church says we shouldn't destroy life. Anyhow, she's dead.'

'MURDERED,' corrected Rachel.

She held his gaze with her own.

'Nay. The Church says we shouldn't destroy life,' he protested.

The shawl dropped from Rachel's head. Fine and dishevelled it rose from the shoddy shawl.

'Oh! And what did the Church do to help her to cherish Life?' asked Rachel. 'Did it fight the things and the folk that made her poor? Or has it not throughout its whole black and bloody history upheld the rotten traditions of them who have the power to go on murdering folk to keep that power? Did it offer her a way out of the damned struggle or did it chuck a tombstone on her Reason, and ask her to wait till the trumpet yelled afore she could find a heaven? Why, man, the Church itself is a Murderer. Right back from Bruno's[67] days. *It never changes.* It's just killed another chap now. I suppose you've never heard of a man called Francisco Ferrer?'[68]

The mountain of industrious fat wilted under her look, the burning vigour of her speech, the force of her challenge.

'The church never shuts its door,' he protested, turning white.

'It does,' said Rachel. 'It shuts 'em up, inside it, like Jonah was shut up, *they say,* in the belly of the whale. It says: "Thou shalt not Reason." It stands by the black faith of the fathers, cradled in fear and ignorance and superstition. It denies the white faith of the children, nay, it preaches of hell to them, and shuts them up, too. And if any reasoning man comes along, like Ferrer, and tries to advance Reason, it shoves him against a wall, and shoots down in cold blood the very symbol of Evolution, the very attribute which divides thinking, feeling men from unreasoning brutes. It says man has a soul, but so soon as that soul challenges *It* – it shoots that soul out of him, as fast it can do, and proves its black materialism. The Church is a Murderer. It murders Truth, Reason, Liberty, and Life, for it backs up all the temporal things that destroy them. So how can it point at that poor woman and condemn her for destroying Life?'

'Eh, lass, where doesta expect to go?' stammered the fat man.

Rachel smiled coldly.

'Not where there's a priest,' she told him. 'Not me.'

'Tha'll think different when tha'rt old.'

She laughed.

'Ay. It's such a coward, your Church – it waits till a man's got senile decay, and cowardice, an' the physical agony of deein', and then it comes an' plays on the lowest part of him – his fear. But, it can't get me. For I was brought up *free* from that sort o' fear.'

'Atheist!' guessed the coffin-maker.

'Free-thinker,' Rachel corrected him. 'One who thinks freely – without anyone saying "Thou shalt go no further."'

'An' what's ta want wi' me?'

'I want a coffin you couldn't see your way to make till you got hold o' half o' the brass,' Rachel told him.

'For thyself,' he asked, trying to get back to normal.

Business was business, anyhow.

'No; for my grandmother.'

'That were thy sister came yesterday?' he asked incredulously.

'Ay.'

'You're as much alike as cheese an' chalk,' he told her.

'Excepting for one thing,' Rachel told him.

'What's that?'

'We're both Socialists, and we both hate your Church – like the hell it stands for – here and hereafter.'

'Well, everyone's a right to his opinions.'

Business was business, anyhow.

'Your Church wouldn't say so,' Rachel gibed. 'It doesn't allow free thought.'

'Well – there's my views.'

'Just at present.'

He stared into her eyes.

'Ah, well,' he said.

'Can you come this afternoon?' asked Rachel, backing out, pulling her shawl over her head. 'Now that we've got the brass?'

He swallowed the reminder.

When she had gone he sat down and smoked a pipe, the coffin lids propped up around him.

'Who were yon?' asked his apprentice coming from below stairs. 'What were she after?'

'A coffin,' said the fat man.

'An' were all *that* about a coffin?'

'No – we were discussing Religion. Jack, tha'd better go up to that woman in Fanny Lane, and tell her if she doesn't pay a bit off that coffin I'll put the bums in. That's the worst o' this trade. Yo' can't fetch the darned stuff back, like furniture.'

Jack stared.

'Hasn't she paid – *yet?*'

'Has she hell?'

'Well, she never will, then, for they've taken her away to dee – in a convalescent home.'

'Come down to these sosinges, afore they're cold,' came the voice from below. Silently the fat man went down to tell his troubles, and wind up with his plaint that he did not know what the world was coming to.

CHAPTER 12

'NEXT!' came the doctor's voice, as he opened the waiting-room door to let out a woman just broken-hearted because Life was again coming to the world.

Hester Martin arose from the dimly-lighted waiting-room filled with the coughing of people who seemed either skimpy or run to fat, people who spoke in hushed whispers of bad trade, the ailments of their children, already in the factory. It was like squeezing through a gang of prisoners, obsessed with the illusion that they were free. Their clothes were as grey as those convicts wore. Their outlook was not much wider. As she went into the room Hester was contrasting them with the inhabitants of 'News from Nowhere.'[69]

Five minutes later the doctor opened the door, with his professional 'Next.'

Hester went out, out into the East Lancashire fog, muffling her mouth with her shawl, breathing through it, stopping sometimes with the fury of the cough shaking her body.

'What did he say?' asked her mother when she got in.

'Nothing much. Run down,' was her answer.

She stood by the window, staring out in the back-yard, fog-filled. She noticed the knot in the clothes-line, which had broken when last they hung out their blouses, she and Rachel.

'Tha mun take thy medicine regular,' said Mrs. Martin.

She knew the medicine she wanted. The doctor had told her. It was beyond her reach. It was the same medicine they had told her father of *at the beginning*. It was clean air, lots of food, no worry – and – *hope*. Also, she must get out of the factory.

'What arta starin' at?' asked Rachel.

'That knot in the clothes-line,' Hester told her.

'Who's that at the door?'

'It'll be the coffin-chap,' said Rachel.

She went to let him in.

She went upstairs whilst he measured Granny for her wooden suit. He tramped down, and made remarks about the weather.

Later that night the coffin came.

Mrs. Martin was out.

'I'll want some packing,' the shroud-maker called. 'Newspapers.'

Hester took them up, and helped her to screw them up. They packed Granny into her coffin, surrounded by the lies of the great Press she had always believed. Hester was coughing as she screwed up the papers.

'That cough sounds like a churchyard,' observed the shroud-maker cheerfully.

Hester smiled.

Later they saw Granny in her shroud, an artificial rose over the heart that had been moulded, and ceased to beat, amidst sordid sorrows.

'She looks very – real – like herself,' said Mary, wiping a tear from her eye.

Hester made no reply.

Rachel held back a retort which her mother would have thought unseemly.

Hester's eyes were studying the already blackening nostrils, the darkening finger-nails. She could smell the faint, horrible scent of body-corruption, triumphant over the camphor-lumps in the saucers. Two foolish lines were throbbing in her brain:

'As I am now
So you will be.'[70]

Such a surging hunger for life was beating in her as she had never known before. Probably a condemned man feels the same as he walks round the prison yard, with his 'wistful look' at the sky. The sheep driven towards the slaughter-house, somehow dimly conscious of the knife at the end of the road, could perhaps tell us of the same. The conscripted men driven out to kill other conscript men, marching along the roads at whose end lies Death, may also have felt the same. To live, to persist – anyhow – the great primitive desire. It was Hester's now. She was young. Dim hopes, folded like flower-buds, all frosted with despairs, stirred within her. The illusion that for her, if not for others, Life could be beautiful, and not a thing of slavery, awoke in her. Physical protest against the sentence she thought had been passed upon her awoke, making her a link with all life, animal and heroic. What places she had dreamed to visit, stirred to travel-hunger by sevenpenny numbers of 'Scenes of the World'! The music she had hoped to bring from the old fiddle! The wistful hunger she had felt when she saw a beautiful baby in a perambulator, or a lamb dancing by the worried sheep. The kiss in the clean, wind-swept darkness of the Long Meadows. All these hopes surged up in her. She was suddenly conscious of her youth, something fair, wonderful, beautiful, despite all its frustrations. She stood, at bay – panic-stricken, yet with a certain desperate courage. Somehow she must get out of the factory. Somehow she must *live*.

In the silences of the night, whilst Rachel and Mrs. Martin slept, near to her, yet apart, it was the face of Sanderson which rose before her sleepless vision. He was the only straw she had to cling to. For Sanderson had ten pounds a week. Sanderson could buy the conditions that were the opposite of those which the doctor had said would kill her.

She slept at last, stirring wearily as the old clickety-clack arose from the flags under the window. Dawn made the room shadowy and grey. Then she slept again.

At the hour she arose, desperate again, an animal fighting to exist. Away, thousands of miles away, a fooled emigrant was waiting outside the General Delivery, one in a line with other fooled emigrants. He had five cents in his pocket. He had slept in a Mission House, having to pretend to save his soul, so that his body should not be a block of ice. The other alternative had been – detention in prison, for this fine land boasted of having no workhouses!

'Anything for Jack Baines?' he asked, as he reached the window.

'Nothing. Nothing at all.'

He dropped out and the queue moved up.

'Nothing. Nothing at all.'

He moved away, aimlessly, the words ringing in his ears.

CHAPTER 13

THE ermine of the Poor lay on the ground. Hills, moors, mill-lands, all were white with it. Black ling and rebellious bilberry bushes pricked through it, and shook it off. The winds blew it up in sparkling, silvery puffs. The feet of hares, rabbits and grouse marked it, in high places under the wide, solitary sky. Sunsets flung mile-wide shades of exquisite colour over it, from blue of shadows to lavender-pink of sunset flush. Sheep, not mankind, moved amidst its glory and its gleam, sheep with snow on their backs, to all appearances, from a distance, eating snow. Sometimes the steps of a poacher, that symbol of the free hunter who claims privileges at least as great as the man who has stolen hills and common lands from the people, broke the white track of crisp snow, followed by the pad-marks of his dog, also claiming rights as great as those in the peerage. The steps of the paid hound of the poacher also wandered across the snow.

In the towns, mill-chimneys poked up like giant, smoking black fingers through the whiteness. The well-housed, and well-fed gained greater appetites from the bite in the air. But the snow soaked through the broken, leaking clogs of Barstocks' burnt-out weavers. Overcoats had been sold. The keen air went through the famished bodies, the threadbare shoddy. It was said that there were men in the town without shirts to their backs, and women without chemises. Shivering men, with a few women, had begun to make collections on Friday nights at the other factory gates. Rachel had stood so once, stung by smarting pride when she heard the pennies chink on the sheets of newspaper spread over the flagstone, and held at the corner by rough stones. Two families had gone to the workhouse. The gayest of the young had ceased their dancing. It was rumoured that Mrs. Barstocks was about to open a soup kitchen. Also that Mr. Barstocks was going to put up for Parliament.

In the moonlight, Brayton's toilers went to their work over the snow – or through it.

Like a procession of ghosts, passed the first stragglers, meeting the knockers-up as they went home to sleep.

Mothers carrying blanket-rolled children under their shawls, stumbled along, dodging the drifts. The stronger carried also a bundle of the child's clothes; the weaker made two journeys of it, child or clothes – or clothes and child. The oldest workers were also out earliest, being unable to hurry in such weather. Old women wheezed and coughed, nervously plodding along by the snow-blown walls, stocking tops over their clogs, to make a fall less probable. Little half-timers, their faces covered by their mother's shawls, were steered along through the cold. By a quarter to six the streets were one long procession, along both flagstones, and down the middle of the road. The kicking off of snow-pads against the house-sides was a constant, echoing sound. The whistle shrieked through the biting air with rasping clearness. The whole scene was like a night scene – lamp, moon, snow, and the black silhouette of the street-wide procession. No painter had ever painted it. The great painters were painting lords, dukes, ladies, sun-splashed Italian villas, and kings and queens in their robes. This was part of the life of a great nation which preserved its equilibrium by ignorance and weariness on the one side and by brute force, diplomacy, and greed on the other. *This* was not worth painting. This was only Lancashire, going to its waged-slavery, through its only ermine – the snow that came through any leaking clogs.

Amongst these workers was Hester Martin.

She had heard from Matty Stiner that a winder at a mill over the 'Switchback' was about to leave, to be confined a month later, one month being the recently-fixed legislative period. Matty said it was a good thing the law had been passed, for one woman at Barstocks last year had had to be carried out of the shed – 'in labour.'

Hester was not hurrying.

She did not need to get over the Switchback by the time the mill started.

She only wanted to make sure she got the place when the woman left.

A shawled woman, hurrying along, told her what to get for her cough.

Hester thanked her, said good-morning, and passed on.

She could not help but think of the weary way it would be, night and morning, in the wintry darkness, backwards and forwards over the

Switchback. There were some places where, when ice was on the ground, workers had gone on their hands and knees to reach work. Still, if she could get work they might pay Sanderson back. Her mother was going to work now – now that the old woman was gone from the corner. With cheerful optimism, Mary Martin asserted that they would soon be on their feet again – if they got working. But she did not know that Hester, going out to work, felt like one accepting, yet struggling against her own doom. Often did Hester stop, on her way over the Switchback.

She felt spent when she reached the mill where the vacancy was to be, according to Matty, who had also said that no one knew the winder was leaving so soon. The dazzling windows with their shadows of flying strap and wheels, their shadows of human spiders crossing and recrossing, made her blink. The light swam before her eyes. But she rallied.

The manager sent for the winding-master, who came down and talked to Hester over the wooden gate between watch-house and mill.

'No. She's not leaving yet,' he told her. 'But there's another devil I'm going to be shut on. Come on up, lass.'

'You're not going to sack anyone for me?' asked Hester, shrinking back.

The light from the watch-house window fell on her pale face with that sensitive pride stamped on it.

'Eh. Tha should think o' thyself not other folk,' he said. 'We've all to look after No. 1 in this world.'

Hester followed him up into the winding-room. It was almost dazzlingly bright after the desolation and darkness of the walk over the Switchback. The stacks of yellow and green bobbins danced before her sight. She saw that there was only one machine running, and this with no one in attendance. The winders were dancing the Lancers in the middle of the room. A few slunk away when the winding master entered. A solitary woman in white stockings approached the machine that was running and half-heartedly pieced up a broken thread and lifted off a bobbin which was being frayed back into waste.

'Get them machines on, you hell-fire devils!' shouted the winding-master. His eyes flared. His face was livid, livid with fear that the manager would come up and reprimand him for this scene. Boss behind boss! Slave behind slave! Each goading the other on, with each a little more power.

'Get 'em on thysel',' called back a young woman with the colouring of a gipsy. There was something superb about her.

The winding-master approached her.

'Thee take thy shawl – an' get down them steps, or I'll damned well punch thee down,' he shouted.

She laughed and snapped fingers and thumb in his face.

'Tha'rt sacked, anyhow,' he told her, rather more calmly.

'Every day'll be Sunday bye and bye,' she answered.

'Tha can go. Tha'rt sacked. This young woman is starting on thy frame,' he said to her.

Perhaps her colour paled a shade.

She stared at Hester, and Hester stared at her, slowly shaking her head.

The winding-room floor seemed to move under Hester's feet. She gazed dazedly from the dark young woman to the winding-master, then felt herself sinking down, hearing as she fell the squeaky cry of an old woman:

'Saints alive! She's goin' ower. The manager! The manager!'

She came to, finding herself in the window-sill, the dark young woman holding her up. The old woman with a squeaky voice was saying: 'Sup this, acushla!'[71] and holding out a can of hot tea. The machine made long slumberous humming. The green and yellow bobbins flew round like discs of flame on the spindles. The winding-master approached her.

'Are you feeling better?' he asked, not unkindly.

Hester nodded.

'You'd best go and sit in the watch-house, till its broad daylight.'

Thus she received the intimation that her services were not required.

The dark young woman, with a glance of triumph at the winding-master, left Hester to the old woman. The winding-master strutted across the floor, hands in pockets, passing from machine to machine.

'She's thick with the manager,' whispered the old Irishwoman. 'He'll never get to sack her. Are you better, acushla?'

Hester nodded.

'Happen he'd let me off for two hours, to see you across the fields, home,' said the old woman.

'Never mind,' Hester told her.

She pulled her shawl about her.

Ten minutes later she set out. As she reached the top of the winding-room steps, the old woman left her machine and panted after her.

'Acushla!' she squeaked. 'They've put me more up then I can eat. Take this and ask Mrs. Thing-em-Bob in the watch-house to chalk you up a pot o' tea – to Bridget Flynn.'

Hester took the newspaper-wrapped food.

She was not hungry.

But she could not refuse Bridget Flynn's gracious gift.

'Oh, you haven't started, then?' asked the woman in the watch-house, as she passed through.

'No.'

She passed out into the dim streets, and back over the Switchback.

'Not got on, Hessie?' asked Mary, when she got in.

'No.'

'Well, never mind, happen we'll be able to do without. I've got sent for. Starting in the morning. An' Rachel's gone up to a meeting. She's gone in a mad hig. I hope she says naught that she'll be sorry for. An' Mr. Sanderson's been and left – eh, tha looks sick. Arta sick. It'll be the cold. Sit down. Canta eat two eggs?'

'Has – has Sanderson laid 'em?' asked Hester, beginning to laugh. Then she broke down, suddenly, and cried. The sobbing throbbed in the silence of the kitchen. Even whilst her mother stared at her, she jumped up from her chair.

'What a life!' ejaculated Hester, tossing off her shawl. 'What a life! Oh – to get out of it. There won't be a Revolution in our time. People just go on, bearing it, hoping, praying, anything but fighting for a better life. The rich'll never be converted. The poor'll never rise up. And us that can see, that can feel all life might be, we're just the prisoners of tyrants, and slaves. If I thought there was a God – I'd ask to be struck dead. But there isn't even that hope. What a life!'

She tore upstairs and flung herself on the bed, face downwards.

Mary went up with a pot of tea and some biscuits.

She stroked Hester's hair.

'Tha can get out of it any time tha likes. Sanderson's axed me for tha,' she said. 'An' he's comin' to-neet to see what tha says.'

She set the pot down on the table and went downstairs.

Hester lay, exhausted on the bed. She fell asleep, and awoke to find the clothes over her – and her clogs off. Then she heard the dinner whistle blowing. The slaves were rushing home to prepare a meal, wash the dust off their faces, pin up their hair anew, lock up their *homes* – and return. *This* was the life she would live, until, like her father, she died prematurely. The devil and the deep sea. Death or life-in-death. And between them stood Sanderson. She laughed half-crazily, covered her face with the clothes, and fell asleep again.

CHAPTER 14

'BUT you said you'd let us have the chapel,' said a little man.

'Well – we found out at the last minute we couldn't,' he was told.

The man went away and told the weavers waiting outside, unable to understand why the door had not been opened half an hour ago.

'They're afraid or summat,' he told the throng.

Disconsolate and already wet-footed with coming from various parts of the town through yellow snow-slush, the weavers grumbled. A few cursed.

'If it had been for a missionary meeting to tell of the woes of savages they'd have let us in,' came Rachel's voice, clear and incisive.

'Ay. They would that.'

'Well – what have we to do?'

'I suggest we go home.'

'Home, Sweet Home, with the fire out,' gibed a young man, with bitterness.

'Let's hold it outside, if it snows cats, dogs, or devils,' suggested Rachel.

'Ay. We can't get much cowder,' shouted a grey-headed man. 'An' happen it'll scare the bobbies – particular if it starts snowin'.'

'What are we goin' to do?' shouted several voices. 'Let's make our minds up. Summat practical.'

'Let's invite ourselves to a good feed at Barstocks',' cried the young man of the bitter tongue. 'We've given him all he has, he shouldn't grudge us a meal.'

'Summat practical,' repeated the voice in the centre of the crowd.

'That's practical,' cried the young man.

'Oh, Jabez, shut up, or tha'll get in bother,' a woman told him. 'They've increased the police force.'

He muttered something and subsided.

'Let's hold it, anyhow,' called Rachel. 'There's no place in the town will hold us but the chapel. We can't get that. If it snows, well, it'll maybe snow to-morrow. Has the speaker come?'

'No; he must ha' missed his train,' grumbled another. 'All these Socialists are alike. They'd be too late for the Revolution, or else put it off because the weather glass was low.'

'Give up haggling,' called Rachel. 'If he doesn't turn up we'll have to speak for ourselves. An' happen it's as well.'

'All them with fires will cower by 'em,' said another.

'Well, we'll talk to ourselves,' shouted Rachel. 'Come on.'

There was a general laugh.

The little man remained outside to wait for the speaker. The rest climbed their way towards the market square. Half-way up the street they passed O'Neill. Someone started singing. The whole crowd took it up.

'Who killed Cock Robin?
I, said the sparrow, with my bow and arrow,
I – killed – Cock Robin.'
'Tottie, will you go?
Tottie will you go?
Down to the banks of the O-I-ho?
Tottie will you go?
Tottie will you go?
Down to the O-I-ho?'[72]

O'Neill, passing by, might have been deaf. The lamplight showed his impassive face. He met the inspector a little further on and they chatted casually.

When the burnt-out weavers reached the square they found the Salvation Army in possession.

'Till Jesus washed my sins away – ,' rasped out the little band of saved.

'We've naught to stand on,' said the man who had held by practicality.

'Come to Jesus. Come to Jesus,' yelled the Captain, a pale-faced man.

'Dear friends – ,' shouted another.

'Another ha'penny on the drum,' said a thin youth who had just picked up a fag-end out of the snow.

'Shut up,' somebody told him. 'They've no damned bishops wi'' thousands a year.'

'Come to Jesus. Come to Jesus,' yelled the Captain.

Bang went the tambourines.

'Go across into "The Scythe",' said the practical man, 'and ask 'em to lend us a chair or summat.'

'It's snowin',' whispered a woman to Rachel.

'Ay.'

'We can give that speaker up, I think.'

Rachel stared across the street. Three of the weavers were bringing not a chair but a large table.

O'Neill came walking up.

'Cock Robin' was sung again.

'Do you think we should aggravate them?' asked the woman of Rachel.

'They want to keep inside, an' not aggravate clemmed folk with the sight o' their great carcases,' was all she got. 'The very sight o' them and what they stand for is enough to aggravate clemmed folk.'

'Now then – we're ready,' said the practical man. 'Who's goin' to stand up an' state the case?'

'Thee!'

The cry arose unanimously from the crowd.

'Well, I'll hold out for about five minutes, then anybody as likes can have a do,' he told them. 'Happen the proper man'll have turned up, then.'

He mounted the table, first shaking it to see that it stood firm.

'Old Barstocks!' ejaculated the woman next to Rachel.

'Well, never heed him,' she was told. She stared at the man on the table. Down below him two stinking kerosene torches, held by a couple of weavers, flickered in the light snow coming down.

'Friends,' said the man on the table. 'I'm no fine talker, as you all know. I'm here to state a plain case, with plain facts, so that we all recognise them clearly, and decide how best to cope with them. As a Trades' Unionist, I realise that there is a class war. If there were not a class war, there would be no Unions.

The Unions are a defensive barricade built up by thousands of men and women to protect their interests against the attacks of the boss to lower wages and the standard of life. The discrepancy between the wages some workers get, and that of others, as, for instance, weavers and farm labourers, is determined by the strength of the workers, and their Unions. Therefore, it is well to be in a Union. At least it is a defence. When the Unions are weak there are always great attacks from the other side. Where they are strong the bosses think twice. I wish you to understand that, first of all. Our case, when the mill was burnt down, does not come under Trade Union rules. The boss had the place insured. He gets his bacon and eggs every morning. The Union is to provide food for us, when the boss starts in to starve us – that is, attack us, to make us work for less wages. It has nothing to do with Capitalist property being burnt down. It's not a fire insurance company – but a fighting organisation. We've only contributed to it on those lines. So it's no good blaming Unions. I put that to this meeting – that the Union is a fighting organisation and not a fire insurance company?'

He stopped, waiting.

'Ay, ay,' went up from the crowd.

'Who, then, is to blame for the state of affairs we are enduring at present?'

'Barstocks!' called a woman's voice.

He waited.

'God!' yelled the bitter young man.

The practical man just glanced at him.

'Man,' corrected the speaker. 'We'll leave God out of it – like the Union. The burning down of the factory was an accident. We were poor before. We shall be poor again, when the factory is built up. And what we have learned when the factory was burned down will, I hope, be remembered when things are at ordinary poverty-line again. *Under Capitalism nothing is certain.* Remember that. Under Capitalism, we are always liable to be flung out of work – to starve and rot. Under Capitalism, if people are unwilling to starve and rot, there is a big police force and a big soldier force, and these men of our own class can be used to shoot us down. The question to-night is not how we are going to get out of this temporary time of clemmin' and fireless homes, but what shall we do when we get back to work again, whether we shall fight Capitalism, and all its forces, or whether we shall just go on in the old way, without making any serious attempts to break Capitalism down by making Trade Unionism not only a defence against attacks, but a great, united, world-wide force of attack on Capitalism. If we have learned how to turn all the bitterness we have felt these past weeks into a constructive force for the final overthrow of Capitalism – the burning down of Barstocks' mill will have been not a bad, but a good thing. If the hunger, the starvation, we have endured now, makes of the men and women here so many thorns in the flesh of Capitalism, and makes them more mutually eager to help other starving folk when a strike is on – the fire of Barstocks' mill has been a great fire. For we have got to realise that the thing which keeps Capitalism alive is not only the selfish courage of the Capitalists, but the cowardly apathy of the workers themselves, who, so long as they have a week's grub before them, are content to go on, in the same old way. Now – I've said all I have to say. Does anybody else like to have a go?'

Nobody did.

They stared sheepishly at each other.

'Tha can gas. Get up,' urged the woman next to Rachel.

'If only Baines had been here,' whispered somebody a few feet from Rachel. The whisper travelled to her, lighting a fire in her blood.

'I'd like to say a few words,' she said.

Then she wished she hadn't said it.

She seemed to crumple at the knees and her heart beat like a hammer as she was hoisted up. She had never known she had so little self-possession. She would have given the world to be down on the ground again. The faces of the crowd seemed to hypnotise her. The first words seemed to be shot out of a gramophone half a mile off, and not to issue from her mouth – .

'Friends,' began Rachel. Then she looked at O'Neill, the Inspector, and Barstocks, and a priest on the edge of the crowd. 'And – Enemies!'

The crowd moved closer together, instinctively. This was a right challenge.

'This is a very small place which we live in. Yet it is typical of the world. You have all around you symbols of two great classes of humanity. There – just over there – you have a symbol of the Church, which tells you you shall not reason. Near him stands Sergeant O'Neill, who makes trouble about small boys pitching and tossing half-pennies, but says nothing of men who gamble with your lives, on the Stock Exchange. Near him is the Inspector, who can, at any time, arm the police if you try to pinch any grub – though all the grub in the world is grown by labour. And near him is a Magistrate, who is also a manufacturer – Mr. Barstocks, who will soon be putting up for Parliament. Of course, you will send Mr. Barstocks to Parliament, to state there what you require. You know how little he has given you for all you have given him. So you will know what to expect when he states your requirements.'

The crowd hitched nearer.

'That is the other class. That is your inveterate enemy. It cannot be anything else. It is the force which holds Capitalism up. It *is* Capitalism. It cannot let Capitalism go. Because then *It* goes. See?'

A little murmur ran through the crowd.

Rachel looked earnestly at the crowd now. Their faces had come out of that strange mist – into focus.

'Then – there are Yourselves,' she said, deliberately. 'I could have said *Ourselves* – but I am not quite your class, either. What do you read? Charles Garvice![73] What do you think? What your newspapers and parsons and churches tell you to think. *You* are content if you've a week's grub beforehand. *You* are content with a semblance of freedom. *You* are content with the idea of your children being no better off, or very little better off, than you are. *You* are content to pay your twopence or sixpence to a Union, and leave its officials to think for you. *You* are content if you've plenty of work, if you bake and scrub and wash, after you've done in the factory. I am not content to have to work till I drop down dead. To work when I'm ill. To work when I'm dog-tired. To work when I'm a little child, when I'm a nursing mother, when I'm a grandmother, just a machine, not a human being, for the interests of such-like monstrosities as O'Neill, and that priest, and old Barstocks. Shall I tell what *I* want? I want Bread – lots of it – so that I don't need to worry about *that*. I want to work, say, *three hours a day*.'

She paused, a smile on her face.

The crowd gasped.

'Three hours,' repeated Rachel. 'Because if everybody worked, that would be enough for all the needs of all the people of the earth, with the resources and knowledge we now have. That is for necessities. Of course, if I wanted to study, or be a musician, or paint, or sing, or make artistic things, after the three hours, I could do so. When you've stood in those muck-wet alleys three hours, you've earned enough to keep yourselves – *well,* if all the other folk were working. That is, policemen, soldiers, servants who keep the rich from needing the Nuisance Inspector, and the unemployed – who can't work because there isn't enough to go round. So all the rest of the time you are forced to put in, is to help a robber like Mr. Barstocks, whom you will send to speak of your needs, in Parliament. Also to support the slaves who help them to uphold such robbery. That is the difference between myself and you. *I* am not content to be a moderately-fed slave. You are. *I* am not content to be a slave at all. I want a Labour Government to get in.[74] If that fails – if any illegal force is used against us when we get that, as no doubt there will be, then it's a straight fighting issue between this class and that class, and I hope we shall have more weapons than they will, seeing we make them, so that there will be as little blood shed as necessary, and that not *our blood,* but the blood of those who would clutch their ill-gotten possessions even into the grave, and beyond! If starving is the only thing that will make you think, change, act, and be the masters of your own fate, I am glad you are starving – *and that I am starving along with you.* Because I am tired of living in a world divided into classes, and nations, all struggling one against the other – when but for the ignorance and apathy of the masses, and the selfishness and determination of the classes, even to-morrow – to-morrow – in twenty-four hours' time, we might see the dawn of peace, plenty, freedom, and human Brotherhood.'

'The speaker,' murmured someone.

O'Neill's voice followed. He had been taking notes.

'This meeting cannot go on,' he said.

Loud hootings greeted his remark.

'Get up, Simpson!' yelled half a dozen voices.

O'Neill approached Rachel.

'If you don't want to see trouble – their trouble – get them to go home.'

'Because *you* say so?' she asked.

The voices of the Salvationists came to them.

'In the sweet – bye – and bye,
We shall meet – on that – beau-tif-ul shore.'

'Heigh up,' cried Simpson, and leaped upon the table.

He assisted Rachel down.

'I must warn you,' began O'Neill.

'Free speech! Free speech!'

The crowd roared the demand.

'As a matter of fact,' Simpson told them, 'there is no such thing, my dear friends. If you had free thought, free speech, free bread, free life, and free death, under Capitalism, Capitalists would sign their own death-warrants. You are not free. You are deluded. If you had even the elements of animal freedom in your lives you would not be starving in a town whose shops are overflowing with good things. You have not even got the basis of free life – enough bread, and free speech comes a very long way after that, being an intellectual freedom.'

O'Neill winked at the Inspector.

'We arrest you,' they told Simpson. He laughed.

'See how free you are,' he gibed.

A roar went up from the crowd.

'In the meantime, I advise you not to become violent,' he said in that slow, calm voice. 'If my arrest will bring home to you the necessity for your own education, for your own unity, for your own progressive determination, when you are hungry, and when you are not hungry, I take my arrest as good wages. Be quiet. Be calm. Be strong. Be determined. Above all recognise that the interests of Capital and Labour are eternally opposed. *They* would like to break your heads. I would like to keep them whole, to see them sound heads, full of challenging ideals, ideas, logic, determination and courage to smash Capitalism. And I will not play *that* game by urging you to have your heads broken. So long!'

He jumped down from the table and went with O'Neill and the Inspector, chaffing as he went.

The crowd dribbled away.

Rachel went home.

Her mother opened the door to let her in, and held up her finger warningly.

Rachel tip-toed into the kitchen.

'Who's in the parlour?' she asked.

'Hester and Mr. Sanderson.'

'No,' protested Rachel.

She stood for a minute, irresolute, strangely irresolute. If Hester wed Sanderson, Jack Baines would come home, sometime, and – .

Then she walked straight down the passage, knocked on the parlour door, and with a sarcastic 'I hope I don't intrude,' opened the door and walked in.

'Oh, hello, Rachel,' greeted Sanderson.

He was smoking a cigar and leaning back in the chair.

'Hello.'

Rachel, in clogs and shawl, sat down, also at her ease.

Hester was sitting rather stiffly in her chair, staring into the fire, but she turned her head, as Rachel spoke, not without some semblance of naturalness.

'Coming courtin' our Hester?' asked Rachel.

She had brought things to a crisis now. She saw it, in Sanderson's flushed face, and Hester's pale one, and Hester's eyes saying unutterable things.

Sanderson broke the painful silence with a laugh.

'Your sister's a corker, Miss Martin,' he said to Hester. 'But I shouldn't dislike her – as a sister-in-law.'

'Only she happens to be spoken for,' Rachel told him, 'to be somebody else's sister-in-law.'

She stared at him with unfeigned dislike.

'She had just been telling me, before you came in, that all that was dead and done with,' said Sanderson.

'I've had interference *once*,' Hester said to Rachel. 'Now I'll not be interfered with. Not by anybody.'

Rachel eyed her in bewilderment. Hester's voice was usually musical. It sounded hard and flat. Hester was rebelling against interference. It had taken several months for the rebellion to work up, and it was bursting out in the wrong place.

'Well, it's naught to do with me,' Rachel told them both, squarely. 'I only thought she happen hadn't the courage to tell you. As long as she knows her own mind I don't care. There's an old saying that it's well to love where money is, in preference to marrying for money.'

She left the room.

Sanderson crossed the cheap carpet.

'You – you won't go back on your word,' he said, bending over Hester.

'What makes you think I would?'

'Because – I don't know. Do you quite know your own mind?'

'You are my only means of escape,' she told him. Sanderson placed finger and thumb in his waistcoat, and stood back to the fire.

'Get all this nonsense about dyin' out of your head,' he told her. He cleared his throat, paced the worn carpet, and made up his mind.

'Because, as a matter of fact, I went down to the doctor's to ascertain if there was anything very serious. He admitted that you were not strong, and, of course, there was your father. But there is no great danger, so long as you don't worry, and get enough to eat. Baines was a six-loom weaver.[75] If you like I'll send him his passage money. I daresay he could keep you – in a way.'

Hester Martin rose out of her chair.

She held out her hand.

Sanderson took it.

'I am tired of being a slave,' she said. 'In any case, I am tired of being a slave. I don't want to spend my life like my mother has spent hers. I don't want to live, dreaming of an awakening in the people which never comes – like my father did. I won't want to go to prison, atoning for the apathy of people content to be slaves. The fact that they'll let their agitators go there and rot for striking their blows, is itself a condemnation of the working-classes. I suppose there is a cause for it all. But it won't be undone in my lifetime. And I want Life – *Now.*'

She looked Sanderson straight in the eyes.

He drew a deep breath.

'You – you will be – my wife?'

'I will be a faithful wife,' Hester told him.

The fireglow meshed them round.

She had not withdrawn her hand from Sanderson's. It seemed as though she might be combating that shrinking his personality gave her. There was something in the way she said 'I will be a faithful wife,' which made Sanderson feel that *this* was the real plighting of her hand – not the ceremony which would follow after.

'I-I don't know what to say. I'll be very good to you. I am very fond of you, by Jove, I am. You shall have the finest ring. What sort of stone do you fancy?'

'Opals.'

'But they're so unlucky, aren't they?'

'They are like dawns or sunsets,' she told him. 'But I wasn't thinking of Things, Mr. Sanderson. I was thinking of *Freedom*. It must be so wonderful to awaken in the morning and feel free. Just to be a free woman, not a slave.'

'You shall be free,' he told her, passionately.

His lips were close to her cheek.

She looked up at him, startled.

They were thick lips and did not seem to close properly.

She leaned a passive cheek towards him. It was not the cheek Baines had touched, almost timidly, with the dark, wet winds blowing around them, the baptism of rain on his hair.

'Now it's sealed in proper orthodox fashion,' said Sanderson.

Hester made no reply.

'There's somebody at the door,' she said.

There was.

'Who's there?' asked Mrs. Martin.

'Sergeant O'Neill.'

Mrs. Martin opened the door.

'What's up?' asked Rachel.

'We want you, Miss Martin.'

'Me? What for?'

'We've a warrant here for your arrest! I'll read it if you like. In effect, it means that you have incited half-famished people. Derry's Stores have been broken into half an hour after your speech.'

Rachel whistled in astonishment.

'You'll find this rather serious, I'm afraid,' O'Neill told her.

'Rachel!'

Mrs. Martin began to cry.

'There shouldn't be any half-famished people,' Rachel told O'Neill. 'There shouldn't be any damned slaves, then there wouldn't be any rebels. My shawl, mother.'

'Rachel!' said Mrs. Martin.

She brought the shawl with shaking hands.

'I'll stand bail, officer.'

It was Sanderson.

O'Neill spoke respectfully.

'Bail isn't allowed.'

Hester went to Rachel.

'Well, ta-ta,' said Rachel throatily.

Then she appeared to shake herself.

'Whatever I've said I'll stand by,' she said. 'Sedition. Incitement. Any old thing. Call it what you like. It was *Truth*. So long as this system remains as it is I'll attack it. If the starving folk have helped themselves, instead of clemming in silence and waiting for the Millennium – they've more courage than I thought they had. I hope they enjoy the tinned salmon they've got from Derry's, but if they wanted the best they should have gone to Thomas's.'

Mrs. Martin rushed to Rachel and tried to hold her by main force.

'Don't do it, mother,' urged Rachel. 'Ta-ta.'

She tore herself away.

The door closed.

'Can I – do anything at all?' stammered Sanderson.

'No,' Hester told him.

'I'll be up to-morrow, probably they're just scaring her, for a warning.'

Hester gave him his hat.

'Eh, if only Jack Baines were here,' sobbed Mrs. Martin, half an hour later.

'Well, he isn't,' Hester told her.

'Thank God tha'rt goin' to get out o' all this scramble and struggle,' said Mary suddenly. 'Oh, God, I do thank Thee for that.'

Hester answered nothing. She sat on the couch, staring into the fire.

Peaceful semi-starvation. Revolt – and prison! Piecemeal reform which but left them more efficient slaves. No. It was too much of a muddle. To sail out of it in the barque of Matrimony was at least definite, rapid and sure. If only, if only one could forget the others – the passive, crushed, bleeding, and gaily valiant – others.

BOOK TWO

CHAPTER 15

TIME – IMP SINGS THE PROLOGUE

Ding-Dong! Ding-Dong!
Ding-Dong-Bell!
Spin the cord strong,
Twist it well.
Let the driven shuttle fly
In and out the mildewed weft.
Let the brittle threads and dry
Mocking taunt the Weavers deft.
Let them struggle as they will,
Bended back and aching sight,
Till the engine crash the mill,
What's corrupt, will ne'er weave right.
Gain and Loss at last shall meet,
Blighted, frayed, ill-woven cloth
Shall be the merchant's winding-sheet,
Proudest ermine bed the moth.
O'er the rifle, sword, and gun
(Bright and pure beyond their mark),
Yet shall rise the People's Sun,
Red, defiant, o'er the Dark.
Ding-Dong! Ding-Dong!
Fast – or slow,
Sure is tolled the Tyrant's Wrong,
Weft and Warp of Long Ago.

Ding-Dong! Ding-Dong!
Ding – Dong – Bell!

Pile the walls strong,
Slavery's Hell.
Priest and scribe, and man-made God,
Diplomats and renegades,
Bishop's mace, and tyrant-rod.
Blood-stained crowns, and war-field spades.
Merchants flinging up the Dice,
Gambling with the People's Lack.
Prim hypocrisy all nice –
Hunger's Fear, and Prison's Rack.
Charlatans who raving start
(Eye upon the cushioned throne)
From the People's bleeding Heart.
Making ladders of *Their Own*.
Pigmied idols raised on high,
Slaves look up, and they – look down,
Making blots upon the sky,
Minstrels, wire-pulled – for renown!
Ding – Dong! Ding – Dong!
All their rods
Cannot break the True and Strong –
Hell shall breed its Undergods.

Let us gather up in our hands, dear reader, the broken threads of six years, wherein some things have changed and some have not. I am sorry if you expected to witness Hester's wedding with Sanderson or the too late return of Jack Baines, who stoked his passage across the Atlantic, when he received Rachel's message asking him to get the next boat. I am sorry if you had expected the curtain to ring down on a beginning which is traditionally the ending of a tale. I am sorry if sometimes you lose sight entirely of the hero and heroine – or rather the two heroines and heroes – or see them jammed at times, helpless units in the mass. Such is life. But in order that the broken threads may be knotted, and the years gathered up, however roughly, we will just glance at some of the people we left six years ago. Behold Hester, who reached the limitations of her endurance of slave-life, the mother of two children, Stephen being a cripple. The verdict of Sanderson's sacked slaves being that the dreamy-faced Stephen is a cripple because Sanderson sacked *them*. Mrs. Martin lives with them. Rachel lodges with the Stiners and is a pugnacious agitator, with a little more satirical, self-preserving subtlety than when she landed herself in prison. Barstocks' mill has long been built up, and the burnt-out weavers have most of them got on their legs again, for there has been a boom of Indian goods for two years. Barstocks himself is M.P. and gives more addresses than ever in chapels. Matty has got on her *feet,* and swears she will never have Stiner back again.

Everybody is so eager to work that practically all Brayton is locked up from morning to night. Only the old women stay at home, worn-out weavers, nursing, washing, cooking for their daughters – when strong enough. When not, the daughters do it for themselves, all save the nursing. Every morning children are carried out, blanket-rolled. Every morning the whistles bring the old rush. A few knockers-up have passed to where no knocking awakens. A few more have taken their places. Bridget the old winder, who gave part of her breakfast to Hester on a far-away morning in Hester's old existence, still creeps to her frame. Sometimes she cries because her hands are so stiff in the morning, that she cannot pull the tight bobbins off the spindles. Then the winders tell her to 'dry up,' and take the too-tight bobbins, and bang them on their own spindles, and give her loose ones. People are making desperate efforts to buy their own houses. Weakly ones spend many shillings a week, to keep up in the fierce struggle. A few foolish bits o' lasses have drowned themselves. All insane, dear reader, all insane. Polly, the winder with the weak heart, dropped dead at her machine on a dark March morning, returning after her confinement. Mrs. Martin's neighbour, who was so kind in the times of their stress, has changed utterly. Somebody or other left her a thousand pounds, since when there's no touching her, and her husband is a mill-manager. Granny has a tombstone and a rose-tree on the top of her. The bitter young man, who would drag in 'God' on the occasion of the weavers' gathering in the town square, has joined an Educational Institution which gives, very cheaply, scholastic attainments to students. He is studying Comparative Religion, Greek Art, and Bourgeois Economics, and is much more fair-minded to 'God' and Capitalism. Allon, camarades! We all travel. Some backwards, some forwards, some in a circle. The man who struck his child for losing a sovereign in the gutter, proposed to Rachel, but was told she was not having a packet, whereupon he said something about Baines, and was told to go home and 'get back into the water,' a working-class slang phrase meaning that his development had not progressed beyond the fish-stage! Matty's boy who read Shakespeare (till he took out papers o' nights) won a scholarship but could not take the chance, for Matty knew she could not send him patched to the Secondary School. The old coffin-maker is laid within one of his own coffins. The old pudding-shop where Hester spent the substance of her playing, in Redburn, has changed hands. The buildings about are knocked down. They call it a Creamery now, and those who want a good feed cheaply, go elsewhere, down other dark, back streets, which are ever a-building.

And the warehouses are filling up with cloth – cloth – cloth!

The markets are full of cloth – cloth – cloth!

Capitalism flaunts its prosperity, and the 'prosperity!' of its slaves, in every newspaper. Man, wife, and child, they rush after the wheels. The boom is on. The boom is on! We are doing well, for we can exist, at least we can exist. And cloth is piling higher, higher, and the wheels run swifter and swifter!

But a few doleful people (who are happy neither when they are worked to death in order to exist nor when they are starved to death because they are not wanted) say that a crash is coming.

And – up goes the curtain.

CHAPTER 16

EVERY night, just at this hour, Stephen dragged the hassock to the window, stood on it, and with his face pressed close to the pane, stared out into the lamplit mists, listening. The sounds were always alike. First came the five o'clock hooter, like Fee-Fo-Fi-Fum, Stephen thought, mumbling and growling. Then the wagons came out from under the shed, groaning over the pavements, and he saw the horses, great, heavy, steaming beasts with the lamplight at the gates making their backs shine. The horses dragged orders, his daddy said. Hester had once told him they were dragging what people made, to clothe other people, over the seas. Always Stephen fancied the wagons were going towards the sea, to the ships. 'Orders' he did not understand. Then there was silence between, and the lamplighters gathering at the house-corner, talking, before they went home. Through the silence all sorts of echoes came, and by peering close through the opened gates he could see little figures flit past, children, like himself, some no bigger, going to stand at the mill-gates and watch for their mothers and fathers coming out. But it was the Feet he liked best to listen to – beginning very slowly, click-clack, click-clack! like slow music, till it beat up to a great chorus, with a deep iron sound in its heart, like some giant striking with a hammer on an anvil of steel. Then, if no one was watching, he would creep away, up and up the many stairs which made his back ache so, till he got to the attic where grandma's furniture was stored till Auntie Rachel got married – which Auntie Rachel said would be when she went 'barmy,' whatever that meant. In the room of shadows, with lamp-gleams from the street, he pressed close to the window, watching these other shadows go by on the lamp-lit walk by the mill-wall. It was like a never-ending picture-book. Some of the outlined Shadows he knew quite well now. The little old woman with the basket. She always wore a bonnet in the coldest weather, bobbing along, bobbing along. The man with the limp, who went down on one side, and the little girl who always ran out of the mill-gates, helter-skelter, like a wild thing let free! Then there was the man, woman, and two little girls, who always walked together, and the woman who never spoke to anyone, and wore a hat and jacket, when all the rest had shawls. Stephen knew them. He watched for them, his Shadows, the Shadows who filled the wagons with the stuff that clothed the people across the seas. He was thinking about them, now. He was creeping softly across the firelit floor, when Hester's voice reached him, stayed him. He tried to laugh, but looked guilty.

'It's cold up in the attic, Steve.'

'I like to watch them so much.'

'It's too cold.'

'Well, tell me about them, then.'

'There is nothing to tell, Steve.'

He crept to her knee, persistent, and stared up into her face.

'Tell me – Hester,' he beseeched.

'You shouldn't call me "Hester," Steve.'

'But why?'

'Oh, father doesn't like it,' Hester told him. 'It – it isn't polite, is it, Steve?'

Steve pondered.

'You were Hester before you were "Mother," weren't you?' he asked.

Hester nodded.

'What's that you're making?'

'A blouse for Auntie Rachel.'

'Was I always here, all the time, when you were just Hester?'

'I don't know what you mean.'

'Did I go about with you when you were just Hester?'

'No. You weren't born.'

'I was.'

'But you couldn't be.'

'I have always been here. I have always been with you,' said Stephen, in sudden, trembling rage. 'I was with you – all the time.'

Hester took his hand in hers.

'But I used to be little like you – and you were not born. How could you be there?'

'I was! I was there. And you couldn't see me. I was a fairy. You're naughty – Hester.'

She pulled him on to her knee, and hugged him.

'I'll tell you something, if you won't tell – .'

Stephen licked his finger.

'You shouldn't do that. It's – .'

'I know it's not eyejenic,' stated Stephen, 'but you used to do it, didn't you? See – it's wet – it's dry – now tell me the secret.'

'Don't tell daddy I used to lick my finger.'

'Why?'

'Because ladies should never tell they once licked their fingers.'

Stephen stared up at her.

'Are you a lady?' he asked.

'I don't know.'

'What is a lady?'

'Oh – Steve. What questions.'

The child on the carpet stared up suddenly, with a gleam of understanding.

'My doll's a lady,' she said. ''Cos Mary said ladies never do anything, and are always clean.'

'Lazy beggars!' said Stephen.

'Oh, Steve!'

'Bob had a horse, an' he said it wouldn't do anything, it was a lazy beggar, and not worth feeding.'

Hester stitched on another button.

'You're growing old, Hester,' cried Stephen suddenly, in a voice of piercing terror.

Hester dropped the blouse.

She stared at him in a startled way. It was true she had sometimes felt *very* old – but – .

'You'll die, Hester,' cried Stephen. 'Well, I shall go where you go.'

'Cry, baby,' said the child on the rug.

'But why am I growing old?' asked Hester.

'White,' said Stephen, shudderingly, and pulled out one long hair.

'O-o-o!' said Hester, and made him laugh.

'They die when they get white hairs,' said Stephen.

'Not always,' she told him.

She dropped the white hair into the fire.

'Promise, then, you won't.'

Hester promised.

'The Feet!' cried Stephen in a hushed voice. 'Listen!' He held up his finger, all else forgotten. The fireglow shone on his frail, velvet-clad body, the face of almost elfin beauty, with its wide, starry eyes, and turned his hair into a halo of burnished gold.

'If I could only tell where they were going!' he murmured.

'They are going home to their teas,' Hester told him.

But the youthful mystic stood by the window, listening to the Feet. They were going somewhere, he believed, not just home to their food.

'Stand over,' cried the child on the rug to the horse. 'Pull – lazy, buddy, thing – or I'll punch thy guts in.'

Hester went on sewing.

'You mustn't go in the yard any more,' she remarked.

A cinder fell on the hearth.

'Cruelty, tyranny, from man to beast, and man to man,' said Hester.

'Is that a poem, Hester?' came from the window.

Hester did not answer.

'Mary says folk are mad who talk to themselves,' came from the window.

Hester laughed softly.

'Come and listen, Hester,' called Stephen. 'Come and listen. The big iron sound is coming up. Listen! But this is the first – .'

He began to hum – a childish nonsense tune, with somehow the beat of the clogs suggested in it.

'What are the words', asked Hester. 'Have you made any words?'

'Yes. But – hush!'

He held her by the hand. They stood in the shadows of the curtains – more like elder sister and younger brother, than parent and child, the un-childishness of Stephen bringing him almost near to Hester – to Hester, still the dreamer.

'Click-clack! Click-clack!
On – on; back – back;

Through the gates and out again.
In the thunder and the rain.
Click-clack! Click-clack!'

Stephen was singing. A shudder of fear ran through Hester. Sanderson said all this imagination business was unhealthy. She had tried to check it in Stephen – but – .

'It isn't thundering, Stephen,' she told him.

'But it comes in the Song the Feet Sing,' he said in a low voice. 'Listen! It's starting, now. Do you hear it, Hester, listen. Low down at first, but if you listen hard, very hard, Hester, there it goes! Boom, boom! Don't you hear it?'

She stared down at him fearfully.

Dreams *might* perish.

Did they arise again in the children – our dreams – and arise more vivid, more strong, more clear, for all their being crushed in ourselves? But he was so frail – so frail.

'Don't sing any more, Steve,' she asked.

'The big iron sound,' hailed Stephen. He listened, lost in rapture, the child of the boss, sympathising unconsciously with the Shadows, the Shadows of Slaves, until they killed his sympathy with schools and snobbery – *if* they could kill it. Revolt had struck a fibre in his soul. Even so was Shelley. All poets hate 'This Slavery', though they do not always recognise it about them, as Steve did, but sing of Slaveries gone.

Then he began to sing again, in his sweet treble.

'Shadows, shadows,
All in a row,
Some say "Yes" and some say "No,"
Shadows, Shadows,
Where will you go?'

Hester laughed, then.

'You've stolen the third line, Steve,' she told him. 'You heard the children singing it in the snow, didn't you?'

Stephen nodded.

'I think that looks like daddy,' he said.

'Yes. So it is,' Hester told him.

They heard him go up to the bathroom.

'Is tea ready, Mary?' asked Hester, humbly.

'Yes, ma'am.'

'Please don't say "Ma'am," Mary,' asked Hester.

'No, ma'am – I mean, No, Mrs. Sanderson.'

Five minutes later Sanderson bobbed into the room. He crossed over to the fire, stood with his back to it. Sanderson had stoutened – coarsened, too.

'Nobody been up, has there, m'dear?' he asked.

'Only the "Self-Denial People."'[76]

'Damn their self-denial. Why should we deny ourselves anything, m'dear? Prosperity is the reward of virtue, industry, brains, initiative and enterprise. Why should we deny ourselves anything? See what I've got for mother, Steve!'

He pitched a box on the table.

Little Ann appeared from under the table and tiptoed. Stephen crept up and looked also.

Hester bent over the box, and opened it.

'Get enthusiastic. Get excited, can't you?'

Sanderson pinched her ear.

Hester looked at the stones.

'But – I've so many, Sandy.'

'Oh, jewels are always good stock. Good as a bank, m'dear. You look nice in that dress, Hester. Have it on to-night. I've got to go up and see Dawson. There's some trouble brewing. And – there may be a delegate from the weavers land up. Give him a good feed, Hester, and the best wine – and – get round him, somehow. Never satisfied, the fools aren't. Don't know when they are doing well. What do y'think, m'dear, they're after another rise? And there's something about the driving in the mills. They can't have thirty shillings a week without working for it. It's that Annan case, fool of a jury censured the system, and brought it off unsatisfactorily. Damn 'em. Tea ready?'

Hester shut up the box.

'Yes.'

'You sound tired, m'dear. You want to use the car more.'

'I'm not tired.'

There was a little silence.

'What was that you said about getting round the delegate, Sandy?'

Their glances met.

Steve stood watching. Then Steve saw Ann taking the box.

'Oh, you needn't lie to him. Tell him I'm considering the matter. We can't afford a strike just now. Let the fools strike when the boom's over. I've got to get that Bombay order out. Must. Stave it off. Pour oil on the troubled waters. Show that we're – in short – human, m'dear. And so we are. So we are, aren't we, Steve?'

Little Ann moved towards the fire.

Steve watched her, curiously.

Sanderson turned Stephen's face up to his.

'Human, aren't we, Steve, eh?'

Stephen puckered his brow.

When released, he went over to the book-shelf for the dictionary.

'We'll put that chap in the Church,' said Sanderson. 'Wants to know the meaning of things, m'dear – see him? And got mysticism enough to cover up 'em, when he gets the meanings. Physical disability's nothing much when you're not out to do manual work. Damn, we'll make him a bishop! Eh, Steve?'

Steve answered nothing.

This was his father's usual Manchester mood.

'Oh, Sandy!' cried Hester.

She had turned pale – frightened.

'What is it?'

'The – the box – I believe Baby's thrown it into the fire.'

'No!' yelled Sanderson.

His voice rang through the house.

He rushed at little Ann.

'No – Sandy – no.'

Hester interposed.

'But they cost – .'

Some of the froth from his lips flew on Hester's cheek.

'Yes, I know – but – see, perhaps they can be got out?'

'Here are the tongs.'

Hester plunged them after the box.

The box toppled further into the heat of the fire.

'Four hundred there,' groaned Sanderson. 'Four hundred.' He almost gnashed his teeth.

'Yes, Sandy – I know.'

'I'll – .'

'No, Sandy – .'

'But – four hundred.'

'Yes – I know.'

'You don't care.'

'I do, Sandy.'

'You don't. You don't value anything.'

'I do, Sandy.'

'You don't.'

The house seemed to shudder.

Hester shut her eyes.

Little Ann was hanging on to her skirts, crying.

'Hester!'

Sanderson suddenly grew calm.

Hester had plunged her hand into the fire, after the box.

'You damned fool?' he yelled. 'You don't think I consider – .'

'It's there,' Hester told him.

She threw the charred box on the table.

'Mary! Oil! Bring some oil!' yelled Sanderson.

'Oh, whatever's the matter?' asked Mary.

'Your mistress has burnt herself,' Sanderson said. 'Oil! Quick.'

'It isn't very bad,' Hester told him. 'I couldn't have done it but for it catching on that coal – and the hollow. Are the stones all right?'

There was no scorn in her voice but she might have been speaking of bits of pot.

'Damn the stones. Mary – .'

Mary arrived with the oil.

They poured it over.

The tips of Hester's fingers were not red – but dried.

'Telephone for the doctor.'

'No, Sandy; it's not necessary.'

'Ring him up, Mary.'

Then Sanderson opened the box.

'Not touched.' he said. 'But I'd sooner you'd let them burn, m'dear – than hurt yourself. Hurt much? I really would sooner you had left them to burn, Hester.'

She tried to believe him.

Then she struck her blow.

'That girl at sixteen, Sandy – you've made more fuss and got more hysterical about those *worthless* stones, than you did about a human life!'

'Hysterical!' gasped Sanderson.

'I said hysterical. Hysteria isn't peculiar to one gender.'

'But she was – mad.'

'The jury didn't say so.'

'The damned jury was mad, too, then. But I'm more concerned about your hand. Let me see!'

Finally they filed in to the tea-table. Hothouse roses and orchids flashed amidst the sparkle of silver. Snowy white linen got up by old and young women at four-pence the hour, dazzled the eye.

'Hurt bad, Hester?'

Stephen was spreading his serviette, pale and subdued. They could hear Ann blubbing in the kitchen.

'Not much.' Hester told him.

Ten minutes later she went out to let the doctor see her fingers. It was the same doctor who had once stood in a poor room, where Granny lay dying.

'It's nothing,' she told him. 'Sanderson would have you come. I'm sorry. You're nearly run off your feet, aren't you?'

He nodded.

'It's a pretty bad burn. Mind you don't get the frost in. You're looking well, Mrs. Sanderson. Send Mary down. You've done the best you can. Best sling it up. I'll send some ointment. Cough still keep away?'

She nodded.

Two hours later the children were abed. Sanderson was off to see Dawson. Hester lay on the couch, the lamp turned low.

'Things!' she murmured to herself. 'Things!'

Things! She had thought that freedom lay in the possession of *things*. *Freedom!* Freedom! *Freedom!* What would it feel like only to be *free* – for a day – only a single day? She had entered the cage of the bourgeois world, and a new slavery, a new servitude.

The burn in her flesh throbbed and blazed.

There was even relief in physical suffering. It deadened the other kind. Mary awoke her, or the burn, or both.

'The delegate, ma'am.'

'What name?'

She sat up, her hair rumpled.

'Tell him to wait a minute in the hall.'

The wife of the boss couldn't see a delegate with rumpled hair.

'I'll tell him, ma'am, Baines – Jack Baines, he says his name is.'

'Mary.'

'Yes, ma'am.'

'Ask him to come when Mr. Sanderson is in.'

'But he's wild already.'

'Wild?'

'Says Sanderson *ought* to have been in. Like his cheek.'

'Well, tell him – .'

'He'd said you'd do as well, ma'am.'

'Very well, then. Ask him to wait.'

Mary went away.

Hester could hear his voice, answering. Panic seized her, rage against Sanderson, against 'marriage' so-called, against the whole of society's lies – so suddenly thrust upon her, in a lightning second. She seized a comb, and with her left hand dragged at her hair, and twisted it up, somehow, anyhow, that burning rage in her heart, those scalding tears in her eyes.

'Where will you see him, ma'am?'

'In the drawing-room. Is the fire all right?'

'Not very good, ma'am,' answered Mary.

'It will do. Don't put any more coals on.'

'No, ma'am.' Then Hester went into the hall, and turned in at the door.

'Good evening, Mrs. Sanderson.'

'Good evening. It's a miserable night, isn't it?'

'Oh – not so bad.'

'But I thought I heard it raining.'

'Yes. But one gets used to it. It's always raining. You used to like the rain, *if I remember*.'

Through the quiet shadows of the great, luxurious room they regarded each other, fencing amidst the conventionalities, swords thrusting in and out the lies.

'Won't you sit down?'

'I don't mind.'

He sat down, carelessly easy, in Sanderson's chair.

'It's about some trouble at the mills, isn't it?'

'Yes. I thought Sanderson would have faced it up.'

'He had to see Dawson on some business.'

'Yes. About the united action in the event of the strike.'

'I hope there won't be a strike,' said Hester.

'Of course. That is natural, isn't it?'

She blanched, a trembling Ambassadress of Capital, having to speak from 'outside' the mill conditions, having to speak from the point of view of financial interests, not human conditions.

'Yes. It is natural that we do not want a strike,' she told him, accepting the ironical position.

She sat down, the width of the Persian rug, which had cost more than the two years' wages of a weaver, between them. Mechanically she pulled the glass screen between herself and the heat of the fire, to protect the complexion which belonged to Sanderson.

'*We* also do not want to strike,' said Baines, out of a little silence. 'We shall want the Union's funds when the great boom is over. When the markets are glutted.'

'Yes,' assented Hester.

Her unburnt hand pulled nervously at the fringe of the silk cover on the small table near her.

'I would rather have seen Sanderson,' Baines told her.

'I can tell him all you say. You can be just as merciless as you please. I will record it faithfully,' came her voice, clear and cold.

'You are quite sure you won't run out of the room,' he jested. Another sword – thrust through the conventionalities. She had told him to be merciless. He had reminded her of her pacifism – years ago. Hester struggled with that fierce rush of scalding tears. For so long she had not cried! Never since that day when she came back over the Switchback, and knew that the brutalities of working-class existence were one too many for her. But the tears were creeping up now, burning geysers under the ice. She was fighting the flood, sitting in her chair, quite still, save for the hand pulling at the silk tassels of the Indian cover, with its peacocks, and butterflies, and roses blazoned on a black ground, like the vanity of the rich woven over the dark sorrows of the poor.

'No. I have learned – not to run away,' she told him.

'Well – then – .'

He put up his hand and ran it through his hair – which made it look wild and defiant. *If she remembered* he used to do that, in that old existence, when she was a slave, amongst slaves – not a slave amongst knaves with the force of the law behind them.

'Were you speaking?' he asked.

It was the beginnings of a half-hysterical laugh she had checked.

'No. I was not speaking.'

'Well, then, the case is this, Mrs. Sanderson. There was no legitimate excuse for the wages being dropped last autumn in the face of the boom continuing again. Seeing that our masters are so prosperous, we surely have a right to have back that five per cent. *now*. That is the opinion of this town, its working section, at least, and of other towns about. Brayton is going to make a stand – *now* – when the boom is on, now, when the great orders are to be got out, not when the work's done and our masters can afford to lock us out. In the event of refusal – there will be a strike – *without notice* of such strike, Mrs. Sanderson. What's the good of notifying the enemy that you are going to hit him and let him prepare – ?'

'*The enemy.*'

The two words stuck in Hester's brain, turning round and round, like burning spindles in a weary machine.

She was the enemy!

At least, she was stuck here to represent it.

What had Sanderson said?

She must get round the delegate, pour oil on the troubled waters, compromise, defer, become part of the Capitalist Diplomatic machine?

'No. It would not be wise to notify the enemy,' she agreed. 'Only – you have just told me.'

'We wish him to know there will be a strike, unless the per cent. is put on *at once*. I have not told you *when* we strike.'

Mary tapped at the door.

'Coffee is ready, ma'am.'

'Bring it in.'

'None for me, thanks,' said Baines swiftly.

'It is quite good coffee.'

'I supped before I came.'

'Very well. Let's get on with the business.'

Mary came with the tray.

'Take it away, Mary. Mr. Baines has supped.'

The wire-pulled puppet took away the tray. Hester was glad to see it go. Supposing she had gulped it, like little Ann had gulped, after the scene some hours before. That would have been so ridiculous! And the great cardinal point in this new Slavery was not to be ridiculous.

'Yes. Let's get on with it.'

Baines spoke hurriedly himself.

It was getting on his nerves, too.

He rumpled his hair again. It heralded another attack. Hester moved in her chair. The fireglow caught the gilded buckles of the slippers she wore. The long link of yellow beads on the indigo velvet dress stood out, and the jewels of a 'slave-bangle' blazed on the whiteness of her arm, the arm a little plumper than in that old existence.

'The other trouble is the driving in *your mills*,' he began. 'The Unions are determined to put a stop to it. That jury who sat on the last case are determined *that* shall be the last. Unfortunately, the people are so eager to work, each harder than his partner – it has gone on a long time. But we're determined it's got to go, with the vicious slate-system of telling workers what each worker earns, and paying overlookers per centage on their workers' wages. *But we mean to put a stop to this girl-murder* – at least, to the *actual and direct murder,* which is clear to be seen. Will you tell Sanderson *that?* Tell him we can't – *yet* – put an end to the indirect Murder and *Prostitution* Capitalism entails, not yet, but we shall do so as soon as we can. Meanwhile we want five per cent. more – NOW – the softening down of this driving – NOW – and the discharge of the manager who told the girl she was not *coming up to the scratch*. You will remember, won't you? Perhaps you had better have taken notes!'

'I can remember,' said Hester.

Her voice was very low, almost a sobbing breath on the air of the room, after the restrained vigour of his speech.

Baines picked up his hat from the frail gilded occasional chair near his.

'And now I'll get out,' he said.

Hester arose from her chair.

She could not see very clearly. The outline of Baines' dark figure was blurred. The fire was blurred.

'Yes. It must be difficult to breathe here, in the same room as Prostitution,' she said.

Baines moved towards the door – then back.

Wild reproaches came to his lips. He thrust them back.

'We try to break Capitalism, not its helpless victims, *unless they stand in the way of its breaking*,' he told her.

Silence answered him.

Then all he had suffered, the memory of that passage, that hellish passage, stoking across the Atlantic, the memory of a fiddle sounding down to that hell-hole at the base of the ship, his deep anxiety, white hopes – and then – black despair, overcame him.

'Has the mess of pottage been worth it, Hester?' he asked.

She stood silent, convulsive, the ignominy of her position throttling her utterance. Traitor to Baines, traitor to Sanderson, traitor to the slaves, and, according to Baines, with some of their blood on her dress. But above all, that intense hatred of the thing which made these treacheries into loyalties, seethed and boiled in her blood.

Then she struck.

'At least I have given my children something nearer childhood than that which I got,' she said. 'At least I have protected them from that which hurt me. At least I have had the joy, the glory, the wonder and the flowers of motherhood, not just the crown of thorns. At least I have not had to pinch and scrape to set Sanderson *his* food, lying and dodging and going short myself. At least I have reduced my Slavery from being a slave of many to being a slave of one, compromising no more than the rest of the slaves do, who compromise with all their bosses, religious, educational, political and economic. You who hold aside your garments believing I have sold myself for a "mess of pottage," you of the virtue, who attack Capitalism, and yet confer with its masters, go-betweens on mere questions of wages, when you should be the advocates of Freedom – of Freedom – *the advocates of the wholesale destruction of Private Interests* – in what way have I compromised more than you? Tell me that. Is the only Prostitution that of the body? When you came here – to talk to Sanderson about *five per cent.* – are you not compromising and prostituting yourself? *Are you trying to put a higher price on Slavery or wipe it out altogether?* Tell me that. Have we to wait hundreds and thousands of years to alter Capitalism? Or are you trying to get it now – Freedom for the People – so that none need sell, and none need buy?'

She stood quite close to him now.

The pallor of her face, the darkness of her eyes, the clenching of her hand, he felt rather than saw them. The vibration of her voice tore at him, shook him, as she challenged him.

'What would you have us do?'

She laughed – uncertainly.

'Nothing. You are always doing nothing – always bargaining for percentages – like the bosses. Perhaps I *fancied* that you might think it more practical to *fight for Freedom* – than haggle with bosses for percentages. But I never had any opinions that were worth anything. Women never have.'

A mocking, pale-faced ghost, with vibrating passion in her voice, she challenged him again, from a new vantage-ground.

'So long as our hair is nicely put up, so long as we attend to the things between the four walls, that is sufficient for boss and slave. So long as we will continue to breed children, whether they are to be bosses or slaves, that is all you care. So long as we are the slaves of slaves, or the slaves of bosses – that is enough. So long as we make a neat job of either boss's-house or slave's-house – that is enough. And if you are the Galahads you would have us believe – you ought to be prepared to do *anything – anything* – to change the lives of women and children from slavery to freedom – even though you had to lay down your own lives to do it. Instead of which you are trying to get five per cent. – five per cent. of the wages of Slavery, increased. And you come here and taunt me. And we have both got our wages of sin, you as a Trades Union official bargaining for five per cent. rises – and I, as the wife of the boss. Shall we shake hands? If I remember – we used to be friends.'

Jack mechanically held out his hand.

He tried to find something to say. The passionate cadences of her voice had paralysed his brain. Then he rallied.

'Anyhow – Hester.'

'Hester Martin,' she told him.

He shook his head.

'Hester Martin,' she repeated, her voice cold and steady now.

'You have lost any chance of striking the tiniest blow for the working-classes. *I am a member of a defensive organisation which may turn into an attacking vanguard.* You – are lost!'

'Who knows?'

Her voice was almost the tired, low voice once so familiar, a music which had echoed through his dreams.

'And I wasn't blaming you. Indeed – I am sorry.'

She flinched away at that.

'I need no pity – .'

He was gathering himself for a last blow.

'You had best keep it for yourself, and when you haggle with the bosses for five per cent. or two per cents. – for little crumbs to alleviate misery – instead of smashing the thing which manufactures it, remember that I, also, pity all you – who, while passing as the advocates of the People's desire for Life, haggle like merchants for percentages! Of course, I am quite helpless, quite lost, but even I can see *your* position and be sorry for it.'

'Well – shake!'

Jack held out his hand.

She placed hers within it.

It was chill as ice, chill as it always was, when emotion tore at her. He held it the customary and regulation moment, then dazed, shaken, chaotic, blundered his way out. The hall-lamp was lit. In the mellow light he saw her face. It was pale still, subdued in expression, but the anger in her eyes seemed to blaze through him.

'Good-night, Mrs. Sanderson,' he said.

'Good-night. There are three steps down – then four.'

He felt a wild desire to laugh.

Three – four – .

To hell with 'This Slavery!'

We ought to be prepared – what had she said?

No matter! Three – four – .

He was laughing, laughing, as he ran into Sanderson.

'Hello. Been to my place?' asked Sanderson.

Baines looked at him, still laughing.

'Go – to hell,' he told Sanderson.

He should have gone back and given a report, but – there was nothing to report. Three – four steps down! Five per cents.! To hell with it, all of it – all of it! He almost ran into O'Neill.

'Evenin', Mr. Baines.'

'Go to hell!'

'After you,' O'Neill told him, pleasantly. Must have been drinking, O'Neill thought. Sounded drunk, anyhow, and his eyes were bloodshot, too! Under the gas-lamp Sergeant O'Neill wrote in his memorandum book the direction Baines had asked him to take, on a certain date – all in the shorthand with which Rachel Martin played such ducks and drakes when she was speaking!

Jack Baines stayed out on the hills. It was bitter cold, all night. The pools were full of stars. The moor awakened at dawn – wild, sombre – the grouse calling ga-bak, ga-bak, ga-bak. Backwards and forwards, all night, till the dawn stole up. Fighting it out, round and round in a circle. Reform or no compromise with Capitalism at all. Hundreds or thousands of years, she had said. Thousands of Hesters sold, then, or starved, in strikes, bad trade, or worked to death, fettered souls all their lives. Children, children, children – generation after generation – bred to oppress or be oppressed. No half-ways. One or the other. Buying or selling. Reform or – . He sat down at last in the dawn, his throbbing brain afire. He felt weak as a kitten. The valley of mists quivered. *The sun was rising.* He watched the confused shadows flee away like wraiths, the fields spread out, the clouds light up with fire; saw the birth of the Dawn, a new day, utterly unlike any day that had gone before it. He took off his hat and stood looking over a valley from which the shadows of night were almost gone. Did the sun compromise with the night? He made his choice. Without mercy, without weakness, without any bond with them, he would strike, strike, strike, making *rebels* – not slaves who wanted merely higher wages.

But he must see this strike through. Yes. Three steps down! He took them through black ling,[77] silvered with dawn-frost. Four steps down – by a clear stream. And there he drank. And the valley was full of Dreams, Dreams with white feet, marching towards the Sun. And even the fact that Sanderson had 'got' Hester could not blacken it!

CHAPTER 17

'Open this door, Hester!'

It was Sanderson's voice.

'It is not locked.'

'Sticking, then.'

He threw his weight against it and entered.

Steve was sitting up in bed, and Hester was sitting on the bed.

'So they sent that mad fool, Baines. What happened?'

'He just stated the case. The driving has to be abated, and they are determined to have the five per cent., and the discharge of the manager,' she told him.

'Oh!'

Sanderson laughed.

'And *when* does the strike come?'

'I don't know.'

'Don't know. Couldn't you make him tell you? Call yourself a female of the species and couldn't get to know that from a man who was once in love with you? Don't you see, that order has got to go through or I'm broke, m'dear. No moonshine. I'm broke. I've staked everything on that order. *Baines.* Why it was Providence sent him here. They told me they were sending Swales. And Baines came – and – you let the chance slip! Couldn't you coax him? Hang it all, we can't afford to be sentimental. The thing's too serious. I've banked everything on that order. It's titanic. It's got to go for a fixed date, or it's left on my hands. And I'm ruined. I'm not like some of the old hands – with my cake baked. Good God! Baines! You had him in your hands, and let him slip through.'

'You would not have me make love to him?' asked Hester.

'Love? Anything! I tell you – it's no bunkum – I'm ruined if that order doesn't land. I shall have gone up like a rocket and come down like the stick. Damn it all, Hester. You might have managed him better.'

'Am I to understand that you think I should have played Delilah[78] to Baines, in order that you can get your order out, Sandy?'

'Faugh! Sentimental piffle, m'dear. I can trust you. I left you to represent our mutual interests, and you talk like a Victorian. The man's nobody. You could have played on him like you play your fiddle – without compromising yourself at all. It was Providence! And you let the chance slip. Didn't you offer him a cigar, some wine – and my chair?'

Hester smiled.

'He took your chair,' she said.

There was a thin note of weary satire in her voice.

'Yes. Mary said you never had the lamp lit.'

'So, you have been in the kitchen – pumping Mary?'

'Oh, no. What words you use, Hester, before the children.'

He paced to and fro.

'The devil take it!' he ejaculated at length. 'Anyhow, I shall not be beaten. I suppose you know which side you are on? At least, you'll not like to be hounded back to the conditions you revolted against?'

'I know which side my bread is buttered on,' Hester told him.

'That will do.'

He left the room.

'Read, Hester,' asked Steve.

And so they went on reading the old, beautiful dream of Morris,[79] Hester translating it as they went into language a child could understand.

'And there were no Poor, Hester?'

'No. None at all.'

'And no rich, Hester?'

'No. None at all.'

'And what did they do with the soldiers and the guns, Hester?'

'The soldiers helped to grow corn, to make bread, and they buried the guns in a deep pit, and sowed corn over them.'

'And they *never* dug them up again, Hester?'

'No, not after the Last Battle.'

'Why had there to be the Last Battle, Hester?'

'Because there were men who had *Things*, and they said these *Things* were theirs, and would not give them up, though they were *Things* the People had made, and could not do without and *must take*, since their lives were in the hands of the men who had the *Things*.'

'Could they not have bought the things back, Hester?'

'They had no money. The man whom they made the *Things* for only gave them enough to keep them alive – always – and till they took the *Things* they had, to go on being Slaves.'

'Is that where the Feet are going, Hester? They always seem to be going – somehow – not just to their teas.'

'Perhaps it *is* where they are going.'

'Shall we be dead, Hester?'

'I don't know, Steve.'

'I would like to have lived there, Hester, wouldn't you? Where they did not look like Shadows. Tell me about the fields, Hester, *there,* and the people working and singing in them. Tell me about the corn, and what we would have done, *there,* Hester.'

And she told him that in that world he would have made pots for the people to drink from, and mats for their feet to rest on, and pictures to hang on their walls.

'And *you,* Hester?'

'I should just have been your mother, Steve, just the same, and I should have woven cloth, too, because everybody would make something – and – .'

'The fiddle! The fiddle!' cried Steve. 'What would you have done with that?'

'On moonlight nights in the Spring, Steve, we would have wandered down the paths between the green corn, and people would have crept to their doors saying, "Hush! The fairies are laughing."'

'You and me, Hester, and the fiddle?'

'Yes.'

'And what would they have given to us?'

'Love,' Hester told him. 'Love and Joy!'

Five minutes later he was asleep.

Hester crept downstairs. Sanderson was sitting before the study fire, thinking how to get that order out before the strike, and how to beat that demand for five per cent. – for five per cent. back from the exploitation he called – Interest on his Capital.

'Mother not come in yet?' he asked.

'No.'

Mrs. Martin came in when supper was almost over. She was dressed according to the establishment in which she lived. But her hair was almost white, and there was an unnatural stiffness in her manner, and the way in which she tried to manage her h's was a tragedy – and a comedy – the Pantomime of 'This Slavery!'

'*Will* there be a strike, Sanderson?' she queried deferentially.

'I hope not, till our order's out – or we go bang!'

He snapped his fingers.

'Well, let's hope not,' she said.

She was going to put some coals on, but remembered she did not have to do such things, now.

'What's that?' she asked, nervously.

'Stephen! He's got a little cough,' Hester told her.

'Diphtheria's going in the town,' she told them.

'Stephen's all right. There are no bad drains *here*.' Sanderson spoke in his matter-of-fact way.

'No. But it spreads from where the bad drains are,' she told him, without deference.

'The child never goes out this weather, so he can't take it,' Sanderson told her. 'Where is the disease going?'

'Finch Row!'

Hester looked at Sanderson.

'Good God!'

'Then – those drains did need attending to, Sandy.'

Hester spoke timidly

'Confound! I suppose so. I'll see the agent.'

'It's broken out in several places,' said Mrs. Martin. 'You see, they sit together in the schools and it spreads.'

'Better have the doctor in every few days, to keep all right here,' said Sanderson and left the room.

Hester and Mrs. Martin sat looking at each other. Quite suddenly Hester arose, crossed the room softly, stood with her hand on her mother's chair, and stooping, kissed her cheek.

'Something the matter, Hessie? What's to do with thy hand?'

'Burnt it getting some stones out of the fire.'

She explained.

'Is it bad?'

'No.'

'I hope Stephen doesn't take it, Hessie. He takes things so.'

Hester stared into the fire.

'The great beauty of it is, that the rich can't wrong the poor without some of the evil travelling back to them.'

'Hessie!'

'At least, there's an elemental Justice runs through Natural Law, which they can't dodge. Oh, Mother, do you never wish we were back again – bad as it was – bad as it was! Think of it! We're having to live on them! To live on them! And I'm sure if I go to Church again I shall rise up and challenge the preacher – but Sandy says it's necessary to go. You see – our cake isn't baked – yet. Oh, if only it were baked, though it were baked into the black sorrows they feel – *all* the time! If only it were baked – to the finish.'

'Shut up, he's coming.'

And so – they shut up.

CHAPTER 18

'DAWSON and a few others are coming, m'dear,' Sanderson told Hester from the depths of his easy chair. 'It would perhaps be better – if – in short – we want to be left alone. And keep Mary out of the way. We don't want any of our decisions to leak out, and things have a way of travelling. How our last move got out I don't know. But Dawson gasses too much, if he gets too much. I shall have to warn him.'

He watched her, as she stood, arranging flowers.

'Mary asked to have a night off to-night,' she told him.

'The devil!'

'I promised.'

'And the other one's off. She didn't look ill. *At least she could have stuck it.* Pretty hole! And – good God! What are we to do?'

'There's plenty of food in the house and fires to cook it,' Hester told him.

'But who the devil will cook it?'

'I'll cook it.'

'But – it's *infra dig,*[80] m'dear. Why should you cook? Tell Mary she's got to stop. Can't have domestics choosing their nights off – just at their convenience, confound 'em.'

'I promised, Sandy.'

'Well – I suppose we shall manage.'

He puffed at his cigar.

She thought ironically of the 'managing' which had gone on in the houses of the strikers – out now these past fourteen weeks. *How it all come back. How it all came back.* The Union pay was exhausted. Three weeks ago the last strike-pay had been paid. Infuriated strikers had besieged the Trades Union office, and Baines had been taunted with his six pounds a week. He had given them his savings, some three hundred pounds, and told them that after the strike was won, though he would be a member of the Union, he would cease to be an official. There had been a great scene. They had carried him shoulder high, marching through the streets, and had stopped outside the house of the boss, singing the challenge which some unknown 'poet' had set to the tune of 'John Brown's Body.'[81]

> 'Our boss's order lies a-mouldering on the shelf,
> Our boss's order lies a-mouldering on the shelf,
> Our boss's order lies a-mouldering on the shelf,
> And we're not downhearted – No!'

Daffodil and narcissus. Pheasant's Eye narcissus! Slender-stemmed, singing of the Spring, she set them in the delicate Venetian glasses. 'Our boss's order lies a-mouldering on the shelf – Our boss's order lies a-mouldering on the shelf.' Just another flower there – to lean over and mirror itself in the bevelled mirror of the Jacobean sideboard – with the Burgundy and port and whisky on it! And the cigars! 'Our boss's order lies a-mouldering on the shelf.' Hester was smiling.

'You see, m'dear, there's only a month now to get that order out. *So they've got to get back.* Made up my mind, m'dear. They've got to get back. Can land it easily. Tim'll run the engine full speed, and fortunately weft and warp are good. We'll land it, you'll see.'

He got up and poured himself another glass of port with shaking hand.

'Hester!' called Stephen.

'What's up with that child?' asked Sanderson. 'Doesn't know of anything that's going on, does he?'

'I've never told him,' protested Hester. 'I wouldn't tell him that people are starving – *on our* account.'

'They've done it themselves. Jolly well off before, if they'd only thought so. What's five per cent., anyhow? But they won't starve, m'dear. We've smashed their damned Union, though. No. They won't starve. *They can live on garbage – that class of people,* m'dear. Yes. You'd better go up.'

Hester went up.

Stephen was sitting up in bed.

The pink-shaded safety lamp cast a warm glow on his pale face.

'The Feet, Hester!' he cried.

'Where, dearie?'

'I can hear them – beat – beat. Listen, Hester.'

She shook her head.

'They are coming, Hester'

'I can hear nothing.'

'You've been dreaming, Steve.'

'I heard them, Hester.'

She sat beside him till he fell asleep. Then she crept downstairs. Sanderson was asleep, asleep like a great, fat ox in the great, fat chair. The heavy gold watch-guard – the sheer ugliness of his well-fed body, gave her a sense of nausea. Manchester hotels, old port, cotton-markets – he exuded their atmosphere. There were men on the 'Change who were not so stout. But they carried the same air of superior, stinking commercialism about with them. Dawson was a specimen of it run to leanness. He always reminded her of a hawk. When he and Sanderson were together, they reminded her – one of the body of Capitalism, the other of its soul. You could see the same type of mind as Dawson's in the faces of the political, Capitalist statesmen. *Keen,* they called it – keen politician – keen business man. Yes, very keen – with the Poor as their chickens. She passed Sanderson's chair with a sense of almost physical sickness, and stood by the vase of flowers – the frail, delicate flowers of Spring, earth-born and beautiful. Then from outside came the sound – the sound of clogs. Click-clack! Click-clack! But the gates were closed. They could not get in. She was thankful, with a sense of physical cowardice, of abhorrence of brute force, that they could not get in. Sanderson snored.

'Silly fools! Never satisfied,' he grunted, and slithered further down into the fatness of the chair. Up from the street it came, a challenge and a murmur.

'Our boss's order lies a-mouldering on the shelf,
Our boss's order lies a-mouldering on the shelf,
Our boss's order lies a-mouldering on the shelf,
And we're not downhearted. *No!'*

Rick-racks began to sound. Sanderson started up.

'What's that, m'dear?' he asked.

'The *Hands* are outside,' Hester told him.

'Can't get in. Gates are locked. And if they do any damage it goes on the rates,' he told her. 'We are well protected.'

'Yes. We are well protected,' Hester agreed.

'They'll give in before we do,' he told her.

'Yes. We have fires and food.'

'Their own fault, m'dear, if they've none. But we've smashed their damned Union – and we'll smash Baines. If he can't keep them in order, so much the worse for him. Pour me another glass of wine – .'

She poured it.

The voices and rick-racks were receding.

'I asked O'Neill to walk round a bit,' said Sanderson. 'I know you don't like policemen, m'dear, but what would you do without 'em, now – eh? Got to keep law and order, and protect ourselves.'

She stood waiting, the glass of wine in her hand, beside his chair.

'Yes, I suppose *we* must protect *ourselves*,' she agreed.

He took the glass and sipped it slowly.

'Such poor straws,' Sanderson said, his eyes half-closed. 'A few policemen and a handful of soldiers – and – presto! They run back into their holes!'

He snapped the fingers and thumb of the hand which did not hold the glass.

He flashed her a look through those half-closed eyes, and laughed.

'"Scuse me, m'dear. Didn't mean to hurt your feelings. True enough, isn't it? And Baines – bah! The poor fool's tryin' to hold them back. They'll sweep him away like chaff! And then he'll get all the discredit for the *force* that is used – and – silly fool, anyhow. Perhaps we'll get him *with us* yet. Used to be in love with him, m'dear – eh? You wait! Drivin' him into a nice corner, we are. You'll shudder at having ever looked at him, m'dear. You see, the funds are done! Silly ass has pitched his earnings to them, but has no more. All that rot about resigning as an official, m'dear – just bunkum. *He'll be asked* to resign, *when we've done with him*. You haven't any sense of humour, have you, Hester? No – never had – never had.'

'Perhaps it is developing,' Hester murmured.

'Come and sit here,' asked Sanderson.

She dragged Stephen's hassock – the little hassock he loved to stand on to look through the window at the shadows – the Shadows – to her husband's feet and sat down. She had promised to be a faithful wife.

'Glad to hear you are developing a sense of humour, m'dear,' Sanderson told her. 'Pretty hair you've got, Hester. Wouldn't like your hair dragged down with the old shawl again, would you? Not that you couldn't wear rags and make them look distinguished. I suppose if we traced you enough back we'd find you came from – .'

'Adam!' jested Hester.

He laughed, and a little of the wine splashed on her.

'Sorry, m'dear!'

She looked down at the wine-splashes.

They were spreading redly over the soft, shimmering whiteness of her evening frock.

'Never mind, m'dear. Give it to Mary. She'll strut in it. They're always glad of our cast-offs, whether it's frocks – or opinions.'

'I must change it, Sandy. Your friends will be here – and they might think we'd been having a vulgar row.' She laughed.

'Yes. Yes, m'dear. Never thought of that. Woman's wit again.'

She ran away – away from the touch of him.

Yes. She must get it off. It looked, not like wine – but *blood – blood – their blood.*

She slipped into a foaming green dress, fastening it with trembling hands. For a mess of pottage. A mess of pottage. And she had thought she could escape! She had taunted Baines with coming to bargain for per cents. She had lost the right to speak one word for her own class. She was in the camp of the Enemy, and the humour of it, the sardonic humour of it, overcame her suddenly. She sat on the bed; the great, plump, satin-ei-derdowned, feather-bed, and laughed – gagging her laughter with a hand-kerchief bordered with Valenciennes.[82] For even now, marching down the rainy streets, with the sad, tearful lamps, they were singing that doggerel – hers, though they did not know it – doggerel – the sole expression of the poetry of the masses, which has its poetic utterances forever throttled at the birth. For the most they were silent, their songs unsung, save for the few who rise like torches in the night of 'This Slavery,' torches which but illumine the sad confusion of the disunited, half-organised ranks, the wretched apathy and the negation of all Social pride. They were marching, singing those defiant words, and fighting for five per cent.! One per cent.

Half per cent.! No per cent.! No matter. For 'the shade of a word, and a thing not seen in the eyes.'[83] She knew now that it was right – that the fight was the thing! For it is only in the fight that it becomes clear, clear to thousands, that the class-war is, and has been from time immemorial, not a war at all, but an armed camp on one side – on the other, a massacre.

When she had conquered her laughter, she took the handkerchief away. There was a queer taste in her mouth. She glanced at the handkerchief. *That* was blood – not wine! Just a drop or two. Not enough to choke one – but enough. She noticed its colour. Yes. Quite enough. Some little sorrow, perhaps; some little fear, but very little. Somewhere, sometime, at some hour – white, shining peace at last, the peace that comes to one who has struck a blow and left the mark upon the walls, a mark which will be seen when the dawn rolls up, when the hearts of men are sifted and Democracy blows its trumpet-blast of Judgment.

She heard the bell ring.

That was Dawson. The rest would soon be here. She must make a good spread. *They* must go on eating. Yes. They would go on eating. And cannibalism was almost stamped out by Christian missionaries!

She met Dawson in the hall.

'How do y'do, Mrs. Sanderson. Sandy in?'

Hester waved her hand towards the drawing-room.

'You're looking pale, Mrs. Sanderson. Don't let it shake your nerves. And that's a cough, you've got, by Jove.'

He stared at her.

She stood, gripping the banister.

A red spot burned on each pale cheek. Her eyes were brilliant.

'It's nothing,' she told him.

Dawson remembered having heard – somewhere – that she was 'going off' when she married Sanderson.

'It's just the mist,' she said. 'How goes the fight?'

'Magnificently! Couldn't be going better. Funds done, you know. Can't hold out much longer, damn 'em! Game they are, poor beggars. They stick it well.'

'Yes. But we stick it better,' she answered, smiling.

He stared – then laughed.

Sanderson heard his laughter, and came out.

Then they went to confer over the fire.

'Both our domestics are away, one is sick, the other's claimed a night out. So you'll have to take pot-luck, Dawson.'

'Don't mention it,' Dawson told him.

'Others coming?' asked Sanderson.

Dawson nodded.

'That's good. I'm going to be in a hole, Dawson, if they don't go in. Fact is, old man, if they're not in in three weeks – .'

He banged his fist on the table.

'No,' protested Dawson.

'True,' Sanderson answered him. 'You fellows will be all right. Your cake is baked. But I shall be done! Small fry, I am, but if this order gets out – no matter! Weakest goes to the wall you know, Dawson. But I've made up my mind they're going back! I'd sooner blow my brains out than lose! The struggle I had to get the capital – loans, mortgages – and now, the first big scoop was coming, the one to set me on my feet, for more. What's the spirit of the devils! Is it breaking?'

Dawson shook his head.

'Fierce?' asked Sanderson.

He stood at the sideboard, pouring out a strong whisky and soda.

'No – *worse*. Steady, cold sort of resolution.'

'Couldn't be provoked?'

'Oh. I won't say that, old man.'

Dawson knocked the ash off his cigar.

'Baines is holding them back?'

'H'm! Very careful not to give the police a chance. He's getting information from some source. Knows all about the reinforcements ready to rush up – it's my opinion. Pointing out the disastrous effect it would have on the fight that's coming along after Brayton's. Constitutional, you know. Telling them that even *if* they go back, the whole of Lancashire will fight the same fight soon – provided no mêlée occurs which will demoralize the rest. So we've published a few leaflets to suggest that he's in our pay, and afraid of their winning. Ha, ha!'

Hester entered.

'And the stuff they're singing,' said Dawson. 'Some fool or other is writing them words to old tunes, and the damned kids are singing it in the streets. Crude stuff, but happens to be a sort of bulletin of all we are doing behind the scenes.'

'Good God!' ejaculated Sanderson.

'It's working-class stuff. Uncultured, you know. But it's my opinion the information is coming from inside our own ranks, and some inartistic, crude mind is setting it into words. It's right, Sanderson. You needn't stare. I heard them singing about the blacklegs coming as I came along!'

'Good God!'

Sanderson sat aghast.

Then he moved instinctively towards the sideboard.

'No, Sandy,' protested Hester.

He patted her shoulder.

'Perhaps you're right, m'dear. But, Good God!'

Then they heard the voices from the street – the voices of the starving.

'Must be a lot of 'em,' said Sanderson.

'Yes. There's a meeting.'

They sat listening.

The starving were singing – singing in bass, treble and contralto. The words echoed into the room.

'Our boss's order lies a-mouldering on the shelf,
Our boss's order lies a-mouldering on the shelf,
Our boss's order lies a-mouldering on the shelf,
And we're not downhearted. *No!*'

'They're going to bring the blacklegs on the black 9–30 train,
They're going to bring the blacklegs on the black 9–30 train,
They're going to bring the blacklegs on the black 9–30 train,
But we're not downhearted. *No!*'

'Jack Baines' knapsack does not hold your bloody crust,
Jack Baines' knapsack does not hold your bloody crust,
Jack Baines' knapsack does not hold your bloody crust,
And the Folk – they know their Own.'

'Good God!'

Sanderson was almost gnashing his teeth.

Dawson sat speechless.

Then up from the street it came – one surging burst of northern singing.

'Glory, glory, hallelujah,
Glory, glory, hallelujah,
Glory, glory, hallelujah,
We are picketing – to-night!'

Then they moved on.

'So – the leaflets were no good,' said Dawson, 'Checkmated, Sandy.'

'If I could find the traitor, I'd have his blood,' said Sanderson.

Dawson was watching Hester.

'You are scaring Mrs. Sanderson,' he said. 'Don't get alarmed, Mrs. Sanderson. We've the police on our side, and, if there's any trouble, they'll rush up a section of the Militia from Redburn. Don't worry.'

'Oh – I wish it was over,' she murmured. 'I wish it was *all over*, Sandy!'

'So do I,' muttered Sanderson. 'So do I. Play for us, Hester Something – soothing. Good God!'

He stared suddenly at Hester.

'That sister of yours doesn't come here any more,' he shouted suddenly. 'She's hand and glove with Baines. And you're so weak – so damned weak, Hester! But she doesn't come here any more – at least not till this mess is done with. I know she's your sister, and all that, but you – you've never told her anything, have you, Hester?'

He jumped up suddenly, seized her by the wrists.

She stared straight at him.

'No,' she almost shouted.

'There – there – I should keep cool, I know, m'dear, but the thought that she might be *ruining us*, you know. Hester's sister has strange ideas, Dawson; can only see one side – the working-class side. Won't believe our interests are mutual – ever. She'd ruin Hester, her mother, and all the lot of us – calling it principle; damned unprincipled, I call it. But she doesn't come here any more – *yet!* Think on.'

'Very well!'

Then she sat down and played them Grieg's 'Cradle Songs.'

'Sing, Hester.'

'Oh, I didn't know Mrs. Sanderson sung.'

So she sang to them, classic cradle songs, very soothing, very sweet, while the babes of the strikers were crying, crying, crying – primitively and unmusically.

And in her heart was great gladness and the certainty of the white and shining peace and a courage growing up within her – a knowledge that her own bonds were breaking. She was learning to fight. The clothes on her back, the food she ate, did not come from Sanderson but from the People. Always she had been theirs. Always she was theirs. Always she would be theirs – . It was the one glory, the one thing incorruptible, the one thing which remained, bitter-sweet, out of the wreckage of her life.

Stephen was crying when she went up after the conference of the bosses, the conference through which she had sat, ostensibly an interested party – .

'Throat, Hessie!'

She called Sanderson up.

'Get the doctor at once.'

So the doctor came.

'Diphtheria!'

'But – we had you two days ago.'

' Yes.'

'But how?'

'It's rampant in the town.'

Sanderson was pale.

'We'll pull the boy through,' said the doctor. 'He's only a little chap, though. But you have everything to get him well, yes, let me see – .'

'A couple of nurses,' yelled Sanderson after him, as he went through the hall.

'Right you are,' said the doctor.

Hester came down.

She and Sanderson stared at each other.

'If Stephen dies, Sandy, you've killed him,' she said.

'Woman!' yelled Sanderson.

She smiled.

'It came from those drains which were made right too late – you were too busy building up your business. And now it's travelled here. There is death in commercialism, Sandy – Death! Death! Death! Nothing but Death and Blood and Tears in it!'

'Mary!' said Sanderson, suddenly. 'She's been crying several times this past week. She's been where it is! She's looked – guilty, too.'

'She has to earn her living,' Hester told him.

'Where's Ann?'

'I've moved her out of the room – but they were playing together.'

'She'll not take it. She's strong. Cheer up.'

Then Mary came in.

There was a terrible scene.

'I-I daren't tell you – my sister – she buried one last week. That w-was w-why I wanted to g-g-go out to-night.'

'You can get out of here altogether,' yelled Sanderson. 'Get out – or I'll throw your stuff into the street. I feed you – house you – and you carry disease into my home. If my child dies, you're a murderess!'

She began to sob again.

'I'd have laid down my life for Master Stephen, but, Oh! don't say I've hurt him – !'

'Why didn't you tell us? We'd have given you your damned wages?'

Hester laid a hand on Mary's shaking shoulders.

'*You* are not to blame, Mary. Don't cry. I'll send word with Bessie how he is going on.'

'Yes, ma'am.'

Fifteen minutes later she went out.

Hester followed her to the door.

'Don't fret, Mary. Don't fret. I'll see you get another place. Good-night, Mary.'

'Good-night, ma'am.'

Hester watched her go – still with bent head – still shaking with sobs.

Sanderson was walking about in the room where Stephen lay – caught in the net. She felt sorry for him, but her mind was quite clear, resolute, and strangely calm.

'Don't you get it,' cried Sanderson.

'Oh, I shan't take it.'

'Let the nurses – .'

She looked at him, working-class motherhood stamped on her face.

'I shall nurse my own child,' she told him. Even then she remembered that most working-class mothers could not nurse their children – save in their *spare* time.

'What's that?' Steve asked.

'Only a train.'

'The 9-30 train,' said Sanderson. 'Now we shall see! Now we shall see!'

CHAPTER 19

THE blackleg train came in, and then, in the words of Rachel, who was there to meet it, the fun began. The blacklegs, poor scourings of humanity, trying to look unmoved by the greeting they received, struggled through the gates, handing in their single tickets with palsied hands. Cringing visibly, half-starved, defeated wreckage of industrialism, they made a tragic, pathetic procession through the shouting crowds. *Scabs!* Yes. Scabs! The sores and the wounds of Industrialism – festering, stinking wounds – corruptions of class virility, class courage, and class honour, so hideous to behold in their lost *morale* that even O'Neill, who was there, with others to protect them, gave one look and then no more. It was not their rags – some of the strikers were almost as ragged – it was the pathetic, slouching gait, the hopeless cringing, the visible symbol of humanity turned traitor to its kind – for bread, just for bread. Where they had come from, none knew. Where they would drift to afterwards, none cared or knew. Somewhere amid the garbage and grime. And yet they were no worse than many who walked clothed in honour and acclaimed. After all, they were only the poor pawns – useful for a time – to be pushed off the board when finished with. It was an object lesson against the revolutionary theory that hunger, carried to extremes, will breed heroes, and not beasts, beasts who can see no further than the animal – needing bread. Down in some underpaid, unorganised circle of slavery, they had been bred. They came now to break an organised strike, police-guarded through a crowd which was an angry crowd, but not a mob.

Children sat on the wall by the railway – one eye on the policeman – ready to fling stones. Pickets wandered about, mist-shrouded figures of control and resolution, warning against violence. Through the crowded streets the blacklegs walked, with bent heads, guarded by the police. Down the roads also marched the pickets. There were banners flying, illumined by torches.

'*More Pickets Wanted.*'

Boos and hisses – defiant songs, shouts for Baines – hoots and cries against Dawson, Sanderson and the others! This was Capitalism – fighting to keep its five per cent.! This was Labour, who created all, demanding five per cent.! And jostled in the crowd, standing with bent head as the blacklegs went by, was Bob Stiner, a little more disreputable, a little more broken – watching with eyes at once more tender and more fierce – the reviled procession of the damned.

'Nay, lass!' he protested, and caught the hand of a young woman, raised – with a stone.

She looked at him by the light of a passing torch. It lit up the tender remonstrance on Stiner's face – the noble, outraged look on her own.

'Don't stone thy own, mate – Jesus Christ! Don't stone 'em. Hell-fire. Look at 'em! Haven't they been stoned enough? If tha wants to throw a stone, hit a bobby!'

It was another sort of scorn – another sort of courage.

'I could tear 'em limb from limb,' she told him. 'I could tear 'em limb from limb – with my own hands. Scum o' th' earth, they are.'

'Ay. But they're our own scum. Not the scum that comes to the top!'

'Our boss's order lies a-mouldering on the shelf,
Our boss's order lies a-mouldering on the shelf,
Our boss's order lies a-mouldering on the shelf,
And we're not downhearted. *No.*'

And Stiner – Stiner was singing also, with bent head, his cap off. Well – not his cap. Another chap had pinched that, and left him this, a 'mile too big for him.' He was singing the words of Morris – with the dream in his heart, glad to be in this skirmish, but knowing it was only a skirmish.

'Whither come they and whence go they?
What is this of which they tell?
In what country are they dwelling,
'Twixt the gates of heaven and hell?
Are they thine or mine for money?
Will they serve a master well?

And the Host – comes marching on.'[84]

When the crowd moved, Stiner moved too, following, following, the old battle-surge in his heart, the one pure passion thrilling him, his blood no longer young and jubilant – but red – red still. He heard someone whistling beside him and peered at her.

'Rachel! By God!' he exclaimed.

'Bob Stiner!'

'Bob Stiner – that's my name,' he admitted.

'Getting to a finish, now,' she told him, staccato fashion.

'Ay. We'll be licked as usual.'

Click-clack! Click-clack! Thousands of clogs, thousands, singing the old tune. Stephen's Feet, marching on. Sanderson's slaves, marching on. The singers of Hester's doggerel bulletins – marching on – to the old impasse.

'How many blacklegs, Rachel?'

Click-clack! Click-clack!

'Oh, about a hundred, I counted.'

'Where the hell will they sleep 'em?'

'Not on their drawing-room floors!'

'No – by God!'

'If this was for Freedom, Stiner!'

'Cheer up.'

'I'm not downhearted – .'

'No, I know tha'rt not.'

Click-clack! Click-etty-clicketty – clack!

'Living with my old girl, aren't ta?'

'Ay.'

'Any chances?'

'Don't think so.'

'Not if I flashed twenty golden sovereigns before her eyes?'

'I don't know.'

'Think it worth while trying?'

'Everything's worth while trying.'

Jumbling on with the crowd she grabbed at Stiner's hand, holding it in her own strong, masterful clasp.

'Never say die,' she told him.

'No, never say die,' echoed Stiner.

The tears sprung to his eyes. An outcast, a doss-house dweller, a drunken fool, a philosopher, a writer of class-challenges on flagstones, sand and snow – that quick, warm-hearted grip had shaken him. He wanted to say something in return for that comradely snatch at his hand, but had no words. He had no words. It was the Fellowship Socialist propaganda had created, the Fellowship of comrades, who, though they now abide under Capitalism, shall shatter it at last, stretching their hands down to the most wretched, recognising nothing but Class Honour, Class Unity, and Class Organisation, and bringing this Trinity to beat at last, with unscarred hands, with mailed fists, on the brass gates whereon is written, 'Ye may not enter.'

'I heard somebody say we had to march up the main road,' Stiner said.

'Well, the police have evidently had their order changed,' Rachel told him. She was bare-headed.

Her voice was very restrained.

'Damn their eyes!'

'They're marching us up past the slaughter-houses,' she told him. 'And there isn't a kick!'

He realised that she was almost sobbing.

'Keep thy wool on, Rachel. Don't let 'em get thee again. I heard about thee finishing thy education in gaol. By God! I did get drunk that night.'

'Oh – I'll keep my wool on,' she told him. 'Shut up. What's that they're singing.'

Away at the head of the procession, orderly even in its chaos, words were travelling along the ranks, and being taken up along the line. Nearer and nearer they came, louder and louder they swelled. It mixed in with the beat of the Feet, and above them. It was the latest bulletin.

'By God! He'll kill her!' Stiner thought he heard Rachel murmur. Then she was listening – her lips moving – and then her strong voice rang out:

'They're bringing the militia – if we don't mind what we do,
They're bringing the militia – if we don't mind what we do,
They're bringing the militia – if we don't mind what we do,

If we don't mind what we do – do – do.'

'Glory, glory hallelujah,
Glory, glory, hallelujah,
Glory, glory, hallelujah,
We are picketing to-night.'

'By God! Rachel!'

'Brute force against constitutionalism,' she told him. 'It only shows itself at times like these – but it's always there.'

'I'm fain I came – though I don't think I've the courage to kill a beetle – at bottom!'

Clicketty-clack! Clicketty-clack! Clicketty-clicketty.

Then the procession at the head halted. They heard O'Neill shouting out his orders.

'All we like sheep – have gone astray,' muttered Rachel.

'Clear the way – clear the way,' called O'Neill.

The crowd lined up, on each side of the road. Feet started stamping to the tune, they were singing about the militia. Empty-stomached, most of them – clogs that had gone a size too large, lately – on the stamping feet. Stiner took his cap off. It was a battle for five per cent.! But – they had guts – his class had guts!

'What is it?' he whispered to Rachel.

'I don't know.'

Then they saw the rival torches and the first forms loomed up out of the mist. The music rose, stirring, the music of tradition, the music of the faith, the old Faith, the faith of the Fathers. It was the procession of the priests and their supporters. There had been a conference. The procession moved slowly, in orderly fashion, along the route between the people. Many caps were removed. Stiner put his on again. He glanced at Rachel. Her face was interesting in its pale scorn and utter contempt. Then he saw her listening. Out of the crowd new words were ringing – surging.

'God! They're singing with the bloody priests!'

'Shut up!' she told him tersely.

She was listening.

Challenging words were rising, rising – to the old tune. What though they set themselves to the music of common mouth-organs? What though they were a little incoherent – the crowd picking them up from mouth to mouth? At last they rang out, clear, distinct – a denial and a challenge – with a little jostling here and there, a few voices raised in conflict, a few caps off, a few faces dogged – unable to deny the faith of tradition, prisoners in its bonds.

'Faith of our children, happy Faith,
We will be true to thee, till death.
Faith of our children, happy Faith,
We will be true to thee – till Death.
What though the skies be blackening o'er us,
What though the road runs red before us?
Faith of our children, happy Faith –
We will – be true – to thee – till Death.'

'The road that runs to Greed and Power,
Doth ever run to deepest hells.
We march where morning light shall shower,
Where Reason, Truth, and Freedom dwells.
What though in Faith you clothe oppression,
What though you march in long procession?
Faith of our children, shining Faith –
At last – at last – shall break your spells.'

They passed – they passed – the Shadows of old heathen power, old heathen worship, in its modern guise. They passed – but their ghosts remained, in the hearts of those who could not break their bonds, their bonds of fear and faith.

Then the split procession of workers moved on again to see where the blacklegs were to be lodged. A shout went up of derision. They were lodging the scabs at the doss-house. They were lodging their strike-breakers at Melrose *Mansions*. They entered by the low door, with its red lamp whereon was written, 'Beds. Men Only.' For ten minutes the crowd serenaded them, then quietly dispersed to their wretched homes.

'Rachel!'

Baines came to her, as she stood talking with Stiner.

'Ay.'

'I'll see thee home,' Jack told her.

'Na, then – .'

Stiner was chaffing, looking from one to the other.

Love! Didn't know much about it himself. Never much romance about Matty, anyhow. Happen working-class existence did not foster it. Still – never say die. Never say die.

'It'll happen be safer,' Jack said.

'Ay. Put it that way,' joked Stiner, slyly.

Rachel stared at them both.

She looked pale in the light from the street-lamp.

'Shut your silly mouths,' she told them, and swung round on her heel.

Baines stared after her in bewilderment. What had he said, anyhow?

Then he slapped Stiner on the back.

'I'm going,' he said. 'She's too irresponsible to be left on her own. She might knock a policeman's hat off.'

'Here!' called Stiner.

'Spit it out,' Jack told him. He was looking after the valiant, lonely, diminishing figure.

Stiner spat it out.

'If that lass isn't in love with thee, I'll eat my shirt – lice and all!' Stiner said. 'Without boiling, too. I will. I'll eat my shirt!'

Jack stared at him.

'Tha'rt too sentimental, Stiner,' he said brusquely. 'The whole movement's too sentimental. *Rachel* – in love with me.'

'Well, I might be mistaken. You never know women. You're surer of dogs. Particular – mongrel dogs.'

Jack stood staring at Stiner.

Then he laughed.

Silly fudge it was! Rachel in love with anyone!

'Where are ta sleeping?' he asked of Stiner.

'In there – .'

Stiner jerked his thumb towards the doss-house door.

'With the scabs?'

'Ay.'

'Come up an' sleep at our house – .'

Stiner shook his head slowly. He started whistling.

'He was despised – rejected – ' then winked one eye, tapped his nose mysteriously and said gravely:

'I've twenty pounds in my pocket. Twenty pounds. Matty can go to hell. I'm going to do my duty. And we'll start with a gallon jug – a flagon[85] of the good-nut-brown – a beaker of Flora, as old Keats had it.[86] Ta-ta! Be good! God's in His heaven. All's right with the world. *Never say die.*'

Jack watched him through the low doorway. Then he ran up the street after Rachel, noticing as he went the policemen guarding the doss-house. *Rachel!* But no. Stiner had always been a sentimental fool. Anyhow, they would both be on picket duty to-night and in the morning. *Rachel.* It was staggering if it was true. After all – why shouldn't he – ? Why? For no reason at all – only the memory of a frail one, who had sold her soul for a mess of pottage – the memory of a kiss, part of Youth's ethereal frailty, so easily smashed, so wonderful, so delicate, so blossom-scented – drifting down the dead years, on a faint, sighing, changing wind. The distance between himself and Rachel lessened. He noticed the plain-clothes policemen. H'm! They wanted trouble – they wanted it. It was part of the game. And it was his duty to prevent it – that futile violence which would pour workers' blood on their own heads. The bosses were playing their last trump card. If that failed – .

They would have to give in.

For Brayton was losing its trade to adjacent towns who were booking orders for Indian goods. A cut-throat system. Oh, to have been born when the murderous scheme of things was shattered! He was dead-tired for sleep, but there was a chance that the bosses would get the blacklegs into the mill before morning, so they must be outside the mill, too, and try to persuade them not to go in.

Poor Stiner! Going to try to corrupt the blacklegs with the twenty quid it had taken him two years to save, going through the tortures of the damned – quite sober, fighting demons of thirst for two years. Somehow he wished Stiner had stayed out of it. A drunken beggar – Stiner – but, drunk or sober, never deluded by boss-logic and knowing class psychology from A to Z. What could Stiner not have done? Of course, he'd done a bit, in his own way. He caught up to Rachel.

'Another over there,' she told him, *sotto voce.*

'H'm.'

They walked on through the shadows.

'I'm going to have my supper with Matty,' he told her. 'Then we can go together.'

'All right.'

'Had I better fetch some chips?

'Ay. Tha'll ha' to go down Anne Street. The other's shut up. The strike's broken it. Wait a minute. I'll bring thee the bowl.'

'Have they come?' asked Matty.

'The blacklegs? Ay!'

'Well, I'm going picketing, too.'

They stared at her.

'She talks for the boss one minute, and then the next for the folk,' gibed Rachel.

'Why shouldn't I go?' she demanded.

'Well, we want plenty,' Baines told her.

'She'll rue afore morning,' Rachel said candidly. 'She gets mixed. It's through reading newspapers in her spare time.'

'Thee shut up. I'm going picketing,' Matty told them, grimly. 'I'm going. She's too much off, she has.' For Rachel was laughing.

'Happen you'll see your loving husband,' Rachel teased her.

'What! Is th' old soldier back?'

Baines nodded.

'Ay. The old soldier's back, Matty. He's joined up with the scabs.'

For a lightning second something stole into Matty's eyes.

'Nay,' she said shortly. 'God in heaven would never make me believe that a' him. He isn't as bad as *that.*'

Baines laughed heartily

'No. We were just plaguing you, Matty,' he told her. 'There's a bit o' love yet, Rachel. I think she'll take him back. Don't blush, Matty.'

'I'll take the long brush to thee – if tha tells me I've blushed,' she answered him.

'An' he's saved twenty pounds,' added Rachel.

'An' I'll not believe that, either,' she told them.

'Well, it's true,' said Rachel.

'Stiner!'

'Your Bob,' teased Jack. 'When a man'll go sober two years, living in doss-houses, and save twenty pounds to get back home, I think he's worked out all the Purgatory he needs to work out. Come, Matty. What has he done – that you should shut your door on him?'

'It's what he hasn't done,' she snapped. 'Allus losing his work and goin' on the rant. Never much above kept himself.'

'A working man can do little above keep himself,' Baines told her. 'That's not his fault, Matty.'

'He doesn't need to waste aught,' she snapped.

'Drink doesn't cause poverty, Matty. You know that.'

'It makes it worse,' said Matty, bitterly.

'I'll grant that,' Baines agreed.

'But it helps to keep folk out o' lunatic asylums,' Rachel told them. 'It gives 'em, from time to time, an illusion that all's well. Like religion.'

'An' – wedding,' suggested Matty.

'H'm,' agreed Rachel.

'Well – what are we going to have to eat? There's naught but loaf-pie (bread)' – Matty told them. 'An' I shouldn't ha' had that but for slutting round at a pig-killing.'

'I'll fetch some chips,' Jack said.

'Here, I'll go,' said Matty, quietly. 'They'll keep warmer under my shawl.'

So she went, with one malicious, sly glance at Rachel, which said she had got her own back. Rachel sat down, on the fender, the fireglow lighting up her strong, striking face. She was reading a scrap of newspaper. They could hear the 'younger end' of Matty's family fighting on the beds, upstairs.

'Thee give up!'

'Not I. Thee give up!'

'Wilta give in?'

'Will I thump.'

'I'm the boss – wilta give in?'

'No – I'll not.'

Rachel jumped up, ran to the foot of the stairs.

There was laughter in her face, in her eyes.

'Ben!' she yelled up the stairs.

'What?' came down, pantingly.

'If tha lets the "boss" lick thee – I'll lick thee myself.'

She came back, to the old seat on the fender. Bump! A loud yell. She ran upstairs. Ben came down with her, bleeding at the nose, but triumphant, and trying not to sniff.

'Get the door key,' she commanded Jack.

'Knocked him out, I did,' said Ben. 'Where's my mother?'

'Gone for some chips.'

'Put it down his back – .'

So they put the key down the curly-headed one's back. He sat on Rachel's knee, looking at her with wondering, adoring eyes. Something of the same look stole into Jack's. But Stiner was such a fool!

'Can I stay up and have some?' asked Ben.

'Tha can stop till thy mother comes and ax her,' Rachel told him.

'He'll happen get cold,' suggested Baines.

'Not he. He's as hard as nails,' Rachel denied. Ben, as hard as nails, and as soft as butter was cuddling Rachel's fingers in his somewhat grimy paws.

'Why don't you wear a ring – like mother?' he asked.

'Because I've more sense,' Rachel told him. 'Keep still. And shut up, or I'll take thee upstairs.'

Then they heard Stiner's knock.

Jack let him in. He could smell Stiner's breath – .

'This is my castle, isn't it?' he asked. 'Where's the old girl?'

'Gone for some chips,' Rachel told him.

'Get out before she comes,' Baines told him.

'Don't let her see tha's broken down. We've done all we can for thee.'

Then they heard the backyard gate – Matty's clogs.

'Tha'll get back if tha'll keep off John Barleycorn,' he said. 'Get out. We're doing all we can.'

'Here –'

Stiner pushed something at Jack, guiltily.

'I found that in the lining o' my pocket. I'm sorry – it had come open. I couldn't help seeing what were written. That made me get drunk. I'm sorry, Baines. Hester Martin gave it me – I forgot it. What the hell does anyone want to turn me into Cupid's messenger for? I'm sorry, Baines.

Tha can kick me if tha likes – .'

Baines came under the lamp and read it.

Faded – blotted – the words danced under his eyes. It was very brief, that undelivered message from the dead years.

'Please do not go. I will marry you – without a penny. Please do not leave me behind.

HESTER.'

Stiner gave one look at Jack's face as he raised his head – and ran. When he looked round, Baines had gone in.

'The moving finger writes,' grumbled Stiner. 'And that inverted bowl – to hell with it. Impotently – as thou – or I – .'

He was still mumbling about the vine, when he passed O'Neill. O'Neill recognised him. Stiner harked back to boyhood. He put his thumb to his nose – and did not run!

CHAPTER 20

STEPHEN was dying. All that could be done had been done. One frail hand lay in Hester's. Sanderson held the other. They did not look at each other. There was utter silence within the room, save for the flicker of the fire. An efficient nurse, an intruder on the scene, stood near. The safety lamps with their gay pictures of dancing bears, cats and frogs, were lit. The darkness had fallen soon this afternoon. The strikers had marched past the house half-an-hour ago, but their feet had not sounded on the turf which had been strewn before the house. They had not sung. The door-knocker was muffled. They had not sung. The poor, even in their famine, and desperate despair, do not war on children. The Great Uncultured, Great Unwashed, have their own unwritten laws of chivalry. In their shoddy rags, from their wrecked homes, they had marched, and, as they passed the house where the boss's kid lay dying they were silent – though their own children were famishing.

'There's a change, Hester,' Sanderson said.

'I know.'

'We've done all we can.'

'Yes.'

'He's suffering – horribly.'

'Yes.'

'Should I ring up the doctor?'

'No. All has been done.'

Stephen stirred.

'Will it soon be morning, Hester?'

'Yes, darling.'

Then he jabbered something incoherent – something about Feet.

The new maid came creeping upstairs.

'Father Galton has come, Sir,' she told Sanderson.

The marble-white figure on the right of Stephen did not move.

But – it spoke.

'Tell him he's come to the wrong house, Fanny.'

'But, m'dear – Dawson – hang it! – the churches aren't *so* far removed.'

Hester realised the position. Dawson was going to help Sandy up again, on certain conditions. She had no emotions. They were cold, dying, dying, like Stephen – slain by the same things. It had all become curiously impersonal and remote, this struggle, something with which she as an individual had nothing to do. Yet, curiously enough, she knew that she could not possibly let the old man waiting in the hall give sacrament to Stephen.

'I'll go down.'

'No, m'dear. I'll go.'

But Hester was half-way down the stairs. Father Galton was waiting. The hall-light shone on his face, its refined, ascetic nobility. As an individual, Father Galton was – like Sandy – human. In the things he stood for, and held, he was unprogressive and inhuman.

'You have come to give Stephen sacrament?' she asked.

He bent his head.

'He has been killed by the spread of disease from the poor quarters of the town. You cannot set frontiers in the air,' she told him. 'And now, you are coming to change bread and wine into the flesh and blood of Christ, who was an agitator if He lived at all, who was an agitator against the oppression of the rich against the poor. So it is all hypocrisy, your miracle, and a symbol of cannibalism. I cannot permit you to administer what you call sacrament, and what I call a burning lie and an ignoble sham, over the body of my child.'

She stood a moment.

Her frailness, her pallor, the lack of emotion in her voice, was suggestive of a corpse speaking. Only in her eyes was the haunting, tortured expression of life, life deprived of all it had been meant to be, but still with something, some spark, yet alive and glowing under the poor clay.

'You are suffering, poor child,' said the old priest.

She smiled wanly.

'People who think and feel must always suffer in a society like this,' she told him.

'Even as He suffered,' said the priest.

'For trying to break corrupt traditions,' she reminded him. 'Corrupt traditions which will only break when the peoples realise that they must save themselves, that none can atone for our omissions. That as individuals, and as a mass we must break our own bonds. I am not brave. I never was very brave. But so far, at least, I am resolute. My child, who dies unsmirched in mind by this rotten social order, needs no "sacrament." Let priests, and those who support Power, say it for themselves, for the token of cannibalism belongs to them by right, since they and those they support feed eternally on the broken bodies of the poor, on the agitators whom they starve and madden, on the artists they murder, on the childhood they break on the wheels of iron, on the poor, broken shards that were men, left on Battlefields, broken as Christ was broken – and by the same Powers! It is a lie! A lie! An eternal lie! Your religion is a lie! Two thousand years! Two thousand years! And all it has achieved has been to keep the poor – the poor – in their places, under the feet of the rich. No. You must go. And go quickly. This house is dark enough, dark and sad and terrible enough, without the shadow of a priest on it. Go! Please go! He is not conscious but if he were your black robes would frighten him, and his mother's arms are the sweetest heaven he has known. Go quickly.'

Her voice was rising, quivering, pulsing now, as though that spark unquenchable was shooting it through with fire. Her eyes burned and blazed out of the whiteness of her face. It was the apathy of the crushed, the bruised, the broken – roused at last.

'I am going,' the priest told her, in his calm, gentle voice. 'I wish I could help you.'

Her laughter, strained and weary, floated after him.

'You can help the People by taking your shadows from their path,' she called. 'You are an integral part of the Church, and wear its bonds in your faith – your faith in the salvation that is for the few. I would rather burn in hell than live in heaven with the Many shut out. You carry your gospel of salvation for a few here, over into the Beyond. For the many must burn there, as they starve here. Your conceptions are a mockery for the Many.'

'Hester! Are you mad?' asked Sanderson, in a low breath. He had come down, amazed.

'No. Sane. Sane at last,' she answered. 'Sane at last.'

The door closed behind Father Galton.

'Think of your child,' he told her.

'I am thinking of all children – all!' she said. 'And men and women, broken and bleeding and deluded – by men like that! Men who claim to be the anointed of God, chloroforming the poor, in the miseries man has made.'

Then she rushed past him and upstairs.

She turned into the silent, marble figure again, leaning over the cot where lay the child. Social degeneracy had sent him into the world crippled in body – and now had finally slain him, even as Mary's sister's baby had been slain. There was no mutual interests between the classes. But the diseases of unhygienic poverty at least could leap, like avenging angels, even where hygiene was. It was Natural Law, rising triumphant above unnatural law, which made of one section of society flesh and of the other fowl.

'Shall I raise him up?'

She appealed to the nurse.

'I'm afraid – he is going, Mrs. Sanderson.'

The heavy silence grew.

Sanderson came up and went down again – then up again – then back to the whisky and soda. Stephen. Sanderson and Son. A dream had broken. Sanderson and Son! Good God! Why had he not attended to those drains? But – Good God! It was all Mary's fault. To carry it into his house, his house. Sanderson and Son! The Indian order. Smashed! If the fools did not go in. And now – Stephen, Stephen who could tell his own father the meaning of words, and ask him questions he could not answer. Another glass. A curse on them, and their five per cents. But the blacklegs would be in on the morrow and Tim would drive the engine like hell!

And Hester – Hester would relent when she saw his interests were bound up in Dawson. Just as she had gone to church with him, against her convictions, she would go to the other church with him. She was very docile. Hypocrisy she called it. But she went. What about churches, anyhow? All alike. One worshipped pictures – the other dolls. But it helped you in business. Yes. Of course, she'd go. He would go up and see Stephen. Terrible to stand helpless and see Stephen suffer like that – *his* child. Mary ought to be smothered. He poured out another glass, with trembling hand. Sanderson and Son! Well, Hester was young.

Pity working-class women could not suffer for those with the money. Couldn't buy that – of course.

The nurse came down.

'Well?'

'He won't last long.'

'No.'

Upstairs Hester stood, still staring down.

Stephen's hand fumbled after something and met hers.

'The Feet – where are they going?' he moaned.

'Into the morning.'

'Where it's all white and shiny, Hessie!'

'Where it's all white and beautiful, and full of Spring, Steve.'

'I can't see you, Hessie.'

'No. It's night, now. It will soon be morning.'

'Am I going with them?'

'I think you will reach them, Stephen – they will hold your hand.'

'They won't – leave me, Hessie? I can't go fast.'

'No, darling, they'll never leave you. They go slow – with those who go slow.'

'Play, Hessie, on your fiddle, and we'll go down the cornfields, like you said, you know, if we had lived in Nowhere like Morry told about – you know – you said – down the paths, in the Spring, Hessie, me a fairy, and you making laughing music. Play, Hessie.'

She went down and took up the fiddle.

The sounds were funereal in her own ears. It was a little laughing melody clear as joy and the sun. Mozart had written it – Mozart who sometimes starved.

'Just you and me, Hessie – eh?'

'Just you and me.'

She played on, and on, watching his face. It was changing. The nostrils were growing pinched. The shadows were creeping into his face, the shadows of death.

'Hold me – tight.'

She laid the fiddle down.

His hands fumbled at her throat, over her face.

'When – it – is – Spring – Hessie,' he said. 'And – the – corn.'

Then he began to gasp.

It was very terrible.

'Tight,' he gasped.

She pressed him close to her.

His head fell forwards.

He gasped something incoherent and his fingers relaxed their grip of her hand.

Stephen was dead.

She had thought she could bear it. She had borne so much, so much.

'No – no –' they heard her shout. 'Let me have him back.'

'M'dear,' said Sanderson, when he got up.

'He's gone,' said the nurse. 'And – oh, Mr. Sanderson, ring up the doctor quick. Your wife – it's – haemorrhage.'

Stiner was trying to chant the Marseillaise[87] and to cook eggs and bacon at the same time. He emphatically denied that he was drunk, even though the pan got ablaze, and an egg slid into the doss-house fire. Anyhow, they were only Chinese eggs.

'Marchons! Marchons!' he roared.

Bill Hayes, the doss-house keeper, asked him not to make a bigger fool of himself than he could help.

'Every wise man is a fool,' Stiner told him, standing pan in hand. 'Come on, lads. Fill yourselves. Eat, drink, and be merry – for to-morrow we die. Come up.'

They shuffled chairs and stools up to the table. Stiner splashed the pint pots full from the gallon jug.

'Here, Stiner – I want thee,' called Bill Hayes. 'How does ta want this meat cooking?'

Stiner stumbled into the back-hole. Hayes shut the door.

'Tha'rt wasting thy brass for naught, old sport,' observed the doss-house keeper. 'Tha's spent a quarter o' thy fortune, now, I'll bet, and there's only six of 'em laid out, yet.'

Stiner winked.

'They'll noan go in the morning,' he said. 'Their heads will be too thick, an' they'll be sick as bow-wows. For they've only been supping the dregs o' pint pots for a weary while. There'll be eighty looms less running in morning. Who says I'm not picketing? Jesus Christ! If we could only get some wagonettes and take 'em back where they came from – I'd die happy.'

'Can't be done,' Hayes told him.

He was strangely moved, this doss-house keeper, standing with the 'waistcoat backs,' otherwise 'picking hands,' otherwise meat at threepence a pound, extended on his hands, waiting for directions how to cook it.

'No; well, we'll do the best we can. If they don't go to work, and can't pay for their beds – how then?'

'Out they go,' Bill told him.

'It's hard lines on 'em,' said Stiner. 'But there's going to be small hell in this town if they don't go soon. What's the game, Bill? Heard anything?'

'The bosses has something up their sleeves – but news isn't leaking as it did.'

'No,' said Stiner.

He stared at the meat, muttered something about blue murder, and staggered into the kitchen, shouting and maudlin. All through the night, whilst a moon like a curved, shining razor shone down on streets cold and dry as white bones, they made merry in the doss-house. They sang 'Home, Sweet Home,' in weary maudlin discord – these 'scum of the earth,' sitting in an atmosphere reeking with kipper-smoke, cheap ale, and the stench of the burnt potatoes to which Stiner had forgotten to attend.

Outside, the policemen kept guard over them, protecting those whom they had, in other days, moved on or summoned for having 'no fixed abode.' They were sacred at last. They were helping Capital to break a little skirmish of Labour's.

'Let's get this upstairs,' Hayes would say, and they would half-carry, half-drag another man up, Stiner groaning the while.

And at last all went to bed.

Stiner and Hayes manipulated the alarm-clocks.

'What is time?' asked Stiner, philosophically, and they pushed the fingers back three hours. Then he went to his bed, his lousy bed, itching and hunting for a while, and then giving up in despair.

'With the half of a broken hope for a pillow at night,' quoted the old soldier. 'With the half of a broken hope for a pillow at night – ,' and, quoting Stevenson,[88] Stiner fell asleep.

He awoke in the early morning to a chorus of groaning which came out of the cold darkness like the lament of outcast souls. Dim shapes, almost nude, writhed about – awakening, awakening to a day which held for them no hope. Rose-flush of dawn on the hills of glory, on God's own hills, sacred to sheep and grouse – to animal life which yet came nearer to its ultimate perfection than the life in these broken bodies. The retching and vomiting of a man with morning catarrh sounded hideously in the long room. Some woke up with curses on their lips, curses against no one in particular and everyone in general.

'What the hell time is it?' said one man.

Nobody knew.

Not many cared.

'Tha's got my trousers,' yelled one scab.

'These are mine,' shouted the other.

Then they were at it – striking at each other. The others, leaping from their beds, naked, chattering with cold, talked, egging them on. Stiner crept downstairs. Bill was blowing the fire up, with a pair of wheezy bellows. They had forgotten to 'slack' it with water the night before. The light showed up the confusion of the great kitchen, where the chairs seemed to have been having an all night sitting of a stormy nature. A broken gallon jug lay in fragments.

'Half-past seven,' grunted Bill, with satisfaction. 'There'll be hell to play, Stiner.'

'Come to my funeral,' invited Stiner.

He leaned against the fireplace, blue with cold. Then they heard the feet of the first scab *bump-bump,* descending the stairs, bump-bump, left foot first every time.

'What the hell time is it?' he asked, entering the room.

Bill Hayes attended to the fire. Stiner said nothing. He was not a fighting man.

'Where's the bloody clock?' asked the scab.

Bill Hayes pointed.

'Half-past seven!' he yelled. 'Lads! Lads! Half-past seven!'

A score of the scabs came rushing, half-dressed, down the staircase.

'How's this?' asked one, menacing.

'Clock got drunk an' all,' Bill told them.

'Well, come on! *We're going*,' asserted one.

Outside the police were waiting. They counted the men going out. Twenty! Then ten. Then five. Then three. They marched them together, a scarecrow remnant. Laughter and shouting arose from the streets. Outside the mill the pickets waited. The moon lingered clear and cold. They came out from the shadows.

'Don't go in,' said Rachel. 'Think what you are doing. Don't go in. Don't be skunks. Be men. Don't go in.'

With bent heads and an attempt at jeering they went in.

She caught one man by his torn, ragged sleeve.

'Don't go in, mate. We're starving, too. Better to starve than be a traitor. We've almost won. Don't go in.'

He hesitated – cursing, asking her to let go of him.

'Don't go in – .'

He tried to shake himself free.

'What do we get if we don't go in?'

She released him.

'We shall think of you, always, as a pal – .'

'Let go,' he almost whined.

But she went on talking to him.

With an oath, he swung himself free at last, took a few steps towards the mill, hesitated, stood still, then turned round and walked out through the gates. He turned round once, and saw Rachel, saluted, and crept away, a shadow among the shadows, returning to the hell from which he had come.

'There's only a handful of them, this morning,' said Baines to Rachel. 'How's Hester?'

'I went up last night. He wouldn't let me in. But the slavey said it was a question of quietness – and she'd probably take a turn in a day or two.'

Baines stared at Rachel.

Then Rachel rushed away, to argue and plead with another scab.

'Not worth setting the right engine on for,' Rachel told Baines, later. 'They're running with the donkey-engine.'

'Is your mother looking after her?' asked Baines.

'Catch my mother leaving her!' said Rachel.

Then they walked over to the other pickets. Matty was there, in clogs and shawl, stamping her feet to warm them. The small crowd in the street began to 'boo.'

'Sanderson!'

He dodged through the gates, followed by hooting, went down into the engine-house and gave instructions to Tim, the engine-driver.

'Now's my chance,' said Rachel to Baines. 'See if I don't get to see my sister! I'll leave thee to picket for two.'

She was off, a flying figure, making for the house. She could hear the new maid singing 'When There's Love at Home.' She knocked at the door, tried it, and finding it unfastened, walked in, right in, to the kitchen, where her mother almost let the saucepan fall.

'Eh, Rachel! He said tha'd not to come in,' gasped Mrs. Martin.

'Well – I'm in. How's our Hester?'

'Eh, Rachel!'

Mrs. Martin turned a sad, worn face.

'And I want to see Steve, too. Both of 'em.'

'Tha mun be quiet, Rachel,' her mother told her. 'She nearly bled to death. Tha morn't upset her. Quietness, no excitement, an' she may pull through, though it may come on again. Still – she's every chance – if Sanderson pulls this order through.'

She faced her daughter, eyeing her narrowly.

'He thinks she's told thee things – and that's how the news has leaked,' she said.

'Let him think,' retorted Rachel, scornfully.

'Well – it's queer how things has got out.'

'Well, happen it's me,' said Rachel. 'Happen it isn't. Which room is she in?'

'The pink room.'

Rachel took off her clogs and left them on the mat at the foot of the stairs.

She crept into the room.

Hester was asleep. Rachel stooped over her. One transparent hand was flung out over the satin quilt. Her cheeks appeared to have sunk. There were dark shadows under her eyes. Was she breathing? Rachel turned cold with dread! She bent lower. Her foot slipped, and she clutched at the bed rails to save herself. Hester started up in bed – sat up like a resurrected corpse, with wide, staring eyes.

'Our Rachel!' murmured Hester.

Rachel laid her back on the pillows.

She surveyed Rachel, panting from sitting up.

'I wanted to see thee – and Steve,' Rachel told her.

She took Hester's hand and cuddled it between hers.

'He's in there.'

Hester's hand motioned to a room beyond, then dropped, listless.

Rachel stole into the room where Stephen lay in his coffin. She didn't stay long. How like Hessie he looked now – like Hessie was at the same age, going to school and sitting reciting 'Three Little Robins Sat on a Wall.' She wiped her eyes on her shawl, then re-entered the room.

'Where's Sandy?'

'Gone to the mill.'

'What have you been doing?'

'Picketing.'

There was a little silence. Curious that Hester said nothing of Stephen, said nothing at all. And how like her father Hester was now, with those hollows in her cheeks, and the feverish sparkle in her eyes.

'I wish I'd bin picketing,' came in a soft, low breath.

Rachel laughed.

But there was a moist, sweet light in her eyes.

'Thee lie still an' get better,' she said.

'I shall never get better,' Hester said.

'Eh. Tha morn't give up.'

'I've given up,' Hester told her. 'An' I'm glad – glad an' fain, Rachel, to be leaving it all.'

'Eh – don't talk like that,' Rachel told her throatily. 'Tha wants to get out o' this bed as soon as tha can. They die in bed. An' screw thyself together.'

Hester smiled languidly.

'I never had much brute courage,' she told Rachel. 'The best that could happen for me would be death. I've just been blown about, Rachel. I hadn't courage to stick it before and *dee,* and now I haven't the courage to stick it and live. I've learned such a lot, Rachel, but it will all die with me. I've passed from sordid slavery to refined slavery, from pillar to post, from individualism to mass-feeling, and now – I'm going. It seems just a bit of a pity, doesn't it?' She laughed weakly. Then she began to pant again, the clothes lifting with each breath.

'Don't let her talk, Rachel,' called Mrs. Martin, anxiously.

'No,' called Rachel.

'But I've such a lot to say,' said Hester. 'Sit down, Rachel.'

Rachel pulled up a chair and sat. The strong, warm hand, and the weak chill one were clasped.

'They were everything to me,' she continued.

She stopped, panting.

'Who?'

'The children, Rachel. They made up for everything. And I was glad at first, to think they'd be out of what we'd known. And then I watched Sandy, driving, an' exploiting, an' I knew my darling would be put in the same mould, and Ann – I saw how Ann would be made into a "lady," and perhaps patronise the poor – you know – nice and kind to them, an' all that – .'

Tears were running down Rachel's cheeks.

'They would be dehumanised, Rachel – as we were by hard labour – in another way.'

'Don't talk,' Rachel sobbed.

'And when my darling was going – I was almost glad. He went – so young and – beautiful. Dreaming – still – and then I wanted him back – and – how's the strike?'

She turned so sharply, so irrelevantly on Rachel that Rachel was startled.

'I can't get to the 'phone here,' she complained. 'Give me something to drink, Rach. I must attend to Sandy's business. Are they singing the songs still! Are they singing the songs?'

Rachel nodded.

'Don't tell Sandy,' she begged of Rachel. 'He'll kill me. Not that death matters. But one prefers not to be killed.'

'They are my songs,' she went on childishly. 'Why are you crying, Rachel?'

'I'll have to go,' said Rachel. 'I'm exciting thee.'

She stroked the hand that was burning now.

'I'm a spy, Rachel,' she confessed in a terrible whisper that froze Rachel's blood. 'A spy! I read all the documents and get the news to the people. In my own husband's house, when he feeds me, and shelters me – I'm a spy! I can't help it. After all, what has he given me? What has he given me – apart from the children?'

'Hester,' begged Rachel. 'Lie still.'

And Hester answered with a remark Bob Stiner once made – which had caught her fancy.

'We shall be a long time dead.'

Then she said in that same feverish, terrible whisper, glancing round as though the walls had ears.

'Don't tell Sandy. And go – go – go – or he'll be back.'

Then they heard the nurse coming upstairs.

'What's ta think about her?' asked Mrs. Martin.

'I don't know,' Rachel told her.

It was rare to hear Rachel say she did not know.

'Go – before *he* gets back,' Mrs. Martin warned her daughter.

'When's the burying?' asked Rachel.

'To-morrow.'

'Does she know?'

'She never axes.'

They regarded each other in bewilderment.

'Do you think she's going wrong in her head?' began Mrs. Martin.

'No,' Rachel told her, definitely. 'I don't. She's ill, an' she's plotting an' scheming – on the right side, an' all. Well, I'll go.'

She tossed her shawl around her, and went out with one long, lingering look of love at her mother. Mrs. Martin sat down and wept.

Half an hour later Sanderson came in.

They heard him at the 'phone.

He seemed brisker, more alert, and only drank one stiff glass of whisky. Mrs. Martin went back to her struggle with English, and the h's. Sanderson went upstairs.

'Don't worry, Hester,' he told his wife. 'We're winning. We're winning. They say they're going in at Dawson's place. Can't starve, m'dear. Can't starve! Now, don't get upset. Of course, m'dear – not actually starving. Can't starve actually. They'll either go in – or there'll be rough work within a week, and if *that* starts, its the end, for we know how to cow 'em. There, m'dear. Go to sleep. And don't worry. We'll get you up in the air of the Swiss Alps this summer. Don't worry, and go to sleep.'

He crept out of the room.

When Mrs. Martin went upstairs Hester was trying to sit up.

She, to whom food had never made a strong appeal, was asking to be fed.

'How long will I be before I can get up?' she beseeched the doctor.

'Now – now.'

'A week?' she begged.

'We'll see – .'

But he shook his head at the nurse.

CHAPTER 21

To STARVE quietly, unobtrusively, and without demonstration is, perhaps, the greatest art civilisation has forced on to the masses. It is the negation of all the instincts of primitive life and society. To pass by windows exhibiting the delicacies and luxuries of an age which has evolved culinary art into something almost impossible to analyse and to pass by with one's savage, primitive hunger controlled by the will to endure, is to give an example of the contradictions in a society where the strong still prey on the weak and the weak starve themselves to grapple with the strong. A society at once controlled and uncontrolled, civilised, and yet bestial as the life of the jungle. The limitations to the endurance of hunger are the limitations of will. The moment comes when the individual, or masses of individuals, grow desperate, civilisation breaks down, temporarily, and the primitive demand for food voices itself in action. The town of Brayton was passing through such a conflict. Could the lids of the stone-boxes wherein the workers lived have been lifted, and a reporting angel have given the bare details of the struggle to live in the thousands of homes – such bare facts would have been in themselves a book of miseries over which men and gods might have wept. Then – a boy in Theobald Street threw a stone which smashed a five-shilling pane in Dawson's glass-houses. A woman in Anne Street, maddened by the eternal crying of five children, 'stole' a pound of black puddings and a hunch of beef. These two 'breaches of the peace' (of that law and order which stands aloof, cold and emotionless, while thousands starve in the effort to assert their rights) were signs and tokens of the conflict raging in men and women. Will yet prevailed, enabling them to starve on passively. Another train-load of blacklegs had been greeted rather more vehemently. The police force was increased to prevent any rough work. They were now working in Sanderson's mill, with the remnants of those he first brought. Numbers gave them some sense of 'moral courage.' Tim was running the engine, according to Sanderson's instructions – 'like hell' – and those looms without blackleg weavers tending them clattered away also, to make the engine's desperate speed safer.

Sanderson himself, police-guarded, was much in evidence at the mill. The blacklegs, coming from a plain-goods town, had to be supervised whilst they wove in the fancy headings.

During these final days of the struggle, Sanderson was a strange combination of lunacy and sanity. He would rush to the mill, toss off his jacket, dash about the alleys, yelling orders into the ears of the blacklegs, stay as long as he could, and rush home to see how Hester was.

He was worried about Hester. Good God! Supposing she was ill years, a semi-invalid! Little Ann had gone to stay with his sister, until the diphtheria epidemic died down. And then – the Bombay order! To be or not to be. To go back, bankrupt, a failure, being a yarn agent when he had got his foot on the first rung of the ladder? That would be a tragedy Sanderson felt unable to face. Stephen had been laid away, and he had been followed to the grave, not by the 'Shadows' he had loved to watch, but by those who had bought and sold these 'Shadows,' gambling with their destinies in that great Hall of Chance, the Stock Exchange. Rachel, an uninvited guest, had watched the last rites of Stephen's burial, standing aloof, a desolate, dominant figure, her shawl blowing in the wet wind, the mud heavy on her clogs. She had watched Stephen buried, herself in the uniform of a striker. Sanderson had turned whiter with rage than he was with grief, to see her come, so attired.

Mrs. Martin, looking down on the tiny coffin in the grave, did not stand there without dark memories. Her husband, her mother, the little sister who had died at nine, entering the mill at seven, by the lie that she was eight – so many who had passed – poor, struggling, enduring – not altogether without joy in their lives, in spite of all – because the human heart is naturally brave and turns to the tiniest flame of sunshine. Now – it was Stephen – Stephen, whom Sanderson said was murdered by working-class ignorance, ignoring the fact that the disease had travelled from the neglected drains in his own property. She saw, as she tottered from the grave-side, choked and speechless – Rachel – aloof, and ignoring as she was ignored.

'Come on, mother,' urged Sanderson.

She stared into his face. It was difficult to read. He left the graveside like one who has lost – yet still clings to the shadow of an empty victory.

She threw an apologetic look at Rachel – Rachel cast out on suspicion of news-carrying – as they went past out of the churchyard. Rachel's smile, faint, proud and sad, came to her dimly through the dark afternoon. When they had all gone, Rachel went to the grave, and before it was filled, threw in what she had brought under her shawl – a little bunch of rosemary, and the woolly lamb she had kept at the Stiner's for Stephen to play with when he came on his rare visits. She noticed the increase of quietly dressed strangers in the town as she passed through the streets. What a black comedy it all was! Police! Soldiers! 'Tecs.! Priests! Newspapers financed to mutilate the truth. Ministers to preach pacificism to the poor, without demanding that the rich do not steal – workhouses jammed with men and women, beggars, weapon-makers, science scratching its brains for new ideas to destroy mankind, diseases which swept life away left half-examined because there was no money for research, political parties at each other's throats, advertisements of quack remedies, new religions in the birth, with the old ideas well preserved, and the occultism and fatalism of the East added!

All to preserve this state of disorder, robbery, indirect murder, and legislative fraud. What a comedy from the past to be played some time in a new age – in some new dawn of reason. But – wearisome to live in, and hard to laugh in – sometimes. Hardest of all to laugh in when one recalled – Hester. What business had Hester to be born in such an age? She did not think long of Hester. To think of her, scheming and planning to make known the moves of the masters, so that they could be checkmated, made her shudder, somehow. She thought of Sanderson, thwarted. No. It would not do to think about. Hester, who in a sane society would have been the gentle, dreaming artist, now become an intriguer, pitting her brain against commercial brains, pitting her gifts against those who bought and sold people, starved and crushed them, and considered them less than cattle.

She walked back 'home' to Stiner's house, with a feeling she rarely had – pessimism, the sense of futility, the sense of the great odds against the folk – and, for once, a sense of spiritual loneliness, and lack of fighting courage. As she opened the door, stumbling over the ragged mat, she heard Stiner's voice.

'Come in, Rachel! Come in, old girl. This is my castle, isn't it?'

And she knew that despite all she and Baines had done to present him as a knight in shining armour, a martyr, and a magnificent picket, he had undone their work. He had come to plead his own hopeless cause – and he had come – drunk.

When Rachel entered the Stiner kitchen, she found Stiner monarch of all he surveyed, and trying to sing 'The Heart Bowed Down.'[89] Failing hopelessly, he tried 'I Dreamt that I Dwelt'[90] – with scarf dangling, two buttons missing from his waistcoat, and a general air of dilapidation. Matty, at the table, was turning the five shillings Baines had given her that morning, into the 'staff' of life – and the multitude stood about her, watching the process. 'Bump-bump' went the tin, as she kneaded the dough, her romantic husband meanwhile making his second attempt at 'There is a Flower that Bloometh.'[91]

'She won't have me chucked at her,' said Stiner mournfully to Rachel. 'I wonder what tha'd have made of me, lass.'

'Either potted meat, or an archangel,' Rachel informed him shortly. She was angry with him for having undone all she and Baines had done to try to get him into harbour.

'By gum! Rachel's mad at me. It's time to hop it,' observed Stiner.

'Here, thee come back. If tha gets any more booze tha'll get into the hands o' the police,' Matty shouted at him. He ambled back, and sat down, a figure of dejection, brooding over the fire.

'I had twenty quids – not long sin',' Stiner remarked. 'An' I corrupted scabs with it – instead o' looking after my own chances. "An' those who," something or other, "the golden grain, and those who flung it to the wind – like rain."'[92]

'Oh, shut up,' Matty told him.

'Damn Omar, anyhow,' muttered Stiner.

He got up and staggered round the kitchen, trod on the cat's tail, and apologised to it for ten minutes.

Someone knocked at the door and came in. His gaze went straight to Rachel. She was sitting on the end of the fender, with Benny leaning against her.

'Something up?' asked Rachel.

'Could I speak with you?' said Jack.

'Go into't parlour,' Matty said quickly.

'Will you come into my parlour, said the spider to the fly,' stammered Stiner.

'Eh, tha'rt a fool,' Matty told him.

She watched Rachel and Jack go into the parlour.

'Are they in love with one another?' asked Stiner.

'How the hangments do I know?' she asked in return.

'Does ta remember them violets I picked for thee? No! Tha't forgotten. "Alas! That Spring should vanish with the rose." Tha's forgotten.'

'Happen not,' said Matty.

He flashed her a wild look of hope, which quickly faded into the old stoic expression.

In the parlour, which now had its curtains pinned together to veil the stripped condition the strike had left it in, Rachel and Jack faced each other.

'I can't see to read it – without a light,' she said.

'Matty might not have any candles. I'll strike a match. Pretty rotten of them to cut the gas off.'

So they read it by the sputtering light of matches, with the darkness falling between. It was printed.

BEWARE.

THE FIRST MOVE TOWARDS VIOLENCE AGAINST
PROPERTY BRINGS THE SOLDIERS. HOLD
THEM BACK. THE BOSSES ARE HOLDING A
MEETING TO DECIDE WHETHER OR NOT TO
GIVE IN.

'What do you make of that?' asked Jack.

'Hold that match up behind the paper,' Rachel told him.

He watched her face. In the flickering light and shadow it assumed strange expressions, tenderness, fear, compassion, admiration.

'Strike another,' she told him.

He did so.

'You can consider that's right,' she said to him. 'That's Sanderson's notepaper and Sanderson's water-mark.'

Jack gasped.

'But how can it be right – if he's sent it?'

'She's sent it,' Rachel answered him.

'Who?'

'Why – who – our Hester!'

He laughed incredulously.

She turned on him like a spitfire.

'She's my sister – and you could cover her with jewels from head to foot – she'd still belong to the folk. She hasn't brute courage, but she's a courage that can defy brute courage. Ever seen Sanderson in a rage? He'll murder her, Jack, if he finds out. He thinks it's me. That's why I don't go. He wouldn't murder me, because I'm not his wife, meaning, I'm not his property. See?'

Jack whistled.

'Then – all these bulletins – ?'

'Hers.'

He stood, pale and moved.

'They've got her downstairs again. She's at it again. She'll go at it till the bitter end.'

There was a moment's silence.

The match spluttered into gloom and the darkness seemed evil and menacing.

'I did not know – she was like that.'

He struck another match.

'She always had a queer, odd sort of courage, all her own. You can be weak in one way and strong in another.'

'It is magnificent.'

Another match – another silence.

'She's very ill, they say.'

'Ill!' sobbed Rachel. 'She's *dying!*'

'No.'

The shuddering protest of his voice told of a memory that would never fade.

Rachel struggled with herself.

'In a way it'll be better for her, but you don't like to lose folk.'

His hand groped its way to hers, and held it for an instant.

'It'll be better for her. Easier. She's married into the Capitalist class, and her early life in the other class won't let it be anything but a torment. Come on! They'll wonder what we're up to.'

So they went out into the kitchen, where Stiner was singing 'Ever of Thee I'm Fondly Dreaming,'[93] to a Matty openly laughing at him.

'What's that?' cried Jack, after ten minutes of rambling conversation with Stiner, during which he told him, in divers ways, that he would never do the Movement any good till he could remain sober.

Clogs were clattering in the dark street. They rushed to the door, all but Stiner. Floored! He was floored! Then he got a bright idea. He'd got threepence – he'd go buy her some flowers – violets, if he could get them. At the door, however, he stopped. He saw it double, that procession going past, composed of women and children.

'To hell with all the bloody struggle,' called Stiner, and pushed his way through Rachel, Jack, Matty and the kids.

'Here! Where are ta going?' asked Matty.

'To get thee some violets,' he told her, and he went off, his bluchers sounding inelegantly.

'I hope he doesn't get into bother,' Matty told Rachel. 'O'Neill might come across him.'

Jack Baines suddenly bounded out and met the procession.

'Where are you going?' he shouted.

They came crowding round him.

And as they crowded he read it out to them – that warning, from memory, holding it up.

'Where were you taking that cross?' he asked of the girl who carried it.

'To nail on Sanderson's door.'

'Give it to me.'

She handed it.

He struck a match and read the crude message nailed upon it. 'We give you 24 hours to clear out.'

'We're winning, I tell you,' he shouted.

'But – we're starving.'

'They're giving in.'

There was the sound of hysterical weeping. He went in and amongst them cheering them up. Slowly they dispersed, going back to their holes. And Stiner, quoting Omar, was gone in quest of violets – and up the street O'Neill was coming, in quest of any trouble he might meet – or make.

CHAPTER 22

THE QUEST of violets with which to touch the heart of an unsentimental wife, and the quest of trouble that shall add a stripe to the sleeve, had, as things turned out, an indirect and ironic relation. Stiner was thinking of nothing as he went down the street – nothing, which, somehow, was Omar, and strikes, and Matty telling him not to make a fool of himself, and little innocent hopes springing up in his heart, blossoming in the memory of the anxious look on her face as she spoke the warning. At least, she cared what happened to him. And, by God, that was something. He started to warble 'Nil Desperandum.'[94] Which way should he go? Where did violets grow? Better to gather than buy them. And after all – an odd pint, before he went dry for the rest of his natural might be handy. And to gather them – there was something taking in the idea. Where the Hanover did violets grow, anyhow? Somewhere down by the river, a chap told him. A chap with a red nose, who ought not, according to the ideas of the Methodists, to have known where violets grew. But he had had some in his button-hole, as he spoke. Stiner stopped – floored with the brilliance of his own sudden wit. Of course. What was the sense of gathering them by the river's brim – when somewhere in the town a chap with some in his coat. So he ambled up towards the 'Scythe.' There he found the owner of the violets. But the owner of the violets was sentimental, too. He had gathered them for his own wife, and how much was Stiner prepared to pay for them?

'This is all my worldly wealth,' Stiner told him.

He planked three pennies down.

'No. I'll take 'em home,' he was told.

'The destiny of a human life depends on those violets,' Stiner told him. 'I'm no fighter, but if tha likes – we'll fight for 'em.'

'I'm a man of peace,' said the other. 'Arta sure that's all tha has?'

Stiner turned his pockets out.

Then he gave a cry.

'It'll be a button,' he said. They both went down seeking it. Stiner pounced on it. It was a shilling.

'There! I'll give thee this shilling and have a drink with thee,' Stiner avowed. 'Here! Let's have 'em. Missus! Have you got a little tissue paper or cotton wool or anything of that nature, to embalm these violets in?'

The landlady turned a smiling face. She brought him some cotton wool.

Stiner, five minutes later, stood up amidst the scornful, genial company of farmers from a country town, passing through to the show.

'Farewell, O waters of Lethe!' he said, holding up his glass. 'Farewell, O waters of dream and poetry. Bacchus is a friend of Love. I have proved it otherwise, gentlemen. Quite otherwise. Henceforth, I am a sadder, soberer, wiser man. Back to the vestal fires of home and to the light of Beauty's eyes, we are faring, armed with violets. "Alas! That Spring should vanish with the rose."[95] Drink, gentlemen, drink. Drink to the sobriety of Bob Stiner – that's my name – and that he may, from this moment, evermore live a sober, virtuous, and – . No, gentlemen, I forbid it. Sober we have not always been. Virtuous – yes – in hell – in every hell – true to one woman, and my hair is grey, and my heart – No, I'm damned if that's grey. Sup up! And the eighteenth of Brumaire[96] will come and I shall celebrate it on water. Good-night, gentlemen. It is a sad world, but we shall live till we dee, if the dogs don't worry us. Good-night.'

He went out to a guffaw of laughter and ironical shouting, and offers of another drink, into the gloomy streets.

Under the street-lamp he examined the violets once, then pushed them back into his pocket. He'd go up by the mill, and see how the pickets were getting on, poor devils. He went, and as he climbed the brow, he saw down into the valley, where from the near towns the flaring lights told of mills that had not stopped, but had left Brayton to fight, on its own. Some day, all that would be ended. Every wheel would stop at once. Some day. When old Bob Stiner was dead. He rambled up by a wall, a vague and shadowy wall, and turned the corner. Sanderson's mill was humming away – humming away. He stared up at the illumined windows. Blackleg shadows crossed them. He forebore to curse. Poor devils, without honour, but not alone – not alone. Then his gaze sank to the ground again, and there on the pavement, lit by the lamp at the corner of the mill-gate, he saw two struggling shadows. There was not a sound, but a terrible struggle was going on. And one – was – O'Neill's. By God! The other shadow was that of a picket. Stiner tossed his coat off and dashed in. The next moment he received a terrific blow on the back of the head. He went down silently, after one groan.

The fight between O'Neill and the picket went on. And then O'Neill's shadow crept away amongst the many shadows – the silent shadows, which could not bear witness. It stopped once – and he shone his light on the man laid out on the pavement, in his ragged shirt sleeves. He leaned down, placing his hand over Stiner's heart. There was no beat. The light strayed over Stiner's face, his wide, reproachful eyes, his clenched hands, fixed as they clawed the pavements. Then O'Neill arose and fled up the back streets. He stopped only once by a lamp and examined his tunic. No spots. Not one. But the face of that dead man! Why had the picket turned nasty at being spoken to? If this should come out! And Stiner's eyes! They burned through the darkness at him. He fled, and fleeing, rushed into the arms of the Inspector.

'What's this?' asked the Inspector.

'A scab attacked one of the pickets,' said O'Neill. 'I believe the man's dead. I took a hand.'

They went back.

The Inspector examined Stiner and the picket.

'Dead as a door nail,' was his first remark.

Then he lifted up the picket.

The man looked at him dazedly. Then his gaze went to O'Neill. He pointed at him, muttered something, and collapsed. They returned to Stiner, examining his pockets. They found a blood-soaked copy of Omar, half under him, a halfpenny, an old envelope with a child's handwriting, and inside a child's curl and the words 'For Daddy, from Benny Stiner,' and the street and the number.

'Stiner!'

The Inspector looked at O'Neill.

'You had to attack him in self-defence?'

'I had.'

'May be awkward, O'Neill.'

They fetched the ambulance and removed the picket to the hospital, suffering from concussion. Then they removed the body of Stiner back to the 'Scythe,' and went down to tell Mrs. Stiner. Rachel heard, from within the house, Matty's scream.

'Oh, whatever's to do?' asked Rachel.

'They say he's got fighting with a picket. Him! *Him!* And *he* had to interfere to save the picket's life! *Him!*' She pointed a shaking finger at O'Neill. 'But it will have to be proved. *Proved.* They won't kill my children's father and *get off* without proving they were innocent.'

Rachel half carried her into the kitchen, and dragged her upon the settee. Later they went to the 'Scythe,' and identified Stiner. When Matty saw the violets she almost collapsed. There was blood upon them – brown spots. She went sick. Rachel turned her head, as she saw Matty lift the dead, calloused hand, stroking it, her eyes aflame, her face dead white, and caught her hoarse words of atonement and promise.

'They shall never say tha were a scab, old lad. I'll borrow brass at a hundred per cent. – first.'

And as they went up the street, homewards, they met Mrs. Martin.

'I think Sanderson's gone mad,' she told Rachel. 'He's persuaded Hessie to go out in the car – to-morrow. In this weather. And she can hardly sit up. What can it mean? What can it mean, Rachel?'

'Hush! Mrs. Stiner's had a shock. Her husband's been killed,' Rachel told her. 'Come on back with us.'

Mrs. Martin stared – shook her head.

'No. Won't have to be long,' she murmured. 'I'll go back.'

She went, walking quickly, like the old Mary Martin, resolute when she had made up her mind. Rachel brooded deeply on this new move of Sanderson's. Then she realised why Sanderson was going to make Hessie ride out in the car. In her black, in her tragedy, she would appeal to the sentiments of the masses, and shake their resolve, their opinion that they were right to fight for self-interest as the bosses did. Knowing the game Hester was playing, the thing assumed a curious, demoniac absurdity to Rachel. He was using her against the people, she, who was risking everything, everything, for them. Hester had not the brute courage to revolt, nor the brute nerve. The woman who had reported every move of the bosses was going to be paraded, a tragic figure, as the boss's wife.

Rebellion meant – anything. Rachel knew it. There would be no open rebellion. But the spirit driven underground to avoid open and brutal conflict, might, very easily might, in a certain desperate mood, go to even greater extremes and fling, in one moment, discretion to the winds.

Mrs. Martin, hurrying back through the streets, was oppressed by sad, dark thoughts. The doctor had urged upon Hester the necessity to be quiet and be careful to take no chill – and here was Sanderson countermanding that order – telling her to pull herself together and have a run out in the car. She could not understand it. She recalled that Rachel had said Bob Stiner had been killed.

Here, in the house of the boss, she and Hessie got no news of their own people, save as that news was repeated by Sanderson – coloured by his outlook. Fanny let her in at the door. How foolish it seemed to ring the bell of the house where you lived – waiting for a paid servant to let you in!

How impossible to be a natural human being, when one had always to be playing hide and seek behind a polite mask. Sometimes, when Sanderson brought 'company' to the house, very refined company, living without working, enunciating every word distinctly, and with manners which seemed to make them curiously stiff and frigid, Mrs. Martin had gone out and sat in the kitchen with Fanny – to Fanny's great horror.

Sometimes she had felt that to go back to the mill, even with white hair, would leave her more free than to abide in this house.

She handed her outdoor things to the maid.

'How is Mrs. Sanderson, Fanny,' asked Mrs. Martin, even while the comical contradiction of calling your own daughter 'Mrs.' and the maid by her Christian name, brought her a sense of the hypocritical unnaturalness of this society in which she now existed.

'I've just taken her a cup of cocoa and some biscuits, ma'am,' Fanny told her. 'That other one's been, but the master would not let her in to see Mrs. Sanderson.'

'You mean Mary?' asked Mrs. Martin.

'Yes, ma'am.'

'She was very fond of Hes – Mrs. Sanderson,' Mrs. Martin said.

'Yes. She cried when he turned her away.'

'I hope there was no scene, Fanny.'

'No. She went off quietly, ma'am.'

From which Mrs. Martin assumed that there would have been a scene had Mary not been willing to go away quietly.

She went into the drawing-room. Hester was asleep. The poor mother rejoiced that she slept. She sat down beside the great Chesterfield,[97] brooding in wild, anxious-eyed, mother-love over her darling. She noted the transparency of the hand flung out on the blue satin of the eiderdown, the gentle, sad expression of the sleeping face. Sleep reveals much. The mask had fallen away from Hester's soul. The gentle, sad regret, the sorrow of life, and resignation to death, was stamped quite clearly on her sleeping countenance. Mrs. Martin lowered her head. Hester was going down to death without one struggle.

She had stopped her from marrying Baines, her natural impulse, and also from being killed by working-class struggle. Would it have killed her, anyhow? She had encouraged her to marry Sanderson – an unnatural impulse, reactionary and desperate – and she was dying, anyhow. Perhaps for those of Hester's calibre there was no health, hope, or joy in either class of society. Odd words, sentences, war-cries of her dead husband's came trickling back into Mrs. Martin's mind.

They took on a deep significance as she sat brooding by Hester – her best beloved child. Her best! Rachel could stand alone, fighting for herself and others. Rachel could meet force with force, challenge with challenge – dominating the dominant. Rachel made friends and enemies, and took her own path, unhindered by either. But Hester had been born fitted only to live in a society where none would have tried to dominate – where no law would have been necessary, save the law of love and service, and where force would not have been a blot on the brotherhood of humanity.

Rachel could defend, and attack, and help to break down the old. It would be such loving, gentle, dreaming souls as Hester's who would build up the new amidst the ruins. Dimly Mrs. Martin saw the vital differences between her girls, as she sat brooding. Fanny brought her a cup of tea and some scones, and inquired if she should light the other lamp.

'No.'

Then the telephone bell rang.

It roused Hester.

She struggled into a sitting position.

'That's a call,' she said.

The doctor had said yesterday that she had wonderful reserves of will. Mrs. Martin saw the daughter who had seemed to be drifting out of life, re-vitalised.

'I'll tell them he's at the mill,' Mrs. Martin said.

'No. I'll attend to it.'

'But, Hessie, you should lie still.'

'If you'll take my arm, I'll attend to it.'

Mrs. Martin piloted Hester to the telephone. She reeled once, and her mother grabbed at her in alarm.

'I'm all right,' Hester told her. She took up the speaker.

'Hello!'

'That Mrs. Sanderson?'

'Yes.'

'Sandy in?'

'At the mill.'

'Well – I can't help but tell you the great news. Damage done again at my place. They're bringing the troops up. All will be over in another few days, at the latest. Are you better?'

'Mending nicely, thanks. Mrs. Dawson and the children all right?'

'Can't hear you!'

'Is Mrs. Dawson quite well. And the children?'

'Quite all right. Take care of yourself.'

'Oh, yes.'

'Don't get excited about the troops. We shall be well protected.'

'I'm not excited.'

'I can't hear you.'

'I'm not excited.'

'That's all right. Shall I ring off?'

'When are they coming?'

'The troops?'

'They are bringing them up from Redburn sometime to-morrow. Good-bye.'

'Good-bye.'

Hester hung up the receiver.

Mrs. Martin helped her back to the couch. She lay down, panting.

'You shouldn't do it, Hessie,' complained her mother, tearfully.

'One must do – all one *can*.'

'Yes. But you must think of yourself.'

'That makes me tired.'

'What's money, what's anything, without health?' asked Mrs. Martin, sorrowfully. 'You should think of getting your health back.'

Hester smiled.

Money had never been anything to her. She had sought for Freedom and found there was none, but at least – one must do all one could. It was difficult to breathe. Weakness, dreadful, frustrating, hindered her. She wiped the sweat of fatigue from her forehead, and panted under the eiderdown. But in her heart was white, shining peace – for at least, *one could go down fighting.*

'Feeling better, m'dear?' inquired Sanderson, later that evening. He was almost boisterous. He had heard.

'Heaps better, Sandy.'

'Going out to-morrow?'

'Yes.'

Mrs. Martin flung him a horrified look. Then she could restrain herself no longer.

'Are you trying to kill her, man? Do you want to be shut of her? The doctor says – .'

'Doctors are fools.'

'Evidently everyone is a fool but – .'

Then she met Hester's gaze and broke off. That look, beseeching, entreating, told Mrs. Martin that Hester wanted to go out, wanted herself to go out – not just because Sanderson wished it.

'Who'll be responsible?' asked Mrs. Martin. 'I won't.'

'I'll be responsible,' said Hester.

She gave her mother another of those quiet, beseeching looks.

'As for wanting to be rid of her,' protested Sanderson, 'that's nonsense. She's getting depressed with staying inside. A sharp drive in the car will buck her up.' He left the room humming.

It was a dark dawn when Hester awakened to find Sanderson dressing, and whistling as he dressed. Fanny came up half an hour later with a cup of tea.

'You're not going out, are you, ma'am?' she questioned with respectful affection, well-disguised and deferential.

'Not now, Fanny,' Hester told her, smiling.

'If you waited a week or two, ma'am, till the weather mended up I think it would be safer. Excuse me, ma'am. It's no business of mine. And I hope you don't mind.'

Hester smiled at her.

Her domestic was apologising for giving an affectionate warning – which could never be paid for in cash. Human nature was nobler than the society it was enmeshed in.

'I'm very self-willed, you know, Fanny – or perhaps you don't know.'

Fanny did not believe it.

'It will do me good to get out of the house,' Hester told her. 'And I'll tell the doctor – after.'

Fanny went downstairs.

At noon the doctor came.

'You're much better, Mrs. Sanderson. Taking your food all right? That's right. Just keep quiet. Sleep all you can, and in the Spring get away to a place I can recommend, and you'll come back as fit as a fiddle.'

She smiled acquiescence.

In the Spring. Spring! The re-birth of the earth's beauty – its Utopia of winter dreaming! All would be passed, in Spring. She knew it. All would be gone by, the bitter striving of poverty, the galling hypocrisies of the life of this house, the little memories which stood out like the white blooms of an age yet to dawn, against the background of an age that was. Sleep – without dreams – rest without a nightmare to break it – and as she went down, the sure and certain hope of a better world to come on the site of this one, sometime, somehow, since nothing could last for ever, and since society, like individuals, decayeth at last to make room for new life. And she was glad.

She was very tired. Blossoms and briars, sordid struggle and blood, stained culture wrenched from the entrails of Labour, mire of the pit, and fiery blood of human nobility which could not be defiled – all would be over, for Hester. She knew it.

But it was sweet to think that the struggle would go on, herself passed from it. The battlefield, where men, half-gods and half-devils, wrestled. Sweet, passing sweet, to think there were men and women like Baines and Rachel left, valiantly contesting, a minority which would one day be a majority. Whatever else she doubted she could not doubt the ultimate victory. Whatever the Winter was, she knew the Spring would break – blossomed, beautiful, dewy and scented, the May Day of Labour the world over. Sure and certain was the resurrection of Labour, coming up out of its tomb of brutal slavery. It was very sweet to fall asleep, in the heart of the strife, with such a dream.

She rested her cheek on little Ann's photograph, and so dreaming, slept. Fanny took the photograph gently away when she went up, and bending over Hester noticed the smile of infinite peace. Awed by that smile, she leaned down, listening for Hester's breathing. Then she saw the clothes lift, and sneaked out of the room, wiping her eyes.

At three in the afternoon, arrayed in costly black apparel, muffled up in Russian furs, and with the crèpe of orthodoxy showing up the whiteness of her face, Hester stepped into the waiting car, the chauffeur, a black band on his sleeve, opening the door for her. The sorrow of the woman who had laid flesh of her flesh, bone of her bone, in the ground, was being paraded to make an appeal to the starving thousands. She knew it, realised it all, and leaned back, a bitter smile under her outward mask of sorrow.

She was glad Stephen was gone from the miseries and hypocrisies of a world like this. But the physical agony of the loss was yet fresh and raw – and this it was which was to be shown to Brayton's moilers – to prove that they were human, these exploiters who would starve thousands in a battle for five per cent.

They drove along the main road, where solitary stragglers, beshawled and wretched, pinched and faint from their emphasised Lent, the never-ending Lent of the poor, stared at the car and nudged each other. Sanderson's car. Sanderson's wife. Hester Martin, who once ran after whistles – their enemy now – in a struggle for profit on one side, and more bread on the other.

The chauffeur was driving slowly, under orders from Sanderson, no doubt. The air felt clammy and sponge-like, and brought to Hester a smarting sensation, with little spasms of pain, through the shoulder-blades.

They drove more slowly, until they reached the town centre. There were hundreds gathered there, apparently waiting for a meeting.

Somebody boo'ed as the car passed, somebody else said 'Hush.' Out of the gloom of the afternoon the whiteness of Hester's face showed cameo-like, ghastly, in its sickly pallor. Then the song struck up. She heard it – a faint smile on her lips.

'Our boss's order lies a-mouldering on the shelf,
Our boss's order lies a-mouldering on the shelf,
Our boss's order lies a-mouldering on the shelf,
And we're not downhearted. No!'

'Stop the car, John.'
'I'd advise you not to, Mrs. Sanderson.'
'Stop it.'
It was almost peremptory – for Hester.
John stopped the car.
He opened the door and helped her out. She stumbled once, but recovered herself. The post-box seemed a thousand miles away, but it came nearer. A little crowd gathered. She dropped the letter into the box, and turned. The sickness of weakness almost overcame the will wrestling with it. John saw it and came towards her. As he came, a small, peak-faced boy blew the horn of the car and ran away. She was halfway back to the car, with its blurred outline, when a woman ran to her, a woman with a skeleton-like face, a woman sharpened by hunger and despair, savage in her desperation.

'My God!' rose her shrill, almost inhuman voice. 'My God! And you can show yourself in your furs and your fine clothes, and your cars, and all of it, and look us in the face. My youngest has died! Died because I couldn't get milk for him. They've put him in a pauper's grave. And my man is dying of heart-disease. We shouldn't have any hearts. We should be made of cast iron and leather, we should! And filled up wi' steel shavings. And you can show yourself – .'

John thrust himself between them menacingly.
'Go home!' he told her.
'Home!'

She echoed his word, and burst into terrible laughter.

'Stand out of the way, John,' Hester said to him.

He touched his cap and moved aside. The two women faced each other.

'I am very much grieved by your sufferings,' Hester told the woman.

'But you live on them!' came the challenge.

The crowd was closing about them.

'Yes. That is true. Unhappily, it is true. I am very much ashamed. One must either suffer with you or live on your sufferings. But I did not make the world. I shall be glad if you win the strike. Please, believe me.'

She panted between the sentences.

The woman was staring at her open-mouthed.

'If we win,' she shouted vociferously, 'your husband will go bust. You'll like that, won't you?'

'I shall be glad if you win,' Hester told her, calmly.

They stared deep into each other's eyes.

Quite suddenly the woman started crying in an uncontrolled way which shook her body. She wiped her eyes on her thin shawl.

'I have just buried one,' said Hester. 'Would you mind letting me go? I am not feeling very well.'

The woman stared into Hester's face, reading something there, a look she had seen not long ago on another face, a little face all drawn, and peaked, famishing for bread and – milk.

'I beg your pardon,' she muttered, very low.

But Hester heard her.

She leaned towards her.

'Whatever you have said – you have the right to hate us,' she breathed huskily. The crowd parted, and John piloted her to the car.

'Which way, ma'am?'

'Anywhere. Out of the world if you like,' she told him, wildly.

'Don't get excited, ma'am.'

So he drove her round, through the dim desolation of the streets, with the wrecks of homes which even at the best were only workshops. There was a very little boo-ing, for it died down at the sight of the ghost-like face surrounded by the blackness that told of bereavement. Then John headed the car for the house.

They carried her into the house.

'Eh, Hessie!' moaned her mother, 'tha shouldn't have gone.'

'I'm glad I went,' she told them.

She was – very, very glad.

The information she had wished to get to Baines had gone. She had not dared to entrust it to John or Fanny with that name and address on the envelope. And her mother would only have worried.

CHAPTER 23

IN THE Stiner kitchen there was dark sorrow, vain regrets and the memory of faded violets, sentimental token of a quest which had ended unsentimentally in death.

Rachel gave the children such meals as they could scrape together, borrowed a half-sovereign from Jack Baines, and again sought the aid of the grocer, giving him her faithful promise that he would be paid 'when the battle is over.' He stared a little at her for calling it a battle, but she went out of the shop with some ham-shanks and ten pounds of peas, telling him that Matty would come for the flour and barm.[98]

Matty would sit brooding, the children staring at her, then jump up, do an odd job and collapse again. They were baking till eleven o'clock on the night following Stiner's exit from the tragic stage of his existence. Then they scraped out the tea-caddy and sat down with a pint pot of tea each. Rachel ate half a hot muffin – but Matty could not eat, yet.

In the course of the baking, the police had paid several visits, asking for particulars of Stiner's 'past,' why he did not live at home, etc.

'What they'll do is to try to make him out a vagabond,' was Rachel's commentary.

'And what have we to do?' asked Matty.

'Well, he was always a member of a union, always worked, or he'd have clemmed, and if he drank a bit, so do his "betters." He never went inside Sanderson's mill, so he could not be a scab. We can prove that, at least. The sham that he attacked the picket will be shown up by the fact that he did time for being in conflict with O'Neill before, for chalking Socialism on the flags. Then the picket may get well, though they say he's given up.'

'If only the picket would get better,' said Matty.

She went upstairs to look at her brood, her sleeping brood. They were the only comfort she had – and there was reproach even in them, for out

206

of those sleeping faces looked memories of Stiner. Benny was most like him. His face was a little puckered as he dreamed, and he had a broken-headed horse on the bed, a reflection of Stiner's love for animals.

'They say the soldiers is at Whitleigh,' said Matty when she came back, wiping her eyes. ' I hope to God there's no rough work.'

Rachel said nothing.

'Are we going to bed to-neet?' asked Matty. 'I'm not particular. I shan't sleep, anyhow.'

'Well – we might as well sham, then,' Rachel told her. She knew that Matty's exhaustion would result in sleep, once she lay down, and so they went to bed.

Silence brooded over the streets as the scabs took their midnight way to the mill. They were running all night to-night, a fresh relay of 'men' having been sent for, and Sanderson was wearing a triumphant look, for in a couple of days the wagons would be loaded, and, guarded by police, driven down to the station *en route* for their destination.

He was at the mill now goading on the scabs. Despondent pickets came quietly out from the shadows as the relay of scabs went in, appealing to those who would listen. The rain was pouring down and washing away the blood on the pavements – the blood of a defamed man, who had yet been 'a man for a' that.'[99]

The house of Sanderson was asleep. Mrs. Martin was very tired, tired with worry and sorrow. Fanny had gone to bed earlier than usual with toothache. The nurse had gone home to see her sick mother, in answer to an urgent wire. Hester awoke at one in the morning, having dreamed that Stephen had come alive and was lisping his dreams to her. Then her gaze fell on the empty cot, and reality rushed back. She saw her mother, in a deep sleep, on the velvet couch at the foot of the bed.

She stealthily set her foot to the floor, trying her strength, calling on her will. Sandy had said he would be at the mill all night. She crept about, finding her dressing-gown, silk-lined. The face of the woman who had attacked her as one of the boss-class, came into her mind.

What was it Sandy had once taunted her with? No sense of humour!

She smiled as she groped her way down the stairs, grateful to the thick luxuriousness of the carpet, not for its cosiness, but because it muted sound. How funny that she should be stealing down, like a thief in the night, in Sandy's house.

How irresistibly funny that she would be dead in Spring, the quick, delicate, wonderful Spring, and yet was creeping down in Sandy's house, intensely interested in documents which had come from Dawson and the others.

How irresistibly funny that she should copy out anything of vital interest and post it to Jack Baines, not because she had any passion or affection for him, but simply because he was the link between herself and the knowledge she could gather – and thousands! But how loathsome, how bestially loathsome, to be driven to plan and scheme and deceive in order to be true to the best that was in her.

She sat down, breathless, panting, when at last she staggered into the drawing-room. The fire was still red. She got up, and raked its embers together cautiously, a fit of shivering taking her. She controlled it, with all the force of her will. When she had conquered it, she opened Sandy's desk, lit the lamp, and sat down to her task. All the life force in her concentrated on that task. She went through many papers, and began to copy out the most important.

She was just putting the papers back in their order, correcting, for once, her tendency for the non-observance of detail when she heard the key turn in the front-door. Panic seized her.

With blanched cheeks and eyes wide and fearful, she heard that familiar sound. It was not lack of moral courage. It was lack of physical courage. Sandy was whistling. He seemed to be in a Manchester mood. He was whistling 'Rule Britannia' in a flat voice, jerky and tuneless – and – he was coming!

What would he do?

She moved towards the desk, put back the papers, and closed the desk, with sweat on her brow. The copied messages she thrust into her slippers. Sandy was almost here. He tumbled against the hall-stand. Then he yawned noisily. She threw herself down on the couch, rubbing her cheeks to give them colour. She felt sick and hysterical, and nearing collapse. Just as she screwed up her courage to assume something like cheerful gaiety, there came a knock at the door.

'Hello!'

It was O'Neill's voice.

Sandy turned back.

'Hullo?' Sandy asked.

'Policeman.'

'Yes. What do you want?'

'I thought burglars were in.'

'No. It's all right.'

'So I see – now.'

'Good-night.'

'Good-night – Oh – could I speak with you – ?'

'At this rotten hour?'

'Oh, all right, Mr. Sanderson.'

'Here – wait a moment.'

She heard Sandy shoot the bolts back. It was her chance. Like a flash, while the white door was swung open and their jumbled voices came to her, she reached the staircase – and the fifth step.

Then she began to gasp, to choke for breath, but the spasm passed quickly as it had come. She reached the head of the stairs, and leaned back against the wall. 'Stiner.' She heard the name. Fanny said Stiner had been killed. What could the policeman be talking to Sandy about him for at this hour? She listened. But the savage throbbing of her heart deafened her. Blood seemed to pulse in her brain. But she waited until that phase of her fright had passed. Then she heard them – weak and exhausted – she heard them.

Nothing open was said. But Sandy had promised to 'scotch anything' against O'Neill. He would say he was not sure if Stiner had worked as a scab at the factory, as they all looked alike, but that his face seemed familiar. Then she tottered into the room just as Mrs. Martin awoke, and she recalled that she had not put out the lamp in the drawing-room.

'Eh, Hessie,' gasped her mother. 'Tha's never bin downstairs?'

How sweet, how pathetic, how full of memories it was when they were alone they dropped back into the old tongue – the tongue spoken by the thousands now clemming.

'I have. I went down to get some wine,' Hester told her. 'And – I forgot to turn out the light. You'll say it was you went down, mother, won't you?'

The terror on Hester's face was past Mrs. Martin's understanding.

'Ay, my lass! I will. Give up shaking,' she urged. 'Cuddle up under the clothes, lass. Of course I'll say it were me.'

Then they heard the door bang after O'Neill.

'Hello!' called Sandy, at the foot of the stairs.

'Hello,' answered Mrs. Martin.

'Who's been down and left the light on – ?'

'I have. Hessie was faint – an' I came down to get her some wine.'

'All right. But it's waste.'

'I'm sorry, Sandy.'

Then she crept back to Hessie.

'Go to sleep, lass,' she crooned. 'I don't know what tha'rt up to, but whatever it is tha can allus ay it was thy mother. Hessie? Arta asleep?'

'No.'

'Tha can allus say it were t ny mother. I'd lay my life down for thee.'

It was Mary Martin's atonement.

The two hands met in a close clasp.

Then Hester's answer came.

'I don't believe I'd be a coward – if the test came,' she said. 'Don't leave me, mother. You'll never leave me, will you? However much you feel in the way – amongst the – swanks – ?'

A tear splashed on Hester's face.

'It's bin hard, lass,' came the broken confession. 'But I'll never leave thee; no, I'll never leave thee.'

Whilst the night crept on in the house of Sanderson; whilst Matty slept and awoke, her pillow wet with tears; whilst Mrs. Martin, anxious-eyed, brooded over Hester; and Rachel was impatiently trying to make sense out of the last chapter of *Das Capital,* too weary to sleep, and too weary to be alert – a young moon was rising through the clouds. The soft, gentle light shone down on the hill-top wood where Hester had once made music.

It shone down on Sanderson's factory, on the steaming lodge and belching chimney, flinging into shadow the wall where the pickets lingered, still clinging to the hope that they could persuade the scabs not to scab. It made into things of beauty the rain-wet roofs of the monotonous rows of houses – those boxes wherein the 'clemmed' tried to sleep, awakened by tantalising dreams of food, food, food – to the nightmare of the struggle for life.

But it shone no more for Bob Stiner – he who no longer needed to be scolded by Matty for his 'language' – language which was a medley of culture, painfully achieved, and the heritage of the doss-house and tramp-shop unrefinement. Never again would he turn the respectable air 'blue,' nor would he again dream dreams of unattainable beauty, nor quote Omar, nor wrestle to convince men in inns of the solidity and science of the theory of Price and Profit. Stiner had passed beyond the eternal shallows of barbarism veneered with respectability, and slept the sleep of one who had gone down in honour.

Matty awoke to find Rachel dressing.

'Why, what time is it?' she asked.

Rachel struck a match and peered at the alarm-clock.

'Half-past two.'

'What arta getting up for?' asked Matty.

Rachel had caught a glimpse of Matty's red-lidded eyes before the match went out.

'Can't sleep. I feel depressed,' admitted Rachel. 'Sort of horrible, creeping feeling that something is going to happen. Unconquered superstition I got from my grandmother, I expect. So I'm going out – for a blow.'

'What could happen?' asked Matty. 'Hasn't enough happened?'

'Oh, I don't know. Nothing ever happens for us – only a strike now and then, just to keep us in working order.'

'But tha can't go out at half-past two in the morning,' expostulated Matty.

'I wonder where I put my top-skirt?' was Rachel's answer. '…I've got it.'

She struggled into it. Matty heard the sound of it being dragged round.

'If tha'rt going out,' said Matty, 'take my shawl. It's thicker nor thine.'

'Thanks.'

Matty was surprised at the humble acceptance. Rachel was a gracious giver but a rather ungracious accepter.

'And don't get in bother, Rachel.'

'I'm just going for a blow.'

'But it's such a queer time to go out walking.'

'Night air is purest,' Rachel told her, and Matty knew she would go. Ten minutes later Matty heard the key turn in the lock, and the echoing sounds of Rachel's clogs faded into silence. Whilst from the other room came the murmur of Benny's voice, repeating in his sleep, his twice-times table.

❧◈❧

Rachel walked quickly through the streets. They were silent as the grave, save for those lurking shadows here and there, the shadows of the preservers of a system where disorders eternally break out.

O'Neill shone his light on her face.

'Strange hour to be taking a stroll, Miss Martin,' he observed.

'All the cats are grey in the dark,' Rachel told him.

'It's scarcely safe,' he warned her.

'I am quite safe. And my doctor has ordered night air,' came Rachel's answer.

O'Neill looked after her.

She was making her way from the houses. He turned to follow, curious, then leaned against the wall, overcome again by that obsession, that out of the shadows – wide, reproachful – Stiner's eyes were staring at him. He walked down, shaken by an inward ague, to meet the Inspector. Terrible if it should come out now – before he was pensioned.

By the time he had reached the Inspector and received the information that the picket was not expected to live another twenty-four hours, Rachel was already walking along the road leading over what was known as the 'Top o' th' Hill.' The clouds had rolled away from the moon. The sandy path glistened in its light. The grasses on each side of it were dim and ghostly. The cries of peewits sounded, and the damp wind touched Rachel's face. She let her shawl slide to her shoulders, and drew a few deep breaths. In the distance she could see the rough, loose, stone walls which divided the half-waste pasturage from the moors.

Black, at the crest of the hill, was Hester's wood. Near by was the stream where on school holidays they had gathered the blossoms of gorse, filling little bottles and carrying them home, to pretend to make perfume with them. She recalled Hester holding yellow gorse-flowers in her hands, smelling them, Hester always eagerly grabbing at the fair things of life – to whom a field of daisies was a carpet of treasure.

But one must not think backwards, to those fresh, fair days when one was only seven and the shadow of the prison-house had not closed in on the dreaming soul. Yet so strong even the memories of this place, not revisited since childhood, that it seemed to Rachel that almost she might see, tripping ahead, a delicate, elfin figure, with the light o' dreams in her eyes, running towards the yellow gorse bushes, saying, 'Lift me up, Rachel; I want to pinch them, then I'll let you smell.' When at last she reached the stream, it was touched by moonshine. She thought of Hester, aged seven, dabbling her hand in the glistening flood, and dashing drops on Rachel, on Rachel who sometimes became furious, until Hester would say, 'I won't do it again. Don't hit me, Rach.' Sad, sweet memories, here in the ghostliness of the old spot, which now seemed smaller, somehow. But the gorse was still there, golden though not profuse, golden in the pale gleam of the dim, blue moonshine.

And on this hill they had danced the old song-game, 'Who shall I marry? Rich man, beggar man, thief. Silk, satin, muslin – rags!' Hester had married silk and a legalised thief, and was dying – glad the game was nearly over. Of what use to weep? Rachel, wrapped in Matty's old shawl, went on her way, almost striding. Through the wood now, where the anemones used to bloom. They had gathered them 'as they grew,' and danced up and down in them, fairy-queens of innocent childhood, blowing meadow-clocks to see if it was half-past five, and time to go home and 'set the table' for mother. She looked for the big boulder, moss-covered, under the shadow of the pines, where they used to keep house, brushing the moss with a heather-broom brought from the moor. There they had sat, nursing old dolls.

Curious, twisted smiles went across Rachel's face. Hester's doll had always been sick, she remembered – and –

She dropped on her knees, by the old boulder, sobbing as she had not sobbed since her 'father' died.

Someone rose out of the shadows, under the deep blackness of the pines.

'Who's that? What's up?' came Baines' voice.

She was up in an instant.

'I didn't think tha'd taken a sleeping-out ticket in this wood,' she told him, resentfully, the tears still smarting in her eyes.

'I thought I should be undisturbed here,' he told her.

'Well, tha art,' she answered him, and turned swiftly. He went as swiftly after her, and overtook her on a knoll of grassy hill which ran up into the glory of the moonshine.

'Here, don't go' he said.

'But Matty'll think I've got "took",' she told him.

She was very resolute.

'What are ta cryin' for?' he asked.

'Just letting the steam off,' she answered.

'Oh, just that. Sort of mechanical bust-up,' he jested.

Then his tone changed.

'It was about Hester,' he guessed.

Silence answered him.

'I was thinking about Hester, too,' he said in a low tone. 'I can't say it will ever be a less tender thing to me, always a beautiful memory, Rachel. Always a dream one never got too near to – and so broke – always an elusive spirit, beckoning on, with sad eyes, when one gets weary of the fight, saying "Remember!"'

They heard the gurgle of the stream, the sigh of the pines, the echo like the sea. The grasses murmured.

'Could you – would you – Rachel – ,' he began haltingly, 'forgive me *that?*'

The grasses were sighing.

Then Rachel held her hand out.

'That and more – ,' she told him. 'Aught, Jack.'

They still held hands as they went down the hill. They looked back.

'Is that – ?' asked Rachel.

'It's the dawn,' Jack told her.

He took off his cap.

'It's a good omen, Rachel,' he said.

'But the night's here, yet,' she answered him.

Jack Baines would certainly never get the chance to forget the sorrows, the struggles and the wrongs of his own class. From the past, and in the present, two very different souls would help him to 'Remember.'

CHAPTER 24

FROM the hills in the dawn-light to the town of murky shadows – that cauldron of seething strife, hate, hunger, misery and injustice, they went down.

They were young. They loved. Warm, strong hand lay in warm, strong hand. It was the mating of the strong. They were types thrown up by Nature, fitted to struggle. Yet it seemed incongruous to have to return, even though they were young, to fight the old battle, even with the glory of the immortal mantle of Love, newly fallen upon them. They went down. But because they were human they did not speak of the struggle, but only the great, new wonderful glory. They murmured the old immortal nothings which shall be murmured, quite unchanged, when such as they have helped to build a world where Love ceases to be a narrow stream of light from one to one, and becomes the force which unites all humanity – after the last battle.

How sorrowful, brooding, and sordid the town seemed.

They lingered slowly, loving the brightening dew-drops on the grass, the chirp of awakening sparrows, the soft, cold kiss of the hill-winds. The little idyll, so real, was left behind; the reality that was unreal and black, lay before them.

'I shall turn in and get a few hours' sleep, if I can,' Jack told Rachel.' 'But I feel all wakened up.'

They stared back at the glory falling on the hills. Always, always, it was a scene that would shine in the memory, unclouded by any grief or shadow – till their shadows passed from the earth that is so beautiful where man's greed has not disfigured it.

'Well, I'll see thee later,' he told her.

'Ay.'

'They're having that meeting to-day.'

'Ay.'

'Happen – there will be a message.'

'She'll do her best.'

'I know that.'

'We ought to have a meeting. Just to keep their pluck up.'

'I'll organise one.'

'Ay. Do. If only the others would have come out in the other towns. They're scabs, too!'

'They don't understand. Don't get bitter, Rachel.'

'I try not to, but it's terrible hard, Jack.'

His hand brushed hers.

He knew that the 'bitterness' in her heart was caused by the sweetness of her love for the Many. She was the great, true-hearted comrade, whose love for the People and their miseries would always help her to see clearly and not to find divinity in millionaires who fed upon the people, nor in those who supported them and the robbery and corruption they symbolised. And Matty's old patched shawl became something more than a shawl to him – more than a bit of shoddy cloth, as Rachel wore it loosely on her head. Barefoot she might walk, but she would always be upright.

'Well, how long are we going to stand fooling here?' she asked, with a smile in her eyes.

'Well, I'll see thee later on.'

'I'll send Benny down about the meeting.'

'Good-morning.'

'Good-morning.'

Each brooded a moment on the other's face, then they separated. He watched her swing away through the shadows. Poor Stiner had been right. Rachel had cared – all the time. And he, he could not tell when it had begun, so imperceptible had been the siege of the great old Democrat, Dame Nature.

His mother met him at the door, anxious-eyed.

'Wherever hasta bin?' she asked.

'On the hills, mother,' he told her.

'It sounds to ha' lifted thy spirits up, sohowbeit,' she answered.

'It has,' he said. 'I found a spirit wandering on the hills. Don't jump. It was well-padded with flesh. And so – .'

He tapped the table with his fingers.

'Rachel?' she asked, shining-eyed.

'H'm.'

She looked at the clock.

'Well, it's hardly a respectable hour,' she said. 'But I'm glad an' fain.'[100] And to show her fainness she promptly began to cry. Then she said, wiping her eyes, 'That's put my nose out o' the joint.'

He shook his head at her.

'Nay,' he told her.

'Well, it's a sensible choice this time,' she said, then stopped.

'That'll do, mother,' he said simply.

And it had to do.

Only a dream, part of an old Spring, but not a breath of the hard world must be breathed upon it.

But when next she looked at him the shadows had passed from his eyes. He was whistling, and taking off his boots. She was very glad, very fain. She rocked in her chair, then gradually ceased rocking and fell asleep herself. She awoke when the cat jumped on her knee, looked at the clock, and rushed to the foot of the stairs calling her son Jerry, who had to cross the Switchback to his work at the brick-kilns. She told Jerry. He lifted his eyebrows, and merely said, 'She's not as nice-looking as the other.'

'An' what good's looks to a working lass, tha fool?' she asked. 'They soon get weared oft.'

'I allus liked t'other,' said Jerry, frankly. 'Happen because she gave me some nuts once, and she'd such soft eyes. I were only a *little* lad,' he said swiftly. Then, 'Rachel's got a will o' her own.'

'And – she'll need it,' was the verdict of Jack's mother. And Jerry laughed through a mouthful of bacon, rationed because he was now the only 'bringer-in.'

'Are you there, mother?'

Mrs. Martin started up guiltily. Had she been asleep?

Yes. Asleep and dreaming, dreaming that she was back in the mill, struggling with a titanic 'float,' and that Hester was a little child, and had come to the mill-gates, in the rainy gloom, to meet her, but had missed her, and was lost, and she herself, heartbroken, went wailing about the town seeking her, going down streets she never meant to go down, stumbling down back alleys, calling 'Hessie! Hessie!'

And suddenly the dream changed, and the back streets turned into

Sanderson's house, and climbing the stairs which swayed as she went up, she had found Hessie, plaiting her hair ready for her half-day at the mill next morning – sitting on a rusted fender, beside a dead fire, with Macaulay's 'Lays of Ancient Rome'[101] beside her – and a sleepy, weary look on her childish face.

Then Hester's voice had trickled through the anxious dream – and she had awakened to find Hester, a married woman, sitting up in bed, in a silk dressing-jacket with lace foaming at the sleeves – the same old Hessie, asking, *'Mother, are you there?'*

'Ay, my lass, I'm here.'

'Is there a little green book on that table?'

'Is this it?'

'Ay. That's it. Do you mind turning the light up a bit? Thanks.'

Still the same old Hessie, grateful as when a tiny child for any little thing done for her, looking at you with a wistful, grateful smile in her eyes.

'What time is it?'

'Three o'clock, my lass.'

'They'll be here – at six.'

'Ay.'

'All the fuss and humbug!' said Hester, turning the pages. 'Never mind. Listen to Matthew Arnold.[102] There's something cold about the beauty of his songs, like the moon shining on snow on high mountains, or statues – marble life arrested for us to examine. He doesn't stir your emotions. He fixes them, like glaciers frozen into everlasting wonder. What shall we read?'

'Eh, I've not had time for much poetry, till it got too late,' Mrs. Martin told her. '"Lucy Gray," "The Rainbow," and "The Last of the Flock," an' "Excelsior"[103] is the most I *remember* of poetry. Thy father used to read it to me, before tha were born, when I sat doing the mending. But – go on.'

The turning of the leaves fluttered in the silence.

A tiny porcelain, hand-painted clock chimed in silvery voice.

'It's terrible dark outside,' said Mrs. Martin.

'Well, we've the blinds drawn against it, so it doesn't matter, does it?' asked Hester.

'No. Happen it doesn't,' answered Mrs. Martin.

She understood Hessie at last. Hessie always darting through the superficial to the reality under it. Dark! Yes. It was dark and terrible outside, in the misted streets where the hunger was, and the hate, and – not Matthew Arnold, but the epic of Want, and Battle, and Hope, wild-eyed as Despair.

'Only – but this is rare,
When a beloved hand is laid on ours,
When maddened by the rush and glare
Of the interminable hours,
Our eyes can in another's eyes read clear.'[104]

Mrs. Martin heard Hester's low voice reading on.

'A bolt is shot back, somewhere in the breast.'

It was a little difficult to make out – but she understood some of it.

'And then there comes a lull in the hot race.'

She listened, with intelligent, homely face, joy in hearing Hessie's voice, and painful effort to understand, written on it. Hester went on.

'An air of coolness plays upon the face.'

Down in the kitchen they heard the cook shouting at Fanny, and Fanny's humble answer.

'And we perceive the course where our life goes,
And the Hills where it rose.'

'It means, I think,' said Mrs. Martin haltingly, Hester's smile encouraging her, 'that we are only ourselves, and know ourselves, when somebody loves us – just for ourselves – and we feel free, then.'

Then Hester turned to 'Iseult of Ireland,'[105] reading the old, fair, tear-blotted story of Iseult coming with spray on cloak and hair to comfort the dying Tristam.

Line after line she read. Then:

'Mother. You're asleep,' came Hester's laughing tone. She laid the book down, still smiling.

'Don't apologise,' she said. 'I'm going to get up. The banquet-hall of Tyntagil awaits. What a place it is to live in. But it's the thought of dying here gets me down. If they only danced – but there'll be Mrs. Dawson sympathetically asking if Sandy's nearly got his order out. And there'll be the long sitting – stuffing ourselves. And all the condolences about Stephen, when I'm glad he's out of it all. And there'll be all the nice polite malignity against the strikers – and the comparing of notes as to how long they can continue to starve. Then I shall play 'em some Bach – Bach's so wonderful, you know, when you understand him.'

'Eh, Hester. Think o' thy position,' remonstrated Mrs. Martin.

But she was glad Hester spoke so lightly.

'I wish I could stop thinking of it,' Hester told her gently. 'I wonder if, in the end, I shall sweep all the food off the table right into their laps? Wouldn't Mrs. Dawson look funny with lobster mayonnaise in her hair? And Sandy shouting for the mess to be cleared up, and sending for a cab for me? He'd telephone for it, of course. And Fanny, as white as chalk, trying to do her duty as a domestic in a mad-house, by pouring humble oil on the troubled carpet! And somewhere, in some small corner – me – singing a Revolutionary song, uncultured, crude and plain. I think I ought to have written a three-act play.'

It was all said light-heartedly, so jestingly gay. Mrs. Martin laughed, too.

'And we'd call it "The First Mrs. Sanderson",' continued Hester.

She was standing brushing her hair, and she tottered a little.

'For, of course, there'll be a second,' she continued. 'I think myself Sandy will marry Dawson's sister, the one with the eye-glasses. Her uncle made a lot o' money – mining interests, I believe, and left it to her, knowing she'd never spend it. It's all right, mother, I can stand.'

Half an hour later the tea-bell rang.

They went downstairs.

Sandy was whistling, back to the fire.

'Nearly got the order completed, Sandy?' asked Hester.

She leaned her cheek towards him.

He gave it the correct domestic kiss.

'She looks well in black, mother,' he told Mrs. Martin. 'Lady-like, black is. They insist on it in the good cafès.'

'What is left of me looks well in black,' Hester said gaily.

'O, come, come! You're improving, m'dear. Isn't she, mother? By the way, Hester. Dawson suggested on the 'phone that it would be wise to take your jewellery to the Bank. Mrs. Dawson's has gone. Safest there. What do you say, m'dear. No telling, you know. So much desperate – .'

'Courage,' prompted Hester, as he paused.

'Now, now! Proper lawless person she is, mother. Had she married that – Baines, isn't the fellow called – Baines, she might have been building barricades across Anne Street now. Ha-ha!'

Mrs. Martin did not look at Hester.

But Sandy did.

'She's blushing, mother. Ashamed to think of those salad days when she was so crude, and dreamed of armies of the night – or was it Monday morning – Hester? – Mustn't get excited, m'dear. Look at the fierce and unholy glitter in her pretty eyes! Just my little jibe, Hester. No ill-feeling!'

Then they sat down to tea.

'What's the joke?' asked Sanderson of Hester.

She was smiling, like a child who has come on some very funny picture.

'Is it that one I told you? Ha-ha!'

She started, as though blasphemy had been brought into something holy.

'See the old Victorian shine out in her, then – mother?' asked Sanderson. He pinched her ear as he went towards the brandy and soda.

'No; it was quite another joke – out of my own head, as Fanny says,' Hester told him. 'Do have one of these cakes, mother. They're charming! Exquisite!'

She overdid it, became an absurd, exquisite caricature of the commercial, refined class.

'I said once you'd no sense of humour,' said Sanderson. 'I take it back, m'dear. But you owe it to me.'

'Thanks.'

Hester's answer was mockingly humble.

Sanderson laughed again.

Mrs. Martin looked from one to the other, bewildered, a little troubled.

This was the splashing of spray, the superficial spray of polite conversation. Supposing deep ever met deep? She took one of the cakes, just to please Hester, and was glad when the bell rang, and Dawson's voice, superior and loud, sounded in the hall, with Fanny's humble 'Yes, Mr. Dawson,' 'No, Mr. Dawson,' answering it like a muted, servile breath.

The house was soon full of people. They filed into the great drawing-room, with its lighted lamps. Mrs. Martin sat stiffly in her chair, answering remarks addressed to her with 'Yes' or 'No,' as occasion demanded. She heard Hester replying in monosyllables to the condolences for the loss of Stephen, and assuring Mrs. Dawson that she herself was really improving in health every day. Fanny, in holy horror, lest she should not conduct herself to the credit of the house, entered with the tea-tray.

There was a pale young man studying for the ministry, who seemed perpetually to be trying to escape from the durance vile of a high collar, and who eventually found some consolation in abusing the novels of H. G. Wells[106] to Dawson, who had never read them. Dawson's sister came as near to animation as Hester had ever seen her in discussing the fly-peril with Mrs. Barstocks, whose 'I agree with you,' punctuated Miss Dawson's sentences at intervals, and who particularly agreed with her when the subject of flies was left behind and they spoke of the falling mining royalties. The young man, still imprisoned in his collar, was by this time indulging in a heated and highly decorative outburst on the immorality of free love.

It was Hester's voice which reached his senses, and reminded him that he was taking up too much of the conversation.

'I am sure, Mr. Findale, there is none here in this room,' she said.

'None?' he asked puzzled.

'None of that immoral thing known as free love,' she explained, smiling. 'Otherwise, Fanny would have disinfected the place – and I'm sure Mr. Dawson is quite respectable. In fact, I think we all are.'

Then Sandy's voice, emphatic and dogmatic, came from the divan corner. '"The Financial Times" is the best paper in the country.'

'But a bit like a cross between a cock-pit and a high-class gambling saloon organ,' came Hester's clear voice.

Sandy laughed.

But he gave her a meaning glance, and she subsided.

'Have another cup of tea, Mr. Findale,' Hester asked.

'Please.'

'And do have a scone.'

'Thanks, awfully.'

'Quite luxuries in these days,' she told him. 'With a strike on.'

He stared at her.

'Oh, surely not as bad as that!'

'These cakes are simply delicious!' cried Mrs. Dawson. 'You must give me the recipe, Mrs. Sanderson.'

One of those lulls in conversation, difficult to account for, fell on the company.

'Couldn't you play for us, Hester?' inquired Sanderson.

'Oh, perhaps – perhaps it's too soon,' said Mrs. Dawson, a little shocked, remembering Stephen and Hester's health.

'Oh, Hester likes to play,' Sanderson assured her.

'If it wouldn't be too great a strain,' said Mr. Findale.

'And sing us one or two of those songs, Hester. "The Little Maiden," and – what's the other? – "The Departing Warrior,"[107] isn't it? Nice little things. Translations she found somewhere, and set to music.'

'You compose music?' asked Mr. Findale. 'How perfectly marvellous, isn't it? So frightfully clever.'

'Did she really and truly ever work in a mill?' asked Miss Dawson of her sister-in-law. There was a babble all about them, and the rattle of the tea-tray. Mrs. Dawson nodded.

Hester's fingers scampered over the keys of the baby Grand, setting the bowl of Christmas roses shaking. Sanderson stood, thumbs in his waistcoat, with much the same cheerful air of pride that a pitman exhibits when showing off his pet canary. Mrs. Martin looked anxiously at Hester. This was the first time she had sung since they picked her up from the bedroom floor – in that pool of blood. Then Hester's voice stole into the room.

'Bulbul, on the little tree,
What is you sing to me,
When the Night winds up her blind,
Leaving half her stars behind?'[108]

'I did not know your daughter sang,' Mr. Barstocks said to Mrs. Martin.

'This one does,' she told him, reminding him of another one – and another scene.

'You – there's another one?' he asked.

'Yes.'

'She – ?'

'She's still in the factory; at least will be, when the strike's over.'

'Is that necessary, with Sanderson manufacturing?'

'She might be in a worse place.'

'Oh, certainly. Of course.'

Then Hester's voice stole into the room again, her fingers tinkling out the valiant, gay music.

'Gaily I take my departure, O world,
Vanquished and vanquishing, hated and blessed.
Sheathed is my sword, and my tossed banner furled,
Peace in my heart, I shall creep to my rest...'

There were the usual compliments, and Hester came back to sit in the little chair beside her mother. The desultory gossip and discussion usual to such parties began. Books and music and the market, and that queer case of the man found dead by the policeman, and the weather. Somehow the time passed, and it was time to dine. The rain beat on the windows. Hester looked out between the curtains once, to stare into a blackness full of the murmuring of rain, rain, rain. They filed into the dining-room, and talked and dined – and dined and talked. Then the ladies went into the drawing-room, and the gentlemen talked cotton over their wine.

Hester played a little, then started them all talking, Miss Dawson back again on flies, Mr. Findale on ethics, and – stole out of the room. Fanny had turned the light down in the hall. Hester could hear her singing 'There is a happy land, far, far away,' as she faced the mountain of crockery. She leaned against the closed door, breathlessly. Once she drew back, but it was only Sandy steering his way to the whisky and soda. She heard Dawson strike a match, and asserting that it was only a question of tactics.

'We're beaten, Sanderson. You know it. Moreover, the whole lot's coming out, soon – very soon – if Brayton doesn't go in. We might as well

– and take it off again – at the first bit of short time. It could be a lock-out, then – and no big loss.'

'My order goes out in two days.'

'If they don't topple it on to the streets before it gets to the station.'

'Oh, they won't do that.'

'There's the possibility.'

'In which case, the soldiers would be here.'

'But your order.'

'H'm.'

'I suggest that we get a Conciliatory Board. This boom'll be over in six months. Pin 'em down to an agreement. Then when the time's up we'll take it off. It'll be a lock-out – till the markets get cleared a bit again.'

She heard a little more, then moved away from the door, and went back to the drawing-room, a smiling hostess, begging their pardon for deserting them. She apologised for having a letter to write, wrote it and placed it in an envelope. Some unquelled childish spirit of comedy made her ask Mr. Findale to post it for her, if he would be such a Christian. Mr. Findale looked rather taken back, being in the middle of an explanation of the spirit of the ancient Spartans. But he could not refuse the flattering invitation to prove himself a Christian. He hurried to the pillar-box, too eager to be out of the rain to glance at the letter. When he came back the drawing-room was full. Hester was singing and playing.

Then – they heard the Feet.

'Good God!'

Sanderson was annoyed.

Miss Dawson distinctly showed a yellow streak.

'No. Don't worry, Miss Dawson. It's only their – rotten serenading again.'

'You're quite sure – they won't come in?'

'Quite; but if you'd feel safer with the doors bolted – ?'

'O, please.'

'Yes. Do, Sandy,' seconded Hester.

They listened to the feet beating through the rain, wind, and darkness. Sanderson bolted and locked the doors. The sound of the feet was an iron chorus now, as he re-entered the drawing room. Dawson sat placid and cynical, but Old Barstocks looked a little perturbed.

'Might be difficult for us to get away,' he said. 'And Mrs. Barstocks is so highly-strung – and gets anxious.'

'Oh, there'll be lots of policemen to take you home,' Hester told him gently.

'Yes, yes. I'm not really nervous – .'

Then the iron chorus of clogs ceased. They were outside, beyond the locked gates. A voice arose.

'Damn 'em!' ejaculated Dawson. 'They're doing it in style this time.'

'Who the devil is it?' asked Sanderson.

He was livid. Queer how they picked him out for all this rotten serenading. Only been at Dawson's once. Of course, he'd got the scabs in.

'It's that pitman, the blind fellow – got hurt in an explosion – and developed a voice. Sang at the Crystal Palace, and then went down because he wouldn't know people, or go out to tea with them – .'

'Do listen,' urged Mrs. Dawson.

It rose out of the darkness, a thrilling tenor voice, clear as a lark's, its natural, untrained beauty carrying its own appeal. The words were quite distinct.

'Here we are again, we dogs of bull-dog breed,
Singing you the old song, give to us more feed;
Whipped and scorned and spat upon in our hour of need,
Singing you this chorus strong – though our hearts may bleed.'

Then the thousand voices ripped it out –

'Here we are again, here we are again,
Laughing at our sadness, mocking at our pain,
Walking on to glory, o'er our own dear slain,
Here we are again. Here we are again.'

The voices conveyed a boisterous good humour. But the pitman's voice rose with a menacing thrill in the next four lines.

'When your guns are rusted, and your ships drift desolate,
When upon the walls you read, "Too Late, Too Late, Too Late,"
When we march with lives in hands, the masters of our fate,
You may hear us singing o'er the thunder of the spate.'

The chorus rolled up, a wild tide of challenge, into the room.

Mr. Barstocks blew his nose. It was quite preposterous. What were the policemen doing?

'Do you think they'll go away now?' asked Miss Dawson, in a whisper, to nobody in particular. Nobody knew. Everybody waited.

Then up from the street it came.

'Three cheers for Sanderson! And Dawson! And Barstocks! And – .'

There was a deafening surge of 'Boo – boo – boo!' from a thousand throats.

Then it came again.

'Three cheers for Hester Martin!'

She turned, a pallid ghost, waiting to have that concentrated sound of challenge and hatred hurled at her, quivering away from it – not for fear – but as from the beating of a thousand beloved hands. But the sound that came was – just a very old song.

'For she's a jolly good fellow,
She's a jolly good fellow,
She's a jolly good fellow,
And so say all of us.'

Had a bomb dropped in the room the effect could not have been more surprising. They were singing again.

'Glory, glory, hallelujah!
Glory, glory, hallelujah!
Glory, glory, hallelujah!
We are taking soup to-night.'

Sanderson's glance travelled from face to face – then to Hester's.

'What the hell do they mean?' he asked her.

'Sanderson!' said Dawson.

Sanderson choked. He had forgotten the ladies. He essayed control.

'Have you been contributing to this Strike Fund?' he asked.

'I'll tell you after, Sandy.'

It came rather faintly, but her voice did not tremble.

'All right, m'dear.'

Somehow, they all came back to the normal, on the surface at any rate. The Feet died away. The voices died away. One by one they went. When the 'mob' had cleared off, with Mr. Findale as a somewhat nervous scout, to see that the coast was clear, the visitors got into their cars and went away. The house quietened down.

'You'll be tired, mother,' Sanderson told Mrs. Martin.

She took the hint.

She went upstairs, but did not undress.

Fanny had wearily gone up before her, and was saying her prayers in the chill bedroom. The cook had gone an hour before. The house was very quiet, save for the eternal murmur of the rain. Hester sat on in the little chair, her hands clasping and unclasping each other.

'Now,' said Sanderson, leaning forward in the fat chair. 'What have you been doing?'

She wanted to say 'Nothing,' just as she had done when her grandmother once discovered her writing with the point of a pen on the old chest.

'You've been giving to their damned strike fund – scabbing on us!' he told her.

She loathed herself vigorously. Inside her was a daredevil chanting to her, 'Tell him. Face it out. Tell him, and take the consequences.'

But Sandy looked very terrible.

'Oh, nothing much,' she faltered. 'Don't look so fierce, Sandy,'

'Tell me.'

'There's really nothing much to tell.'

'They don't fling their damned gratitude at you for nothing,' he told her. 'You've cheated, Hester. You've struck a blow for them, and that's against me – against us, I mean. You're a treacherous devil – and I want to know the extent of your treachery. It's no good trembling. That damned Baines – I expect he put you up to it, when he came that night.

He's infected you. Now, what have you given them? What have you given them? How much?'

He leaned forward and gripped her hard.

The confession came with a throaty laugh.

'Everything, Sandy.'

'Everything, you she-devil! What do you mean?'

'All I had.'

'All you had – what had you? I picked you up out of the gutter.'

'Not quite, Sandy.'

'Out of the gutter. What have you given them?'

'Everything I had – I tell you.'

It was strange to have such terror in one's heart, such futile childish terror, to know you were defeated, and to be able to laugh at your own defeat.

'Stop your damned laughing.'

'What had you to give?'

'I gave them – .'

'Come on. Tell me.'

'Don't grab my wrist.'

'I'll break you into little bits if you don't tell me.'

'I gave them the jewellery you gave to me.'

'You – .'

He turned almost green.

'Hester! You're getting a bit of your own back. You – you never gave them – ?'

'I've told you.'

'But how – ?'

'They are taking soup to-night,' she told him. 'They are emulating the example of a famous Queen of History, who had pearls in her wine. They are eating and drinking diamonds, and rubies, and emeralds, and opals! Haven't you any sense of humour, Sandy?'

'Good God!'

He released her.

'But – .'

'I had nothing else to give.'

It seemed so silly to be telling Sandy this over and over again. She set her foot to the floor, to get up, and move away. But even as she moved, his hands came down on her shoulders.

'Oh, no; you don't get off so easily.'

'What are you going to do, Sandy?'

He had picked her up.

'I am going to pitch you out into the street.'

'You needn't. I'll walk out.'

'I prefer to pitch you out.'

'But you gave me the things.'

'Don't argue. I'm going to pitch you out.'

She beat at him futilely with trembling hands.

'I'm pitching you out into the streets, where you belong. You can wait till Baines comes and picks the bits up.'

She was slung over his shoulders – still beating at him. They passed through the doorway, down the passage, through the vestibule – and he opened the door. The rain sounded on the garden walk. She hit him with all the force she had.

'Now – you're going – .'

'No. Sandy – .'

She clung to him frantically. There were so many steps down.

'Let me walk out.'

'I'm pitching you out.'

One – two – – three!

Then she went, with a faint, shuddering cry of terror, and a hysterical wonder as to when she would – crash! The earth came up. A door closed. The bolt was shot. Bruised and shaken, with stinging pain, mad, stinging pain, she lay. She had not fainted. But she lay a little while, trying to find out if any part of her had been broken. Then she arose – creeping first on hands and knees. She stood up at last, in her evening dress, her hair down her back, the rain drenching her. 'Till Baines picked the bits up,' he had said. She rubbed her forehead. There was a lump on it like a small pigeon egg, and her nose was bleeding. 'Till Baines picked the bits up.' She opened the gate and went out into the street.

It was very quiet. The rain sounded on the road and the flagstones. She had a dim memory that somewhere from the house, as she had crashed, her mother's voice had called 'Hessie!' A motor passed, its headlights shining on her. Her nose was still bleeding. She had no handkerchief. The fact that she had no hairpins either, worried her. She fumbled and found one, still clinging in her hair, and stood in the shadows fastening it up in one big knot. The rain-drops splattered on her bare neck. One thought beat in on her brain – she could not walk in the main streets like this.

So she turned up the back streets, and wandering about for some time found that she had been going round in a circle. There were lights, voices, in Sanderson's garden. She turned, and fled back into the back streets, running as she had not thought she could run. Quite suddenly all her strength went. She groped her way to the deepest shadows, found some steps and sat down, trying to think.

But it was quite impossible. A voice out of the blackness startled her. She realised it was a man – drunk – and ran off again, trying to think where women did go when they had no money, and did not want to go back to their friends. She tried to pull the velvet dress higher, holding it with one numbed hand, and still running, till she came out into the lamplit streets. A policeman stood near a lamp. A ray of penetration lit up her mind. He was a new one. He would not know her.

'Could you tell me where Mr. Jack Baines lives?'

He caught a brief glimpse of a woman, bare-headed, with white gleaming neck.

'Here – do you know you're bleeding – ?'

'I've fallen. That's all. Do you know where he lives?'

For she could not think of the street, or the number.

'Vinter Street – first to your right, second to your left, then to your left again.'

'Thanks.'

'I say – .'

But she had flashed away.

She was drumming it into her brain as she ran, Vinter Street, first to your right, second to your left, then to your left again – and there was something about 'bits' – somebody picking up the 'bits' – but it was not quite clear. She could not quite remember what relation there was between Vinter Street and bits being picked up.

CHAPTER 25

JACK BAINES sat writing in the kitchen. Mrs. Baines had had gone to bed. Jerry was out.

The table was littered with papers. He was sending out another appeal to the General Executive to act – and act at once, and to stop scabbing in Brayton. It was couched in very official language. But it's challenge was plain. He drew a deep breath as he pushed it into the envelope, fastened it up, and ran his fingers through his hair. Something was rotten in the State of Denmark! After this little job was over, propaganda for Jack Baines! inside and outside the union, too – and not only when strikes were on, all the time. Not only when they were putting up members for Parliament, but all the time.

Poor old Stiner! Stiner used to say that that was what should be done. He'd done his little lot, Stiner – in his own way. Map out the country, map out all countries. Have hundreds of men scouring their cities, towns, hamlets, villages, and hill-sides.

He filled his pipe, yawned wearily, and sat down in his mother's chair. Wide was the field, and few the labourers. He stretched his limbs out, preparatory to sleep. The door was unlocked. If any trouble was on, they'd find him there. He took a few pulls at the old pipe. Queer how you got fond of an old pipe. How kindly it came to the hand, the old, familiar, seasoned friend. It brought all the old dreams circling about you in the smoke clouds. Queer how conservative one was in things like pipes.

He held the pipe before him, staring at it curiously. The first time he had smoked that was on a rainy, windy evening.

Was it quite fair to keep that old pipe?

He took it between his hands, smashed it, and tossed it into the fire, raking the cinders over it. Then he had to read for half an hour. 'Bleak House.'[109] The Court of Chancery rose up through the fog, and he was smiling. And yet wasn't all life a Court of Chancery? The book slid from his hand at last, making the cat jump. He slept heavily, dog-tired. There was a mouse running about. The cat stole after it, stealthily. The wind rattled the window-sashes. The rain lashed the panes. Jack thought it was the tap-tap of the window blind he heard. There was something – tap-tap – weaving its sound in with his troubled dreams. Tap-tap! Through the fantastic dream he heard its echo. Tap-tap.

He half opened his eyes, then closed them again, wearily. Tap-tap! Sometimes Tibby beat her tail against the door, when outside. He opened his eyes. Tibby was washing herself, sitting on the fender. Tap-tap!

Baines felt annoyed. He was very tired. He got up from his chair. How it was raining! He hoped no one was sleeping out on a night like this – but he knew that was not impossible. He yawned as he went down the lobby. Tap-tap! Sounded like a child. But no child would be out at this hour – -unless it was a lost child! That made him open the door swiftly.

A swirl of rain beat in on him. He stared out into empty darkness, and pressing forwards – stumbling against her.

'Hello! What's up? What is it?' he asked, bending down. 'Who is it?'

There was no answer.

He went back into the house for a box of matches, and returning, struck one. Her chin had fallen forwards. He could only see an evening dress, a white neck. Some poor prostitute, some piece of wreckage washed up by the tidal waves on a grim shore. That was his thought.

'Here – !'

He grabbed her shoulder.

It was very thin, painfully thin. The match had gone out.

'Pull yourself together.'

Perhaps she was drunk?

And what if she were? Wasn't she a sister of his?

'Pull yourself together,' he repeated.

The woman on the step seemed to hear. Familiar words Sandy had often spoken, subconsciously she obeyed. She staggered to her feet and faced him as he struck the other match. Its brief light flickered over her features.

'Hessie!' he gasped.

'It's – only me,' she told him.

Only me!

'Is – is something the matter?'

A silly, futile sort of speech have humans when paralysed by great emotion.

'No – there's nothing the matter. Sandy said I'd to wait till you came and picked the bits up. But it was *so* cold; so cold!'

In the darkness his face took on that inscrutable expression which made the employers complain of Baines that he was hard to deal with.

'Shall I carry the "bits" in?' he asked her.

'No. I'll walk in.'

She walked in. He saw that she did not notice any of the details around her, but by the instinct of the physically starved, turned with shuddering eagerness to the fire, rubbing one frozen hand with the other. She was sodden with rain. The steam rose round her in a cloud, as she stood by the fire. She had something of the look of a woman he had once seen walking in her sleep. She answered like one speaking in her sleep, too – without consciousness of the real meaning of questions or answers. She stood up, until he asked her to sit down.

'How long have you been wandering about?'

She did not know.

But some realisation of time returned dully, with his question. She looked around for a clock, found it – and forgot to concentrate on the time it showed.

'I'll make you a cup of tea.'

'No, don't trouble. It's only that it's – a little cold outside.'

She stared at him in a strange way. He was something that had been in the Past, and was in the Present, but had nothing to do with To-morrow. Just a link, somehow connecting her with all she had ever loved, did love, and ever would love.

Baines was pushing the kettle down into the hot cinders. He found the bellows and blew the fire into redder heat. The cheerful singing of the kettle came to him with an alien sound. Then he took out a cup and saucer, and a little plate, cleared a place on the paper-littered table, and found a canister of biscuits in the cupboard.

'It's ready, Hessie,' he reminded her.

She stared at the solitary cup – and jumped in a startled way at the sound of his voice.

'Aren't you having any?'

So he fetched another cup and plate, and they sat up to the table pretending to eat. But she sipped at the hot tea. A cinder falling on the hearth made her slop the tea, and she gave him an apologetic look, a look he had once seen on the face of a beggar his mother had taken in out of the winter cold.

'I'm afraid I'm not hungry,' he told her.

'I'm so sorry I've disturbed you,' she said, after a silence, speaking with the enunciation of Sanderson's class – the class she had lived with all these years. And as she spoke, the false smile of that class played on her features – the smile without meaning.

Bits! Yes. Bits! Certainly bits!

Shattered a long way from the heart's desire, but still the bits of his own class, surviving through a dead language, a dead life, and the phantom show of unsplendid miseries. He handed her his mother's shoulder-shawl, a woollen antimacassar. She put it on, her teeth making an attempt not to chatter.

He made an attack on the strange unconsciousness she showed of her own position. Somehow, he had got to rouse her. There were all the conventions to be thought of!

'What's that bump on your head?'

'I fell.'

'Here's a handkerchief.'

He took one from the clothes-rack above his head.

'Did you hurt yourself?'

'Yes. I think so.'

The beautiful conventions!

'How are your children?'

Then he could have bitten his tongue out. He had forgotten that one was dead, just for the moment.

'The little girl is very well. The other died.'

She rose from the chair and cast a restless, wavering glance at the door. Her children! That had roused her.

'Yes – but – sit down, Hessie. We've got to talk this out.'

She obeyed, with that distressed look still on her face, her human emotions struggling through mental coma at the mention of her children.

Then he heard his mother moving upstairs. He went to circumvent her.

'Whoever is it, Jack?' she asked, as he waited at the foot of the stairs.

'It's only – a bit of Waste Sanderson's sent me, after it's been devilled up in his mill,' he told her enigmatically. She stared at him. The light of the candle she carried revealed his face. Was *this* her son's face? Or had her son's face been hidden from her until this moment? Her brain was homely, but it could leap at truth.

'Not – ?' she asked.

'Ay. It's Hessie!'

She opened her lips –

He held up a warning finger.

'And yon keep out of it,' he told her, calmly, determinedly. 'I know all I owe you. But you must keep out of it. The older generations are always throwing barricades between us and – the path we should tread. You do it for the best, to save us, but it becomes the worst.'

The candle swerved uncertainly, he caught a sobbing breath, and was on the stairs beside her. The lights and shadows flickered and blurred the two faces, alike yet unlike. Then he grabbed the hand that did not hold the candle, the dear, worn hand, marked with common labour, the sign of toiling motherhood the wide world over. He kissed her for the first time since his boyhood.

'But for God's sake – don't stand in the way,' he begged, humbly.

She answered him through the tears of the grey-haired. 'Well – consider it all round, Jack – and – be careful.'

It was the voice of the Old World speaking to that which would build a new one – speaking out of its grey sorrows, grey experience, and grey fears, and also – out of its hard-won serenity, wisdom, and infinite compassion. Whilst between them for 'consideration' stood the symbol of the Soul of the People, broken and confused, cold and hungry, divided against itself, sick with old wounds, shrinking from new ones to come, saying in its heart of sorrows, 'How long shall this endure? Would that the Spring were here!' Waiting patiently with drooping head, hearing, muddled and afar, these echoes of voices on the stairs, which in some way had something to do with its destiny, its terrible, wonderful, stained and frustrated destiny.

CHAPTER 26

IT WAS at the public telephone, in the little coffin-like box with the glass door, where 'ghosts' talk to each other whilst the world wags by, licking postage stamps, just beyond.

'Hello!'

Jack's face was the face of one who has passed a sleepless night.

'Hello.'

'Is that Sanderson?'

'Yes. That you, Dawson?'

'No. This is *Baines*.'

'Oh.'

'I wanted to tell you Sanderson – .'

'Are you speaking officially?'

The taunt came over the wires.

'No.'

'Well?'

'There was a consignment of "bits" you sent along to Vinter Street last night.'

'Oh, they landed, did they?'

'Yes. Quite safely.'

'Well?'

'*Thanks.*'

'Anything more to say?'

'Yes. Just this – .'

'I'm waiting.'

'If you'll condescend to come round to a working-class back-yard I'll give you compound interest on the time you've had those "bits."'

'Sounds like a text-book, Baines.'

'H'm. But not a Ready Reckoner! Are you coming?'

'Yes – with the car. Awfully good of you, Baines, to have taken care of

Mrs. Sanderson – .'

'Sanderson.'

'Yes.'

'I'll break your head if you come near her.'

'I shall bring a constable.'

'All right. If you try force – possibly you'll be met with *force*.'

'Thought you were a constitutionalist, Baines?'

'Try us and see!'

'How many are there of you?'

'Oh, Oh! Come and see!'

'The soldiers are at Whitleigh.'

'Quite aware of it! This town contains the stuff for a small revolution, Sanderson!'

'Sounds as if you Socialists have private interests of your own – and we are not the only class that makes pawns of the mob.'

Baines stood still, the receiver at his ear, with a shattered look on his face. Out of the mouths of our enemies truth *sometimes* issues.

Private Interests!

Should a Socialist have any, that are not an integral part of Mass-Interest – He had just threatened to use the passions of his class, to hold and keep his own broken, precious 'bits.'

'I'll be round with the car in half an hour, Baines. So – long!'

Baines hung up the receiver.

Half an hour!

He dashed out into the street. He had a crazy idea that if he could see Rachel, somehow daylight would dawn on this unholy jumble in which he found himself. Rachel, the new Dream, which had somehow gone down before the onrush of an older Dream. But Rachel would understand. Whatever he was not sure of, he was sure of that.

The Shadows of the 'Mob' passed about him, despondent men, desperate men, draggled women, half-famished children, and he saw them pass, penned in a little particular hell of his own.

Then across the chaos of a torn soul Rachel's strong voice called to him – from across the street, from across a gulf wide as the world.

'Going home – or away from it?'

'Rachel – !'

She came over to him.

'Don't talk to me about it. I've been. Your mother sent for me.'

'Well?'

'Get an impartial Committee on it, Jack. I'm too near it.'

'But I relied on you – .'

'I daren't. I daren't. I would if I dared. Ask me to shoulder a rifle, when they land from Whitleigh. And find me the rifle – and I'll shoulder it. But this is a thing I can't meddle in. My own Private Interests might bias me. You can't choose for other folk when you're not sure of yourself. I wish I could have helped – but – consider me outside of it! Out of it altogether. I just daren't, Jack. We've all of us interfered with Hessie – too much. At the last ditch, *I* daren't.'

And he realised through his desolation that she was thinking not of himself at all, but of Hessie.

A blue-faced clock in the market tower showed him the time.

'The only thing to do is to *leave it to her.*'

Queer! He had never thought of that.

It was Hessie who had to decide – she who was the pivot – just as the People's Soul is the pivot of every battle, swung this way and that, balanced from one end then the other, the balance preserved by someone, anyone standing in the middle of the see-saw.

'All right.'

She seized his hand.

He recognised her, then, the soul that was big enough to stand out of the way.

Then she was gone.

He wished he had been in a calmer state. One should decide these things calmly. That is, if the big things could ever be decided calmly – without upheaval. Could they? History said 'No.'

His mother opened the door.

'Rachel's been here.'

She tried to look innocent.

It was too small a thing to bother about. He let it pass. He went into the parlour, with the fire burning, there Hessie sat in her motley, an evening-dress from which his mother had sponged the blood-stains, and the old working-class shawl. Then he shut the door.

'Have you had your breakfast?'

She was in her right mind now. He saw that. The 'bits' were weakly coming together. Consciousness had returned.

'Yes.'

'Much?'

'Oh – quite a lot.'

'You've got to eat. You've got to hope. You've got to learn to live. And I'm going to teach you *how*.'

She stared at him.

'Is that something anyone can teach us?' she asked.

'Yes. It can be taught. It shall be taught. And the results shall be the proof.'

'A tired thing?' she asked.

She stared down at her hands – snowflakes which would melt in the Springtime.

'A broken, worn-out piece of mechanism – waiting to be scrapped?' she asked.

'All that is true of you, is true also of the Masses!' he told her, doggedly.

'Without feeling – ,' she added. 'Quite content to go on – to the end? Passivity which has compromised with Capitalism (meaning Sandy) and only left it when it was pitched out,' she added, very quietly. 'Oh – what a fool! What a fool!'

'Every agitator born has been a fool,' he told her. 'My faith in my fooled class is in you. Can you betray it?'

She began to tremble, then. She belied herself when she spoke of having no feelings left.

'Sandy's bringing the car round. It will be here in twenty minutes.'

She staggered out of the chair.

Then she asked 'What did you say to him?'

'I threatened force.'

'Force?'

'Force against his force – .'

'To hold me here, as he would hold me there – ?'

'To defend you against him.'

'Perhaps – weak as I am – I am not weak enough to need a defender.'

'Five minutes have gone,' he told her, laying his watch on the table.

'If you have a mind – choose between us.'

'Would you mind going out whilst I decide?' she queried. She handed him the watch.

He looked round the room. Was there anything she could hurt herself with? With that uncanny penetration she had when fully conscious, and not dreaming, she handed him the knife and fork off the breakfast tray, smiling in faint satire.

'Five minutes,' he told her. 'And remember, I've used no eloquence. It hasn't been box-oratory. If I liked – .'

She knew quite well the sort of eloquence he could have used, if he had liked. It had been used, all through the ages, by lovers, patriots, comrades, and rebels, leading with the masses – half-dead in the House of Bondage!

He stood outside, waiting the passing of the eternal five minutes, his watch in one hand and the ridiculous knife and fork in the other. All was very still.

'The time's up,' he told her, in a tense voice.

He opened the door – and went in.

'Well – ?'

Silence answered.

'Don't keep me waiting – .'

She spoke very deliberately.

'I have considered it all – all, pushing myself *quite* outside of it. I keep my bond with Sandy.'

'Your bondage – you mean.'

'*My bond.*'

'Your bondage,' he repeated. 'Oh, Hessie! Oh, Hessie!'

He knew now how very precious, even in its fragments, that old Dream had been!

'Till some Force bigger than either of you – frees me,' she told him. 'Bigger than either of you.'

When the car came she was ready. Sanderson had brought the fur-lined cloak, the fur-lined gloves, a hat, and Fanny, who looked as though she had not slept all night, either.

'Where's my mother?' asked Hessie.

She asked it of Fanny.

'She's left, ma'am – .'

'Where's she gone?'

'I don't know, ma'am.'

She was quite alone. Quite alone, with her bond, and her bondage.

'I can't see you home, Hester,' Sanderson told her. 'They're loading the wagons. I must get back to the mill.'

Yes. He must get back to the mill.

The dominant factor dominated the victor as well as the victim. He walked away with a triumphant glance at Baines.

As Hester was driven home, the car passed two men, carrying a coffin.

'That's for that man who was killed fighting the picket,' Fanny told Hester. 'The picket who killed him is dead, too. They say O'Neill has never been himself since that night. A woman told me his wife says she's scared of him. She thinks he's going queer.'

'A lot of policemen go mad,' Hester said.

John sat driving.

Nothing was said of the previous night.

CHAPTER 27

JACOB'S Ladder. That was not the technical name for it but what the winders called it, when they went 'stealing' tallow[110] to make the cops skewer more easily. It went down from the sizing-hole into the place where the donkey-engine throbbed and shook the winding-room floor. It was dark where Jacob's Ladder hung. A reeking, sickly smell of heat, and grease, and tallow, and the mixing of size,[111] was the atmosphere with which it was surrounded.

Scrambling hand over hand was a little man, more like a monkey than a man, in shoddy rags, on whose face, the dim light falling showed what man had made of man. One sentence was burning in his brain, his brain not far removed from apedom, in spite of the facts of science and the fine art of the world. He could hear the heavy wheels of the wagons rumbling under the sheds in the yard. The engine-throbs were repeating that sentence to him, in Sanderson's voice.

'You dirty skunk! I'll soon have done with the lot of you. Jump at it! Get those picks in.'

Inside the shed the scabs were 'weaving up.'

They were waiting in the warehouse to 'look' the last cloth off the looms, and toss it on the wagons. Then it was done with and the scabs were done with.

That which should have been 'human' looked down, and saw the disappearing form of Tim. He dropped down, unrolled a bundle of waste from his pockets, and rubbed it round in the tallow-box.

'You dirty skunk!'

That was the thanks of Capitalism – the wages of scabdom. Yet he had been called many names. Far back in his nightmare of a memory various names stuck out. *Bastard* was the one he remembered first. *Oil-can* came next. He recalled the whistling of the pit-wagons as they went past him, waiting for the oil from his can. Other names, all as dignified, throbbed in his memory. But to be called a dirty skunk after having made one of a stinking army, to save an 'order,' to have withstood one's own manhood, when pickets pleaded, and to be called 'a skunk' for it! Round and round the tallow-box. He found a bottle of paraffin. He heard Tim whistling 'Maggie Murphy's Home,' and climbed up Jacob's Ladder. He got back into the shed, somehow. Sanderson was raging about. He flew to his looms and set them clattering on, an upturned weft-can covering waste, tallow and paraffin. He was very humble when Sanderson came to him. He was putting the last picks into the cloth. Sanderson was pulling a lot of cloth off one of the looms and a scab was waiting to receive it. Scabs were loading the wagons. And it was in his brain that the whole place was a scab, a sore on the face of the earth. The jibe of burning it all down, himself included – and all the others appealed to him with grim fascination.

'Here – carry this,' Sanderson yelled at him.

The last picks were in.

The scab picked up the roll of cloth. Poor Hindoos whose fatalism is not confined to the mysterious East, would wear that cloth on their heads and say their prayers on little mats, and hope to reach Nirvana! They would go through all the mummeries of 'caste,' salaaming and prostrating themselves to Tradition, with that rag on their heads. The East of the West, and the East of the East, are not quite the poles apart that our jingoes would have us believe.

Sanderson rushed out of the alley, into another where another scab was 'coving.'[112]

The man who had been up and down Jacob's Ladder panted into the warehouse.

He stood close to the middle counter, as they looked the cloth. He leaned down to tie his broken boot-lace. He struck a match for his pipe.

'Mind them sparks,' called the man looking the cloth. Then he had the cloth over the frame, on a strong light, looking for faults. Everybody was rushing about. The wagons were waiting, all but one, which stood with its load, covered with tarpaulin to keep it dry.

They were out loading, swearing at the horses, while the little flame was creeping up, and up, and up – curling about like a serpent and shooting out to see what it might destroy.

CHAPTER 28

'ARE you asleep, ma'am?'

It was Fanny's voice, respectful, but excited.

'No.'

'I'm sorry, ma'am – .'

'What is it?'

'The mill's burning down. Mr. Sanderson's just told me on the 'phone. And he says you are to go in the car and tell O'Neill and get the soldiers here. The fire engine's going.'

A few ticks of the china clock.

'All right, Fanny.'

'Mr. Sanderson said if you weren't fit to go, I'd to go. The car's waiting.'

'All right, Fanny. Tell John to take the car into the garage. I'll walk. You see there's a lot of excitement.'

She climbed up into the attic where Stephen had loved to watch the Shadows. She opened the old box, and a smell of mould came out, years of mould, as from a grave. Dimly she saw Morris and Liebknecht staring at her, their faces dust-spotted, gentle and determined faces! She was smiling gently. She dragged out the old skirt, the shawl, green with mould.

Fanny had followed, and stood staring.

'This is the best way to go, Fanny.'

Fanny remembered afterwards the curious emphasis on the word 'best.'

'Perhaps you're right, ma'am.'

'I am certain I am right.'

'And I'll go out by the back entrance, Fanny.'

'Yes, ma'am.'

'Brush the mould off, Fanny.'

'But they're damp.'

'Never mind. Brush the mould off.'

'Do you think you're fit to go by yourself, ma'am?'

'Quite fit.'

'I'll have the bottle in the bed, ma'am.'

'All right, Fanny.'

She took a look round the attic – the attic with its Shadows – and those dust-spotted faces of their old pictures.

'You've been so upset lately, ma'am. It will soon be over. Keep your heart up.'

It was the human being peeping out from the domestic.

'You've always been very kind, Fanny.'

Fanny's eyes filled with tears, suddenly.

'They say, you know, them jumped-up working-classes is harder nor anyone. But I – you've never given me a cross word, ma'am.'

'And yet you always called me "ma'am."'

'Oh, yes, ma'am. I was brought up to remember my manners.'

'How do I look in this get-up, Fanny?'

Fanny was silent.

Hester laughed.

'I wore these a long time – these sort of rags – could you fasten the clasps, Fanny?'

Fanny knelt down and fastened the clog-clasps.

'Now, just say this after me – it's just a sick fancy – so humour me. Say, "God speed you, Hester Martin."'

Fanny said it.

'Now, I'm off.'

She went down the steps, and out by the servants' entrance, and into the dark streets. It was raining again. She heard a group of women saying that O'Neill had gone mad, and given himself up for murder. It came to her as part of the dark comedy. She went to a public telephone. She had taken just enough money for the call. She got through to the Union offices. It was Baines' voice which answered hers.

'Sandy's mill is on fire. They're getting the soldiers. Warn everybody to keep inside.'

'We've a meeting in ten minutes. The crowd's waiting now. Where are you?'

'Public telephone.'

Then she hung up the receiver.

Amongst the others, she passed on to the place of meeting. They were singing when she arrived – singing 'When Wilt Thou Save The People.'[113] They were waiting for Baines. The scabs came filing past, their work was done, saved from the mill-fire, and some of them crept near, listening to the man who was trying to keep the crowd good-humoured till Baines came. Out of whose hand flew the stone? Nobody knew. But there was fighting – and a police-call – and the call sent out for the soldiers.

Baines landed in the thick of it, just as Barstock came up with the police, to read the Riot Act. He read it. Riot Acts. How many have been read? How many more will be read? Baines tried to get a hearing, but they were singing. He yelled at them, but his voice went down in a surging flood of revolutionary songs. It was tragic to see him struggling to govern hell let loose – trying to save them from themselves.

One or two, more controlled, saw the tragedy of it.

Someone leaped up out of the singing mass, a bit of a thing in a mouldy shawl, up on to the wagon. The flare of a torch lit her face in the dark afternoon.

'It's Hester Martin.'

They started to cheer.

How prone they were to hero worship! All part of 'This Slavery.'

They realised the strange significance in the appearance of Hester in clogs and shawl. Reason could not make them listen. Drama could. There was a dead hush.

'The soldiers will soon be here,' she told them.

'Speak up.'

'The soldiers will soon be here.'

'Let 'em come.'

A tearing cry of readiness for anything went up. They failed to grasp what it meant.

Then another hush.

'To destroy our victory?'

'Victory!'

It came in a cry of protest.

'You have won. The bosses are giving in.'

They heard that.

'Is it God's Truth?' called a voice.

'It is human Truth,' she answered. 'Go back to the places you call *Homes*. Don't give them a chance. Here's the proof.'

She tossed half-a-dozen documents amongst them.

The proof! They jumbled about, passing the proof from hand to hand.

Then they heard the tramp of the soldiers.

They couldn't have been at Whitleigh then. They were coming. The soldiers were coming. Rum-tum-a-tum! The drums sounded. They were marching in on Brayton. They began to scatter – but it was hard to get out when you'd once got in – and whilst they scattered, those who could, the soldiers streamed into the streets, surrounding the square. Their red jackets made a menacing scarlet amidst the grey shoddy.

'God!'

Baines ejaculated it, his eyes ablaze.

His voice rose then, surging over the shoddy and the uniformed militarists.

'These people are peaceful. Let them go to their homes.'

'Disperse!' yelled the regimental sergeant. The soldiers began to push the crowd about. Blows were exchanged. Baines jumped down into the struggling mass, he was striking with bare fists at everything military he could see. And somewhere the first rifle went up.

Then Hester's voice rang out, wild and piercing.

'Brothers in bondage, comrades of poverty. *Don't shoot your own.*'

He had been in India. He was a little barmy, they called it. The surging, struggling crowd made a mad picture in his eyes. Other surging scenes jostled in his brain. Arabs, and – others.

'Let no one shoot,' yelled the regimental sergeant, even as the Inspector said, 'Take her up for Sedition.'

But before they could 'take her' the rifle had sounded its shot, a puff of blue smoke curled in the air. She went down, like a shot bird. And the crowd fought its way out, helter-skelter through the streets, with the rifle shots sounding in the air, to quicken its speed. The police had Baines in handcuffs – dragged along, away from that waggon where a little heap of nothing lay. But Rachel was there – weeping, without a rifle!

Realising that Hester – and not she – had saved the folk from their own blood.

And it passed away, like our tale which is told. Just a fantastic human story, symbolising Society – and all its struggling types. Let it pass. As some day 'This Slavery' will pass. When the triumphant armies of Democracy march past the old 'forts of folly' they will see on those walls strange marks, the blows of thousands of obscure men and women. As the dawn rolls up in its thunderous glory, which all the striving shadows cannot stay, these words may stand clear in the dawn-light, the message of those who have struck their blows, and passed.

'Democracy! Serene-browed, triumphant, peaceful-eyed, look up and read our message on these, *their walls*. Even we, fettered and half-blind and half-dumb, have served thee, O Democracy! Whilst thou wert yet in the dust – and uncrowned – save by thorns. Not Caesar! But thou, Democracy! Not Power – but the People. With frail human hands, calloused hands, blundering hands, illiterate hands, vain hands, even with the hands of hate, as with the hands of love, *we, unremembered, unhonoured, have served even thee.* Garland thy spears with blossoms. Build thy new World. And forget us, quickly, the Shadows of Yesterday. Make us no altars. Worship us not. Such is of the Past. March on triumphant, and forget the echoes of our strife. For in all that we were – and we were very human – we had but one glory. We were of thee, Democracy. Of thy Blood, of thy Bone, of thy Heart, of thy Soul. We salute thee, Democracy – and bid thee forget us. We are but the Shadows of thy Yesterday. March on – electric with Love. Serve – as we have served.'

THE END

NOTES

1. William Morris (1834–96), author, designer and poet, one of the principal founders of the Arts and Crafts movement and a pioneer socialist who co-founded the Socialist League, a breakaway group from the 1881 Social Democratic Federation, in 1885.

2. Probably William Liebknecht (1826–1900), German Social Democrat and one of the founders of the Social Democratic Party of Germany, rather than his son, Karl Liebknecht (1871–1919), German Socialist and co-founder of the KPD (the German Communist Party) who was murdered along with Rosa Luxemburg after the Spartacist Uprising in Berlin in 1919. Prints of popular left-wing figures could be readily obtained through weeklies like the *Clarion*, the *Labour Leader*, and the *Christian Commonwealth*.

3. Edward Clodd (1840–1930), well-known agnostic, rationalist, and influential populariser of scientific naturalism. His books, like *The Childhood of the World: A Simple Account of Man in Early Times* (1873) aimed to introduce children and young adults to current developments in evolutionary theory and sold in huge numbers. Rachel appears to be reading the best-selling *The Story of Creation: A Plain Account of Evolution*, first published in 1888.

4. Psalm 23.

5. There are several biblical analogues, the closest probably being Deuteronomy 8. 3, 'And he humbled thee, and suffered thee to hunger, and fed thee with manna'.

6. Starved.

7. The Social Democratic Federation (S.D.F.), founded in 1881, a vanguard organisation intent on educating the workers in economic theory and the fundamental importance of the class struggle. Though never a mass organisation, it had a stronghold in Lancashire. Burnley, close to Carnie Holdsworth's family home in Great Harwood, boasted one of the strongest S.D.F. branches in the country and came

close to electing the group's founder, H.M.Hyndman, as an MP in the 1906 General Election. Though Hyndman considered himself to be a Marxist, Karl Marx thought him 'theoretically backward'. William Morris and Eleanor Marx (Karl Marx's youngest daughter) broke from Hyndman in 1884 and formed the Socialist League.

8. A process in the stretching of cotton before it is spun into yarn, resulting in a finer cloth. A delicate job involving winding roving (slivers of spun cotton) onto a spindle in an ovoid ball (cop), then when it is of sufficient size sliding it off, skewering it, and placing it in the creel of the spinning machine.

9. The mythical king of Phrygia, son of Zeus, condemned to stand in water for perpetuity for revealing the secrets of the Gods, and haunted by the proximity of the food and drink which he cannot reach.

10. From *The Rubáiyát of Omar Khayyám* (lxxxviii).

11. The ancient Greek underworld.

12. The capital city of Lesbos, often associated with the classical Greek female poet Sappho (c. 630–12 BC–c. 570 BC).

13. A one pound coin, made of gold.

14. Strong leather half-boots or shoes.

15. Omar Khayyám (1048–1131), Persian philosopher, mathematician and astronomer whose poetry, preoccupied with questions of mortality and transience, was popularized by Dante Gabriel Rossetti's championing of Edward Fitzgerald's translation, *The Rubáiyát of Omar Khayyám* (1859).

16. Open to question because of the ambiguous date of the text. It may refer to the 'July Revolution' (or the 'Tragic Week') in Barcelona in July 1909, when over six hundred men and women involved in a General Strike were killed by the authorities.

17. Anthem of the International and British Labour Movements, written by the Irishman Jim Connell (1852–1929) in 1889.

18. The British Empire, with its free trade monopolies and ability to flood the markets of its colonies, was a great boon to the Lancashire cotton industry. After the Industrial Revolution, British mechanised production could import raw cotton from America (in the early nineteenth century this was predominantly from the southern

slave plantations), spin and weave it in the factories of Lancashire, and sell it in India at lower prices than local producers could offer. In the nineteenth century, when 'cotton was king', the Indian textile trade was the largest single item in British export trade.

19. The personification of riches and greed in the form of a false god. 'No one can serve two masters, for either he will hate the one, and love the other; or else he will hold to the one, and despise the other. Ye cannot serve God and Mammon' (Matthew 6. 24).

20. Odin, a war God from Norse mythology, and Thor, his son, the great, red-bearded warrior and God of Thunder.

21. Wat Tyler (1341–81), leader of the English Peasants' Revolt of 1381 which made its way from Kent to London in reaction to the King's levying of poll tax. Tyler was eventually killed in an interview with the King at Smithfield, London.

22. The alienation of paid, contracted labour is a classic tenet of Marxist theory.

23. Lancashire term for a substantial snack.

24. In Greek myth, Lethe is a river in Hades that causes forgetfulness in those who drink its waters.

25. William Morris, 'The March of the Workers', collected in *Chants for Socialists*, published by the Socialist League in 1885.

26. Percy Bysshe Shelley (1792–1822), libertarian and hero of the left in the nineteenth century. English Romantic poet whose works demonstrated progressive ideals of social reform.

27. In the biblical story the hungry Esau sells his birthright for a 'mess of pottage', a pot of stew (Genesis 25. 29–34).

28. The garden in Jerusalem where Christ was betrayed, leading on the next day to his Crucifixion (Matthew 26. 36–56).

29. Typical of the critiques levelled at the Workers Educational Association by proponents of the Independent Working-Class Education Movement (run through the National Council of Labour Colleges), which reached its zenith in the 1920s. As a teacher at Bebel House Women's College and Socialist Education Centre (the Labour College institute for working-class women) Carnie Holdsworth was a fierce adherent of its policies.

30. Written by the Irish poet Thomas Moore (1779–1852) and set to

music by Sir John Stevenson (1761–1833).

31. J.M.W. Turner (1775–1851), Romantic landscape painter, known for his powerful paintings of catastrophes and the 'sublime' forces of nature.

32. The wolf and the lamb are often used as symbols of evil and goodness in the Bible. This passage implies that leisure will come to the factory workers only through death.

33. The first volume of Karl Marx's (1818–83) critical analysis of capitalism was published in 1867. He had written the second and third volumes in draft form when he died from bronchitis and pleurisy. These were then edited by Friedrich Engels (1820–95) and published in 1885 and 1894.

34. Popular music hall song.

35. Evangelical protestant charitable movement, founded in 1865 by William Booth with the initial aim of feeding and housing the poor of London.

36. A marching song written by the English socialist poet Edward Carpenter (1844–1929), collected in *The Clarion Songbook*, ed. by Georgia Pierce (Clarion Press: 1906).

37. Welsh song and military march traditionally said to refer to the seven year English siege of Harlech Castle from 1461–8, the longest siege in the history of the British Isles.

38. I have been unable to identify this hymn. Possibly a reference to Robert Nichols (1893–1944), one of the realistic soldier-poets of the First World War.

39. Field Marshall Kitchener, Earl Kitchener of Khartoum (1850–1916), imperial soldier and first Secretary of State for War in World War One.

40. In Greek mythology, the monstrous watchdog of the underworld, usually said to have three heads.

41. Andrew Carnegie (1835–1919), steel magnate and philanthropist, published *Triumphant Democracy: or, Fifty Years' March of the Republic* in 1886, expounding his theories of philanthropy and republicanism. The book caused a furore in Britain, especially in the face of Carnegie's notoriously ruthless business tactics in his steel works which drove the unions out of his mills. Carnegie accumulated a great

personal fortune. His benefactions totalled over $350 million by the time of his death.

42. Fanny Hawthorn is the heroine of Stanley Houghton's popular and sexually liberal play of 1912, *Hindle Wakes*, which takes place in 'Wakes Week'—the traditional summer holiday in the Lancashire mill towns when the factories close down. The play was adapted for film in 1918, 1927, 1931 and again in 1952.

43. Agricultural work, stripping a field of the produce left behind by the regular gatherers. The Martin grandmother's agricultural background points to the common heritage of many nineteenth and twentieth-century urban cotton workers. Prior to the Industrial Revolution, the majority of British people worked in agriculture.

44. Written and composed by the American hymn-writer and gospel singer, Philip Paul Bliss (1838–76).

45. A mean, miserly person.

46. A mortgage.

47. A name symbolically applied to Israel by the prophet in the Bible (Isaiah 62. 4). Used in the hymn 'Beulah Land' written by Edgar Stites and John Sweney in 1876.

48. Popular religious hymns of the late nineteenth century.

49. Tin or metal drinking cup.

50. Bread.

51. Hymn, words by Thomas Taylor (1836), music by Arthur Sullivan (1872).

52. Spoken by King Lear in his 'madness' (*King Lear*, IV. 6. 164–5).

53. Also known as 'Miserere Mei, Deus' ('Have mercy on me, O God'), a setting of Psalm 51, one of the penitential psalms, composed by Gregorio Allegri around 1638.

54. Most probably based on Blackburn, a boomtown of the industrial revolution and internationally renowned as a cotton centre at the beginning of the twentieth century. In 1907 the town boasted 79,405 running looms.

55. Portia and Jessica are the central figures in Shakespeare's *The Merchant of Venice*. *A Royal Divorce*, written by W.G.Wills in 1891, is a sensational historical-romance centring on the romantic triangle of Napoleon Bonaparte, Josephine (his first wife), and Marie Louise

(his second).

56. From the *Rubáiyát of Omar Khayyám* (xxviii and xxix).

57. 'Christabel' by Samuel Taylor Coleridge (1797 and 1800), and 'Lamia' by John Keats (1819) are gothic poems in which unearthly figures are encountered in woodland settings.

58. From *Hamlet* (I. 2. 203–4) when Marcellus and Bernardo, the two watchmen, first see the ghost of Hamlet's father.

59. William Morris, 'The Day is Coming', in his *Chants for Socialists* (1885).

60. John Ball (c. 1330–81), radical preacher, counsellor, and one of the leaders of the rebels in the English Peasant Revolt of 1381.

61. Ernest Jones (1819–69), Chartist radical and writer, imprisoned in 1848 for seditious behaviour, who made several unsuccessful attempts to enter parliament.

62. Robert Owen (1771–1858), social reformer and philanthropist. Believing in the determining impact of environment upon character, Owen sought to improve the living and working conditions of his factory workers at the 'happy valley' of New Lanark. *A New View of Society, or, Essays on the Principle of the Formation of the Human Character* (1813–14) proposed a system of national education to prevent idleness, poverty and crime.

63. Heinrich Heine (1797–1856), German journalist, romantic poet, and utopian socialist.

64. William Blake (1757–1827), artist, printer and poet, critical of the established church and influenced by the ideals of the American and French revolutions.

65. *The Rights of Man* (1791) by Thomas Paine (1737–1809), written in response to Edmund Burke's hostile *Reflections on the Revolution in France* (1790), is a seminal libertarian text expressing the ideal of human equality.

66. A reference to Shakespeare's *Macbeth*, where themes of death, deception, and the disruption of sleep ('Methought I heard a voice cry "Sleep no more! / Macbeth doth murder sleep"', ii. 2. 35–6) are central to the play. Rachel's words may be a mis-quote from memory; they are not from the play itself.

67. Giordano Bruno (1548–1600), Italian philosopher, cosmologist and

priest, a believer in the plurality of worlds. Imprisoned on charges of blasphemy and heresy and burnt at the stake during the Roman Inquisition.

68. Francisco Ferrer (Francesc Ferrer y Guàrdia) (1859–1909), Spanish-Catalan free-thinker and atheist, founder of the International League of Rational Education. Ferrer's socially progressive educational practices and philosophy brought him into conflict with the Roman Catholic Church in Spain. He was shot by a firing squad after the authorities declared him the leader of the 'July Revolution' in Barcelona in 1909. Ferrer was not in Barcelona at the time of the insurrection, and his trial and execution at the hands of a military court provoked international fury. Ferrer's *The Origins and Ideals of the Modern School*, translated into English by Joseph McCabe, was published in 1913.

69. *News from Nowhere, or, an Epoch of Rest: Being Some Chapters from a Utopian Romance* by William Morris (1890) was of tremendous importance to the socialist imagination.

70. Possibly a reference to John, chapters 14-15, where Jesus promises his disciples the Holy Spirit.

71. Acushla (Anglo-Irish), 'darling' or 'dear heart'.

72. 'Who killed Cock Robin?' is an English folk song, often said to refer to the death of the folk hero Robin Hood. The 'Tottie' song may be a version of the murder ballad 'Banks of the Ohio'. The running together of the songs may be a comic amalgam of the time.

73. Charles Garvice (1850–1920), prolific novelist, writer of romances and morally 'healthy' adventures for the new mass reading public of the late nineteenth and early twentieth century. In 1911 the *Daily Chronicle* estimated his readership to be six million.

74. The Labour Representation Committee (L. R. C.) was formed in 1900 from an amalgam of left-wing groups to support Parliamentary candidates. In 1906, after the L. R. C. won 29 seats at the General Election, the name of 'The Labour Party' was adopted. The first Labour Government held office in 1924.

75. Men's wages were often around four shillings a week higher than women's in the Lancashire weaving towns because they worked more loom machines. Weavers were paid according to a piecework

list, with wages calculated according to the minute details of loom widths, number of weft threads etc.

76. Self-denial was an important tenet of the Utilitarian movement, the doctrine that the greatest happiness of the greatest number should be the guiding principle of conduct.

77. Northern English name for heather.

78. In the bible Delilah uses her feminine wiles to betray Samson to the Philistines (Judges 16. 4–20).

79. This is William Morris's socialist utopia depicted in *News from Nowhere*.

80. Beneath one's dignity (from the Latin *infra dignitatem*).

81. A well-known folk song and popular Union marching song of the American Civil War. The 'poet' here adopts the famous line, 'John Brown's body lies a-mouldering in the grave'.

82. A variety of lace from the celebrated lace-making town of Valenciennes in Northern France.

83. From the poem 'If This Were Faith' by Robert Louis Stevenson, *Songs of Travel and Other Verses* (1896).

84. From William Morris's 'The March of the Workers', *Chants for Socialists* (1885).

85. A large vessel for holding liquor such as wine or ale.

86. In John Keat's 'Ode to a Nightingale' (1819) the speaker calls for 'a draught of vintage! [...] Tasting of Flora and the country green / [...] Oh for a beaker full of the warm South' (11–15).

87. The French national anthem, composed in 1792 during the French Revolution and repeatedly banned during the Napoleonic era and much of the nineteenth century because of its revolutionary associations.

88. Robert Louis Stevenson, 'If This Were Faith', from *Songs of Travel*.

89. Late nineteenth-century ballad by the popular Welsh baritone and early recording artist, John W. Myers (c.1865–c.1919).

90. Possibly John W. Myers's 'I Dreamt that I Dwelt in Marble Halls' (1904).

91. Ballad from the popular opera *Maritana*, composed by William Vincent Wallace (1846).

92. 'And those who husbanded the Golden Grain, / And those who

flung it to the Winds like Rain', from *The Rubáiyát of Omar Khayyám* (xvii).

93. Popular song written and composed by George Linley (c. 1830).
94. Dance music for brass band, from the popular fantasia of Henry Round.
95. From *The Rubáiyát of Omar Khayyám* (lxxii).
96. Napoleon Bonaparte's coup d'état of 1799 which marked the beginnings of the end of the French Revolution. In 1852 Karl Marx published *The Eighteenth Brumaire of Louis Bonaparte*, an account of the 1851 coup by Napoleon's nephew.
97. Grand leather chair, signifying the status of its owner.
98. Yeast.
99. Title of a popular egalitarian song by the Scots writer Robert Burns (1759–96), otherwise known as 'Is There for Honest Poverty'.
100. Delighted, overjoyed.
101. A collection of heroic ballads about ancient Rome, written by Lord Thomas Babbington Macauley and published in 1842. They became set reading for school children and were popularly recited throughout the Victorian era.
102. Matthew Arnold (1822–88), English poet, cultural critic and inspector of schools.
103. Lyrical poems by William Wordsworth (1770–1850). 'Excelsior' is a brief poem written by Henry Wadsworth Longfellow (1807–82) in 1841.
104. 'The Buried Life' by Matthew Arnold (1852). The poem expresses the redeeming quality of love for the self in a world of alienation, hypocrisy, and misunderstanding.
105. Part II of Matthew Arnold's Arthurian 'Tristram and Iseult' poems (1852).
106. H. G. Wells (1866–1946), novelist, socialist, and pacifist. *Ann Veronica, A Modern Love Story* (1909) and *The New Machiavelli* (1911), both of which deal with 'modern' questions of sexuality, caused much public outrage and were banned by some libraries.
107. The 'departing warrior' is a character in *The Kalevala*, the national epic of Finland first assembled in the 1840s and translated into English by John Addison Porter in 1868. 'The Little Maiden' most

likely refers to one of the characters in this poem.

108. The Bulbul is the Eastern name for a nightingale. This is possibly taken from an Indonesian children's song.

109. Novel by Charles Dickens (1812–70) published in 1853. Cheap reprints of Dickens's novels became widely available in the late nineteenth and early twentieth century.

110. Hard animal fat, used for making candles, soap.

111. Prepared from materials similar to those which make up glue.

112. The probable meaning of 'coving' here, as per OED, 'cove, v.', is sheltering or leaning into.

113. Hymn, words by Ebenezer Elliot (1850) and music by Josiah Booth (1888). See 'The People's Anthem', in Mark Storey (ed), *Selected Poetry of Ebenezer Elliott* (Cranbury, NJ: Associated University Presses, 2008) pp. 206–7.